Apc  s

Homecoming
Episodes 7-8-9

By

Joe Nobody

Copyright © 2019
Kemah Bay Marketing, LLC
All rights reserved.
Edited by: E.T. Ivester
Researched by: D.W. Hall

www.joenobodybooks.com

Other Books by Joe Nobody:

Tainted Robes
Apocalypse Trails: Episode 1
Apocalypse Trails: Episode 2
Apocalypse Trails: Episode 3
Apocalypse Trails: Episode 4
Apocalypse Trails: Episode 5
Apocalypse Trails: Episode 6
Secession: The Storm
Secession II: The Flood
Secession III: The Surge
The Archangel Drones
Holding Your Ground: Preparing for Defense if it All Falls Apart
The TEOTWAWKI Tuxedo: Formal Survival Attire
Without Rule of Law: Advanced Skills to Help You Survive
Holding Their Own: A Story of Survival
Holding Their Own II: The Independents
Holding Their Own III: Pedestals of Ash
Holding Their Own IV: The Ascent
Holding Their Own V: The Alpha Chronicles
Holding Their Own VI: Bishop's Song
Holding Their Own VII: Phoenix Star
Holding Their Own VIII: The Directives
Holding Their Own IX: The Salt War
Holding Their Own X: The Toymaker
Holding Their Own XI: Hearts and Minds
Holding Their Own XII: Copperheads
Holding Their Own XIII: Renegade
Holding Their Own XIV: Forest Mist
Holding Their Own XV: Bloodlust
The Home Schooled Shootist: Training to Fight with a Carbine
Apocalypse Drift
The Little River Otter
The Olympus Device: Book One
The Olympus Device: Book Two
The Olympus Device: Book Three
The Ebola Wall

Prologue

Captain Alex Bascom grimaced in annoyance at his bedside cell phone; its alarm-tone screeching a poor imitation of the rock classic, *Sweet Home Alabama*.

As usual, the tune pulled his sleepy mind back to the land of the Crimson Tide and his alma mater, the University of Alabama. Despite a lifetime of accomplishments and accolades, he still reminisced about those days on the Tuscaloosa campus. He had played football there, enjoying a few glorious moments during his senior year. While his size and speed weren't quite impressive enough to draw the attention of the pro scouts, he was respected by both his teammates and several attractive co-eds in his wide circle of friends. Those had been good years.

Not that being drafted into the NFL would have mattered. The United States Air Force was paying Alex's tuition. He attended class at the pleasure of the local ROTC commander. He had to repay Uncle Sam with four years of his life. Cadet Bascom considered it a fair trade.

Within a year of his graduation from the university, he was flying. He was offered command of his first squadron less than five years after that.

Over the next twenty-five years, Alex had flown combat missions, experimental craft, and practically every class of airplane in the US Air Force's significant arsenal. Along the way, the breast of his uniform had been adorned with an impressive and varied "tossed salad" of medals and awards.

Like so many Air Force pilots, Alex loved flying and flying machines more than anything. He craved time with the stick while immersing himself in the underlying engineering that allowed those miraculous, man-made birds to soar through the skies. He

3

excelled and was repeatedly acknowledged for his dedication and effort.

Driven by this passion, Alex's focus throughout his military career had been narrow. He didn't like strategic studies, had no interest in logistics, and wasn't concerned with the other aspects and nuances of command. His single-mindedness created a permanent glass ceiling, a limit to the potential altitude of his rank.

The US Air Force wanted well-rounded officers on its general staff. Those who would lead the service into the next era needed a broad range of skills and experience. After reaching the rank of full colonel, Alex was bypassed for promotion twice. The proverbial handwriting was on the wall... in bold, flashing neon lights. He was forced into retirement at forty-eight years of age.

He traveled for a year, visited distant relatives, and refreshed old memories of his childhood and formative years. He was bored, single, and for the first time in his adult life, he had no mission or purpose.

At exactly eleven months to the day after hanging up his uniform for the last time, Alex called an old service buddy who now worked for a large commercial airline. "Are you hiring pilots? I just want to fly again. I'm not ready to be grounded."

Bascom was immediately snatched up, his pedigree in high demand. Just a few months after joining the airline, he was flying business owners and vacationers around the United States, smiling politely as they disembarked his Boeing 737, and spending most of his nights in airport hotels. He was, at worst, content.

He was in Austin, Texas when his alarm's rendition of the southern rock classic pulled him from the depths of slumber. He had a 10:05 a.m. departure to Las Vegas, then another leg to John Wayne Airport in Santa Anna. He wanted to get in a workout at the hotel's gym before starting his day.

As was his habit, Captain Bascom's first act was to check the weather. After scouring the nondescript hotel room for the television's remote, he fumbled with the buttons until the screen came to life. A few moments later, he had found a cable station that was broadcasting a forecast.

Coffee was the next order of business, the room equipped with a miniature machine that would brew two cups at a time. Again, sleepy fingers fumbled with the tiny canister of java, tap water filling the reserve.

He was about to enter the bathroom when the television newscaster's tone drew his attention. As the coffeemaker hissed and popped, Captain Bascom's focus was riveted on the small TV. Yellowstone was erupting. It was a massive event like none seen before.

Within five minutes, the former Air Force officer knew the world had just been changed forever. The untouched pot of black caffeine was still simmering thirty minutes later when the bedside phone's loud report pulled him from the horrific images of massive ash clouds and reports of widespread destruction.

"They're grounding all flights," the airline's regional manager announced. "You might as well stay in your room. I'll call you as soon as I know more."

By noon, Alex realized the super volcano's wrath was going to result in more than just a few delayed travelers. He had been grounded by eruptions before, both by Mount Saint Helens and a 2010 event in Iceland that had covered Europe in a cloud of ash. From what he gleaned from the boob tube, Captain Bascom fully realized the magnitude of the maelstrom streaming toward mankind.

By mid-afternoon, he was taking the hotel's shuttle to the airline offices at Austin-Bergstrom International's main terminal. "We've got about three days to do something," he informed the shell-shocked staff huddled around a small screen. "That ash cloud will take about that long to circumnavigate the globe. After that, we're

5

all going to all die from simply breathing the air. We need to act quickly if we are to survive."

Chapter 38

Jack was getting close, just a few more agonizing miles, and it would all be over. He would know. He would have the answers to the questions that had burdened his mind for weeks. He would know if his family had survived, or if he were alone in this grey, lifeless world. He wanted nothing more than to share a future with his wife and daughters. His countless hours of soul searching, internal strife, and deep reflection would soon be resolved.

His wife, Mylie, was either dead or alive. She would either welcome him back or not. It was all that simple according to Jack's thinking. He had boiled down the situation while the journey of more than a thousand miles had passed. The isolation of his existence, combined with the pewter skies of the apocalypse, had enabled him to draw off any fat surrounding their relationship and cast it aside. Now it was pure, only meat and bone… she would either embrace his return or exile her husband to the wilderness.

Somehow, as the commander had laid awake night after night, he had bundled his wife and daughters together. As Mylie went, so went the girls. They were tethered in a symbiotic relationship. In this ash-covered world, there were no visitation rights or court-enforced decrees. He saw himself in a very all-or-nothing position regarding his entire family. Inside Jack's weary mind, it was just that binary.

Central Texas was now a distant memory in the fog of his exhausted, numb mind.

The flat plains of the Lone Star State had been a blessing of sorts, providing a temporary reprise for his aching knees and overworked, undernourished muscles. Still, pedaling day after day through the grey hell of Yellowstone's aftermath held its challenges, no matter how forgiving the terrain.

Avoiding even the smallest of towns had created a major obstacle. Bypassing those communities resulted in mile after mile of traveling desolate country roads and adding days to his itinerary. Given his experiences with surviving humanity so far, he considered the added wear and tear on his lower body as a wise investment. "Better sore and tired than dead and cold," he had reminded himself a dozen times.

As he rolled east, the map displayed an ever-increasing density of ink, both in the number and size of the communities in his path.

Having survived a multitude of dangerous situations during his journey solidified his belief that major population centers like Midland, Odessa, and San Angelo were his greatest remaining threats. Detouring an overweight bicycle around sprawling metropolitan areas had proven challenging and had already significantly delayed his return to his family. Jack was thankful none of Texas's major population centers were in his path. It would take ten days to go around Houston… or Dallas… or San Antonio.

He survived off canned food from Heather's cellar, water from isolated springs, and the grit of sheer determination. Glancing down at his thin arms and boney hands gripping the handlebars, Jack doubted he weighed more than 150 pounds. Between the constant exercise of riding and the lack of calories, he had lost a quarter of his mass in less than two months.

Unlike the previous achievements in his life, Jack felt no sense of accomplishment from having survived the most grueling adventure imaginable. Hunger, pain, danger, and fear were behind him now, stored in a mental filing cabinet burgeoning with a growing catalogue of newly mundane experiences. For a moment, he wondered what kind of person doomsday had forced him to become.

Competition had always been his game. Crossing the finish line first, hitting the winning shot, or having the best time were what had pegged his gratification meter. Graduating from the Academy had been his single greatest accomplishment. There had been promotion, command, and a long list of successful endeavors. The old Jack Cisco would have been a strutting rooster at the end of this cross-country voyage.

Instead, Jack found himself wanting nothing more than simple closure. Alive or dead. Yes or no. Stay or go. Family man or lonely wanderer?

A few days ago, the terrain had confirmed he was getting close. As he struggled up the first hill he'd seen since New Mexico, Jack knew his father-in-law's ranch was finally within reach. He barely had enough food and water to complete this last leg of the trip. Luckily, there were only a handful of towns to avoid, so the journey was quite straightforward. As long as his legs and the bicycle's tires held out, he would make it. A sudden calm overcame the commander. His apprehension evaporated, the gut-wrenching fear of the unknown melting away. All of his life's important questions soon would be answered.

As he approached the western edge of the Texas Hill Country, the roadway changed as drastically as his attitude. Gone were the long, flat straightaways, gradually replaced by inclines, curves, and undulations. Through the low light of the darkened sky, Jack could discern the hazy outline of hilltops and shadowy valleys ahead.

He had passed a road sign advertising Enchanted Rock and its associated state park. He and Mylie had hiked there on one of their return trips to her homestead. He remembered the impressive domed mountain that looked like a giant bald head rising sticking out of the surrounding countryside. It was the largest single hunk of pink granite in the United States, and now it was probably covered by a toupee of grey ash.

Anticipating the familiarity of the landmark engendered a swell of emotions in Jack's troubled mind. He had joined his family at the ranch for only a few of those holidays. The Christmas lights and the Thanksgiving turkeys were now distant images that he

9

found difficult to pull out of his memory banks. Most years, he'd been at sea and unable to attend the festivities. He had been a man repeatedly forced to choose between the demands of Uncle Sam and the women he loved. Like so many things in his marriage, memories of those holidays were a mixture of good and bad, emotional homecomings and missed celebrations.

Even when the family was all together at the ranch, Mylie quickly became restless. After a day of hugs, greetings, and smiles, Jack would catch his wife wandering the property, exploring the barns and outbuildings, and acting as if she was already bored. "Let's ask Dad to go with us into town tonight for dinner," she'd suggest. Or, "Let's go shopping later this afternoon."

"But we just got here?" Jack would offer, secretly questioning if he were the catalyst for her uneasiness… Was she trying to avoid spending time with him?

"I know. I guess I get bored too quickly," she would rationalize, followed by that killer smile she used to escape uncomfortable situations. "You know my mantra – a rolling stone gathers no moss."

Had Mylie gotten bored with their relationship? Was his dedication to career and service just an excuse for a woman who was constantly in need of stimulation, or who was always looking for something better? Had their time apart permanently damaged their relationship? Was his wife tired of spending so much time alone? Jack would know where he stood soon enough, he supposed.

Bypassing Fredericksburg hadn't been all that difficult, at least not physically. Upon seeing a billboard that advertised a familiar, local restaurant, another fountain of conflicting sentiments swelled inside him. He had met his wife there, had fond remembrances of the place. At the intersection of two lonely state highways, the commander paused to pensively gaze west toward the distant community. He wondered how the welcoming tourist town had fared after Yellowstone's temper tantrum. Licking his lips, he remembered how cold and tasty the beer had been during Octoberfest that year. He could almost smell the sausage and sauerkraut so popular with the ancestors of the German immigrants who had settled the village.

With a shrug, he continued, always heading south and east, melancholy in the knowledge that he would probably never taste anything like those simple pleasures again.

He stopped pedaling in the middle of the road, unconcerned about traffic. While there was always the possibility of an ambush by preying highwaymen, the commander's surroundings were desolate and remote. He had learned to trust his senses, and they were signaling the all clear.

With a flurry of practiced movements, Jack stepped off the bike, nudged down the kickstand, and withdrew a map from his breast pocket. Next, he carefully adjusted the cotton towel that was today's breathing filter. Again, the commander frowned, wondering if he would ever be able to draw air without his mouth and nose being hostage to a cloth mask. His full beard had long ago passed the stubble stage and was the only thing that protected his face from being rubbed raw.

Glancing at the dog-eared map, Jack then scanned the surrounding countryside. Identifying no landmarks, he strode to the highway sign and brushed off the thin coating of pumice obscuring the white letters beneath.

The town of Clover Springs was twelve miles ahead, the bustling metropolis of Driftwood an additional five miles travel. His dirty finger tapped the spot on the map where he stood.

His gaze returned to the highway and then the utility lines that had supplied electrical power to the homesteads and ranches in the area. He was looking for a wire heading off into the surrounding hills that would signal a driveway. "The ranch's lane should be right along here," he announced, clearly puzzled. "I'm positive I'm in the right place."

Frustration and confusion caused Jack's neurons to misfire in rapid succession, his brain now muddled, his posture stiffening from the stress. He turned to stare back in the direction he'd just come. It had been a few years since he'd stayed at the ranch. Things looked so different now, all the vegetation brown and dead, the hills a monotone hue. "Hell, it's not as though I can feel for the moss on the north side of trees," he grumbled.

He decided to continue, cursing his lack of attention during earlier visits. Mylie had always been with him, navigating the rural region from the rental's passenger seat, directing him right and left. He tried to recall every little detail from his memories.

Ned Armstrong, his father-in-law, had inherited the 390-acre property from his dad. In fact, the Lazy A had been in Mylie's family for four generations.

In the Lone Star State, sprawling ranches were customarily marked by weathered metal signs suspended over the property's main entrance, proudly welcoming guests and pinpointing the driveway. These gate signs allowed the locals an opportunity to personalize their patches of earth in any way they wished. A unique form of marketing, ranchers often identified their brands with pastoral titles like Whispering Pines, Cattail Hollow, or Fox Run. Other landowners took a more whimsical tactic, choosing slogans like Pushin' Up Daisies, All Mosta Ranch, or The Big Kahuna. Ned Armstrong took a more pragmatic approach, displaying the ranch's incorporated name, "The Lazy A Ranch," and a leaning, capital "A," signaled the outfit's logo.

Jack couldn't even find the driveway, let alone the gate sign or the thick rock pillars that had held it in place. Would Ned have taken down the placard to hide the existence of his spread? Had it fallen during one of the intense storms that now pounded the earth's surface?

Rounding the next bend, all of Jack's concerns evaporated when he spotted the outline of the rusty red gate sign in the distance. Cursing his paranoia, he pedaled faster now, the finish line in sight.

He stopped at the entrance, his eyes scanning the area, following the narrow driveway as it wound up the side of a massive hill. He knew that the Lazy A occupied the valley on the far side, spreading out for as far as the eye could see.

Flashes from earlier trips filled his mind... the picturesque ranch home with its charming, attached courtyard, the crimson-colored barn and stables, the wood-weathered corral surrounded by a collection of long-standing outbuildings... Massive oaks supplied ample shade for the main house. A small lake located on the far side of the toolshed was visible from the low metal roof of the whitewashed bunkhouse. Tie-up rails separated the back porch from the big outdoors. Together, the mental image formed the quintessential prototype of a working, well-kept ranch.

A man perpetually tied to the sea, he had always been in awe of the splendor that was the Lazy A. He remembered even telling Mylie that her father's spread was postcard perfect. "Norman Rockwell himself could not have dreamt of a more picturesque spot," Jack had insisted.

Shaking his head to clear those old images, Jack braced himself. The Lazy A wasn't going to look anything at all like it did the last time he was here. He forced himself to imagine the centuries-old, tree-lined drive inky black and lifeless, the pristine green pond to be covered in pewter-colored goo, the yard a carpet of ash.

"Worse yet, your whole family might be dead," he whispered as a melancholy expression crossed his face, sobering his mood even more. His mind raced down a murky path as he contemplated the many circumstances he might face. The ranch could have been raided... the house may have been hit by lightning and burned to the ground; desperados may have invaded... or any number of other disasters may have occurred. "You might find your wife and daughters' bones, Commander. Are you ready for that?"

13

He resumed his journey, pedaling up the steep terrain until the wheels sank into the ashy ground cover. Dismounting his two-wheeled steed, Jack began walking the bike up the lane.

Just short of reaching the top, he knocked down the kickstand and let the bike rest. Taking his rifle, he hiked up the last yards to the crest, his heart pounding like a jackhammer in his chest. After his months' long journey, he had made it! His soul leapt with the anticipation of finally seeing the Armstrong homestead and his beloved family.

His highest hope, the best-case scenario, was to see movement in the valley below. Tracks in the ash, smoke drifting from the chimney, or any sign of life would be welcome. Ned Armstrong knew the old ways. He knew how to survive without the comforts of modern society. He was a tough, old Texas cattleman with an iron will. Miley and the girls would have been safe here.

Hurrying to the top of the ridge, Jack could hardly wait for his first glimpse of home. Reaching the apex, he blinked twice and then inhaled sharply. His eyes flew wide with shock, his heart beat wildly, and a cold sweat covered his brow.

On the other side of the hill, a lake stretched before him, its smooth, pewter surface interrupted only by the peak of the barn's roofline and the skeletal remains of several trees. The commander was stunned, his brain unable to process what his eyes were taking in.

His first reaction was to turn and look back down the lane. Was he in the right place? Had he bumbled up the wrong driveway? Where was the valley? Where was the ranch? Where was his family?

His brain unable to reconcile his memory with the landscape before him, he jogged ahead for a better vantage. He needed to get closer. *After journeying halfway across a post-apocalyptic United States, your tortured mind is playing tricks on you, Commander. You are like the dehydrated desert traveler who sees a mirage in front of him. This is not reality.*

Halfway down the far side of the lane, Jack pulled up short. The lake's shoreline stretched ahead of him, several pieces of blond driftwood lying along the edge. The "water" was like every other pond he'd seen since Yellowstone's explosion, filled with a substance resembling thick coffee, covered by an opaque film that looked like the patina on old coins.

Reeling from shock, Jack stared at the scene in front of him, his brain no longer able to will his body to move. Nothing within his view made any sense. "This isn't right," he protested. "Clearly, you can't even find your way home without GPS, Commander," he muttered.

Shaking his head to clear the fog of confusion, he focused on the fifteen feet of the barn's roof protruding from the surface of the muck. A weather vane was mounted at the ridge, a rusty, leaning "A" clearly visible against the hazy backdrop of the darkening sky. The Lazy A. He wasn't lost or mistaken.

"Mylie?" he groaned between the outbursts of emotion. "My girls?" he managed a minute later. Suddenly, Jack's legs would no longer hold his weight. Sitting in the middle of the lane, the commander buried his face in his hands, uncontrolled sobs racking his frame.

"Did you drown? Were you even here? What has become of you?" he continued, a thousand images and questions swirling through his head.

Jack's face burned hot with tears. "I came all this way for nothing?" he spat, his pity party beginning. A moment later, overwhelming guilt surpassed his frustration. "I wasn't in time to save you! I wasn't fast enough!"

For nearly an hour, Commander Jack Cisco sat, waves of distress and anguish bombarding his soul, his legs unable or unwilling to move. He ignored the thirst in his throat, didn't care that nightfall was fast approaching.

Finally, drawn and weak, Jack rose. His motions were clumsy, his face hollow and sunken. From a lack of any other reasonable option, he stumbled toward his only companion for the last several weeks, the filthy bicycle with the worn pack strapped to its frame.

The use of his muscles and lungs helped to clear Jack's thoughts. By the time he made it back to the bike, he was beginning to sensibly process what he had seen. "Where had the new lake come from? How quickly had the water risen? Would Mylie and his daughters have had time to bug out? Where would they have taken shelter?"

Fleeting moments of optimism flashed through the commander's brain. "They would have had time to get out," he reasoned. "Hell, they might be at a neighbor's… or friend's nearby ranch."

Disengaging the kickstand, Jack scanned the surrounding hills. He'd never met any of Ned's neighbors, couldn't recall Mylie talking about any close friends or schoolmates who lived in the area.

As he descended from the ridge, exhaustion and cold began to take their toll on Jack's already weakened frame. At the bottom, less than one hundred yards from the road, he spied an outcropping of rocks surrounded by a thick patch of dead scrub.

A quick check of the sky indicated it would be dusk very soon. He was beat, hungry, thirsty, and in need of shelter. Those rocks would be his home for the night.

His mind relaxed for a moment, distracted by his survival routine. He made camp, careful to build his fire where it wasn't visible from the road. Instead of pitching his tent, he draped the worn canvas over two stone pillars, creating a space just large enough to insert his weary frame. He heated half a jar of canned beans and opened the last of his salt.

Ordinarily, the commander would have carefully measured out a modest amount of the spice, only using enough to make the food palatable. This evening, he carefully tore the corner of the packet and stared at the single-serve packet in his palm, his mind continuing to process the events and emotions of the day.

Mylie and his girls were all that had kept him going since the fall of civilization. All his dreams were officially extinct, having vanished beneath the surface of a lake that shouldn't exist. His future, his hope, his reason for being no longer existed.

His body heaved with the weight of his sigh. He was a man whose heart had been broken beyond repair. He poured the remaining beans into the pot and then sprinkled his entire stash of spice on the meal.

It wasn't much of a last supper, but it would have to do.

He would join his family in the afterlife, the thought comforting in its own dejected way. *After all*, he reasoned, *what justification could there be for taking his next breath, climbing the next hill, or struggling to overcome the next obstacle*? There was no one to share his life with, no one to fight for. Additionally, even the simple pleasures of this world had been destroyed. There were no green, grassy meadows, color-streaked sunsets, or hopeful dawns.

The experiences of human life that generated dopamine were distant memories. Chocolate, love, hot showers, football, the smell of his daughter's hair, the sound of Mylie's laughter... all of it had vanished, buried under a layer of grey, lifeless pumice. They had traveled to the other side. Why shouldn't he join them?

Or had they?

Suicide wasn't in Jack Cisco's DNA. Giving up all hope was incongruent with a man who had conquered some of mankind's most difficult obstacles. He had never felt so low and worthless; yet, pulling the pistol from his belt and pressing it against his temple simply didn't seem right. He had come so far. Worked so hard. Overcome every challenge blocking his route.

Mylie and his daughters could still be alive. There was no solid evidence to the contrary. He forced himself to focus, to play the role of post-apocalyptic detective. Where would they go? Who would they turn to for help? His wife was a strong woman, his father-in-law a tough, old bastard. For a man like Ned Armstrong, words like surrender, quit, retreat, or give up did not exist. "I need to be just as resilient… just as ornery… just as hardnosed," Jack whispered to the dying fire.

He realized that it would take him weeks to search the surrounding area. Homes in this part of the country were far and few between. "Elbow room," he remembered Ned declaring, "I need a lot of elbow room, and cities just don't have a lot of that. Hell, I don't even like going into town to pay my taxes once a year."

Even if he did mount a door to door search, approaching post-apocalyptic homesteads without being known or invited would be extremely dangerous. If any of the surrounding ranchers had survived, they probably weren't rolling out the red carpet for vagabond bike riders. "You don't need to put that barrel in your mouth," the commander chuckled. "They would be happy to do the job for you."

The grim prospects prompted Jack to consider turning around and heading back west. After all, he had always known that finding his family was a remote possibility. Had it always been, in fact, a fool's errand that would only result in his own painful, grizzly death? Food and water were rare commodities. Nothing was growing, and probably wouldn't for years. There were few renewable supplies of nourishment, and eventually, what hadn't been consumed after the eruption would be gone. He was probably better off in one of the communities he had discovered that had developed sustainable food resources.

Jack thought about Archie and Dr. Reagan, Toni and her eggs in Pinemont, and of course, the beautiful Carmen in Carlsbad. There were still people out there fighting to survive, folks who had a chance of making a life for themselves. Should he turn around and go back? Abandon this irrational quest?

The commander removed the beans from the fire, stirring his meal to make sure it was evenly heated. The food provided instant and much needed fuel for his debilitated body and spirit. His thoughts turned back to his family.

Suddenly, Jack brightened, remembering a recurring argument between Mylie and her dad. In truth, the old codger would never leave the ranch if he had his way. Still, every year, Miley practically dragged Ned kicking and screaming to Sunday service, the local grocery store, or a movie theatre.

"Town? Would they have headed to town when the water began rising?"

Sure, the old man didn't like being around other people, but he would have Mylie and the two girls to care for. Would that responsibility have forced him to reconsider his hermit ways?

Even if the Armstrong clan hadn't resettled in the community, someone there might know their location or intended bug-out plan. "Or," Jack frowned, "they may have helped bury my family."

By the firelight, Jack again consulted the map to refresh his memory. "Clover Springs," he nodded, now remembering the tiny community that was less than ten miles away. He and Mylie had gone there once, to the local co-op to pick up a part for a tractor. As best he could recall, less than a thousand people called the village home.

"But where did the lake come from?" he questioned again. "This part of the country is arid."

Again, the map provided an explanation. "The Pedernales River," he noted, tapping the chart just north of his current position. "The ash... or an earthquake... or debris must have changed its course, and the Lazy A was in the way."

"I need water anyway," Jack observed, shaking the plastic gallon milk jug that was part of his kit. "Maybe Clover Spring's flow will taste better than the last place I stopped."

With a new objective and restated purpose pushing aside his disappointment, Jack's body finally began to relax. Sleep eventually squeezed the troubles from his mind.

Chapter 39

A mile outside of Clover Springs, Jack was beginning to doubt his new mission. This close, he would have expected to see tracks in the ash, or smell smoke from a campfire, or hear some sign of human activity. "The local residents probably have you in their cross-hairs," he mumbled. "They're just waiting for you to venture a little closer, so they don't waste any ammo."

Buildings began to appear in the distance, a scattering of dark outlines revealing the occasional roofline of a business or home. The blanket of pumice covering the pavement was completely undisturbed.

The first structure he passed was a modest outlet selling lawnmowers and other small machines. Next, he spotted an antique store, that business sited next door to the Dairy King. It was the type of place that would have been bustling with carhops rushing trays filled with burgers and fries to waiting pickups. "Looks like the typical Texas town," Jack mumbled as he scanned for any sign of life. "I bet a hot fudge sundae was pretty tasty on those humid, summer evenings back in the day."

Lifting his carbine from the handlebars, Jack began steering the bike with one hand, the other keeping his weapon ready.

As he traveled further into the center of town, the density of roadside homes and businesses increased. By the time he reached the main business district, he was completely walled in by two-story brick facades that sported signage advertising everything from women's clothing to a small pharmacy.

Coasting to a stop, Jack dismounted and leaned his ride against the outer wall of a second-hand furniture shop. With weapon in hand, he began exploring the deserted community.

His critical need was to locate the springs for which the town was named. He needed water, and as always, food. He was also praying for information.

Crossing Texas had taught him that most of the winding creeks in the region had become state parks or other government-owned recreational areas. In town after town, he spotted signs indicating that such-and-such park could be found after taking a right or left turn. There were no such markers here.

Sticking close to the buildings, he was ready to use any doorway or corner as cover – if somebody started shooting. The commander began looking for a chamber of commerce, library, or one of those metal stands holding tourist brochures often found inside of mom and pop businesses. He needed local knowledge and a more detailed map, if possible.

At the pharmacy, Jack used his hand to clean a little circle through the coating of grit and dust on the window. Peeking inside, he was surprised to see a neat row of shelves. Yes, they were mostly empty, having been stripped of anything valuable. What was so shocking was the fact that there was no broken glass, strewn debris, or evidence of anything other than an orderly day of intense shopping. Had the drug store gone out of business before Yellowstone spewed her fury?

Blinking with confusion, Jack then realized that he hadn't spotted a single broken window in the entire town. That was weird. Every other city he'd visited showed signs of civil unrest, looting, vandalism, and absolute chaos.

Stepping to the pharmacy's door, Jack tried the heavy, old brass knob. The place was locked tight. No one had bothered to jimmy the lock or bust a window. The mystery deepened.

The Liquor Barn anchored the next intersection. "No way that place survived untouched," Jack whispered, making his way carefully toward the oddly-shaped, little alcohol market.

Again, he found the interior completely empty and the door secured. A pile of unfolded cardboard boxes was stacked near the entrance, a half-empty roll of packing tape lying nearby. It had been an orderly retreat, a planned exodus. "What the hell?" he quipped. "Can't a man get a drink in this one-horse town?"

The city hall was his next objective, the modest, single-story building one of the newer structures in the area. There were two ash-covered police cars parked in the lot.

He read the sign, "Clover Springs City Management Offices" as he climbed the three front steps. A moment later, Jack had his answer.

"All citizens are hereby directed to report to Clover Springs High School," declared a photocopied sheet of paper taped to the glass door. "This is an emergency evacuation order! Bring as much food and medical supplies as possible. Only one small bag of personal items per resident will be allowed."

A photocopied map directed the reader to the school, the mandate endorsed by the signatures of the city manager, sheriff, police chief, and several members of the city council.

"They knew it was coming," Jack considered. "Impressive. A well-organized response. I wonder how many of them survived?"

For a few moments, Jack stood on the top step and visualized the hastily called town meeting. Everyone, even in the sleepiest of hamlets, would have known about Yellowstone's eruption. Every television and radio station on the planet was probably broadcasting scenarios of gloom and doom.

The commander had to chuckle, his mind-movie bringing to life the fierce debates, arguments, and fear that must have dominated that last town meeting. There would have been detractors, stubborn citizens who weren't going to abandon their property, no matter what their elected officials demanded. Yet, from what he had seen in the tiny community's major business district, the town's officials must have been very persuasive. It was the first place Jack had visited that hadn't been completely sacked. There weren't any decaying bodies in the street, piles of broken store glass, or mounds of burnt rubble.

His eyes returning to the posted notice, Jack scanned the provided map. For a second, hope welled inside his core. "Did the

Armstrong clan evacuate to the high school when the water started rising?" he whispered. "Are Mylie and the girls sleeping on a cot in the science lab?"

The facility was apparently sited on the edge of town, according to the map. Jack pivoted quickly, the purpose in his stride having suddenly returned.

Before he'd traveled the short distance to his bike, the commander began to question that flicker of hope. "Ned Armstrong would've died before he hunkered down with hundreds of other people. But… would he have sent the girls to safety? Did he deliver them to the shelter?"

There was only one way to find out. With a renewed vigor, Jack began pedaling toward the school.

A quarter mile from the facility, the commander again dismounted and started pushing his bike through the thin coating of grey, volcanic spew. Caution, learned over the last 1400 miles, was his new companion.

At 300 yards, he leaned the bike against a utility pole and raised his weapon to use the magnification of his optic.

Taking in the limestone block walls, modern style windows, and green metal roof, he observed that the high school was of newer construction. "Hays County Independent School District. Clover Springs High School. Home of the Tigers!" announced the large sign at the main entrance.

There was a depiction of a ferocious-looking feline flexing its bulging muscles beneath the white letters.

Jack took in the parking lot and the dozens of yellow buses, pickups, cars, and minivans residing there. Several police cars, three fire trucks, and at least two dozen large semi-trailers were lined up on the far side of the facility. He scanned the goal posts and bleachers in the rear, the field surrounded by a paved running track. "Nice campus," he whispered. "I bet this was the place to be for Friday night football games. Probably had some real barn burners."

Despite the obvious organization and widespread response of the community, Jack felt a sense of lifelessness as he studied facility. "Those trucks were probably full of food and supplies," he considered. "Somebody was planning for the long term, but did it do any good?"

While he wasn't close enough to detect any tracks in the ash, the commander couldn't help but think the worse.

Bracing himself for what was sure to be another chapter in a long book of horrific memories and images, Jack began pushing his bike toward the school. As an afterthought, just to appear less hostile, he tugged on the carbine's sling so that it rested across his back. "I'm not aggressive," he mumbled. "I'm a peaceful traveler."

At fifty yards away, he noted the first unusual feature. There, at the corner of the school's grounds, someone had created a makeshift guard post. A series of metal desks had been turned on their sides and then reinforced with sandbags. "A machine gun nest?" Jack questioned. The outpost, however, was unoccupied, the carpet of ash surrounding the bunker smooth and undisturbed.

A moment later, Jack spied a similar post at the drive leading to the main entrance. "They were worried about something," he offered.

Continuing unchallenged toward the large, double-wide glass doors, the commander started looking for the nearest cover – just in case his arrival was met with hostility.

Neither challenge nor high-velocity lead came his way as Jack mounted the four wide steps leading to the threshold. Glancing inside the dark entrance through the glass, he unable to discern anything other than an oversized trophy case and several colorful banners hanging on the wall.

When the door's handle offered no resistance, Jack's eyebrows immediately soared skyward, his senses on high alert. Astonishingly, the building was unlocked.

He was halfway through the doorway, inhaling to shout out, "Hello?" when the odor hit him. So strong was the rancid scent, the commander staggered backward. "Oh my God," he panted, drinking in the fresh air outside to clear the stench from his nostrils.

The reeking smell prompted a childhood memory to surface, that of his having visited a cemetery one spring afternoon. Young Jack Cisco had accompanied his aunt to the church graveyard, his fist clasped tightly around a bunch of freshly-picked daffodils. His grandmother had been laid to rest in a modest-sized mausoleum, alongside her husband and his parents. Jack had never visited an above-ground crypt before and did not expect to smell the putrid odor of the decaying corpse inside. The kindergarten-aged child immediately realized the value of dead folks being covered with six feet of earth. "Give me a burial at sea any day," the commander added. "Better to swim with the fishes than create this kind of lasting impression. Nothing else on earth smells quite like death," he muttered.

He paused for several seconds more, allowing his watering eyes to clear, trying to identify the odor currently assaulting his senses. No doubt decaying flesh was the primary component of the malodorous bouquet, but there was another, equally offensive ingredient yet to be recognized that took this stench to another whole level. *What is that?* he wondered, gingerly sniffing at the gases that escaped from the lobby. But the mystery scent defied explanation. "Whatever it is," he muttered, "it smells like a mixture of old campfire smoke, burning chemicals, and spilled cleaning supplies.

Jack had encountered his share of dead bodies during his journey. From the base at San Diego onward, the ground had often been littered with blackened corpses or the skin-covered bones of the deceased. He had yet to happen upon a still-decomposing cadaver; however, he didn't expect to. "The body's internal bacteria finish their smelly work within ten to fourteen days, depending on the environment," *Utah*'s senior corpsman had advised his shipmates after they had first come across several dead bodies in San Diego. That news was a relief as the burial details were being formed. "The ash may preserve certain tissues, but the unpleasant odor should be long gone after a couple of weeks. You can thank Mother Nature for that small blessing."

Yet, Jack had never been so sickened, and he was wearing a mask to boot. He struggled to keep his gag reflex in check.

He would have liked nothing better than to turn and walk away from what seemed to be the final resting place of the population of Clover Springs, but that simply wasn't an option. What if Mylie and his daughters were there? The commander *had* to know what was in that building. Even if his family were not inside, valuable supplies, bottled water, or medications might be stored in there.

Reaching for his pack, he remembered a piece of peppermint he'd salvaged while on the road. Digging to the bottom of a front pocket, he soon produced the prized sweet.

Licking a finger under his mask, he rubbed the hard candy and then transferred the aromatic fragrance to the cloth covering his nose. He repeated the process three times, his nostrils now filled with the fresh scent.

He made his way through the school's lobby, never bothering to raise his weapon. Whoever was left inside had met his maker a long, long time ago.

The corridor led to a series of double doors, each equipped with a small rectangular window reinforced with chicken wire. Peering inside, Jack realized he was looking into the gymnasium.

The basketball goals, with their white nets, were clearly visible in the low light. The court, however, was covered with cots, blankets, suitcases, and other items associated with emergency shelter. He didn't see a single body. It was like the occupants had all vanished into thin air.

Pulling open the door, Jack cautiously inhaled the air inside the gym and quickly concluded that the arena wasn't the source of the foul odor.

As he moved back to let the door close, a desk just beyond the court's boundary caught his eye.

There, on the surface, a three-ring binder laid next to a coffee cup full of ink pens. "I wonder..." the commander mumbled, moving back inside, and reaching for the notebook.

Sure enough, Jack found several pages of handwritten names and addresses. The large, bold letters "Registration" scrolled across the top.

Snatching up the prize, the commander hustled back to the front glass doors, wanting to utilize the marginally-brighter outside light. He began flipping through the pages, his finger following the column of names, his eyes alert for either Armstrong or Cisco.

At the end of the second page, Jack paused his search and wondered which name Mylie would have registered under. Technically, they weren't divorced, yet he was sure his wife was already mentally reverting to her maiden name. Or was she?

The list encompassed about twenty pages, each containing about twenty-five lines. Five hundred or more people had been documented, none of whom were named Armstrong or Cisco. Where had his family gone?

With a sense of relief, Jack closed the book. His family wasn't here, or at least had never registered. As organized as the town of Clover Springs appeared to be, he was convinced that every single soul at the school would have been accounted for. There was a chance Mylie and the girls were still alive.

Now, the only mystery involving the school was what had happened to all these people?

Returning the binder to the desk, Jack continued walking along the wide corridor. As he approached the first classroom, he noticed a homemade sign taped to the door announcing "Police."

Across the hall, another placard written by the same hand read "Maintenance."

"They were repurposing the classrooms to be various offices and services," Jack nodded. "Whoever was running the show here had their shit in one, neat bag."

The improvised police station was locked, the maintenance office housing nothing but two empty desks and a bookshelf full of service manuals.

As he headed down the hall, Jack spotted the offices of the mayor and the chaplain. As they were unlocked, he checked each one and found no human remains inside. However, he did notice that the air inside the classrooms was much more breathable than the foul stench in the hall.

Just past those rooms, Jack spied a makeshift day care center organized in what had been the school's library. The commander could not help but be fascinated by what he found inside. Many of the tables had been neatly cleared to the side, opening up a large space for the children. The room was full of toys. Dozens of children's books littered the floor. A long, rectangular table in the middle of the room was covered with debris from an afternoon's finger-painting project on one end, a hodge-podge assortment of preschool-age musical instruments on the other. The reading nook, furnished with colorful and cushy lounge furniture, had been embellished with two cribs and a stack of blankets. It looked like a wonderful playroom. He could almost hear the cackles and laughter of boisterous kids at play. In truth, the eerie silence gave the commander goosebumps. He wondered if that sound would ever reach his ears again.

Next, he approached a main junction, an intersection of two wide hallways. There, taped to the wall, a single sheet boasted an oversized red cross and the word "Medical" pointing to the right. Another marker indicated that straight ahead were the "Single Male Dorm" and "Single Female Dorm."

While Jack approached every area of the building as if he were about to be ambushed, he was relatively sure the place was deserted. Always on the lookout for any antibiotics or other valuable supplies, Jack followed the first sign and took a right turn. *I can check the living quarters later,* he thought. *First things first.*

After wandering past what seemed to be two blocks of lockers, the commander spotted a large glass wall at the end of the hall. Long sections of white craft paper were stretched across the full-length windows, apparently to supply some privacy for those inside. *I wouldn't want to be in your shoes when the cheerleaders see what you have done with their banner-making supplies,* the commander mused.

At the door, Jack read a small, plastic plaque that indicated the huge room had originally been the cafeteria. The dark interior was furnished wall to wall with cots, many of them still cradling rumpled blankets and sheets. As he took a few steps inside, he spotted deep purple and black stains on the two of the closest beds. Someone had been bleeding… heavily.

Subconsciously pulling the mask tighter against his face, Jack continued inside. The offensive smell was stronger in here. The windows' covers obscured the light, and the space emitted a sinister, foreboding vibe that made the commander want to pivot and retreat to the corridor.

Pulling his flashlight, he paused before flicking on the torch. Batteries were extremely rare and he had a limited supply. Was it worth it? Deciding that he had to know what had happened here, the commander engaged the light.

The last row of cots was still occupied… the shrunken, black limbs and the heads of human cadavers half covered by blood-stained sheets evidence that they had crossed the great divide. The scene was so grotesque, Jack quickly moved the beam to explore elsewhere.

Along the back of the room stainless steel counters held stacks of food trays and the assorted equipment used in a serving line.

A wave of nausea welled up inside the commander's gut, followed a moment later by a spell of dizziness. Jack wondered if it were the morbid setting or a side effect of some lingering chemical odor that made him feel ill. His instincts warned that he should get back outside sooner, rather than later.

He spied a doorway in the corner, the round circle of his flashlight illuminating another cadaver seated at a simple, oak, office table. The deceased wore a white smock, a stethoscope dangling from its shriveled neck.

Pushing aside his urge to run from the morbid scene, the commander stepped gingerly toward the opening.

Once he'd reached the threshold, he realized that there were actually three sets of remains, all sitting around the same table, all of them holding hands as if participating in a séance. From the length of their still-visible hair, the commander assumed two were females. What the hell?

In the middle of the modest piece of furniture laid a book that reminded Jack of a diary his oldest daughter kept on her bedside table. Reaching carefully across the dead, he picked it up and directed the beam at the first page.

Sure enough, it was a log, authored by one Dr. Rena Faraz. A quick flick of his flashlight onto the corpse with the white smock confirmed as much, the navy blue, embroidered letters above her breast spelling out her name.

Fascinated and curious, Jack's inner archeologist overcame his urge to flee the death-chamber as soon as possible. He thumbed back to the first page and began reading:

> "At last count, there were 581 desperate souls at the school. Two late-stage pregnancies, thirty-seven adolescents, and a host of elderly with chronic conditions. I am most concerned about the diabetics and cardio patients who are in need of proper nutrition and sustained medication. The mayor and sheriff have done a wonderful

job convincing people to come here... almost too good of a job."

Fully engrossed by the recorded events, Jack continued to read, flipping a few pages, and steadying his light:

"DAY 4 -- An argument broke out today. The ash began falling in earnest a few hours ago, some of the councilmen demanding that the sheriff begin sealing the doors, but there are still deputies out patrolling and gathering citizens. The mayor disagreed with the other leaders, saying we couldn't turn people away. Tensions are mounting. We are all wondering how bad the ash will be. The AM radio station in Austin stopped broadcasting an hour ago."

Often, the narrative was disjointed, as if the doctor were pushed for time, scribbling notes rather than composing a historical account.

"DAY 5 -- I was in the management meeting this morning. We have about seventy-five days' worth of food left. Why didn't I take that job at Austin General? Why did I want to contribute at a small-town clinic? Everybody wants to know if the ash is dangerous... if it will make them sick. How am I supposed to know?"

Peering up at the dead doctor, Jack shook his head. "You found out just how dangerous it was, didn't you?"

Not receiving any answer from the deceased physician, Jack again flipped a few pages and continued reading.

"DAY 8 -- The electricity went out last night. I have two patients coughing up blood. I don't know why. Both are healthy, twenty-something males, one of them a deputy. They are drowning in their own fluids. I wish I knew what to do and why this was happening! I have isolated both of them, but we don't have the facilities for a proper quarantine. I'm frightened. We all are. There has been no contact from the outside world. I hope help arrives soon."

Pausing, Jack looked around the sparsely-furnished office and spied a microscope on a corner desk. "Probably scavenged from the science lab," he surmised.

Next to the device laid a stack of small, translucent glass slides. "You had the right idea, Doc," he whispered. "Just a little behind Yellowstone's curve." Returning to the diary, Jack continued reading.

> "DAY 11 – We had our first death last night. The deputy, one of the last people outside, passed away. I now have sixty-seven patients, most of them suffering from the same symptoms. I think this illness is airborne. I'm going to start gathering samples. Where is FEMA? Where is the CDC?"

> "DAY 12 – Three more have died, another dozen now coughing up blood. We are in trouble. The microscope shows that there are minute, jagged particles of glass present in the ash, even from the samples taken from inside the school. The air filters on this building aren't dense enough to protect us. I've ordered everyone to cover the nose and mouth. I didn't see this coming. I hope I'm not too late."

Sighing, Jack knew what the rest of the story would be. Flipping to the end of the diary, he read the last entry:

> "There are only three of us left that can still walk. I'm so weak, both from exhaustion and blood loss, that I can't take care of anyone else. The remaining patients are alone and miserable, but there's little we can do. We're all so frightened, the coughing so painful, death so lonely. We've made a pact. We're going to end the suffering. I pray that it is quick and painless. God help us all."

Staring once more at the trio of corpses, Jack now understood why they were holding hands. He frowned, "A suicide pact." The full impact of what had happened there made him break out in a cold sweat.

Tucking the log book under his arm, Jack moved to the doorway, his mind trying to reconcile what he had just read. These people had done everything right, had executed an impressive, mass evacuation to the best shelter available. They had quickly established an orderly society. They were providing for their friends and neighbors. Yet, it hadn't been enough.

Just thinking about the organized, yet failed attempt to survive, made the commander's head ache. The events at Clover Springs High School were demoralizing. What chance did Mylie and the girls have? How could any society, in any place, sustain itself? How could mankind ever recover?

Still, Jack reminded himself that people *had* survived. He had helped Archie tend a small, indoor garden. He had eaten eggs laid by live chickens. He had discovered hundreds of people still living in underground structures and caves. Would they be enough to sustain the human race?

As he crossed the threshold, his flashlight illuminated several large containers against the far wall. "What the hell?"

Stepping quickly to get a closer look, Jack inhaled sharply when he spied what appeared to be a moonshiner's still. "Well, now that's what I call turning lemons into lemonade," he smirked, wondering what bootleg whiskey would bring in a post-apocalyptic market.

His levity was brief. Bewilderment returned to Jack's expression when his beam landed on an oversized, plastic drum labeled "Chlorine Bleach."

Now more curious than ever, he focused on another plastic container prominently adorned with a black skull and crossbones, the bold label warning that the contents were poisonous. His lips moved as he read the next word "ACID."

"Bleach and acid?" Jack mumbled just as his eyes opened wide in recognition.

Holding his breath while his legs pumped toward the building's entrance, Jack nearly panicked when he realized that Dr. Faraz and the last few survivors had killed themselves using poison gas. That was the source of the unidentifiable odor he had first smelled when he opened the main door. He had been breathing in the same air!

Calm down, Commander, he told himself. Time must have dissipated the cloud, diluted the vapors. He would already be dead if there were still a danger… wouldn't he?

Suddenly, a very disconcerting thought occurred to him. Maybe his newly acquired headache, his dizziness, and the cold sweat that hung on his brow might have had more nefarious meaning than simply the stress of his current situation. By the time he rounded the corner and headed toward the entrance, Jack's heart was hammering, his lungs struggled for air, and his legs ached.

His feet felt like they were made of lead, and his pace had slowed even more by the time he recognized the front lobby ahead. It was his own proverbial light at the end of the tunnel, Jack realizing that freedom and survival were just outside.

Thirty feet, Commander, he reminded himself. *Just thirty feet stand between you and the Grim Reaper.* He thought of Miley and the girls. He couldn't quit now.

Twenty feet. In his mind, he knew he was a survivor, incapable of just giving up when times were tough. His feet, however, didn't seem to share this same realization, barely clearing the floor and nearly stumbling over his own shoestrings. He regained his balance and aimed for the door.

Ten feet. His neurons were beginning to misfire, his brain struggling to cope. Suddenly, his Academy instructor's shrill voice cut through his mental fog as it rapidly screamed in succession, "Let's go! Let's go! Let's go!" A career military man, Jack's conditioned response was to immediately demand his body perform at a higher level… even when his muscles swore that it was impossible to do so. While he couldn't sprint to the door, he resolved he wasn't going to fall on his sword either.

Five feet, Commander! His objective almost within his reach, he stretched out his hand to press the release bar. Pushing against the door, he mustered his last ounce of strength to survive. He had made it!

As Jack continued to suck air into his oxygen-starved chest, his mind raced with horrors of the invisible death he'd just avoided. His head was now pounding with the echo of each heartbeat, his stomach still rolling. Stress, exertion, and chemical residue could all be to blame.

Five minutes later, after breathing in fresh air, the commander's symptoms began to clear. "That was close," he whispered.

Relieved, his mind returned to the scene in the cafeteria. He could understand Dr. Faraz's decision, could relate to her mindset. How often had he thought about ending it all? The never-ending grey skies combined with the isolation and lack of hope for any reasonable future were enough to drive anyone to the edge. The folks inside Clover Springs High School had to deal with all that, plus a boatload of death and suffering.

Not wanting to take any chances, he ignored the desire to search the school for valuable supplies, food, or other goodies. It wasn't worth the risk. There could still be pockets of deadly fumes floating around inside. Clearly, a strong odor and enough chemicals lingered to cause him a brush with death.

Finally recuperated, Jack turned and stepped toward his bike. "You need water, Commander Cisco. And food. And someplace to shelter tonight. And a plan to find what happened to your wife and daughters."

Chapter 40

The first order of business, as always, was water.

As Jack rode his bike back into Clover Springs, he prioritized his needs and began formulating a plan to satisfy them.

He was almost back to the primary business district when he squeezed the brakes hard, his tires skidding in the thin coating of pumice covering the pavement.

He'd been following his original tire track through the ash. Now, ahead, there were two sets of markings. Somebody... or something had been following him.

In a flash, the commander turned his bike sideways and let it fall. His rifle was up, his body going prone behind the pack strapped to the frame. It was the best cover available in a moment's notice.

Several small businesses lined each side of the road, a handful of modest homes checkering the charcoal-colored landscape beyond. Slowly, methodically, Jack began scanning his surroundings through his optic.

The new tracks had cut down a side street just a few yards ahead. The imprint left in the ash was wide, flat, and odd. It was almost as if someone were dragging a box with sharp edges through the ash. "Or they're covering the evidence of their journey, the way Archie did at his driveway."

He quickly ruled out several possibilities. From a considerable distance away, his ears would have alerted him to the roar of any internal combustion engine. Jack lived in a silent world, without birds, insects, or any other form of noise pollution. Most days, the only sound was the howl of the wind. Besides, the pumice could defeat any engine filter. He'd seen plenty of evidence of that.

Regardless of their mode of transportation, whoever was out there knew of the commander's presence. Yet, they had cut off the main drag well before the high school. Were they circling around? Socially awkward or easily frightened? A traveler like himself who tried to avoid trouble or confrontation?

Given his experience with post-apocalyptic mankind, Jack was no longer the trusting sort. Sure, there were still good people out there. He'd met them.

However, some of the worst examples of humanity also roamed the earth. He'd run into his share of the darkness that filled some people's souls. In this case, it really didn't matter. Either side of the species coin was prone to shoot first and ask questions later.

It took him nearly half an hour to check every window, nook, and cranny. Even then, Jack knew it was impossible to detect someone who didn't want to be seen. There were a thousand places in an urban environment that could be disguising a lone individual… or their rifle barrel.

Still, he couldn't just lie in the middle of the road forever. Cautiously, he rose, lifted his bike, and began walking it toward the center of town.

He stayed to the left, stretching his arms long to steer the handlebars, trying to keep the thick pack between where the stranger had turned and his center mass. A good shot could still pick him off. He'd need a fair amount of luck to survive a bushwhacker hiding on either side of the street.

No shot rang out; no lead pierced his body.

Finally, back in front of the City Hall, the commander exhaled deeply and shrugged. He'd be vigilant and keep his eyes and ears on a higher alert, but that was about the best he could do. He pushed the bicycle between the two parked police cars and did a quick, 360-degree scan.

As much as he wanted to flush out his stalker, the top priority was to find a spring. He couldn't survive long without water.

Across from the town's former center of government, Jack noticed a little diner. Pushing down the kickstand, Jack hefted his rifle and quickly jogged across the open pavement. At the restaurant's front door, he wiped away a coating of volcanic dust and peered inside. Just inside the glass, a modest, metal fixture was stuffed with brochures promoting local attractions.

Jack pushed and pulled on the double doors, finding them locked tight. "This is the only community I've seen that has not been looted to the rafters," he whispered, glancing around for something to pry open the entrance. He could have blown apart the lock with his weapon, but that would have informed everyone within three miles that a burglary was in process. "I can just see Deputy Barney Fife come out of the woodwork at the sound of a gunshot," the commander smiled. "That is definitely not the best way to meet the neighbors."

All the while, the commander couldn't shake the feeling that he was being watched.

"You're being silly, Cisco," he whispered, scanning everything in the area from doorways to rooftops. "You saw a weird set of tracks. Don't get all paranoid. The hills do not have eyes."

At the next alley, he spotted a hunk of concrete, complete with a six-inch piece of rebar protruding from one end. Hefting the weighty club, he strolled back to the café's front door.

"I hate doing this," he grumbled, coiling to strike the glass while turning his head away from any potential airborne shards.

With a powerful blow, Jack bludgeoned the door's glass into a spiderweb. A quick kick with his boot finished the work, creating a narrow opening.

Careful not to cut his skin or clothing, the commander stepped inside and skimmed the colorful brochures. He didn't care about the nearby dude ranch or the four-star bed and breakfast. On the second row of leaflets, he found what he was looking for. "Visit Franklin Springs!" it read. "Swim in a natural limestone pool of spring water."

The pictures looked perfect, a small, stickman map indicating the local swimming hole was situated just outside of town. After glancing at the nearest highway sign, Jack headed back to his bicycle and mounted the seat. He needed to hurry. Dusk promised to arrive in a few hours.

He pushed the pedals at a faster than normal clip, trying to beat twilight's onset while at the same time hoping to make his thin frame a problematic target.

Again, the road in front of him was clear of any tracks or signs of occupation. Only slight waves in the ash were visible, courtesy of the swirling gusts of wind.

Still, Jack remained vigilant. Constantly glancing over his shoulder while keeping a tight grip on his carbine, the commander's head was on a swivel. All the while, he felt like he was being shadowed, his neck hairs tingling with the sensation of prying eyes.

Finally, long after the density of Clover Springs had faded, Jack approached a charming, rustic sign with the words "Welcome to Franklin Springs" carved into it. Apparently, family-friendly fun could be had for $10 per carload. A site directory offered a map to hiking trails, picnic areas, restrooms, and the swimming area. The list of attractions included a concession stand; open from 9 a.m. to dusk. *Just in time for a burger and fries,* Cisco quipped.

Jack turned into the driveway and then pulled behind a board that reiterated the park rules. Peeking around the sign, he examined the road behind him for nearly a minute. No nefarious vehicle appeared; no mysterious stalker became visible.

Ahead, several hundred yards off the pavement, Jack spied a series of rooftops bordering what appeared to be a sizable parking lot. He cycled past an outhouse-sized shack with a sliding glass window. "Do you accept credit cards?" he asked the empty ticket booth.

He continued riding, always glancing right and left, front and back. It was if he was the only living soul on the planet.

Finally arriving at the main parking area, Jack spotted a series of wooden signs. The picnic area was located to the left, the restrooms and snack bar to the right. "I wonder if they have spicy mustard for their hotdogs?" the commander joked.

The pool and spring were straight ahead.

Loosening the two plastic milk jugs that were his primary water containers, Jack started walking down the steep path. *Thank heavens somebody shelled out the dough for a poured-concrete trail.*

He was now on high alert, his grip on the M4 tight, his arms ready to bring the weapon to his shoulder at the snap of a twig. Since Yellowstone's blast, many people had succumbed to dehydration, and unfortunately, fresh sources of potable water were rare. Any survivors in the area would know of the spring's existence and might even dedicate resources to protect it from outsiders. After all, simply trying to secure a drink had gotten Jack into trouble before.

At the bottom of the trail, he spotted a large, Olympic-sized pool, including a generous sundeck covered with paver stones, several lounge chairs, and a single diving board. The water looked crystal clear, a reassuring sign.

With his rifle in the crook of his arms, Jack began to circle the pool. At the far end, a round, stone structure the size and shape of a wishing well was stationed about ten feet beyond the diving board. Two rock-lined channels led from the monument, one returning to the pool, the other continuing downhill. Both were flowing with a considerable stream of pristine, bubbling water. A brass plaque had been embedded in the limestone nearby.

Brushing aside the pumice and dead leaves, Jack read, "Franklin Spring. Registered as a Texas Historical Site. Discovered in 1821 by Isaiah D. Franklin, one of the first Europeans to explore what is now known as Hays County. The spring was a welcome stopover on the Trans-Pecos cattle drive route. It is believed to have been used by native Americans for hundreds of years as a meeting place for important powwows and other ceremonies."

41

Jack's reading was interrupted by the distant crunch of a broken branch. He scurried behind the stone structure in a flash, his rifle up and ready to engage.

He didn't breathe or blink, his eyes scanning the dead woods stretching off to the east. Had the sound been just the normal surrender of decaying wood? Was someone trying to track him? Had he really heard the noise?

For nearly five minutes, the commander didn't move. His ears and eyes were piqued, but nothing else hit his radar. Only the hypnotic burbling of the running water disturbed the silent forest.

Cautiously, he rose from behind his cover and began following the other manmade channel down the hill. The route was easy, a wide sidewalk provided by the owners of Franklin Spring.

A short distance later, the concrete path branched to the left, another of the matching, wooden signs indicating the direction of the tank.

Shrugging, Jack followed the provided trail.

After hiking for a bit, he noticed a series of stone steps carved into the ground, their gentle spiral leading down a steep wall of a limestone cliff. Frowning at the unexpected feature, he again elected to play tourist and began his descent.

He wound his way down, carefully taking what had to be over seventy steps. As he neared the end of the slope, he heard an unusual sound that was a cross between slapping water and a dull rumble.

At the bottom, he emerged on a massive flat rock that was at least half the size of a basketball court. Peering up, Jack smiled at an unspoiled waterfall dropping into what appeared to be a crater carved out of solid stone. "This must be the tank," he whispered, in awe of the natural beauty of the place. "This is what really pulled customers in."

Mesmerized by the crashing water, Jack stepped slowly around the pool, his mind completely captivated by the amazing sight before him. He wondered if there had ever been any native fish, curious if they might have survived. Nothing was swimming, croaking, or disturbing the gorgeous pool today.

As he walked the shoreline, the commander realized that he hadn't stopped smiling. It was such a wonderful setting, a perfect blend of formation, sound, and sculpture. "What's the term the Chinese use?" Jack whispered. "Feng shui? The harmony of people in their surrounding environment?"

He was sure the Native Americans must have felt the same sensation. "This is holy ground," he continued.

With darkness quickly approaching, Jack decided to camp here, regardless of the dangers associated with the proximity of a water source. "There were no footprints at all," he reasoned. "This isn't a regular stop for the locals… if any of them survived."

Jack climbed the steps, panting hard by the time he reached the top. Pushing his bike, he then made the return trip to the tank, the wheels bumping down one step at a time.

His next chore was gathering firewood. There was no shortage of dead timber, but the effort left him perspiring despite the cold.

Now hot in his multiple layers, Jack considered taking a swim. How long had it been since he'd had a bath? How filthy were his clothes? How could he wear a mask while enjoying a dip?

The thought made Jack remember a wooden cabinet he'd seen by the manmade pool above. With a grimace, he reclimbed the staircase and approached the locker-like bin. Sure enough, the inside was full of folded beach towels. There was a money box on the door, requesting two dollars to rent a towel. "Do you take IOUs?" he chuckled.

With an armload of terrycloth in his arms, the commander descended the steps again. He then built an extra-large fire and erected his shelter just as darkness was settling in.

Careful to keep his breathing cloth over his face, Jack then began shucking off his clothing. He had a spare, less-dirty set of clothes in his pack and knew that he would need their warmth once he finished his swim. He would take the opportunity to wash the worst of his wardrobe and dry it over the fire.

Second thoughts filled the commander's mind as he stuck that first foot in the water. "Damn, that's cold!" he barked. Yet, the clear pool was so inviting.

He dove in, pressing the cotton mask tight against his face like a kid jumping off a pool's edge while squeezing his nose. The shock of the icy water passed quickly, surpassed by the pleasurable feeling of the soft liquid against his body.

With one hand keeping his air filter in place, Jack began rubbing his skin with the other. It was a glorious experience.

Once acclimated, the pool actually felt warm. Jack remembered reading that most caves and springs maintained a constant temperature of their air and water. He guessed it was about seventy degrees.

After five minutes, he knew it was time to get out. He didn't want to lower his core temperature too much, didn't want to risk catching a cold or worse.

He then pulled his clothing into the pool. First, he rinsed the glass fragments from the cloth under the relentless flow of the waterfall. Then, sense he didn't have any detergent, he settled on briskly rubbing the soiled garments on the stone bottom. Finally, after a twisting motion to remove as much water as possible, he tossed his wardrobe onto the rocks.

Stepping onto the bank, he reached for a towel and took in a large chest full of air. He would hold his breath while he dried his face.

A shadow appeared along the cliff face, Jack pivoting toward his campfire. A human shape stepped forward, backlit by the flames and embers. There was a rifle in the stranger's hands.

Jack froze, his dripping, naked body instantly beginning to shiver in the frigid air. Or was it fear that caused him to shake?

Stepping closer, the human outline kept its weapon steady, pointed directly at Jack's chest. Fury and rage took command of his emotions. Why had he been so stupid? Why had he let his guard down?

"Go ahead," a female voice ordered. "Finish drying off. You're turning blue."

A woman? Jack thought. *"Where in the hell did she come from?"*

He did as she instructed, quickly wiping off the rest of his frame with the soft towel and then reaching for a clean mask. A moment later, his face was the only part of his body that wasn't exposed.

"Go ahead, get dressed. I'm not a pervert, and you're a little skinny for my taste anyway," she chided, pointing at a pile of spare clothing near the fire. "But... just to be clear, I have unloaded your rifle, and your pistol is in my back pocket. If you even think about making a move for your knife, I'll cut you in half. Are we clear?"

"Yes," Jack answered, padding barefoot toward his camp. He then slipped on his spare outfit, glad for the warmth. Neither he, nor his captor uttered a word. While he dressed, the commander managed to get a good look at the stranger.

She was a tall woman, nearly six feet in height. Given the fall of civilization, she appeared to be remarkably fit, wearing a dark blue jumpsuit marked with an American Flag on the sleeve. A black ski mask covered her face and hair, an AR15 style rifle in her hand. She sported a thick, duty belt, the kind typical of military personnel. A large knife, pistol, and three pouches dangled from her waist.

Finally, as he pulled on his boots, she spoke, "I didn't expect you to take a bath. That kind of surprised me," she paused, and even with the cover obscuring most of her face, Jack thought he detected a slight smirk. "I was going to wait and approach while you were sleeping, but I couldn't pass up such a prime opportunity. Who are you?"

"My name is Commander Jack Cisco, United States Navy," he replied.

His response seemed to surprise her. While he couldn't see her eyebrows under the mask, he was sure they had traveled skyward.

"Commander? Navy? Are you out of Corpus Christi?" she asked.

Jack knew the Navy had a large base in that southern Texas city, but he had never been there. That facility was used to train naval aviators, not submariners. "No," he replied honestly. "I came from San Diego."

This time her reaction was visible, her eyes blinking several times in the firelight. "San Diego? As in California?"

"Yes."

"You're telling me you rode that bicycle all the way from the West Coast... after the eruption?"

"Yes. I was aboard a submarine in the Pacific, the USS Utah. When we docked a few months ago, the world had changed... for the worst, I might add," Jack explained.

"That's no shit," she barked, her tone indicating both a sense of disbelief as well as a hint of humor. "And just why, Commander, did you decide to pedal across half a post-apocalyptic continent? I'm sure it wasn't just to take a bath in Franklin Pool."

"My wife and daughters were supposed to be staying at my father-in-law's ranch," Jack replied. "I had to get here. I had to find them."

Tilting her head, she responded, "Were supposed to be staying at the ranch? You mean they weren't there?"

"The ranch is under water. I think the ash caused a river to change course or overflow. I don't know if they had time to escape or where they are," the commander stated, his voice gloomy and low.

While she digested his response, Jack took a step toward the fire and began rubbing his hands. It then dawned on the commander that their conversation had been all one-sided.

Somehow, he didn't think she was out to do him harm, but these days, there never were any guarantees.

"What's your name and story?" he finally asked.

She grunted before deftly changing the subject, "Aren't you going to ask if I come here often? Don't you want to know my zodiac sign?"

He laughed, despite having a rifle pointed at his chest. That seemed to relax her just a bit.

"My name is Hannah. Hannah Middleton. I worked for the… I used to work for Uncle Sam, just like you, Commander. I was a TSA agent at the Austin airport before the world went to hell."

"A TSA agent? You mean one of the officers who searched luggage and ran a wand under people's arms?"

She chuckled at the crude job description, then answered, "Well… yes and no. My actual assignment was perimeter security. I'd only been on the job for a few months before Yellowstone exploded. Before that, I'd been in the US Army for eight years. I was an MP."

"Nice to meet you, Hannah Middleton," Jack replied, taking a step toward her and offering his hand.

She didn't bite, her weapon snapping up as she moved back. "Not *that* nice, Commander Cisco. Stay back, or I'll arrange for that to have been your last bath."

Withdrawing his hand, Jack shook his head. "You dry-gultched *me*, lady."

Ignoring his slang western term, she changed the subject. "What did you find inside of that high school?"

It was Jack's turned to be surprised. "You've been following me since when?"

"I have the gun. I ask the questions," she answered.

Despite the harsh rhetoric, Jack once again suspected the hint of a smile behind her mask.

"Whatever," he shrugged. "I found a bunch of dead people and a cloud of poison gas… or at least the remnants of one. After I came across that, I didn't hang around very long," he sighed as he remembered how close he had come to being permanently interred in the Clover Springs High School. Shaking off the bad vibe, it was his turn to redirect the conversation. "So, I guess those were your tracks I saw in the street, weren't they?"

Again, she ignored his question, at least at first. "I didn't *think* you were in there long enough to thoroughly search the place. What was the source of the poison?"

Despite Hannah having the drop on him, Jack was growing tired of the one-sided conversation. He said as much, "I'm tired and so hungry my vocal cords are having trouble working. Shoot me if you're going to; otherwise, I want to put more logs on that fire and fix a meal. You're welcome to dine in, leave, or murder me and take my stuff. Your call."

Hannah tilted her head again, her grip tightening on the rifle. For a second, Jack thought she might really pull the trigger. She then chuckled, and said, "A man who can cook? Now, you don't see that every day!"

Nodding toward his pack, he responded, "Well, I am no chef; that's for sure. But I have canned corn, beans, and one last pickle that I was saving to share with my daughters. I'm running low on chow at the moment, but you're welcome to half."

The lady gunman hesitated like a woman taking her time to assess her options. In a voice dripping with sarcasm, she answered, "Now, don't take this the wrong way… especially since we are getting along so well and all, but I need you to prove that you're actually a commander in the United States Navy. Can you do that?"

"My dog tags are in my pack," Cisco responded. "I can show them to you, or you can dig them out of that front pocket."

For a second, Hannah seemed to be judging distances and angles. Finally, she indicated the pack with her chin and said, "Go ahead… but slow. Real slow."

As Jack took a step forward, he heard the safety click on her weapon. As promised, a second later, he produced the metal identification, holding the shiny tags up in the firelight.

"Toss them over here," she ordered.

Jack gave them an easy toss, Hannah catching them with a cat-like pass of her hand. After reading the tiny, raised letters, she said, "You could have picked these up from any old dead body along the road. Do you have any real proof?"

Returning to the same compartment of his pack, Jack fished around for a moment before producing his wallet. "You're getting on my nerves, Miss TSA Agent, just like at the airports. I'm sorry there aren't any handicapped grandmothers around so you could perform a body cavity search."

"I don't see that you have much choice, Mr. Navy man. Toss your billfold over here, *please*."

Jack complied and then watched as she pulled out his laminated picture ID. Her eyes darted between the photograph and the man standing before her, then she flipped the plastic sleeve and came to what Jack knew was a picture of him, Mylie, and the girls. It was a photograph that he cherished.

She threw the wallet back and then lowered her weapon. "I'm sorry Jack, but a girl can't be too cautious these days. I believe you are who you say you are." It was the closest to an apology Hannah had ever come. "By the way, you have a beautiful family."

There was an unspoken communication between them in that moment. Two complete strangers, survivors in a world gone mad, meeting in an extremely unlikely place. Neither could afford to trust the other, yet they did. Perhaps it was the fact that he hadn't talked to another human being in weeks, but Jack found himself liking the woman standing next to the fire, weapon or not.

"Thank you," he replied, returning his dog tags and wallet to the pack. "Are you going to stay for dinner?"

"Yes, if the invite is still open," she nodded. "But I've got my own food. Maybe we can *pool* our resources and set up a buffet?"

Jack thought the play on words was funny. "Cute," he nodded after a chuckle. "I'll throw some wood on the fire, and we can **dive** right in."

She returned a bit later, carrying a backpack stuffed to the brim. As she began emptying her rations, Jack noticed an oddly packaged meal. It reminded him of an MRE, but the wrapping was all wrong. As she pulled the plastic off the small, cardboard tray, the commander saw a pint-sized steak, asparagus, and what appeared to be a slice of apple cobbler.

Thirty minutes later, they both had a plate of food. Each choosing a rock for a seat, they began shoveling the chow into their mouths. Not since serving on the *Utah* had the commander tasted anything so scrumptious.

"I'm embarrassed," he began between mouthfuls. "This steak is excellent. I'm afraid my small contribution of veggies is left wanting."

"I disagree," Hannah retorted between chewing and swallowing. "I've not tasted fresh corn or beans since before Yellowstone blew. I'm sick of this airline food. It's good to have something homegrown."

"Airline food?"

Nodding as she swallowed another fork full of grub, Hannah continued, "That's about all we have left, and even that supply is beginning to run low. That's why I'm scouting the area. We're running out of food and water."

"Who is we?" Jack asked, impressed by both Hannah's food and skill.

"That, Commander, is a long story," she sighed, trying to corral the last few kernels of corn onto her fork.

Chapter 41

"Just about 400 other people and I owe our lives to an airline pilot named Captain Alex Bascom," Hannah began. "We've been holed up inside the Austin International airport since Mother Nature threw her little temper tantrum."

Jack was awestruck. A million questions flooded his mind at the same instant. An airport? Were they privy to any government communications there? How did they keep out the ash? How have they survived?

Instead of continuing her story, Hannah stood up and sauntered to the water's edge. There, she took a knee and began washing her plate and utensils.

After finishing the chore, she stood and returned to the fire. Jack could see from her eyes that his companion was someplace else… reliving a time in the past.

"I'll never forget that day," she began in a monotone. "All flights, both incoming and outgoing had been canceled, all the terminals closed. The Austin police were handling the people both inside and out of the secured area. We didn't have any passengers to screen, so I was in the TSA's employee breakroom, shoulder to shoulder with everybody else, watching cable news on the television."

She paused just then, her gaze dropping to the ground as more memories surfaced. "By late in the afternoon, I knew the entire planet was in trouble. There had already been a church roof collapse in Denver, the weight of the blizzard-like ash causing all kinds of problems. There were reports of thousands of dead in Rapid City, South Dakota, one reporter claiming a poison gas cloud the size of Vermont was rolling east."

"I was under about a mile of Pacific Ocean at the time," Jack interjected. "I missed all of that. Just lucky, I guess."

"Yes," she replied. "I think ignorance would have been bliss those first few days. It seemed like every few minutes, there was a breaking news story of another catastrophe. Large chunks of California were falling into the sea. There were earthquakes all over, most of Hawaii and Alaska wiped out by a tsunami. The New Madrid fault line shook so bad, the arch in St. Louis collapsed. Omaha had two feet of ash by the time the sun was setting. I wondered if it was going to rise the next morning."

She stopped again, her mind obviously struggling to pick which words to use next. Jack let her go. He understood the trauma life-changing memories could invoke. Hell, he'd have a tough time recounting any number of the experiences he'd had since he left the *Utah*.

"I didn't know what to do, where to go, or how to act. Here we were, at work and away from our families, all absolutely stunned by this incredible breaking news. Some of the early reports made it sound like maybe 20% of the United States would feel the damaging effects of this eruption, but it was not likely to seriously impact Texas at all. I remember seeing a map that showed a highlighted box extending from Washington state to North Dakota, then south to Nebraska and west to California. Originally, most of the experts thought that was the area that would be affected. Other news stations broadcast a real "end of the world" story... interviewing some guy who sounded like a nut job because what he was predicting was so unbelievable... but was that really just a ploy for higher ratings? With all the constant updates and conflicting reports, it was hard to know what to believe. What was the real reach of this event? How long would it last? I thought I had rather be with my family up in Texarkana, but I called, and I couldn't get through. I thought about going home to my apartment, but I didn't want to be alone. I can't ever remember feeling so lost and hopeless... and I wasn't the only one."

Returning to her rock-chair, Hannah then managed a smile. "About then is when one of the airline reps knocked on the door.

He said that their people were organizing, preparing a plan to make the terminal building a shelter, and wanted to know if we wanted to attend the meeting. That was the first time I met Captain Bascom."

"He is a striking man," she soon added. "A true leader who strode to the front of a room full of anxious people and immediately established calm. He said that if we all acted quickly and worked together, we could survive. He claimed to have a plan. He was so reassuring and firm in his resolve. I'll never forget that first gathering."

"How did you seal the terminal against the ash?" Jack inquired. "I was just in the school, and their filtration system didn't keep the lethal stuff out. How did you manage clean air?"

"There were dozens of commercial jets attached to the building. We divided up into work details, each equipped with rolls of tape and all the plastic trash bags we could carry. While we went about taping shut every door, window, opening, and duct, Bascom was working with the mechanics and other pilots to modify all the parked aircraft. They configured the planes' circulation systems to create an overpressure inside the terminal. I'm not an engineer. I don't know the details, but it worked."

Rubbing his chin, Jack suddenly stood and began pacing around the fire. Hannah's story was amazing and a little hard to believe. Yet, given his rudimentary knowledge of jet aircraft, it was possible.

Modern planes used a method called engine bleed to pressurize their cabins during flight at higher altitudes. The commander knew this because he'd been part of a study conducted by the Navy that considered using a similar technology on submarines.

If Captain Bascom had managed to increase the air pressure inside the terminal, even just a few fractions of a pound over the outside air, it would have kept the ash and its deadly slivers of glass, at bay. Still, Cisco had lots of issues with the entire concept.

"To do that, he would've had to keep the jets running. The pumice would have shredded those turbofans into scrap metal in no time at all. That's why all the flights were grounded in the first place," he spouted, unable to disguise the skepticism in his voice.

"They only had to run the aircrafts' engines at a very, very low speed. The ground crews covered them with some sort of cowl which let in enough air to function at a low level for several days."

Jack was lost in thought, and pacing seemed to help him think. "Yes," he eventually conceded. "I suppose that might be enough positive pressure to work. And of course, the airlines had warehouses full of food, delivery trucks stuffed with trays of the stuff, and probably a huge supply of water, medical supplies, and the other essentials of survival."

Without making eye contact, Hannah replied, "Not all the essentials. We lost a lot of people those first two months. Some to sickness, others to violence. We had several that completely lost their marbles and escaped to the outside. It was rough going there for a while."

"I understand," Jack whispered. "I've seen things these last few months that no man should ever witness."

Both of their gazes shifted to the fire, the flickering flames seeming to pull them both into a trance. It was Jack who broke the silence, "I've also seen miracles," he proclaimed, trying to dig himself out of the melancholy funk. "I've encountered inspiring, strong people along the way. There is still good in the world. There is still hope."

"Really?" she brightened. "You're not trying to pull the wool over my eyes, are you?"

"We both already have wool over our faces," Jack countered, making them both chuckle.

Jack told her about Archie and the underground society in Carlsbad. He spoke about the cliff house and the cattle that still survived there. "There was also violence," he then added. "But there's always a top and a bottom... a front and a back to everything. We, as a species, can't seem to manage good without evil."

"I know what you're saying. The airport is close to Austin, and when the situation in the city reached a really, really desperate level, we had people who tried to shoot their way into the terminal. The violence threatened the integrity of our building and endangered our lives. We had to turn the airport into a fortress of sorts, just to survive...." Her voice faltered, and the commander realized he had struck a nerve. A minute later, she continued, "You know, Jack, I served in the military. I get defending the Constitution of the United States, but I am telling you that battling with fellow citizens... other people just like me who wanted nothing more than to raise their kids, visit grandma on the weekends... live the American dream.... Nobody should have to do that. So many people died during those skirmishes. More than once, we barely held on."

"I believe it," Jack replied, his mind summoning the images from the firefights that took place at the San Diego Naval Base before the *Utah* arrived. He'd seen the aftermath and destruction.

They fell silent, the fire holding both of thoughts for several minutes. Again, it was Cisco who interrupted the crackling embers. "You saw the picture of my family. Is there any chance they came to the airport? Or would someone there possibly know where refugees were going at the time?"

Shaking her head, Hannah said, "No, we didn't let anyone in after the ash began to fall. Captain Bascom, however, might know something. He values information more than anything else, other than food and water, of course. I've seen him barter with travelers before. Since the pumice has become less dangerous, we've been sending out scouts like me. Sometimes they come back with a visitor. Sometimes, they don't come back at all. You need to go and speak with him. He'll be very interested in your travels, and who knows, he might be able to point you in the right direction."

Jack was curious about something she had said, "The danger from the ash has declined?"

"Oh, yes," she replied. "For the first three weeks, it took a very special mask to keep your lungs clear. At about two months, we discovered that it was safe to go outside with just a cloth over your nose and mouth. We also have seen that not every area received the same amount of accumulation. Along the coast, we've heard, there is hardly any ash cover at all. Captain Bascom believes that is due to the onshore breeze that occurs along most of the Gulf. There are rumors that some people living shoreside never had *any* glass in their air, but we don't believe them. Some people just like to talk a lot, I've discovered."

That was welcome news to Jack. He had seen dozens of people who had survived the worst of it, and that meant Mylie and the girls might still be alive. Plus, he had already speculated a hundred times that the environment's situation might be improving. The possibility of being reunited with his girls, coupled with the possibility of mankind's comeback lifted his spirits. Hannah's words provided him with more hope than he'd experienced in weeks.

Catching his guest stifling a yawn, Jack suggested, "We don't have to catch up on the entire apocalypse tonight. We can compare notes again in the morning. But right now, we should get some rest."

"Are you going with me back to the airport tomorrow?" she asked, reaching to unroll her tent.

"I don't know just yet. I really need to find my family, but I might find out more by talking to the people there than knocking on random doors here. Let me sleep on it," Jack replied, unzipping his own shelter.

Jack awoke just after dawn, the commander's outlook murky and his heart heavy. Despite the meal and pleasant conversation he had enjoyed the night before, his dreams had been filled with worrisome images of his missing wife and daughters.

Hannah's story had helped a little, keeping alive a dim glimmer of hope in the commander's mind. Time and again, he had been amazed at the resiliency of the human animal, and her story was a prime example.

Exiting his tent, he detected a delightful aroma drifting from the rejuvenated campfire. Hannah was already up and at it, kneeling by the crackling wood. "Is that coffee I smell?" he asked, sniffing the air.

"Yes, it is. I thought you might appreciate a cup," she said.

"That, young lady, is about the nicest thing anybody's offered me in a very long time," he nodded, reaching for his metal cup and extending it toward the dark liquid heating over the flames.

Returning to his rock perch, Jack sipped the brew, more from wanting to prolong the experience than any concern over burning his mouth. After swallowing that first bit, he rolled his eyes while tilting his head backward. "Oh... my... goodness," he cooed. "I had forgotten how good legally addictive stimulants could be first thing in the morning. Paradise. Amazing. Thank you. I needed that after the night I had."

"How long has it been since you've had a cup of joe?" she inquired, a smile forming under her mask.

"I don't know. Months. Years. Decades? At least it seems like it's been at least that long."

"There was a warehouse of coffee at the airport, enough for a month of flights carrying a couple of hundred people each. It was one of the first things we confiscated after the eruption."

"Same thing with that meal you fixed last night?" Jack asked.

"Yes. The airport at Austin was going through this big public relations effort to go green. They had just installed wind turbines along one side of the property. We rerouted the electricity to power the food storage facilities. There were freezers full of prepared meals inside," she explained.

"So, you had a building you could seal enough to create an over-pressure, tons of food and coffee, and a built-in security force. That was pretty damned lucky, Hannah."

Nodding, she added to the commander's list. "We had an airport full of travelers as well. Among them we had a doctor, nurses, engineers… folks from all walks of life were marooned there. More than once their presence and skills have saved our bacon."

Jack struggled to hold his tongue. He wanted to unleash the hurt that festered in his soul. He wanted to say, "Lucky you. My wife and daughters probably fought back a lake of ash while you dined on meat and potatoes in the airport lounge!" Somehow, he crushed the urge to let the harsh words tumble out. None of this was Hannah's fault. There was no need to heap guilt on someone who was simply in the right place at the right time. Sometimes in life, luck was more important than skill. Still, it was a bitter pill to swallow. Mylie flew into that same airport several times a year. She would have passed through just a few months before Yellowstone's eruption.

Somehow, the airport scout seemed to sense his feelings even though his face was covered. "You can have the rest of the brew," she offered in a sweet voice. "I'm good for the day."

After savoring his last drop of java, Jack began packing his kit. "The coffee did it," he said a short time later. "I'm cheap and easy. I can be bribed with caffeine. If the offer is still open, I'll go back to the airport with you."

"That's great!" she said. "I'm sure Captain Bascom will want to hear every detail of what you've encountered on your journey. He might also have information that can help you find your wife."

That decision made Jack think of another nagging question that had plagued his thoughts. "What is your mode of transportation? I noticed some odd tracks back in Clover Springs… what kind of vehicles are you using?"

He detected a huge grin under her mask, accompanied by a twinkle in her eye. "I'll show you," she replied, hefting her pack onto a shoulder.

Pushing his own bike up the steps, Jack waited in anticipation at the top while Hannah walked ahead. "I left my wheels on the far side of that hill so you wouldn't see any evidence of my stalking, but there is more..." she began, "hold on. I'll be right back."

A few minutes later, the commander recognized Hannah's head, encased in a lime-green helmet, bouncing along the trail. She was riding what appeared to be a motorcycle, yet there wasn't a sound from any engine. "What the hell?" he grunted.

Pulling to a stop in front of an amazed Jack, she announced, "It's electric. It runs off batteries, just like a golf cart. I get about a hundred miles per charge."

"Where on God's earth did you get that?" Jack asked, stepping around to admire the vehicle.

"I told you before that the airport was going green, right? The TSA, always looking to improve its public image, joined the effort by purchasing a handful of these electric motorcycles. We used them to patrol the perimeter fences and to buzz around the grounds. It's actually faster than a regular bike, and best of all, it doesn't give a rat's ass about the ash," she stated with pride.

Jack had never heard of such a thing. It looked like the typical mid-sized, dirt bike, including a "gas tank" that he assumed held batteries instead of fuel. "It doesn't have a transmission, just brakes," Hannah added. "It's very easy to ride. We use the wind generators to recharge them. Captain Bascom assigned all of the scouts their own bikes. As long as I don't venture any further from my post than half the battery's life, this little scooter is a real gem."

"Wow," the commander replied, a bit of envy in his voice. "A stealth dirt bike. Perfect for the post-apocalyptic rider." Still, he couldn't have used such a machine on his trip. There would have been no way to recharge the beast.

Jack remembered Dr. Reagan's electric golf cart and how helpful that device had been. So far, battery and steam power seemed to be the only methods of transportation that had survived. *I should apply for a job selling hybrid cars*, he thought.

As he walked around the battery-powered chariot, he noticed it was pulling a small, makeshift sled made from a sheet of plastic and several metal rods. "That explains the odd tracks I saw in the street," he whispered.

Nodding, Hannah added, "If I find valuable supplies, I can load them up. We call this 'Santa's sleigh.'"

"And it covers your tracks pretty well," Jack conceded.

A few minutes later, the duo was riding back toward Clover Springs. Jack, pedaling at his usual pace, worried that he was holding Hannah back. She didn't seem to mind.

They reentered the town, carefully checking the roadway for any sign of life. Only the original imprints of Jack's tires were visible in the ash.

With Hannah leading the way, they turned toward the east, a road sign indicating Austin was thirty-one miles away. After less than a block of travel, she pulled to the side and stopped. "The airport is on the southeastern edge of the city," she explained. "We'll have to take a slight detour to avoid a couple of suburbs. We occasionally clash with people living there. They have been incredibly hostile in the past. My job isn't to fight, just scout. I try to avoid confrontation if possible."

"I'm with you there," he replied. "Always better to go around than through."

"If you don't mind, I want to take a slightly different route back home. There is somebody I want you to meet. He might know something about your wife and daughters. At least that might salvage something out of my trip."

"You've found an excellent source of water," Jack offered, pointing with his thumb, back toward the spring.

"It's too far away to be utilized. We would have to have large-capacity water trucks to transport it to the airport. Over four hundred people consume a lot of liquids."

Jack flashed with embarrassment. The scope and scale of Hannah's problems were far greater than his own. She was out trying to support hundreds of survivors. It was daunting even to consider.

Changing the subject, Hannah said, "The road I want to take east will add a couple of miles to the trip. Are you sure you're okay pedaling the extra distance?"

It was the commander's turn to counter with the obvious. "I don't think a couple more miles will be the straw that breaks my back," he grinned. "What's an extra twenty minutes of pedaling in the grand scheme of things?"

Shaking her head, Hannah replied, "Sorry. I guess we come from two completely different worlds."

Scanning the pewter sky, Jack added, "And they both suck."

They continued east, Hannah zooming ahead at every hill and curve, scouting to make sure the road was clear of bandits or other hazards. Jack had been doing the same thing on his own since leaving San Diego. However, having a partner with a super-fast ride who could provide intel in advance eliminated the need for Jack to constantly pause his journey to scout an upcoming area. Having Hannah accelerated the process, their pace as a team significantly faster than Cisco was able to accomplish alone.

They had traveled just over ten miles when a steep hill caused the commander to make a breaking motion with his hands. "I need to rest," he informed his new companion. "That last incline was a real muscle burner."

Nodding her agreement, Hannah pulled alongside and kicked down her bike's stand. "I need to powder my nose," she informed Jack, pulling a small pack and her rifle from her electric chariot's rack.

"I won't look," Jack quipped, instantly regretting the smartass remark.

He thought he'd really made a mistake when Hannah racked the charging handle of her rifle, an obvious motion intended to let him know she was chambering a round into the weapon. "I know you won't," she teased.

As he stretched his overworked legs, Jack pulled water from his Camelbak and studied the road ahead. This was hilly country, the pavement winding and weaving through ridges that he estimated were 750 to 1,500 feet high. He'd never noticed the terrain while cruising comfortably in a car. On a bike, every rise was agony.

Just as Jack was closing the hose of his water bladder, gunshots rang out from the east, the blasts echoing as they rolled through the valley ahead. The commander's weapon was up and ready before his brain finished calculating the volume and distance involved. Whoever was shooting was far away. The noise was dull, and not that loud.

Hannah, concern wrinkling her face beneath the mask, reached his side a moment later. Before she could speak, another string of reports sounded. "Somebody's in a fight," Jack grunted.

"They aren't hunting; that's for sure," she responded.

Another volley of gunfire rolled through the valley, the echo of at least a dozen clear shots reaching the duo.

Throwing a troubled glance at the commander, Hannah moaned, "Shit! That might be coming from Sheng's place. It's so hard to tell with all the gorges and valleys."

"Sheng?"

"The man I was taking you to meet. He is Chinese. His name is Sheng," Hannah replied as she moved to mount her bike. "He's an artist... an eccentric... and older than these hills."

It took Jack a moment to realize that his new traveling companion was about to rush headlong into what sounded like an intense firefight, and that seemed an incredibly bad idea. "But you don't know it's your friend's place? Right?"

"There's no one else living out here as far as I know. It has to be Sheng's house," she stated in a rush. "I need to help him. He's got to be close to eighty years of age!"

"Okay, okay, hold on. You can move a lot faster than I can. Shouldn't we approach this as a team?"

Before she could answer, another exchange of gunfire rattled through the countryside. Hannah's eyes, wide with adrenaline, answered Jack's question before she formed any words. "It might be over by the time you get there. He's an old man... and alone. Look, stay on this road. You'll go over one more hill and then cross a railroad track. The lane leading to Sheng's home is the next drive to the right. Don't try to approach his house... stay back and snipe if you can. He has booby-traps all over the place. Hurry."

Without waiting for the commander's response, she was off, the front of her bike going into a high wheelie as she twisted the throttle and zoomed away. Jack watched, super-impressed by not only her riding skills, but by the bravery obvious from her actions. "She's *that* loyal to a friend that she hardly knows?" he questioned, "Is that foolhardy... or a sign of good character?"

Reaching for his pack, Jack quickly pulled out the heavy load vest he'd acquired from the Marines' arsenal back in San Diego. With pouches on the outside and armor plates in the lining, he hefted the heavy piece of kit over his shoulders and secured the straps.

Pushing off, Jack began pedaling hard, his mind tortured with the worry that he'd be too late. Finding his new friend dead would only add to what had been a grueling couple of days. As he rode, the commander realized that he really liked Hannah. "Don't start getting all mushy, Cisco," he chided himself. "You don't have the best track record with women for sure. You don't know where Mylie and the girls are, and you're still on the rebound from Heather kicking you to the curb. Man up."

More gunshots rumbled across the valley. Jack, now closer, thought he could make out at least three different weapons… maybe four. "Hannah should be there by now," he hissed. "Get some, girl."

The next hill didn't seem to be as difficult a climb, the prospect of entering a battle refreshing his stamina. His heart was pumping at double time, redirecting blood to his starving muscles, and his mind was focused.

Down into the next basin he plunged, the bike picking up speed as the reports of more weapons sounded from below. "As I ride into the valley of death…" he mumbled, fear's icy hand making itself known.

Yet, Jack's mind remained calm, his thoughts orderly. He'd been through so much in the last few months. He'd lost count of the firefights, violent confrontations, and near-death experiences. He was a veteran… a man who knew and respected combat, as well as his own abilities.

A minute after hitting the valley floor, he approached a railroad crossing. Sure enough, the gunfire originated from his right, just like Hannah had predicted. Dismounting, Jack quickly concealed his bike behind a pile of scrub next to the elevated train track. From here, he would continue on foot.

Plenty of dead trees and head-high brush bordered Sheng's driveway. Even so, the commander could easily make out dozens of footprints in the ash. At the crest of a small rise, he spotted Hannah's motorcycle resting near an outcropping of rocks. She hadn't taken the time to hide her ride.

Now the gunshots were loud, a series of bullets seeming to zip, pop and boom just around the bend, as they ricocheted off the rocks of the nearby hills. Quickly determining that hiking straight up the main lane wasn't the wisest tactic in the book, the commander cut up a narrow draw and broke into a fast jog.

The terrain was rockier here, and soon he found himself face to face with a thirty-foot high mound of protruding stone. Peering up at the elevated spot near the top, Jack concluded that he needed to know the lay of the land before barging headfirst into the middle of the skirmish. Hannah's warning about booby-traps flashed through his mind. "You might be able to identify opportunities for snares and trip wires from above and plan around them, Commander," he whispered.

He reached the summit quickly, and then gradually worked his way around to gain a view of the territory below. What he saw made the commander inhale sharply.

Less than two football fields away, a single-story, modest home jutted from the hillside. At least he thought it was a home. It looked more like a dugout at a baseball stadium than a country residence, half of the structure embedded in the rock. He could make out the metal roof of a porch, but instead of a swing or lawn chairs, mounds of dirt blocked the entire front of the residence. Jack thought they looked like a recent addition as there was no dead vegetation or ground cover visible from his vantage.

An ash-covered pickup sat in the driveway next to a crudely-constructed, lean-to shed and three heavily oxidized shipping containers. A short distance away, a large barn rounded out the structures. He couldn't be sure, but it looked like part of the barn's roof was missing.

Next to the outbuildings, a front-loading tractor was parked. "Well, that explains the piles of dirt," Jack muttered.

Only a narrow opening led to the home, the entry looking more like a small cave than a welcoming sidewalk or path. "Sheng used his tractor to create a fall-out shelter," Jack whispered. "Smart. Very smart."

Small patches of exposed tin sheeting explained what had happened to the barn's former roof, the galvanized metal repurposed as the entrance tunnel's ceiling before being covered with a thin layer of earth.

The surrounding grounds, for 200 meters in every direction, were a sprawling junkyard.

Dozens of old cars, tractors, delivery trucks, and miscellaneous farm implements littered the ground in a haphazard fashion. Jack even spotted the derrick from an oil well lying on its side, right next to a school bus that was covered in pumice. In fact, the entire area was nothing but scrap metal, derelict vehicles, mounds of wheels and tires, and rusted appliances. Debris and clutter were strewn all over the grounds, most of the junk partially covered with brown, dead vegetation and clumps of pewter-colored weeds.

"Wonder what the homeowners' association says about this?" Jack whispered, taking in the scene. "Maybe this guy is an artist *and* a hoarder?"

As he watched, Jack spied the blue puff of a gun firing from the cave's entrance. He assumed that was the Chinese owner defending his property.

Movement at the front of the scrap yard drew the commander's eye, a human shape popping up to return fire at the house. Another man appeared from behind the school bus, a burning torch in his hand. Running hard toward the main residence, it was clear he intended to set the place on fire.

On cue, three other attackers stood and began shooting at the opening, obviously trying to keep Sheng's head down while the torchbearer charged in close enough to launch his flaming missile.

It occurred to the commander that the attackers were all dressed the same. Each of the men he'd spotted so far was wearing identical, faded and stained yellow overalls. Their faces were covered by breathing cloths, odd-looking hats protected their heads.

A million questions raced through Jack's head as he raised his rifle. Could he make the shot? Was he giving away his position too soon? Would the attackers turn and trap him high on this towering rock? How in the hell were he and Hannah ever going to root all the black hats out of that scrap heap?

Before the commander could center his optic on the running arsonist, the torch bearer pulled up short, let out a howl of distress, and then crumpled awkwardly to the ground, his body writhing in agony.

Scanning the fallen man, Jack sucked in a chest full of air when his optic focused on the distressed fighter's leg. There, just below the knee, the clutching jaws of a massive bear trap clamped tight on his calf.

Streaks of crimson were already running down the victim's leg as he screamed again and again, his hands trying desperately to pull apart the sharp teeth that were consuming his limb. "That's what Hannah meant by booby-traps," Jack hissed. "Nasty... effective... but nasty."

Hannah appeared on the far side of the barn, just as two of the trapped man's friends rushed to help their wounded, shrieking comrade. Her rifle barked, cutting one of scurrying rescuers down with three shots.

"Yes!" Jack hissed in celebration, "Nice shooting!"

As she disappeared back around the corner, the wooden planks of the barn exploded with splinters and dust as a hailstorm of gunfire chased after her. The commander prayed she had gone low, or that the barn's weathered façade was thicker than it looked.

After one last look to get his bearings on where the nearest invaders were stationed, Jack began climbing down. He would come up behind them and put an end to their siege.

Working his way through the rocks and scrub, Jack noted that the tempo of the gunfire had slowed. "Their main plan of burning Sheng out has failed, and now they know Hannah is there. The equation has changed. They're trying to figure out a new plan."

Bent at the waist and running low, Jack hustled to a refrigerator-sized boulder less than one hundred yards from where he'd spotted the primary grouping of bad actors. His pace was slowed by having to step in existing footprints, images of the bear trap's jagged teeth still fresh in his mind. Carefully, he peeked around and saw four men right where he'd expected.

They had taken cover behind an old hay wagon that was missing two wheels. They all had long guns, each taking turns occasionally popping up and loosing a poorly aimed shot at the house. All the while, Jack could see their shoulders and heads moving as if a heated discussion was in progress.

Raising his weapon, the commander centered on the closest foe's back, leveling his aim at the unaware gent's shoulder blades. As his finger began to tighten on the trigger, he suddenly had second thoughts. "How do I know for sure these are the bad guys?" he wondered. "All I have is Hannah's word that Sheng is in the right."

For a nanosecond, Jack paused. While trying to burn anyone out of their home was a serious indictment of wrongdoing, for all the commander knew, Sheng had been stealing their food, or raping their women, or worse.

His hesitation passed in a flash, Jack realizing that he trusted Hannah for some unknown reason. "She's fighting them, so they must be the black hats. I have to fight them," he mumbled.

Focusing back on his optic, Jack pulled the trigger.

Twice his M4 carbine barked, the two rounds slamming into the shooter's back and knocking him into the hay wagon's frame. Before the dying man's friends could reconcile what had just happened, Jack centered on his next target and sent three more ballistic messages. A loud shriek of agony filled the air as the commander's second victim flopped to the ground.

The rock next to Jack's head exploded into stinging shards as the remaining two foes recovered. When he ducked back behind cover, the commander caught a glimpse of both shooters hauling ass toward a rusty van.

High-velocity lead from his carbine chased them all the way to their new position, Jack's weapon spitting a steady string of rounds their way. He missed the ducking, bobbing targets, grimacing as he watched them dive behind what had once been an ambulance in years past. "The irony," he grunted, retreating behind the cover of his rock fortress.

More shots from across the grounds followed, Hannah engaging with a target the commander couldn't see, followed by another salvo from the house.

Jack didn't know Sheng. He was here for Hannah. Jack pivoted and ran for a position closer to his new friend.

Changing directions twice as he hustled for an old tractor, Jack felt a bullet snap past his head, the round so close he was sure it had cut off some of his hair. He dove headfirst, praying there wasn't another steel-toothed monster lying under the ash. His body twisted awkwardly when his shoulder landed hard on two old tire rims obscured by the weeds.

Pushing aside the lightning-like bolts of pain burning through his frame, the commander rolled hard and came to a knee next to the rear axle of an Alice Chalmers tractor that was probably four times his age.

More bullets whizzed and pinged off the old workhorse's frame, flecks of metal and orange paint puffing into the air. Sheng's salvage yard was now a confusing, whirlwind of flying lead, screaming throats, and blasting weapons. Adding to the nightmarish blizzard of projectiles, every footfall was a terror. "It's like trying to square dance in a minefield," Jack quipped.

The combatants had ample cover, both sides moving, shooting, yelling, and scrambling in every direction. There were no lines dividing friend from foe, no plan of attack or strategy involved. It was every man for himself in a rolling furball of chaotic gunfire.

Jack fired twice at the old ambulance, that effort rewarded by incoming rounds from his right. Hannah responded, her AR15 pelting the oxidized remains of an archaic gas pump. She, in turn, narrowly avoided a volley of lead coming from somewhere on the far side of the junkyard.

To his left, Jack spied movement, Hannah making a break for the house, shouting, "Sheng, I'm coming in!" as she burst from her hide.

She was halfway across an open area when another human form appeared. Rising from behind an old oven, a man tracked the scurrying woman with his barrel, his finger tightening on the trigger.

Snap-firing two rounds, Jack hit the shooter just as a ball of red flame erupted from his shotgun. The commander's target, stunned at being hit from behind, half turned, trying to bring the 12-gauge to bear.

Rising to get a better shot over the old tractor's hood, Jack's carbine pushed against his shoulder. An expanding cloud of red mist and white bone fragments replaced the hombre's masked head, his scattergun flying wildly into the air.

Before the commander could duck back down, a sledgehammer slammed into his back, knocking the air from his lungs in a whoosh of expulsion. Jack tried to turn, but his legs wouldn't respond. He was falling, the tractor's frame rushing toward his face.

Everything went black.

Chapter 42

He was certain that old tractor was sitting on top of his head, its running engine sending vibrations of pain through his skull and spine. He had to get out from underneath it. The effort to move sent white-hot streaks of agony through the commander's body, his eyes fluttering as he struggled to remain conscious.

When his vision cleared, Jack was staring into the almond-shaped eyes belonging to an old man. Crevices of time and wrinkles of age surrounded the dark gaze that seemed to be studying his soul. Long, silver strands of unkempt hair framed the patchy, salt and pepper beard that covered the hovering face. "Sheng?" the commander managed in a hoarse whisper.

"He's awake," the old man announced. "His eyes aren't right. His brain is swollen."

Hannah's worried expression appeared over the old man's shoulder. "There you are. You had me worried, Commander."

Jack tried to stand, the attempt causing him to inhale and grimace at the same time. "That was a bad idea," he croaked, returning to the pillow. "What happened? Did we win?"

"The miners gave up," Sheng announced with a slight grin. "Your arrival broke their attack. They'll be back, of that I'm sure."

"Miners? Why were they shooting at..." Jack began, his question interrupted by a surge of nausea doing back flips through his stomach.

The urge to vomit passed a few moments later. "Did I get shot?"

"This one is full of questions," Sheng informed Hannah. "You said he was a sailor?"

"Yes, he's an officer... or *was* an officer in the US Navy," Hannah replied, her AR15 resting in the crook of her elbows. Then, turning her attention back to the patient, she continued, "You were shot in the back, but your body armor stopped the round. When you fell, you hit your head. You've got a nasty gash and probably a concussion. Just lay still. You're not going anywhere for a while."

Jack decided that a nod was the best response, but even that motion pulsated waves of pain through his cracked cranium. He'd never felt so miserable.

Sheng, evidently done with his examination of the wounded man, rose quickly from his perch. "I will make some tea; that will help with his discomfort."

His eyes following Sheng, Jack noted a slightly hunched, tiny man who stood maybe five feet and four inches at most. A long ponytail of silver hair hung from the back of his head. He was thin, perhaps a hundred pounds, yet walked with a visible spring in his step. Hannah's earlier estimate of his age seemed spot on.

Leaning her weapon against the wall, Hannah took Sheng's place on the bedside stool. Behind her mask, Jack could see the concern in her eyes. "That was a close one," she whispered. "Another inch lower and the bullet would have hit your spine. You took an awful risk, my friend…. But thank you for helping us."

The aroma of a wood fire wafted past as Hannah removed a bloody bandage from the commander's forehead. A minute later, Jack detected an unusual, earthy scent that reminded him of ginger with a touch of cinnamon.

Sheng then appeared in the commander's peripheral vision, the old man carrying a butcher knife when he walked past. As Jack watched, his host hobbled to a nearby wall and approached what appeared to be several clusters of roots and stalks hanging from hooks. With a deft hand, he sliced several times and then strolled out of view.

"Sheng is an herbalist," Hannah whispered, seeing the questions already forming in Jack's mind. "He knows more about the local vegetation than most biologists. He also eats better than anybody else I've met."

Jack's gaze returned to the spot where the man had just performed his handiwork. Dozens of different colors and shapes of tubers hung there. A realization quickly formed, the commander understanding what probably prompted the firefight. "Wow. That makes all the sense in the world. I never thought about roots as a food source. Anything below ground would probably still be edible. I just never...."

"With the covering of ash and cooler temperatures, all the earth is now one big root cellar," Sheng announced from the woodburning stove where he continued to toil. "Nature will always provide for those who know where to look and how to use her bounty... at least for a while."

"I've been trying to talk Sheng into returning to the airport with me," Hannah continued. "We have a large population of survivors with varied and extensive skills. He could teach us all about what roots to look for and how to prepare them. His teachings could help save our species."

"The miners know I eat until my stomach is full, every day," the old Chinaman added. "They are starving and want what I have. If I leave, they will pick my place clean, and I cannot allow that."

"You've been fighting with them since the eruption?" Jack asked from his cot.

"No," Sheng said with a sad tone. "Today is the first time they brought guns and tried to raid my home. Before this, they threatened and bullied me. At first, about a month after the ash began falling... after it was safe to go back outside, I gave them food. They kept coming back, begging for more. I offered to teach them how to harvest their own food on their own land, but they showed no real interest. Later, I noticed them trying to track me in the hills. When that didn't work, they grew desperate... and mean."

Frowning, Jack tried to make sense of it all. "You keep calling them miners. I didn't know there was any mining in this part of Texas. Were they digging coal?"

"No," Sheng stated bluntly. "They moved here a few years ago, to the valley over by Saddle Mountain. They were from a new

73

company that manufactures rare earth magnets. They were digging minerals whose names I can't even pronounce."

From his military background, Jack knew the strategic importance of rare earth magnets. They were used in everything from superconductors to electric motors to computer disk drives. He had also read that the United States was behind the curve when it came to their manufacture. Evidently, some smart, venture capitalist or eager entrepreneur had decided to rectify that situation. Over the past few decades, Central Texas had become an incubator for hundreds of high-tech startups. The commander had heard his father-in-law complaining about Austin's constant expansion and unbridled growth.

That thought brought Jack back to the here and now. "Sheng, did you know a rancher named Armstrong who lived about fifteen miles north of here?"

The old timer had to think for a second, "Yes. The Lazy A, if I recall?"

Jack's heart rate jumped, "Yes! That's the man."

"Ned? Yes, I knew him. I hauled away an old planter from his property some years ago. Why do you ask?"

"He is my father-in-law. I think my wife and daughters were staying at his ranch when Yellowstone blew. Have you seen or heard anything about them?"

Shaking his head, Sheng said, "The river changed course a few months after the eruption. I think that whole area is now a lake. I've not seen anyone from around there since the grey skies came, but then again, I didn't see very many people before the volcano either."

Sheng's words discouraged the commander, and he didn't bother to ask any more questions. For the Nth time, he wondered if his family were even still alive. The throbbing in his head didn't help his mood.

Sheng arrived with a steaming cup of some foul-smelling liquid. "Drink this. All of it. It will help with your pain and make your brain shrink back to regular size," he ordered.

Taking a sip, Jack stilled himself not to react – an effort to be polite. The taste, fortunately, wasn't nearly as bad as the odor. From some distant recess of his memory, the old song about a spoonful of sugar helping the medicine go down popped into his thoughts. He was, again, reminded of his daughters. These days, everything seemed to do just that.

After the tea, Jack grew sleepy. Sheng's brew seemed to be helping, at least in that regard. Hannah, perceptive as usual, noticed his exhaustion. "By the way, where did you leave your bicycle?" she asked.

"On the far side of the railroad track, behind a patch of thick scrub," he remembered, glad she had reminded him.

"It's still too dangerous out there to retrieve it. Sounds like you stashed it away well enough that the miners won't find it."

"I agree," Jack replied, his head still spinning. "Besides, what would they want with a filthy, old bike?"

Exhaustion overcame the commander, the day's hectic bicycle sprint, combat, and his subsequent injuries all taking their toll. Ten minutes later, Jack was asleep.

Captain Bascom walked to the ticket counter and extended his index finger. Preparing for the worst by drawing in a chest full of air, he swiped the smooth surface. The only thing missing was a white glove.

Examining the tip, he found a thin, barely detectable layer of grit covering the ridges of his fingerprint. "Is it pumice or just regular, old dust?" he pondered.

Every day since the eruption, the ex-fighter jock had performed an identical ritual. During the first few months, he'd repeated the procedure in multiple locations throughout the terminal. He was concerned that the deadly ash was making its way past the seals so hastily erected around the massive structure. Today's coating was just another in a long list of the captain's worries.

Pivoting smartly, Alex navigated the cavernous area where rushing travelers had once plied with a frenzy, towing suitcases and carry-on bags while clutching boarding passes in their anxious hands. Now, it was a hollow, empty place, depleted of its energy and soul.

Only unused rows of molded plastic chairs met his gaze. The lofty ceilings no longer echoed with the hustle and bustle of a busy airport. There were no flight announcements, no airline personnel asking for passengers to "Please pick up a white courtesy phone." Austin International was a silent, haunted space.

What had once been a gateway of freedom was now a prison of sorts. The hundreds of people trapped here often referred to themselves as "Yellowstone's convicts." Bascom disliked the label but had to agree that it was appropriate in so many ways.

Stepping toward the wall of glass surrounding what had been the terminal's main entrance, Bascom eyed the abandoned curbside check-in kiosks, briefly wondering what had happened to the platoon of skycaps who had once made a living helping passengers check their bags. Noting that the depth of outside ash hadn't changed since yesterday, his mind's work returned to the dust still resting on his finger.

Was it thicker today? The same? Harmful or not? There wasn't any process or method to be sure. He would speak with the doctor about what he had found. The sawbones would respond by complaining about the lack of resources and equipment, just as he did every day. The physician's rant would then turn, as it always did, to the lack of medicinal acholic beverages available. Alex had to admit, there were days where a good, stiff shot of single-malt would have made things more tolerable.

Checking the wide, glass doors that had once opened automatically for arriving and departing passengers, Alex focused on the edges. Around each was a thick coating that consisted of multiple layers of duct tape. All the seals appeared to be intact. The maintenance crew was, as expected, keeping up with their most critical assignment. Bascom wondered how long it would be before that task was no longer necessary? Months? Years? Decades?

"We won't last years or decades," he whispered with a frown.

His eyes then shifted to the world beyond the dirty windows, scanning the terminal's exterior for the hundredth time. He could see the wide, paved approach that had once been snarled with vehicles and policemen blowing whistles to direct the motorists. Past that, a parking garage rose high from the ground, and then an expanse of poured concrete lots spread out in all directions. Barely visible in the distance was the outline of several hotels that bordered the property. As usual, the longing that always accompanied any view of the outside world threatened to overwhelm him. Most days, he struggled against the urge to cast all caution aside and rush into the open air.

The community called them "jailbreakers," another slang term developed after months of living inside the same four walls. For a moment, Alex tried to remember the first kid who had torn away a sheet of plastic and made his escape to the wild gray yonder.

Shaking his head, Bascom couldn't form an image of the seventeen-year-old's face. Nor could he remember the teenager's name. Had it been that long? Had death become so common that his mind was becoming callused? Uncaring? Immune?

Three days later, coughing up blood and barely able to breathe, the kid had returned. They heard him pounding on a window, his eyes desperate and wild. "Please!" he had begged between fits of respiratory convulsions. "I'm sorry! Please! Let me in!"

That episode had been the first time the captain had been forced to issue a death sentence on another human being. It wouldn't be the last.

"We can't let him back in," Alex had ordered. "He put us all at risk by breaking the seals. Letting him return will pollute our air even more, and besides, he's already dead."

77

At the time, Bascom couldn't understand why the kid had flipped out and bolted. Now, months later, he not only got it, but he often felt compelled to do so himself. As huge as the terminal was, it was still the confinement that twisted and tortured the human psyche more than the captain would have ever imagined.

"We are housecats," one woman stated grumbled long ago. "We can never go outside, feel the grass under our feet or the wind against our faces. We can only stare wistfully out the window and wish that we were free to chase mice."

As the time passed, he was sure there would have been many, many more jailbreakers if not for the scouts.

Organizing that elite squad of explorers had helped. Their limited forays into the unknown world beyond the glass walls of the airport had quickly become wildly popular events. After the first explorers had ventured forth, Bascom noted how everyone gathered around the returning travelers, hanging on every word of their reports, firing salvos of questions about what was now a denied existence. The captain had eventually made their debriefings a public event, a theatrical production of sorts. Beyond boosting the inhabitants' dwindling morale, it was a necessary step to quell the rumors that seemed to swirl like the ash outside.

There were no newscasts, morning papers, or internet browsing available to the community. People craved information, as well as entertainment. Even more important was their need for hope, a commodity that was in short supply. Seeing a few of their own ride off into the ash-wilderness and return with news of the outside world was a key step. It was progress toward normalcy, or so they all prayed.

Pivoting away from the tall windows, the captain's stride took him down a wide corridor and past the long-abandoned security checkpoint. Again, his mind drifted back to what now seemed like ancient memories. He could barely recall the long lines of people here, waiting to have their bags x-rayed, their bodies scanned by a metal detector. All that equipment was dark now, just like the monitors that hung from the walls and the rows of advertising signs that had once glowed so brightly.

Pausing, Bascom scanned one of those advertisements. There was a picture of an elephant and a tiger imprinted on the plastic face, the words "Visit the Austin Zoo," in a bold font. It was his favorite.

Before the eruption, the captain had walked right past hundreds of such ads. He, like so many airport passengers, had never appreciated their bright colors and backlit hue. In fact, he couldn't remember ever noticing them at all.

Now, as he made his rounds, his reaction to their depictions and images was more akin to visiting an art museum. They were like rare, classic paintings of a bygone era, full of images that no longer existed in the real world. He wondered for a moment if any lions or tigers or bears had survived. "Probably not," he mumbled. "Most likely, only cockroaches and turtles still walk the earth."

Approaching what everyone called, "the inner barrier," Bascom looked up to examine the large tarps draped across the passageway. Six weeks after Yellowstone's eruption, one of these hastily erected curtains of plastic had become unattached and fallen, sending a wave of panic through the occupants of the gates. Had the ash gotten inside? Were they breathing poisoned air?

In the days following that failure, every little cough had caused mounting fear to gush through the survivors' ranks. The very air they inhaled was a catalyst of death.

Bascom continued his stroll through the main terminal, passing the first gate, number 10.

Despite the early hour, a flurry of activity had already begun around the jetway, two sleepy-looking men both nodding a greeting as the captain mouthed, "Good morning." The aircraft docked at Gates 10 and 11 were for single males, each supplying shelter for about fifty individuals. The interior of each fuselage was now divided by a matrix of cardboard walls and bedsheet curtains, each man doing his best to create a private space.

Next came the "Team Green" space, a tongue in cheek tribute to the pre-apocalyptic, mandated plan to reduce the environmental footprint of the airport. Like any bureaucratic program imposed on an otherwise well-functioning organization, the green strategy had a few hiccups, making it somewhat unpopular with the staff. Bascom didn't like the nickname, but he understood that the verbal jab at the previous administration released a little steam from the pressure cooker of his little colony. As a result, the normally-spacious terminal was now cluttered with a small mountain of over 400 seats unbolted from the interiors of the two 737 planes. Those once-proud birds had been forced into service as hotels, every inch of interior space repurposed to house the survivors. This was also where mounds of plastic bags full of refuge resided, including the food wrappers, discarded cups, and heaps of suitcases that had been thoroughly searched over the weeks and months. It was essentially the community's landfill, without the land.

Bascom pined for the day when the air would be clean enough to remove discarded hardware and garbage, or even better yet, for the survivors to move outside.

He continued, passing the next two gates that housed the single female dorm planes. Strategically sited between Team Green and Gate 12's ticket counter stood the laundry area. A series of clotheslines had been erected across the hall from the bathrooms, creating a spot for the the rainbow of freshly washed garments to dry. In the first few months following Yellowstone's event, Bascom had relished the fragrance of detergent on laundry day. That small pleasure was no longer available. They had run out of soap several weeks ago.

Bascom's ears automatically piqued as he walked, his senses focusing on the distant whine of two jet engines running outside the building. A quick check of his wristwatch confirmed that the 757 at Gate 13, currently serving as the facility's air pump, had one more hour left of its shift. The plane at the next gate would follow, its eight-hour runtime scheduled to begin just after breakfast.

He listened for any sign of mechanical stress, altered tone, or other indication of trouble coming from the idling turbofans. There had been more failures lately, the community having lost two of the critical engines in the last month alone. Still, Bascom was surprised the jets had lasted this long.

Eventually arriving at a heavy, metal door, Captain Bascom turned the handle and entered what had once been the crew's lounge. Austin International was a newer airport, with features designed according to how airlines and their personnel operated in the modern era.

Along one wall, a handful of tiny studios, each with a single bed, private shower, and couch had been constructed for crews needing accommodations while on extended holdovers. Directly in front of the entrance, a spacious area welcomed crew into a breakroom complete with microwave, refrigerator and sink. Along the other wall, a weather office had supplied cockpit officers the latest forecasts and conditions. The larger office had once been used as a simple infirmary… the kind where if you could slap a bandage on it or swallow an aspirin for it, you could find a cure.

Bascom had designated the area as the community's medical facility.

Entering what had been the lounge, Alex found the doctor working on some unknown task, his back to the door. A white lab coat hung loosely from his slumped shoulders, wisps of grey hair covering the physician's temples. A wide bald spot acted as the doc's crown, the earpieces of an always-present stethoscope visible around his neck, the black frames of thick eyeglasses tucked around his ears.

"Good morning, Doctor," the pilot announced, carefully shutting the door behind him. "I trust you slept well?"

Dr. Leland didn't bother to turn around, his hands busy with a beaker of liquid. A gravelly grunt of "Morn'n," the only response.

"I found more dust on the ticket counter this morning, Doc. If you have a moment, I'd like to speak with you about it," Bascom continued.

"What is there to speak about?" grumbled the physician. "There's nothing further we can do… no additional preventative measures to be taken, at least from a medical perspective."

The captain, accustomed to the doctor's foul demeanor, only smiled. The crusty old physician's personality had probably been gruff and condescending long before Yellowstone had made the planet into a living hell. "I want to talk about testing the air, trying to determine if it is still dangerous," Bascom offered. "We could all be confined here for no good reason. For all we know, the dangerous part of the ash has settled or dissipated to a safe level."

"Glass doesn't dissipate, young man. If there is still ash on the ground, then it's still dangerous outside. It's all that simple," Leland responded, his tone resembling an impatient professor scolding an inattentive student.

Sighing, Bascom moved to stand closer to the old grouch, somehow thinking that making eye contact would help persuade the foul-tempered sawbones. "We don't know that, Doc. If what you're saying were true, then past volcanic eruptions would have been far deadlier than they were. We all know that from Mount St. Helens to Kilauea in Hawaii, the ash dispersed and settled. People could breathe in the area after just a brief time. Yellowstone has to adhere to the same laws of nature, doesn't it?"

Finally glancing up from his work, a deep scowl sculptured the skin of Leland's face. "I'm not a volcanologist, sir, I am a country doctor who retired three years ago and was absolutely content with the daily objective of destroying my liver. I was on my way to Palm Springs to play golf, consume large quantities of hard liquor, and smoke vastly overpriced cigars. I had no intent of ever practicing medicine again, let alone analyzing a volcano that is over a thousand miles away."

The captain had heard Leland's rant a hundred times and ignored it. "There has to be some way… some method to test the air, Doc. I can send the scouts to retrieve lab equipment, or supplies, or virtually anything you would need. We're losing this battle, and you know that as well as anyone."

Leland sighed deeply, his frustration mounting, his elderly shoulders somehow managing to slump even closer to the floor. Finally, in a softer voice, he answered, "We've gone over this a dozen times, Captain. As long as there is ash on the ground, the wind will stir up and recirculate the glass and other deadly compounds it contains. It may be a hundred years before we can breathe without protection. I could have the finest research facility in the Northern Hemisphere, and it wouldn't change a damn thing."

Shaking his head, Bascom wasn't convinced. "We're not only facing a food shortage, Leland, but a serious mental health issue as well. We need to show those people out there progress… we need to give them hope that things are getting better. I'm going to have to cut rations again if the scouts don't find a large cache of food soon, and we both know that will drive morale even lower."

"But rehashing this topic doesn't change our reality. I wouldn't know how to operate a mass spectrometer if you brought me one with a pretty red bow on top. If you want to test the air, you're going to need not only the right instruments, but a scientist who knows how to use them."

Irritated that their conversation was following the exact path it always did, Bascom began rubbing his chin. "Before Yellowstone blew, I used to hear air quality reports on the local newscasts. They would supply pollen counts and other information. Can't we create something similar to measure how much glass is still in the atmosphere?"

"Perhaps. Perhaps not. Why do you keep asking me questions that I can't answer, Captain? I'm not any smarter today than I was yesterday... or last week. I can't tell you what I don't know. This isn't a coal mine. We can't send somebody outside with a canary to see if the bird dies."

"You're right," Bascom admitted. "You'll have to pardon my desperation, Doc. I get like this whenever I realize that the lives of so many people are in my hands."

"Speaking of lives," the physician offered, "I suppose you should be the first to know... given your responsibilities. We have our first pregnancy. I'm not sure if that's uplifting news or not."

Bascom's body fairly snapped to attention, announcing his surprise. "Where did they find a place to..." he mumbled, but he never finished the question. Privacy was in very short supply in the terminal. His next question sought information pertinent to the colony. "Who is it?"

"That's confidential, I'm afraid. The expecting parents are supposed to stop by today. I'll ask their permission to let you know who they are."

A plethora of questions raced through the captain's mind, most of them having potentially negative answers. "I'm sorry, Leland, but that answer is not going to cut it... not in today's world. I need to know who these people are for a dozen distinct reasons, not the least of which is security concerns. Please tell me that the mother and father aren't married – to other people?"

Grunting with a slight grin, Leland shook his head. "Isn't it amazing how human beings have been driven to have sex for thousands of centuries, regardless of starvation, drought, or plague? Don't panic, Captain. These are both single, consenting adults."

Relieved, Bascom flashed his own smile. "Thank God. All we need right now is a pedophile, or ugly domestic issue, or rapist on the loose."

"Still, I'm not sure about how the community is going to react to this news once it leaks out," Leland offered. "What kind of future could the child possibly have? I'm sure some of the more negative members of our clan will complain about another mouth to feed while others will worry about the resources the baby will require."

Frowning at the doctor's pessimism, Bascom disagreed. "I think that overall, this news will be welcomed. Our species, despite great adversity, is still reproducing. That's a good thing, right?"

"Maybe. A lot depends on the newborn's health. Who knows what Yellowstone's exhaust has done to our bodies? I may be delivering a two-headed mutant... or worse... six months from now."

"Are you seriously worried about that, Doc?"

"No," the physician replied with a smirk. "What concerns me the most is when you're going to have those high-and-mighty scouts of yours go out and scrounge up some properly aged whiskey. I need to throw back a stiff one... or two."

Jack blinked away his sixteen hours of sleep, the welcome aroma of coffee now filling his nose. His head still hurt, but the constant jackhammering between his ears was fading.

Rising gingerly to one elbow, he took in the dim surroundings, trying to reconcile time and location while separating dreams from reality.

"Want some java?" Hannah offered, her voice hoarse from the morning air.

"What a ridiculous question," he croaked, his throat still unlubricated.

Looking around, Jack soon realized they were alone. "Where's Sheng?"

"He's out on patrol right now. We took turns standing guard throughout the night. He should be back shortly."

"You should have woken me," Jack protested. "I would have taken a watch."

"You needed your rest," she cooed, bringing him a steaming cup of joe.

On cue, four light knocks tapped on the front door. Hannah rushed to undo the latch, allowing Sheng's masked face to enter. In his hand dangled a cluster of tubers that Jack thought looked like sweet potatoes. "I stopped and got breakfast out of my root cellar. I don't normally eat this early, but I thought you both might be hungry."

"Are those turnips?" Hannah asked, licking her lips.

"No," he grinned. "Better. These are greenbrier roots."

Frowning, Jack balked at the suggestion, "Hold on. I thought greenbrier was a weed? I am pretty sure I had to put out poison to keep it out of my yard."

Shaking his head in disappointment, Sheng replied, "See if you think it's a weed after breakfast."

Carefully navigating to a sitting position, Jack had to pause after being upright. For a few seconds, the room was spinning, his primary concern being not to spill a single drop of his morning caffeine.

After a few deep breaths, things settled down, and Jack felt almost steady. His head was throbbing again, his lower back feeling stiff and bruised. Rubbing his temple, he asked, "Did you find my bike?"

"No, I didn't go looking for it. You said it was well-hidden, so I let it be for the time being."

"What about my pack?" Jack inquired. "There is a medical kit in my pack. I have a few aspirins left. I was thinking it might be an appropriate time to indulge," he stated.

Hannah turned to point out the location of the commander's belongings a few feet away, when Sheng snapped, "Save your pills, I have something more effective for pain."

"Oh?" Jack replied.

"Cannabis," the old Chinaman smiled. "It cures many ills."

"Marijuana?" Jack asked, amazement thick in his tone, his eyes wide and eyebrows arching skyward.

"Yes," Sheng grinned. "I always keep a stash for those times when these old bones complain about a chill. We rarely have damp weather here, but when we do, my joints don't like it. I'll be glad to mix a little in as I cook this greenbrier. I will help with both your head and sore back."

"Interesting. For breakfast, the menu includes 'weeds' with a side order of 'pot.' I am beginning to believe you might be a bad influence on me, Hannah. I have never tried marijuana before."

"You've never smoked pot?" Hannah chuckled. "Were you raised in a convent?"

Shaking his head caused Jack to grimace in pain, but he continued, "No. I was a jock in high school, and wanted to stay in peak physical condition. At the Academy, they required urine tests on a regular basis. I always wondered what it was like, but I never indulged. Still, I don't think today is the best time to satisfy my adolescent curiosity. I have a feeling I'm going to need what few wits I have left. Thank you very much, but I'll use my aspirin."

Shrugging, Sheng went back to his root-slicing.

With Hannah standing by just in case, Jack managed to stand. Again, a wave of dizziness caused him to falter, but the feeling passed quickly. Nodding his thanks to her, the commander then took a few careful steps toward his pack.

Finally upright, he had the first opportunity to study his temporary home.

Sheng's cabin was one large, long room built from logs and some sort of filling mortar. Exposed timber formed the ceiling as well. The front door stood in the middle of the wall, flanked by windows on each side. They were the only source of natural light, but the dirt stacked across the porch made the interior dim, so the botanist used candles and a single lantern burning some sort of oil to see.

A fireplace anchored the back wall, the stone façade probably repurposed rock from the surrounding countryside. In fact, the entire rear of Sheng's fortress was made of the same limestone. Jack then remembered the dugout shape he'd noted during the firefight and the fact that half of the structure was embedded in the hillside.

The floors were wooden plank, dark with age and bearing the scars collected over the decades.

Along the north wall, not far from his cot, was a rather sparse kitchen. A black iron, box-shaped, woodburning stove sat there, its tin chimney pipe disappearing into the wall. A wash basin was located next to it, the worn, red handle of a pump signaling that Sheng had a well.

Above the sink hung two shelves, each containing a mismatched variety of cookware. Hand towels, spatulas, and an assortment of wooden spoons hung from a series of nails.

What really drew the commander's eyes, however, were the sculptures.

Every corner was home to a metal creation – most of them depicting birds, animals, or insects. They were fashioned from scrap, Jack able to identify gas caps, hood ornaments, engine components, and various other parts salvaged from the junk outside.

Hannah had been right – Sheng was truly an artist.

Forgetting about his aspirin, Jack strolled to a nearby piece and dropped to one knee to study what was clearly a praying mantis. A waist-high masterpiece, the sculpture was constructed entirely out of tarnished metal components that had originally been part of an automobile. The bulb-like eyes were dash gauges, the head having been born as a brake cylinder. The short upper arms were door handles.

The entire work had been carefully welded together. It was rugged, yet delicate. Plain, yet ornate. Somehow, the different surfaces, textures, and colors worked perfectly. "This is remarkable," Jack observed, "I've never seen anything quite like it."

"Thank you," Sheng replied from the kitchen. "That was one of my earlier pieces. It holds a lot of sentimental value."

Jack could see a dozen of the metal masterpieces strewn about the interior, each displaying a unique sense of grace and beauty. There was a bird taking flight, a doe and fawn grazing, an ant carrying a large leaf with its mandibles. "You are very talented, sir," the commander informed his host.

"My larger creations are out in the barn. I don't like sculpting while wearing a mask to breathe… it just seems to dampen my inspiration. I hope the air cleanses itself soon. I miss my work."

"Sheng has exhibited in the Austin Museum of Modern Art, and in Houston and Dallas as well," Hannah bragged from her perch near the fireplace. "He's well known in artistic circles."

"I would imagine so," Jack nodded, his mind returning to his pack and the aspirin within. As he crossed the room, another feature drew the commander's attention. There, next to his kit, sat a pile of weapons. Knives, rifles, pistols, binoculars, magazines, and other tools of the fighting trade were heaped near the corner as if someone had dumped the small arsenal out of a box.

"We killed six of the miners," Hannah explained. "Those were their effects."

"And the bodies?" Jack inquired.

"We dragged them down to the road where their friends can find them… if they're interested. If not, they'll eventually rot," Hannah continued.

"We won't be able to smell them up here," Sheng added, his words carrying the confidence of experience.

"How many of them are left? Could you see any tracks or blood trails?" Jack asked, his eyes moving to the window.

"I think there were ten total that attacked Sheng. Given what I saw outside, I would say we wounded one more, but I have no idea how badly. The other three seemed to be helping the injured man escape," Hannah said in a low tone.

"So, they'll be wanting revenge," Jack offered.

"What they want is my root cellar," Sheng inserted. "Trying to help them was a mistake. I let one of them see inside my secret stash. Now they want my food for themselves."

After throwing two white tablets to the back of his throat and swallowing, Jack moved to stand where he could see what Sheng was doing.

A large, cast-iron skillet heated on the stove, some sort of fat or grease coating the bottom. Sheng deftly manipulated a large knife, slicing one of the greenbrier roots into thin sections. "You cook them until the outer skin turns black, then you cut it away and mash the soft insides. Then you clean out the fibers, and you have something akin to what you would call 'mashed potatoes.' These, however, are much, much tastier in my opinion. And they have a lot of iron, which is good for the blood."

As Jack watched, Sheng tossed the first batch into the pan, the tubers instantly sizzling and steaming. A tempting aroma filled the dugout. The commander's stomach growled, letting him know it had been too long since he'd eaten.

Twenty minutes later, each of the three were sitting with a plate of hot food. Tenderly putting the first fork of greenbrier into his mouth, Jack chewed carefully for a few seconds before a wide grin broke out on his face.

His palate was treated to a unique flavor, somewhere between a radish and a cucumber, a hint of root beer adding just enough spice. Sheng had been correct – the texture was identical to mashed potatoes. It was delicious.

Shoveling the wonderful treat into his mouth, the commander then forced himself to slow down. He wanted the take advantage of the opportunity to savor every morsel. Meals like this were rare in Yellowstone's aftermath. "There is plenty where that came from," Sheng announced from the stove. "I dug up about 150 pounds the other day. Greenbriar is one of the most common plants in North America. It grows practically everywhere that there are trees. The Indians used to make flour out of the tubers. When blooming, the tender young stems and leaves make a great salad."

For a moment, Jack wondered how many potential calories he had bypassed during his ride. *You were probably pedaling right through a banquet hall of deliciousness without even knowing,* he thought.

"How do you identify each plant now that they don't have any leaves or color?" the commander asked.

"Greenbriar is easy to spot, even in the winter. It's the only plant that has vines and thorns," the ancient Asian responded. "Even my old eyes can still find it. But... the tubers aren't going to last forever. Right now, they think it is winter and are hibernating. At some point, they are going to begin to degrade and rot. I've been trying to stockpile as much as possible, but my cellar is full, and my bones are tired. I'm very worried about the future, and now those miners are making things worse."

What Sheng was saying made sense to Jack. Right now, the cold temperatures and sunless skies had fooled the plants into thinking it was time to take a seasonal pause in their cycle of life. How long would that charade last?

Jack did little but sleep and eat over the next few days, his body gradually healing. During the few hours when he did feel capable, Cisco busied himself with small chores. He cleaned his weapon, washed his clothes, and inventoried the ammunition and firearms taken from the dead miners. The commander's expended ammunition was replaced from the salvaged cache.

On his fourth morning at Sheng's dugout, Jack announced that he was taking a turn patrolling the Chinaman's perimeter. "I've got to get outside," he whispered to Hannah. "I've been living under open skies for most of the last few months. I'm getting cabin fever, and besides, I want to retrieve my bike."

"Before you go, let me draw you a map, showing you where not to walk. I've set up a few booby-traps that you would find most unpleasant," Sheng announced.

With a clean breathing mask and toting a full carbine, load vest, and pack, Jack stepped out of the manmade tunnel and into Sheng's collection of relics. He didn't think it was fair to call the collection junk anymore, not after seeing what the man could do with corroded iron and scrap steel.

It felt good to work his muscles, the commander taking his time as he toured the grounds. The miners hadn't returned and perhaps had given up. Jack and Hannah's surprise appearance was no doubt affecting their plans, causing them to question whether or not a stash of roots was worth dying for.

"Maybe they're watching from the hills," Jack mumbled, scanning the surrounding elevations with his optic. "Maybe they're hoping Hannah and I will leave soon."

It occurred to the commander that he might be able to judge the enemy's level of activity by checking to see if they had retrieved their dead. Sheng and Hannah had left the bodies by the railroad tracks, not far from where he'd stashed his bicycle. Were they still there?

Anticipating the smell of decaying flesh, Jack adjusted his mask a bit tighter and headed for a slight rise that would allow him to overlook the makeshift graveyard.

The climb was steeper than he'd anticipated, but the commander was undeterred. He had been mostly horizontal for the last few days. He needed to stretch his muscles and verify he had healed before attempting the journey to the airport with Hannah.

Finally arriving at the crest, Jack scanned the area with his optic while catching his breath. Sure enough, the outlines of several dead bodies were still visible below, a thin coating of wind-blown ash acting as the only sign of their burial grounds.

"Maybe they're not the big threat that we thought they were?" Jack whispered, lowering his weapon.

Pivoting with the idea of retrieving his bicycle, Jack descended the rise with caution. Broken legs or twisted ankles were not in his plans. He'd suffered enough aches the last few days.

The commander's heart sank as he approached the brush pile where he'd stashed his bike. Even before he circled the hide, he knew his wheels were gone.

There were dozens of footprints around the area, as well as the narrow indentations of his bike's tires. "Shit!" he barked, anger swelling in his gut. "Why would anybody steal a man's bike? Don't these assholes know we hang horse thieves in Texas?"

A mixture of rage and concern boiled up inside Jack. He was furious at the loss, cursing his own stupidity and laziness while at the same time wondering how he would ever manage to find his wife and daughters without the bike. That simple machine had been with him through hell and high water, had saved his life multiple times, and was his only companion during countless dark, lonely nights.

For a dozen steps, Jack followed the fresh tire tracks, the impression's age impossible to judge. "You sons of bitches," he raged. "I should have killed you all."

It occurred to the commander that the miners might have simply pushed the bike to a safer place to search the bags and panniers. "They're probably eating all my food this very minute," he spat.

With his bloodlust barely under control, Jack began stalking the hijackers, his carbine ready to engage. From the tracks in the ash, he assessed that there were three of the bastards. "A fair fight," he grunted.

Two miles passed, the commander's fury increasing with every step. "They're just not after my food," he growled. "They are stealing my life-line… my wheels… absconding with any hope I have left of finding my girls."

The parallel with the Old West wasn't lost on Jack, despite his boiling temper. More than once while growing up, he had been watching an old cowboy movie and wondered why horse thieves were always summarily hanged. "The punishment didn't fit the crime," he observed on multiple occasions. "Two men could shoot up a saloon full of patrons, and the sheriff would look the other way. But steal a horse? The hangman's rope was standard issue, along with the posse, pitchforks, and torches."

Now, years later and with ankle-deep ash slowing his pace, Jack understood. His bike was the same as the cowboy's trusty steed. Just like in the horse operas he'd watched as a kid, it represented freedom, mobility, and an unconditional friend who remained loyal and by your side during the worst of times.

Rounding a bend, Jack observed the bike tracks take a left turn along what appeared to be a game trail. Here, the slag was packed, a sure sign of a high-traffic area. "I'm close to the mine," he reasoned. "They've taken my wheels back to their outlaw's lair. Bastards!"

The fog of indecision clouded the commander's head, his mind trying to reason his next best step. Logic dictated that he should turn around and seek Hannah and Sheng's advice. Maybe the old man would provide some roots for a trade. Perhaps the miners had taken his horse-bike as a hostage and would soon negotiate a ransom.

Shaking his head, Jack chided himself for thinking of his chain-driven companion as if it were something more than an inanimate object. "You can find another bike, Cisco," he reasoned. "Besides, you hated riding the damn thing more often than not. How many times did you complain of a sore ass or aching legs? It's not worth risking your life over."

Still, he couldn't push aside his attachment to the machine. More than once, he'd had thoughts of hanging the two-wheeled contraption on the wall once life returned to normal and men rode around in gas-powered luxury. He'd even humored himself on the lonely road, daydreaming about putting the bike out to pasture and letting it breed tricycles.

After a few minutes of reflection, Jack concluded that he was going to get his bicycle back. He'd spent the last 1400 miles avoiding confrontation whenever possible, skirting around as many possible conflicts as he could.

Sure, he'd been sucked into a few scuffles and bad situations along the way. Those episodes had not been by his choice, and he was getting tired of playing the demure role. Mylie and his daughters had always been the primary goal, an objective that kept his aching legs and exhausted muscles pushing on the pedals. Now, that mission was in question, perhaps out of reach.

"Those miners have taken the only thing of any value that I have left," he growled, "and I'm sick of being the victim. It's about time I stood up for myself!"

With his carbine high and ready, Jack began stalking the trail with revenge in his eye.

At the base of a 2,000-foot hill, Jack reached the end of the trail. There, cut into an outcropping of rocks, he spotted the entrance to the mine.

A high, chain-link fence surrounded the business, guarding a gravel parking lot that held a surprising number of pickup trucks and other vehicles. A mobile home flanked one side, a sign identifying the main office still visible through the coating of ash.

A poured concrete apron led to a tunnel that had been cut out of the hill's stone face. It was about ten feet high and twice as wide, obviously not a natural cave or opening. From his hide, Jack could tell that the area had seen a lot of foot traffic, most of it leading into the dark mouth of the excavation.

Two metal storage buildings rounded out the mine's above-ground presence, the commander assuming those facilities had housed fuel, spare parts, and other necessary equipment. There weren't nearly as many footprints on that side of the grounds, the wooden steps leading to the office also unmarred. "They must be living underground," Jack concluded. "Like the Cliff house and Carlsbad, that's how they survived."

Just as Jack started to move closer, he spied a single man exiting the hole. The commander went prone, his rifle's optic centering on the new threat.

Stretching as if he'd just been woken from a deep sleep, the miner then stood and studied the parking lot and fence line. Jack noted the shotgun hanging by a sling from the dude's shoulder. Given his relaxed, almost-bored movements, the commander assumed that sentry duty had become a mundane task. "Let's change that," he grunted, backing away on his stomach.

The wind started picking up as Jack circled around to a spot behind the office-trailer, the commander approaching the chain link barrier with caution. He was thankful for the breeze and that its whine would help cover any noise he might make. He dropped to one knee near the fence, taking one last opportunity to scope out the lay of the land. After looking toward the west, Jack froze again with indecision. The sky looked dark. Was there a storm on the way?

His fury and indignation burning white hot, Jack didn't care about anything but retrieval and revenge. Refocusing on the fence, it took him only a few seconds to find what he was looking for.

There, hidden from view by the mobile office space, was a twenty-inch gap between the bottom of the chain link barrier and the ground. The Hill Country terrain was lumpy with rocks and troughs, those undulations making it nearly impossible to mate the fence tight with the earth.

After making sure the sentry was still stationed by the entrance, the commander easily slid under the chain link and hustled for the cover of the trailer. By the time he reached its aluminum skin, the wind was buffeting and rocking the mobile office. The ash was being driven hard enough to sting the eyes.

Taking a few deep breaths, Jack chanced a quick glance around the corner. Sure enough, the lackadaisical sentry hadn't moved. He too was glancing westward; his eyes focused on the approaching clouds.

The plots of old cowboy flicks rushed back into Jack's brain. "Wasn't the guard always distracted by a thrown rock? Didn't that always work?" he whispered under the increasing drone of the wind.

A quick search of the ground left Jack holding a baseball-sized stone, perfect for throwing against the wind.

As he peered around the trailer's rear bumper, the commander coiled to fling his missile.

A streak of lightning flashed through the sky, followed a second later by a rolling crack of thunder. With the rock cocked and ready, Jack relaxed when he spied the sentry turn and begin hurrying back toward the entrance to the mine. "Damn... sometimes it's better to be lucky than good," he mumbled, dropping the projectile.

The guard was two steps inside the rock opening when Jack's charging-shoulder slammed into the unaware man's back. The miner hit the stone floor hard, his shotgun rattling out of reach. By the time he realized what had happened, the commander's snarling face was leering over him, the muzzle of his carbine looking like a giant, black hole of death.

"Where is my bicycle?" Jack snarled from under his mask.

"I don't... it's... we took it into the mine," the stunned sentry stammered, his eyes darting left and right in sheer terror.

"Take me to it... now!" Jack barked, his voice barely discernable over the screaming wind.

While intent on following Jack's instructions, the guard's eyes remained trained on the battle rifle threatening his life. He stood up, somewhat awkwardly, stumbling as he backed further into the tunnel. Regaining his posture, he continued his half-backward, half-sidestep further inside the cavern.

Soon enough, they were deep in what was essentially a circular tunnel, corrugated metal lining the interior roof and walls. The ceilings were low, a narrow-gauge rail line running along one side of the corridor. In so many ways, the confined space reminded Jack of being in a submarine.

There was a dim light gleaming from above, an odd hue of yellow emitting from what appeared to be a tube-like fixture screwed into the supports. The commander followed his captive, being led toward what looked to be a miniature train, several small cars resting on a pair of iron tracks.

"This is the mule," the recovering sentry announced. "It will take us to the bottom of the shaft."

The miner stepped to the front, taking a seat on a boxy-looking unit that had a few simple controls and gauges. Jack took a minute to examine the locomotive before taking a seat in the first open car. There were at least a dozen similar units coupled together, hitched behind the engine, just like a regular train. Only slightly larger than a grocery store's shopping cart, he climbed in it and perched on top.

With his weapon nearly touching the nervous guard's ear, there was no need for Jack to remind the miner that there would be no funny business allowed. Instead, Cisco simply tapped the shoulder of the man with the carbine and said, "Let's go."

The driver, reaching for the controls, punched a button and the turned a dial. The mule started rolling.

With glass-smooth torque, the train accelerated, the track clearly angled downward. Soon, they reached an impressive speed, and Jack found himself swaying with the curves, a rhythmic clacking sounding from the small wheels and metal track.

The commander paid close attention to the overhead lights that illuminated the tunnel for as far as he could see. Despite the knots in his stomach from having to venture into the enemies' enclave and the fact that he had never been in a mine before,

Jack couldn't help but wonder how the men below were enjoying so much electricity.

He decided to ask his guide. "How are you generating electrical power?" Jack inquired.

"Those are chemical lights," sounded the miner over his shoulder. "We don't have enough fuel left to run the electric generators except to power the ventilation system and the mule. We have siphoned all we can get out of the cars and trucks in the parking lot, but it goes fast."

It seemed like a mile of the corrugated tunnel passed, the commander feeling like he was traveling through an oversized sewer pipe. Twice, his ears popped from the pressure as the air grew warmer during the descent.

Finally, the train glided to a stop. Jack made sure his captive again felt the cold barrel of a gun behind his ear. "Where is my bicycle?" Jack asked again, wanting to make sure his new friend didn't lose focus.

"It's down on the next level," the miner announced. "We're not very far away."

To get to the bike, the two men climbed down a series of metal ladders, each taking Jack and his hostage deeper into the bowels of the earth. The commander had no idea how far below ground they had traveled and was beginning to grow concerned. Was his captive intentionally trying to get him lost? Was he leading Jack into a trap?

Still, he had little choice but to follow.

Below the surface seems to be the hottest trend in real estate these days, Jack thought, his mind revisiting his journeys to the caravans at Carlsbad, the Cliff House, and the Marines' underground base. *So much for my investments in oceanside properties.*

They approached a rock room, one wall full of metal lockers that would have been at home in any public high school. A shelf held dozens of hardhats, each filthy with grime and equipped with a large flashlight above the bill.

Below each hardhat hung a mask of the design Jack had never seen. His bicycle was resting against a rock wall.

"Why are you helping that murderer, Sheng?" the frightened sentry asked. "He tried to kill us all."

"What?" Jack replied, the skepticism evident in his tone. "That one, little, old man tried to murder all of you? That's a little hard to believe."

"We made a deal with him," the guard insisted. "He took us into the woods and showed us what plants to pick. You can ask the woman, Hannah. She was with him. When we ate those roots, we all got sick as hell. I thought I was going to die. Cam says Sheng tried to poison us."

"Given what I saw a few days ago, I don't blame the old grouch for trying. You guys seemed pretty damned intent on burning him out of his homestead. I can understand Sheng being a little defensive," Jack countered.

"We weren't trying to kill him. That would be stupid," the guard stammered in defense. "We were only trying to scare the shit out of the old bastard… trying to convince him to honor the deal he had made. He knows too much to die. That would be a waste."

Something in the man's voice convinced Jack that he was telling the truth, or at least as much of it as he knew. "Who is Cam?" Jack asked.

A voice sounded from the other side of the room, "I am Camaro Butler. I am the mine boss of this operation."

The commander spun, his weapon centering on a man entering from an opening in the far wall. The newcomer was twice Jack's age, with leathery skin, close-cropped hair, and years of wisdom wrinkling his eyes. With no apparent regard for the weapon pointed at his chest, he strolled to a wooden table in the center of the room and took a seat on a metal folding chair.

"Take a load off, Commander," the raspy voice offered. "Despite the fact that you killed two of my men the other day and have now invaded our home, I hold no ill will, Jack Cisco. After we're done talking, you have my word that you and your bicycle will be returned to the surface, unharmed."

Jack started to ask how the fellow knew his name, but then answered his own question. "The saddlebags on my bicycle. You searched them."

Nodding, Camaro admitted as much. "I wanted to know who the new shooter was. For all we knew, you were a relation to Sheng, or perhaps a hired gun that crazy, old fart had dug up somewhere."

Jack didn't move for several seconds, his eyes studying Mr. Butler with suspicion. To reiterate his offer of a powwow, Cam again pointed toward an empty chair. "You have my word, Commander. No harm."

With his weapon never leaving the mine boss's chest, Jack pulled the metal chair to a safe distance and then sat at an angle where he could watch both entrances, the sentry, and the mine boss all at the same time.

"Good," the older man said. "Let's start over again, shall we? My name is Camaro Butler," he began. "I am the head cheese of this operation. Welcome to our mine."

"Commander Jack Cisco, US Navy. I came here only to retrieve my property and nothing more."

"I see," Cam grunted, his expression neither hostile nor friendly. "That took a rather-large pair of balls to come into our mine alone, Commander. Have you ever worked underground before?"

"In a way," Jack replied. "I am... was a submariner. I was the executive officer aboard the *USS Utah* before the fall of good society."

"Interesting," Cam replied, his eyes intently studying Jack top to bottom, finally deciding that his guest wasn't likely to freak out given the subterranean confinement. He'd seen grown men completely freak out before.

There was a pause, almost as if the mine boss was trying to decide what to do next. Finally, he pointed at the guard and said, "With the commander's leave, go and retrieve his saddlebags and belongings. They're in the breakroom, against the back wall."

Jack didn't like Butler's plan and said so, "I don't think that's a clever idea. You might bring several armed friends back with you or sound the alarm so your buddies can set an ambush for me on the way out."

"My, my, you are the suspicious type, Commander," Butler grunted.

"That's how I've managed to survive the last few months, sir. Trust is a rare commodity these days," Jack quipped.

"I will be happy to remain here as your hostage, and I will personally travel with you back to the surface. Would that be enough assurance?"

Weighing his options, Jack still didn't like letting either man out of his sight. "Let's *all* go retrieve my belongings. I don't mind the exercise."

"As you wish," Butler shrugged, rising from his chair.

With Jack at the rear, the three men left the locker room and traveled less than a couple dozen steps to another chamber. Like the previous room sporting the lockers and masks, the area was carved out of solid rock and illuminated by chemical lights mounted to the ceiling. There were several wooden benches and tables scattered here and there.

Just inside the door, a small figure darted from the shadows, drawing the barrel of Jack's weapon. The commander, seeing the movement, was just shy of applying enough pressure to break the trigger, when a tiny voice shouted, "Uncle Cam!"

The child ran to Camaro, wrapping his arms around the mine boss's legs in an embrace. Exhaling, Jack raised his weapon's aim, more than a little relieved that he hadn't shot the kid. "That was close," he whispered.

"Hi there, Timmy," Camaro greeted, patting the youngster on the head. "Now's not a good time to play."

"We have food, Uncle Cam. It tastes so good. Did you eat some yet?" the undeterred child asked.

"No, I haven't had time, but I'm glad you got something to eat," Cam replied.

A woman then appeared, followed by a concerned-looking man with a long, black beard. "Timmy, get back over here and leave Mr. Butler alone," the lady chided. Then, after noticing Jack and his carbine, her voice became even more demanding. "Now, young man!"

The tot did as he was told, trudging toward his mother. She tried to snuggle the child in a protective embrace but didn't have the strength to do it. Dad, alerted by the tone of his wife's voice, stepped between Jack and his family. "Who is... what is he doing here," the defensive father growled.

"It's okay, Mike," Butler soothed. "This is Commander Cisco. He's come for his bicycle and equipment."

Understanding took a moment, Mike finally nodding as his eyes bore into the commander with beams of pure hatred.

"I just want my gear," Jack repeated, nodding toward the contents of his pack that were strewn across the top of a wooden table.

"I'm sorry, Commander, but we've already distributed the food we found in your pack," the woman confessed, her tone thick with embarrassment.

"No problem," Jack replied, then motioning to the sentry, he continued, "Repack my belongings, and then I'll take my leave."

As Jack's saddlebags were refilled with his equipment, the commander took a moment to study the miners.

They were all rail thin and had sunken eyes. Cisco also noted that they all seemed exhausted, slouching hard, and taking advantage of any nearby support. The mother couldn't lift her child, despite the boy being little more than skin and bone.

Mike's focus and concentration seemed to be an issue. Even now, with a hostile invader holding a gun on his family, his eyes appeared to drift around some undefined point or empty space. When anyone spoke, there was an extra pause before the words seemed to register with the audience.

Jack thought back to his initial contact with the sentry. The commander had spotted the man stretching and yawning. He had supposed that the guard had been sleeping just before coming on duty... but now he doubted his assumption. And when he followed the sentry down into the mine, he'd noticed the man having difficulty with any physical task. Walking had seemed to require extreme concentration, the two of them traversing the ladders painfully slow.

Cisco's mind worked to assimilate his observations and adjust his impressions. Thinking back even further, he had believed the attackers to be amateurs during the battle at Sheng's, either poorly led or having zero combat experience. Now, he was second-guessing that theory as well. The sentry claimed that they were only trying to scare Sheng, and that might explain some of what happened. While Jack tended to believe the man, he was also convinced there was more to the story than the man had disclosed.

As he waited for his gear to be returned, he took the opportunity to replay every little detail of his encounters with the miners. Their motor skills were obviously restricted. He watched as Camaro tried to tie his boot. It took the miner three attempts to make a simple loop and cross, his fingers struggling as if the shoelaces were oily snakes trying to escape. If he didn't know better, Jack would have thought the man was severely intoxicated.

They are starving, the commander realized. *They are weak... without energy or reserve. They're losing their motor skills and reflexes.* Jack was reminded of pre-eruption television commercials trying to raise donations for famine-stricken parts of the world, the depicted victims having delayed reflexes and hollow stares.

Yet, there were some stark contrasts to those old charity broadcasts. Jack noted that everyone's hair was reasonably clean, as were their clothes. He hadn't detected any body odor. Other than Blackbeard, the other men he'd interacted with today had all recently shaved.

"Sheng tried to kill us all," Camaro blurted out, apparently as a last-ditch attempt to influence Jack. "After our food supplies ran out, we went to him for help. We offered respirator equipment, clean water, and access to our medical supplies. He agreed to help us. He took some of my men and showed them which plants to harvest and told us how to prepare them. But when we ate the roots, we nearly died. That old bastard tried to poison us all."

Jack's first reaction, as before, was disbelief and he said as much. "There must have been some sort of misunderstanding or mistake," the commander stated. "I hardly know the man. I only met him a few days ago, but he doesn't strike me as mass murderer... not by any stretch of the imagination."

"We followed his instructions to the letter," Mike blurted with emotion in his voice. "We all nearly died after eating that shit that old bastard had us dig up. Timmy stopped breathing twice. If one of the men hadn't been an EMT, we would have lost him."

Shaking his head, Jack asked, "Why? Why would he do such a thing? That doesn't make sense."

Camaro had an answer, "Before Yellowstone, Sheng filed a complaint against the mine with the EPA and the county government. He claimed that we were poisoning the creek, made a big stink about how all the plants he watered using the stream died because of something we were dumping in the water. The mining company's lawyers fought him off."

Pondering the miner's response for several moments, Jack still couldn't fathom Sheng doing such a thing. "I'm having trouble wrapping my head around what you're saying, Mr. Butler. I also can't imagine Hannah being associated with a sociopathic killer.

She's like me, sure that Sheng is a straight-up guy. He's fed and cared for me since the shootout. If he wanted me dead, he's had ample opportunity."

"That woman was involved as well," Camaro offered. "She helped him. She wants all of us dead for some reason."

"How can you be so sure?" Jack pushed back, now even more apprehensive over what he was being told. "Why? Why would she do such a thing? Like the old man, she's done absolutely nothing to raise my suspicions or indicate any sort of criminal behavior."

"I can't answer that. Believe me, I've tried to understand their actions a hundred times since this went down. And even if you don't believe us, fact is, we aren't trying to kill Sheng. That would be very short-sighted. We only want him to show us how to harvest what's left out there so we can eat. Look at that child. We have a dozen more of the little ones like Timmy, all of them starving to death right before our eyes. We only want that Chinese bastard to tell us the truth this time. We have the right to eat."

Again, Jack scanned the people in the room as the last pouch on his pannier was pulled shut. Camaro wasn't lying about the starvation part. That much was clear, even to a blind man.

The sentry patted Jack's bag, "It's all back in there... except for the food, of course."

"Bring it along," Jack ordered, waving Camaro and the sentry toward the entrance with his rifle barrel.

As the two miners moved to do his bidding, Jack had no choice but to turn his back on the remaining occupants of the mine. Confused, and still feeling the adrenaline dump from his son almost being killed, Mike drew a long knife from the small of his back. He lunged at the invader, slashing at Jack's back with a vicious stroke.

Surprised by the assault, Jack survived only because his body armor deflected the strike. Pivoting, the commander's first thought was to raise his rifle and fire, but there was neither the time nor the space.

Recovering quickly, Mike stepped in for a second try with his blade, his eyes filled with hatred and wrath.

With his foe too close for the long barrel of his weapon, Jack sidestepped the extended thrust while grasping the attacker's arm with both hands. Extending his hip into the wielder's mid-section, the commander twisted and pulled in the same motion.

The miner's weight went onto Jack's hip, his feet dangling above the floor for a fraction of a second. With a twist and a jerk, the hapless attacker was flipped into the air, thrown at the legs of the onlooking miners. His grip on the knife failed as his body seemed to defy gravity, the weapon clattering onto the rock floor.

A whoosh of air gushed from the downed man's chest as he slammed into the hard surface, tumbling into the knees and shins of Camaro and the sentry.

Jack, seizing the opening, scooped up the blade as he rolled across the floor. In a flash, the knifepoint was poised at Mike's neck, shimmering in the chemical light.

Coiled to kill, the commander paused as if trying to determine his foe's fate. "Dad!" the boy's voice shrieked, followed a moment later by the wife pleading. "No! Mister, please! No!"

The fury surging through Jack's veins began to diminish as he regrouped from the ambush. While he had been driven to kill the man who had blindsided him, the commander couldn't bring himself to cut the bushwhacker's throat.

That was too easy, flashed through Jack's mind. *This guy doesn't weigh ninety pounds soaking wet with a brick in each hand. It was like grappling with a rag doll. He's weak, slow, and hardly worth the effort.*

"I can't kill a man in front of his children, no matter how foolish he might be," Jack hissed, the blade still threatening Mike's jugular.

Pausing just long enough to make his point, Jack then withdrew the knife and stood up. Tossing the weapon aside, he raised his rifle and growled, "The next time somebody gets frisky, I'm going to start pulling the trigger. There will be hot lead bouncing off the walls and shredding flesh. I won't stop until my mag is empty. Is that clear?"

Every head in the room nodded their understanding, including Mike, who wisely remained on the stone floor.

Once Jack was convinced that his message had been received, he nodded toward Camaro and said, "Take me out of here before I change my mind."

Leaving Mike and his family behind, Jack and the remaining two miners returned to the locker room. Once there, Jack's eye was drawn to the row of sophisticated masks hanging from the wall. He moved toward them, reaching to examine the complex-looking device.

They were the most sophisticated breathing apparatus the naval officer had seen outside of a fighter pilot's headgear... or an astronaut's spacesuit. Making eye contact with Camaro, he asked, "Okay if I look at one of these?"

"Suit yourself," the mine boss replied, looking confused about where the commander was going.

Lifting the mask from its peg, Jack studied the unit for nearly a minute. "Can this filter poison gas?" he asked.

"Yes," Butler answered in a curt tone. "Their protection rating is equal to the military's M50 system. We even have special cups that allow us to drink water without removing the mask."

"Interesting," Jack nodded, replacing the unit on the wall. "How many do you have?"

The question seemed to frighten the mine boss, almost as if he thought Jack was going to demand the masks as reparation. His eyes narrowed to slits as his voice dropped to barely a whisper, Camaro confided, "More than enough. Many of our coworkers have died since the eruption. You and your lady friend have killed even more. If you want one, take it, but please, leave us enough for our people."

"The men I fought with at Sheng's weren't wearing masks like these," Jack responded, ignoring Cam's concerns. "Neither was the sentry above."

"We don't wear them outside any longer. We only have so many replacement filters, and if there is a follow-on eruption, the ash will get worse again," Cam explained.

"That's very astute," Jack acknowledged with a nod. "I have never even considered that Yellowstone might not be done spitting death."

Motioning for Camaro to push the bicycle, Jack said, "Escort me out of here, Mr. Butler. I'm afraid I've worn out my welcome."

Nodding, Cam took the pack and began pushing the bicycle. Turning to the sentry, Jack said, "Try anything stupid, and your boss gets the first bullet. Are we clear about that?"

The disgruntled guard merely nodded and stepped back for Jack to pass.

Catching up with Camaro, Jack maintained a wary eye as the two men negotiated the matrix of tunnels and ladders. Pulling the bicycle up through the various levels was a pain, but the miners kept plenty of ropes on hand. Finally arriving back at the mule, the commander motioned for the mine boss to operate the controls.

Taking the seat directly behind the locomotive, Jack was beginning to relax as they started the return ride to the surface. Halfway there, he noticed the first flashes of strobing light. "What the hell?"

Over the click and clack of the rails, Jack then heard the unmistakable sound of nearly continuous thunder. "You've got to be shitting me," he growled as the mule approached the opening. "What terrible timing."

The two men stepped toward the entrance, both watching in amazement as nearly continuous sheets of rain slammed into the Texas Hill Country followed on by a heavenly display that would have rivaled the best of laser light shows. Jack had seen these storms before, unconsciously wincing at the memory of nearly being buried alive just outside of San Diego. Were it not for Archie's timely rescue, his body would probably still be trapped under the rubble.

"You can't travel in this," Camaro yelled over the roar of the thunder.

"No kidding," Jack responded. "I suppose you and I will just have to stay here and wait it out."

They moved further into the mine, wandering far enough inside that the thunder wasn't assaulting their ears. For several minutes, the duo simply stood and listened to the raging weather.

"So tell me... what is a naval commander doing in the Texas Hill Country?" Butler finally asked.

"I rode that bicycle here from San Diego to find my family," Jack replied.

"California? All that way after the eruption? That's hard to believe," Camaro ventured.

"Believe what you will, but that's how I got here. My wife's family owned a nearby ranch. She was supposed to have been staying there when Yellowstone blew. After my boat docked in San Diego, and we learned that the government no longer existed, I took a leave and set off to find them."

"Is there much left out there?" Camaro inquired, a hint of hope creeping into his voice.

"There are survivors all over the country," Jack offered. "I've encountered entire communities along the way. Some are even growing food."

"How? There's no way anything will grow without sunlight. All the animals are dead," Cam frowned unable to keep the disbelief out of his voice.

Shaking his head, Jack said, "For a bunch of guys who are smart enough to have survived this long, you all sure seem a bit short-sighted when it comes to putting grub in your stomachs."

Camaro sighed, obviously regretting the harshness of his tone. "I'm sorry. The truth hurts. I have mined minerals on three continents, Commander. My adult life has been spent dealing with poison gases, poor ventilation, and the dangerous pressures involved in working underground. I've been doing this for nearly four decades. Breathing, given our equipment and training, has been manageable. Securing nutrition, however, doesn't seem to be our forte. I guess I would have to admit that there isn't a farmer or a rancher among us all."

"Where do you get water?" Jack asked, his curiosity unchecked by his pending doom.

"We commonly dig through various reservoirs and veins of water," Camaro shrugged. "Normally, we seal them off or pump it out. What was once a headache and an unwelcome expense now allows us to drink and bathe. Accessible water has kept us alive... barely. We have scavenged every empty ranch and home. My men have ventured far and wide, bringing back what they could find. We're running out of options."

"Survival of the fittest... or the smartest," Jack whispered, always amazed at mankind's ingenuity. After reflecting for a moment, he then continued, "I still don't know what to make of the conflict between you and Sheng. Nothing makes any sense about the entire affair. Either it was a simple mistake or a misunderstanding, I can't see that old goat trying to kill anybody, let alone children."

A grimace crossed the mine boss's face, "Look, I don't know what he told you, but my men found Sheng digging in the woods one day. He claimed to be able to identify edible plants even though all the surface greenery was dead. We made a deal with him and did exactly as he instructed. He wanted propane and one of our cutting torches for his sculping. We delivered. Ask your lady friend; she was there. When we got sick, we didn't trust him anymore, so we demanded that he give us food from his own cellar. We figured he wouldn't have any poison grub there. I'm with you, though. I thought we could help each other survive. I had believed that together, we would be stronger."

"You said Hannah was there?"

"Yes. She went with Sheng and my crew into the countryside. She even helped us dig. Ask her when you get back. If she has an ounce of decency, she'll confirm my side of the story. We have 187 people living in this mine, Jack. Nearly half are women and children, family members my men brought here to survive after Yellowstone blew. The cans from your pack were the first bites of food they've had in a week."

The conversation was interrupted by an especially close lightning strike, the follow-on thunder vibrating the rock behind their backs. "Yellowstone is the gift that keeps on giving," Jack quipped after the rumbling had subsided.

"This could go on for hours," Camaro noted. "And it's going to be dark soon. You may end up being my guest for the evening, Commander."

The thought of staying up and alert all night didn't sit well with Jack, his expression making that clear. There was no way he was going to close his eyes and sleep while surrounded by a bunch of hostile miners.

"I give you my word, Jack. No harm will come to you. There have been enough dead bodies already."

Wanting to believe the man beside him, Jack knew he could never take that chance. The Sandman never came under those conditions, and yet, he was starting to feel the drain of exhaustion.

On the other hand, traveling through the storm wasn't an option. Walking through unknown territory at night wasn't at the top of his Christmas list either. Then there was the approach to Sheng's minefield of booby-traps in the dark or the reception a nocturnal visitor might receive from Hannah's AR15.

An idea then came to Jack, "Do you still have the keys to the office trailer outside?"

Nodding, Camaro responded, "Why yes, I do. They are on a hook, hanging in my quarters."

"Take the mule and go back. Get those keys, and we'll spend the night together above ground. If you come back with your men, a lot of people are going to die. You believe that, don't you?"

With a knowing grimace, Butler responded, "Yes, I'm sure you would be able to kill several of us before our numbers overwhelmed you. We're not fighting men, Commander; we're miners."

"Then that's the plan. You and I will wait out the storm right here. After it has passed, we'll move into the trailer and spend the night," Jack announced.

"I don't know if that's such a hot idea," Camaro frowned. "What if my boys dig up a sudden load of courage and decide to come and rescue me? I can issue all the orders I want, but you know how men's minds can work in the middle of the night."

"Bring back two of those fancy breathing systems with you," Jack grinned. "Those will be my insurance policy."

Camaro had to think about that for a moment before he responded, "I don't savvy, Commander? Those masks are valuable, but we have a lot of them. How are they going to keep my guys at bay?"

"Because tomorrow morning, you and I are going to use them to find food… a lot of food. Tell your crew that I'm going to help you, that you convinced me that Sheng had done you wrong. Tell them that I know where there is a stash of groceries. That will give them something to think about before charging up here and shooting up the trailer."

"Are you serious? You know where there is a stockpile of groceries?" Camaro asked, his eyes holding more hope than Jack could have imagined.

"Yes. I can't be positive how much, but I came across what might be sizable stash during my travels. It will be worth the hike, Mr. Butler. Of that, I'm reasonably sure."

Chapter 43

Hannah's pacing seemed to bother Sheng. "He'll either be back... or he won't," the old man stated. "The world is a very dangerous place. Listen to that storm rage."

Pulling up short, Hannah's scowl made it clear that her friend's attitude wasn't appreciated. "He risked his life to save you and your home," she snapped. "He's a good man... the kind we're all going to need if there's to be any future for the human race."

"You said you just met him," Sheng pushed back. "How could you possibly know so much about him?"

"He came to your rescue without having ever met you before. He did so just on my word. Trust like that is rare these days, Sheng. You, of all people, should know that."

The old man wasn't convinced. "For all we know, he just stole something from my yard and ran off. You can't trust anyone, young woman. *You*, of all people, should *know* that. As far as coming to help me, I don't think my ancient bones had anything to do with his bravery. I think it was you he was trying to impress... you and your breasts."

Dismissing the debate with a wave of her hand, Hannah returned to her pacing. She had tried to stop Jack, mostly out of concern that he hadn't given himself enough time to mend. Maybe Sheng was right. Maybe the naval officer had run off.

That line of reasoning, however, didn't make any sense. There were food and shelter here. There was a chance Captain Bascom would know something about Jack's family. The commander wouldn't just slink away. He was still on his quest and needed information to know where to start. Bascom might deliver that.

Then she speculated for a moment why she was so worried about a man she barely knew. After all, most of her encounters with people outside the airport had turned violent. Most survivors had become little more than wild animals, feral beasts who

115

thought of nothing but their own needs and were no longer restrained by the rule of law or threat of punishment. Jack had been different. She had first sensed it while stalking him through Clover Springs.

Was it the fact that he had made a superhuman effort to reunite with his family? How many men would do that? Didn't that speak to some inner code of honor or morality that had become a rare commodity in a world covered by ash? How many men were capable of such loyalty in today's environment?

It then dawned on Hannah why she felt such a strange kinship to the commander. There was a bond between them that would be difficult to explain to anyone who hadn't traveled through the apocalyptic landscape. They were both explorers… pioneers. They had overcome the dread of the unknown and traveled what had become a new wilderness. Being caged inside, paralyzed by fear, was unacceptable to members of their creed. Both survived where others wouldn't dare venture. It was a brotherhood of sorts, probably not unlike the feelings shared between those who had endured combat together.

Before Hannah's analysis could continue, a loud clap of thunder vibrated the dugout's floor. *If Jack is caught out in this storm, I hope he can find shelter,* she thought.

For another two hours, Hannah walked the floor while the weather raged. Ten minutes after the final thunderclap had echoed through the Hill Country valley, the scout was pulling on her gear.

"Where are you going?" Sheng asked, despite already knowing the answer.

"I'm going to see if I can find Jack," she replied. "There is a little light left. He might be wounded, or lost, or trapped in one of those damn contraptions of yours. Are you coming with me?"

"I am telling you… most likely he has stolen something before slithering off the way thieves always do," the old man declared. "I will not waste my time and energy looking such a man, nor will I help him again if he is found. I have shared enough of my wealth already."

Hannah was again disappointed in her host, the term "greedy old bastard," forming in her throat. In a huff, she stomped out the door, weapon in her hand. "I'll be back in a bit. Let's hope that a little solitude helps your outlook."

Navigating the junkyard, Hannah's eyes strained to pick up Jack's trail in the ash. The storm had swept most of the footprints clean, only a few indentations visible in the low light. The ash would not reveal its secrets.

"He said he was going to retrieve his bicycle," she remembered. "That's where I'll start looking."

Convinced that foul play might be afoot, she proceeded with caution, her weapon always ready. Finally, she approached the railroad tracks and the pile of scrub where Jack had hidden his bike.

She knew that the hide was located along the route that the miners typically used when traveling to Sheng's property. It came as no surprise that the area was ripe with tracks.

Most of the signs had been partially filled by the wind-blown ash, and again, Hannah cursed the storm. About the only thing that was recognizable was the straight, line-like impression left by the bicycle's tires.

Despite being almost obscured by the storm's blow, Hannah could clearly spot where Jack's bicycle had been pushed through the pumice. For a fleeting moment, she thought Sheng might be right. Had the commander changed his mind and bugged out? Why would he do that? Her heart sank at the thought that he wouldn't at least say goodbye or offer an explanation.

Following the bicycle's trail for a half mile, her brain tried to reconcile Jack's actions. At that point, the train tracks entered a concrete viaduct, a county road passing overhead. Inside, the trail hadn't been touched by the wind.

117

Hannah could see several footprints associated with the bike's passing. One of them was from the military-issue boots that Jack wore. She had tracked the commander all through Clover Springs. She recognized the pattern of the sole.

"They've captured Jack," she hissed, raising her head to see that the path continued toward the location where the mine's main entrance was located. "Those bastards!"

"They waited for Jack at the bicycle. They knew he would be coming back to retrieve his wheels, and they ambushed him," she concluded.

For a few moments, Hannah considered following the the tracks and attempting a rescue, but she quickly dismissed the idea. Dusk was fast approaching. She had never been inside the mine. She would end up dead or a prisoner herself. Frustrated, she turned around and began the hike back to Sheng's.

Twinges of concern tormented her, her concern for Jack growing with each step. *Would they kill him quickly? Would they torture him to find out where Sheng's booby-traps were hidden, or force their prisoner to reveal how much ammunition was left in the dugout?*

It then dawned on her that perhaps the miners deserved more credit than what she was giving them. "They have a hostage," she whispered. "They will try to negotiate a trade."

The old man's words echoed in the recesses of her memory, and again, sadness filled her up. "There's no way Sheng is going to give up anything to save Jack's hide. What a selfish coot."

After the secret knock, Hannah entered the dugout to find Sheng warming himself by the fire. "Well?" he asked after looking up.

"The miners have captured Jack. From the tracks I found, it looks like they were waiting in ambush by his bicycle. I know he *was* alive... I followed his footprints for a considerable distance. They led back toward the mine."

"And?" Sheng asked, apparently not overly concerned.

"And what if they torture Jack and he tells them where your booby-traps are hidden?" Hannah barked, her frustration growing. "A war party could be in that front door before we ever knew they were coming. Do you want to wake up tonight with a gun barrel in your mouth?"

Her words caused the old man to scowl. "I will move the traps," he announced, springing to his feet with a surprising amount of energy. "I will keep those men away from my home, even if I have to work all night."

"In the dark? Can you do that safely? And what if they are out there, right now, watching, waiting for you to come out the door?" Hannah countered.

Her logic prompted Sheng to hesitate, allowing Hannah to pour it on, "Even if Jack told them where all the booby-traps are hidden, they might think he's lying. That's too risky. If I were in their shoes, I don't think I would try to attack us at night. I would try to negotiate a ransom instead. That is what I would do if I had a hostage."

"I'm not going to make any deal with them," the old man stated with conviction. "They won't honor any agreement... we both know that. They can't be trusted. I tried to help them once already and look at how that act of kindness was repaid. Why would they bother doing the work of digging and cleaning? They will just come here and raid my supply. I'm not going to make any agreement with them under any circumstances. They have proven themselves unworthy."

"I do not want to help them," he repeated after a few deep breaths. "Given a chance, they will kill us both."

"So, you're just going to throw Jack under the bus? You're just going to let them kill a man who risked his life to help you?" Hannah asked, her anger barely contained.

"I did not ask for his help... or yours," Sheng replied, his ire building by the second. "I will not give up my hard-earned stores... not for you... not for anybody."

Shaking her head in disgust, Hannah tried to think of a way out. She knew that the miners were as pig-headed as her friend, perhaps even more narrowminded. They were starving, desperate, and without hope. Before the apocalypse, none of the miners would have considered kidnapping or any other serious crime to solve their problems. It was amazing what hunger could do to the human mind.

In a way, the men holding Jack were a preview of what her community would soon become. If Captain Bascom's scouts didn't find a sizable food source in the next few weeks, the people at the airport would eventually become just as reckless and aggressive as the miners.

Sheng's reaction to Jack's abduction compounded the problem.

Or did it?

She had been gradually working to win the old man over since discovering his dugout over two months ago. As far as she was concerned, Sheng's extensive knowledge of roots and tubers was the answer to all her people's problems. Was this the time? Were the circumstances now right? Had the stars finally aligned?

She had been hoping that he would return with her to Austin and teach them all how to harvest what was left. She had been counting on the information from him offering a critical piece of the nourishment puzzle.

The old man's unwillingness to help others was deeply disappointing, and if she didn't play along with his wishes, there was no way in hell Sheng would help the colony at the airport.

"I don't have very much ammunition left, and neither do you," she began. "We can't hold out much longer if they lay siege to your home. They may already know where a lot of your traps are located, and you can't move them all. They learned a hard lesson the last time and won't make the same mistakes again. I'm sorry, but that's the reality of the situation."

Crossing his arms in defiance, he repeated his stance. "I won't help them again. I will die first."

"My people are counting on me, Sheng. They need me. They depend on me. I can't stay here… can't risk dying for your cause when there is a straightforward way out. We can fix this once and for all. There is a solution."

Hannah could tell Sheng was getting worried now. "What way out? Surrender to those rats who live down in a hole?"

"I have a different idea," Hannah cooed softly. "Why don't you return to the airport with me, first thing in the morning. We can be packed and out of here before the miners know we're gone."

"But my home… my collection… my work," the old man protested, his arm sweeping the interior.

Taking his hand in a gentle embrace, Hannah continued to sell her offer. "There are people at the airport, beautiful children, singing birds, and other things you've not seen since the eruption. I know Captain Bascom will be happy to provide you with a studio for your work. You can teach at our school, pass on your skills to a new generation, and create a legacy for your art and your knowledge. All the while, you'll be a hero. You will save hundreds of lives and have the eternal gratitude of all those souls."

For a second, Hannah thought her words were missing the mark. Sheng turned away, pulling his hand free. "Why is it so important that I go back with you?" he asked. "Why can't you bring those that want to learn back here?"

"There are too many to bring here," Hannah replied. "The children can't travel outside because it would be too dangerous for them. Besides, I don't want to leave you here alone. The miners are going to try again and again and again, Sheng. They will wear you down and eventually take what they want."

"Yes… yes, I suppose that is true," he sighed. "But I don't want to leave my home. Everything that I am is here. The fruits of all my labor… the purpose of my existence is right here."

"If you don't like living at the airport, then I will bring you back. I promise. I'll even try to persuade Captain Bascom to send some armed men with me so we can protect you from the miners if that is what you wish."

For nearly ten minutes, Sheng paced around the dugout, his footsteps and the crackling fire the only sounds. Finally, he stopped and stood erect. "It would be good to see new sights and hear new sounds," he whispered." Seeing animals again might inspire my tired, old mind to create. Do you I have your word that you will deliver me to my back home if I don't like it at your airport?"

"I do," Hannah smiled.

"Then we should begin packing," he declared. "We have a long journey ahead of us."

Captain Bascom exited the cockpit of the 757 aircraft, stepping carefully onto jetway. His eyes automatically scanned the makeshift seal that mated the plane's aluminum skin to the padded opening of the mobile ramp, looking for even the smallest breach or tear.

If he remained absolutely still, he could feel the slightest breeze exiting the aircraft. In reality, it was more akin to circulating air than any semblance of wind. Still, there was movement, and that was what had kept them alive.

When he'd first conceived of creating an over-pressure situation inside the terminal, Alex had been thinking in terms of days rather than months. The last few newscasts, before the airwaves had gone silent, had included experts who warned of microscopic glass shards and other dangerous elements in the ash. People had been advised to stay inside, to cover their mouths and noses, and not to drink any water exposed to the deadly blanket of volcanic spew now circling the earth. Two of the fundamental elements of life, air and water, were now considered deadly.

The captain had known that completely sealing the interior of a space the size of an airport was impossible. His first idea was to order everyone to take shelter inside the parked planes. The pilots could run the engines at the lowest possible speed to keep up with the ventilation requirements of the occupants. Idling at low power might keep the jets from being damaged by the ash… might keep them running long enough.

That proposal was quickly rejected as the size and scope of Yellowstone's eruption became clear. Being trapped inside those airliners would have been a horrendous experience. Even the fanciest of flying machines had been designed for only a few hours of habitation, not days or weeks. The toilets would fail quickly, the water tanks unable to support the needs of an extended existence.

Fortunately, one of the benefits of being at a busy airport was the broad availability of knowledge and expertise. The passengers and flight crews included engineers, professors, retired military, and even a couple of scientists.

"We only need a little overpressure," one man had suggested. "Just a few millibars will do the trick. If we seal the building's doors and vents as tightly as possible, running the aircraft's pressurization systems might keep the ash out."

They had formed work crews, quickly scavenging every bit of tape, plastic sheeting, cardboard, and plywood available. Again, luck was on their side, one of the nearby cargo facilities undergoing remodeling and expansion. The materials scavenged from the construction site had been extremely useful.

Rolls of fiberglass insulation had been repurposed, as had the truckload of lumber found near the hangar. Every window, door, HVAC vent, and opening had been modified. Jetways were tightly secured to fuselages, exhaust fans closed off, doors welded shut, and the baggage handling areas completely enclosed. All the while, a team of men with carpentry skills had been tasked with building "filter boxes" that could be attached to the aircrafts' intakes.

The concept was simple enough. Air from outside would be sucked into the airplane's pressurization system, passing through five cubic feet of fiberglass insulation before being pumped out to circulate throughout the building.

Instruments were scavenged from the airport's weather monitoring office. Their first tests showed that four jet engines, running at idle speed, increased the terminal's internal air pressure by just a few millibars. Not enough to make any ears pop, but an amount sufficient to keep ash from getting inside the building.

The captain had just started another set of engines, the day's second shift. Sitting in the cockpit for a quarter of an hour after initializing the powerful turbofans, he had carefully monitored the gauges and dials, alert for any sign of trouble. The plane's pressurization system was now working hard to fill the cabin with enough air to satisfy its preconfigured goal. Having the 757's door wide open meant the system would continue to work to meet its objective… and in doing so would filter the colony's air.

For the Nth time, Alex fretted over how long the jet engines would hold out. They had plenty of fuel, but the mechanics reported more and more deterioration of the turbofan's blades due to the ash and grit being sucked inside. They had already experienced several failures.

Pushing aside that concern, Bascom continued his journey up the mobile corridor. He nodded politely to two middle-aged men returning to the dorm. Like everyone else in the terminal, he knew their names and stories. Both had been on business trips. Both had families back east. Every single day, both wondered if their spouses, children, or relatives had survived.

They shared a sad tale, one often repeated throughout the weeks and months of confinement at Austin International. "Yellowstone's convicts," the captain whispered as he entered the main terminal.

Before he could reflect further, a familiar voice rang out from Gate 12. "Captain Bascom, sir, one of the scouts just radioed in," sounded the report. "He's returning. Should be here in five minutes."

Alex turned toward the former TSA agent, a middle-aged gent named Deiter who was hurrying to catch up with the captain while clutching one of the community's portable radios. Those devices, once used by the government agency to communicate between terminals and checkpoints, were now used by the scouts to announce their return or to call for help if they were in range.

"Did he give any further details, Deiter?" Bascom inquired, unable to keep a wee bit of hope from entering his voice.

"No, sir, he did not. From his tone, I don't think he had a successful trip. But… that's just my read," the ex-agent reported.

Given Deiter had stated that a male was returning, and thus eliminating Hannah, Bascom realized T.J. Pierce was coming in.

The two men then stepped to one of the floor-to-ceiling windows that overlooked the main tarmac. There, a wide expanse of open concrete met their gaze. They could see the fuel trucks parked below, as well as two of the electric carts used by the mechanics. Off in the distance, near the giant hangars at the fringe of the grounds, sat three dark planes that had once hauled freight. They had already been cannibalized for spare parts.

While they waited, Bascom and Deiter made small talk. "Why didn't you leave the airport and go home when Yellowstone blew?" the captain asked his second in command. "You and I have worked countless hours together, and it just occurred to me that I've never asked you that question."

The TSA worker smiled shyly at his superior, the inquiry a common one for those who lived in the Austin area. Those traveling through the central Texas city didn't have much choice after the eruption. Many of the locals did.

"My wife died of breast cancer a few years ago, sir. After I left the Army, I moved to Austin to start over again and took a job at the TSA. I really didn't have anything to go home to… any real reason to leave. We never had any children, and the few distant relatives on my side of the family are scattered all over the country."

Bascom had heard comparable stories from several of the locals, unmarried individuals who didn't have much of a social life outside their workplace. After learning just how deadly the volcano's impact would be, a few of the married employees had left the airport and brought their families back to the facility. "My wife and I lived in a small apartment," one baggage handler had recalled. "We lived from paycheck to paycheck and didn't have any food put back. Everybody was going insane out there. It was pure chaos, so we came back here."

Others had returned with brothers and sisters. Some had brought back boxes of supplies, packing the limited provisions from their homes, and returning to the only reasonably safe environment they knew.

"You should receive the credit, Captain," Deiter stated with confidence. "You came in here the day of the eruption and took over. All of us owe our lives to you. Without your leadership, everybody in here would have surely died."

"I only did what was necessary," Alex sighed. "Some of those early decisions were the most difficult I've ever made. We lost a lot of people those first few months. I think about them often."

Always uncomfortable with praise, Bascom was relieved when T.J.'s motorcycle appeared outside the window and interrupted the conversation. There, speeding across the open expanses of the tarmac, a lone figure appeared, gradually slowing the electric machine as he approached the main baggage door.

Glancing up, the rider waved at the two men observing his return. With his face covered by a mask and his eyes hidden behind thick goggles, the captain couldn't read the scout's expression.

Behind the motorcycle, secured by two lengths of rope, trailed a makeshift sled. Bascom's eyes moved to visually inspect the two cardboard boxes secured there, his mind automatically wondering if the scout had made a major discovery or had merely scavenged a few containers of supplies.

The silent bike came to a stop outside a set of large, metal panels embedded in the concrete-block wall, the entrance resembling a common household garage door. "Beep. Beep," sounded the motorcycle's horn, followed a moment later by the rumbling of the heavy barrier as it was being lifted open.

"Get everyone together," Bascom said. "We'll have the debriefing in ninety minutes."

The captain watched as Deiter nodded and then headed off to spread the word. "I hope T.J. brought back some good news," he added before heading for the stairway.

Stopping in front of a heavy-duty, steel door, Bascom bent and rummaged in a box next to the entrance. Inside were several pieces of cloth designated as "breathing rags." Quickly wrapping what had been a dish towel around his head, the captain made sure that the filter was tight against his nose and mouth.

Satisfied with his mask, he then descended two flights of stairs before arriving in what had been the terminal's baggage handling and maintenance area. This was a place that passengers rarely visited.

He found T.J. undressing in the clean room, a small office that served as a makeshift airlock. One door led to the unsecured, unfiltered section of the building, another opening located behind the ash barrier that had been erected. All people entering or leaving the pressurized section of the terminal had to change their clothing and cleanse any exposed skin or hair. The mechanics and scouts had taken to referring to the process as detox.

While the entire procedure reminded Bascom of a science fiction movie, it spoke volumes regarding the fear Yellowstone's spew had invoked.

Tapping lightly on the glass, Bascom waved and smiled at the returning scout. T.J. returned the gesture without providing any hint about the success or failure of his mission.

A few minutes later, the inner door opened, and Pierce emerged. "Morning, Captain," he greeted, extending his hand.

"Morning, T.J.," Bascom replied. "As usual, everyone is gathering to hear what you discovered. I thought I would exercise the privilege of rank and ask you for a brief preview, if you would be so kind."

Shaking his head, the scout confessed, "I didn't find any large food caches, sir. I did, however, manage to scavenge a couple of boxes of medical supplies for the doctor."

His eyes widening, Bascom asked, "Real medications, or those that come in a large, glass bottle?"

Chuckling, T.J. replied, "Real pills, Captain. I found them in a delivery truck up on I-35 about fifteen miles north of the city. It was parked behind a pharmacy that had been thoroughly ransacked. Evidently, the looters didn't think to look in the rusty, old Ford van sitting outside."

"Good job, T.J. Did you encounter any people?"

"Nothing face to face. Somebody took a few shots at me on the feeder road. I thought had given the Forbidden Zone a wide berth, but evidently, they have expanded their territory again. I saw new signs painted on an overpass, the typical skull and crossbones as well as written warnings to keep out. Fortunately, they missed badly, probably because I had the bike maxed trying to get the hell out of there. I didn't see any footprints or other signs of life, but with the wind, that doesn't mean a whole lot. I'll show you on the map later, if you wish."

"So, they're expanding? This is getting out of hand, T.J. Pretty soon, they'll have us hemmed in on three sides." Bascom was clearly worried by the scout's report.

"It appears so. They've gotten bolder since trading fire with our salvage team last month. I wish we knew who they were," the scout replied.

"Probably gang members who took over their neighborhood after the police collapsed," Bascom speculated. "Maybe an outlaw biker club. Whoever they are, they organized quickly and are damn ruthless. You were wise to scoot out of the area as fast as possible."

"I'll warn the other scouts about the new section of the Forbidden Zone," Pierce added.

"And the ash?" Bascom inquired.

"My read is that it is dissipating," the scout stated with a shrug. "With the wind the last few days, it was difficult to be sure, but it seemed like I had to clean off my goggles less often than even the last time out. Maybe it's just wishful thinking on my part?"

Bascom accepted the report with a grain of salt. One of the key job requirements of being a scout was having a positive attitude. While that attribute hadn't been publicly discussed, the captain had made sure that those assigned to that critical task were all individuals who would look at the glass as being half full. They were the new source of information about the outside world. Their reporting on the situation and conditions beyond the little colony was critical for the community's morale.

"Let's hope not," Alex commented. "Go ahead and get something to eat or whatever you need. You're on stage in an hour. Break a leg."

"Thank you, sir," T.J. responded. "Oh, and Captain, I brought you this," the scout announced, reaching to the small of his back and producing a thin book.

Accepting the offering, a huge grin spread across Bascom's face. "The Farmers' Almanac," the pilot read. It was an edition from last year. "Where did you find this?"

"It was in the office of a convenience store I was searching. I know it's not much, sir, but it was the best I could do."

If there was one consistent adage Captain Bascom was known for, it was the saying, "Knowledge is the only thing that will save us all." Over and again, Alex had used that wisdom as the foundation for practically every major decision the community had faced. One of the scout's highest priorities was to find guides, texts, reference materials, and other information that would help the community.

"I'll add it to our library," the pilot nodded. "Thank you."

"If you would authorize entry into the Forbidden Zone, sir, we could scour the university's library. We know it was a huge facility, probably tens of thousands of books and other reference materials."

A dark scowl painted Bascom's face, the expression indicative of frustration and anger. The Forbidden Zone basically encompassed Austin's north side, an area dominated by the University of Texas. While the school's sprawling campus was no doubt full of potential solutions to a host of mankind's problems, it had proven to be a very deadly place. The fact that homicidal Neanderthals controlled that territory and the information housed there irritated him to no end.

Little was known about the occupants of the massive college's complex. Someone had nicknamed the survivors the "Horns," after the famous school's mascot, the Texas Longhorns. The handle had stuck, even though there wasn't a shred of evidence indicating that students or faculty were involved. In fact, every attempt to contact the people there had been met with gunfire, ambushes, or booby-traps.

Barricades had been erected in many areas, entire streets blocked by vehicles and intentionally downed trees... and in one case, a row of heavy, steel dumpsters. Occasionally, masked men carrying long guns had been spotted patrolling the university's grounds. Bascom's scouts had tried white flags, written messages tied to thrown rocks, and every frequency on the radios in an attempt to establish friendly contact. All to no avail.

Sensing that his leader was pondering his request, Pierce expanded on his logic. "They may be like us, Captain. We sealed off the airport right after the eruption and wouldn't let anybody in. They probably had to do the same to survive when anarchy ruled the streets. They might still be living by that same protective mindset. I've been talking with the other scouts, and we think it might be time to try and approach them again."

Bascom clearly didn't like the idea of risking any more lives and said as much. "I'll consider it, T.J., but now seems like a bad time. We need every scout focused on finding calories, and that has to be our priority for the moment. If we don't locate a food source, all the knowledge in the world isn't going to save us. After you're done with your public briefing, I'm going to announce another cut in rations. That's not going to sit well with a lot of our people."

Nodding, the disappointed scout dejectedly responded, "Yes, sir, I understand."

Turning back toward the staircase, the captain began his ascent with a frown. He had maintained high hopes for T.J.'s excursion and was now disappointed in the results. While he was sure the doctor could put any scavenged medications to good use, it was food that they so desperately needed. Now it was up to Hannah, and she was past due.

When the idea of forming the scouts had first been conceived, Bascom had sketched out a basic set of qualifications. The recruits had to be between twenty-five and forty years old, in excellent physical condition, and have some sort of professional skill with firearms. Experience riding a motorcycle was also necessary, as well as good communications. After all, one of their primary goals was to contact other surviving communities or individuals.

"Groceries and information are our highest priorities," Bascom had lectured the first group of volunteers. "You're not raiders or looters, but scouts and ambassadors. We will *not* shoot first and ask questions later. We will *not* take anything, valuable or not, from others."

Two Austin police officers had been the first to volunteer. They had been assigned to the small substation tasked with airport duty before the collapse, and really didn't have any place else to go after everything went to hell.

There had been a handful of ex-military among the passengers, as well as the TSA agents who had remained at the facility. T.J. had been a hunting guide at one of the large Texas ranches where customers paid huge sums of money to stalk big game.

Initially, Bascom had high hopes for the excursions. Isolated in their bubble of pressurized atmosphere, the people at the airport had no idea what was going on in the world around them. They were as starved for information as castaways on a remote island, cut off from any external presence or interaction.

At that time, many believed that other pockets of people had to exist. "We can't be the only ones in the entire city who survived," folks commonly believed.

Others in the community had even higher expectations in those early days. "The government has to exist on some level. The entire federal, state, and local infrastructure couldn't have just vanished into thin air."

"No," Bascom said as he continued up the stairs. "They vanished into *thick* air."

The first scouts had been assigned to visit city hall, the state capital building, the police station, and other centers of government. Their reports had been astonishing, even to the most jaded of the airport's survivors.

"We found hundreds and hundreds of dead bodies, most killed during what appeared to be riots or violent clashes. At the state capital building, we found dozens of dead cops lying behind a barricade. The interior had been looted and burned," Hannah had reported. "We didn't see a single living human, bird, dog, cat, or insect. It is a desert out there, void of life."

"City hall was worse," another scout had piped in. "It was mostly rubble."

"We found Texas National Guard vehicles surrounding the police station," the third scout chimed in. "It looked like one of those old Western movies where the pioneers circled their wagons. There were lots of dead people from both sides, stacked waist high in the street. Clearly, the last few days out there were brutal."

"Every storefront, business, house, and building appear to have been looted or ransacked," Hannah continued. "I passed by two grocery stores and saw nothing inside but bare shelves. Same with the pharmacies and liquor stores."

Still, Bascom wasn't ready to give up. Their next mission was to scout the university and two local hospitals. It was on that next excursion when they had lost the first scout.

One of the hospitals had burned to the ground, nothing but a hollowed-out shell of scorched limestone remaining. The other was full of decaying corpses and broken glass, and they had been completely vandalized. "Hundreds and hundreds of people had lined up outside the ER entrance," the scout had reported. "The line wound around the building and down the block. I guess some of those people got desperate for medical attention and decided they were going inside, one way or another."

It was at the University of Texas that the scout was killed. Bascom and his people would never know what happened for sure. Most blamed the Horns.

His name was Thomas, a former infantryman in the Army who had joined the Austin Police Department just a few months prior to the eruption. He was young, strong, fast, and had more combat experience than all the other scouts combined. Captain Bascom had often wondered if his courage hadn't been the young man's undoing.

When Thomas hadn't returned from his assigned area, two more scouts were assigned to look for him. There was speculation that his motorcycle might have broken down, or that the rider had experienced an accident and needed a rescue.

Following his tracks around campus, they discovered his bullet-ridden body beside a fountain at the foot of the school's administration building. His weapon was missing, as was the victim's pack, gear, and motorcycle. There *were* survivors after all, and they weren't friendly.

As the rescue party loaded the dead scout onto a sled, a volley of gunfire had erupted, several masked men appearing out of nowhere. Bascom's people had fought back but were clearly outnumbered and outgunned. They barely managed to escape, their dead comrade in tow.

Since that first skirmish, there had been four other attempts to contact the Horns. Those diplomatic missions had resulted in two more scouts being killed. From that point on, Bascom had declared that the north side was forbidden.

Arriving at the main terminal level, Alex continued his trek, his goal a small storage room that now housed his office. There, on the wall, was a large map of the Austin metropolitan area salvaged from a rental car counter on the ground floor.

Taking a handful pushpins from a cup on his desk, the captain inserted four colorful markers into the chart, outlining the area where T.J. had explored.

The scouts had now ventured into all of the state capital's downtown area, as well as most of the east side. Hannah was exploring the far west, no doubt roaming country roads and small towns, looking for a warehouse or any other storage facility housing a significant amount of food.

"If anybody is going to bail us out of this mess, it's Hannah," the captain whispered. "Be safe, young lady. Come back to us with good news."

Jack remained vigilant as Camaro gathered his gear. After learning how the breathing apparatus functioned, the commander said, "We had similar equipment on our submarines for firefighting. I think it will work for us today."

"I'm ready," the older man stated, his expression reflecting hope.

Turning to the mine boss, Jack said, "One way or the other, food or no food, I will turn you loose and be on my way. Don't try to follow me. Don't even think about being heroic. As long as you don't try anything clever, you'll be fine."

Jack sent Cam outside the mobile office first, the commander watching for any sign of an attempted rescue from the mine. It would be daylight in a few minutes, but there was no sign of any activity from the entrance. "They followed my orders," the mine boss announced.

Once outside, Jack scouted the area carefully before pointing with his rifle barrel. "Secure your pack on the bicycle's rack. You're going to push the bike while I stay back here. Head west," Jack instructed.

Over the next hour, the two men trudged through the ash, following a county road through the hills and valleys of Central Texas. Cam pushed the bike, Jack staying a few untrusting steps behind.

Camaro's stride was slow, his steps uneven and unsure. It reminded Jack of a sailor who had consumed too much rum while on liberty and was now trying to make his way back to base without being stopped by the Shore Patrol.

Twice the older man had been forced to stop and rest, his malnourished body suffering from the exertion required to walk. "He's not used to it," the commander whispered, adding, "and the ash isn't making it any easier."

"This is ridiculous. Where are you taking me?" the mine boss eventually complained. "If you're going to shoot me, why don't you just get it over with?"

"I'm not going to kill you, Mr. Butler. I'm going to try to save you and your people," Jack reassured, amazed at how quickly the mine boss had lost his ray of hope.

Finally reaching the outskirts of Clover Springs, Jack pointed to his bicycle tracks that were still visible in the street. "I came through here before," he stated. "We're close now."

"My men searched this town. They said it had been picked clean," Cam offered.

"They were right about that," Jack grinned. "There's probably not a crumb to be found in this entire village. That was what struck me as odd and caused me to poke around a little more. No offense, but your guys didn't dig deep enough… no pun intended."

The commander was sincerely worried about his hostage by the time they reached the high school. Again, with Camaro leaning against a signpost, the duo paused for a rest. "The last few people inside that building committed suicide via some sort of poison gas. They were dying in droves from the glass in the air, and I'm hopeful that there might still be a significant supply of food inside."

"Why didn't you take it yourself?" Camaro asked.

"I was getting light headed by the time I figured out that the air might be poison in there. With just a cloth mask, I didn't want to chance it. Your breathing apparatus, however, should protect us… at least that's what I'm counting on."

Nodding, Camaro reached into his pack and produced two of the masks. "These will do the job," he declared. "Let's get this over with."

It required several minutes of adjustment before Jack was staring through the thick glass lenses of the mining mask, each breath sounding like a distant waterfall in his ears. He detected a faint taste of plastic while his chest worked just a little harder to fill with air. It felt odd to be outside without some sort of towel or cloth around his face.

Jack's second entrance into the high school was a lot more relaxed. Again, seeing only his tracks in the ash confirmed that no one had visited the facility since he was last there.

"I think we should check the loading dock back by the cafeteria," the commander suggested, pointing the way with his carbine's muzzle.

"You're the boss, Commander," Camaro shrugged.

Passing the gym and several classrooms, Jack gave a running narrative of the facility, his voice full of respect for what the people of Clover Springs had tried to accomplish. "I've walked through two dozen towns since leaving San Diego," the commander stated. "Every single one of those communities had been absolute chaos after the eruption. These people, on the other hand, had their shit in one neat, well-packed bag. Were it not for the invisible killer glass in the air, they probably would still be doing well."

"We were lucky," Camaro admitted. "The right place at the right time with the right gear made the difference."

The mention of equipment reminded Jack to take a deep breath as a test before they ventured further into the bowels of the school. He was reassured by the lack of chemical odor or taste.

The two men approached the cafeteria, Jack pointing toward the canisters and makeshift still that the last occupants had erected to end their lives. "I'm pretty sure that's the source of the poison gas."

Camaro bent to check the labels and apparatus. "Chlorine is very toxic when mixed like this," the miner stated. "I doubt the concentration, at deadly levels, would have lasted more than a few days in here. Regardless, if they had tried to seal the doors or vents, it might have been longer. I'm not a chemist... and there's no way to be sure."

"I think I'll keep this mask on a little longer," Jack said.

"Me, too," Butler agreed. "No need in taking any unnecessary risks."

Working their way past the food preparation area, they approached a heavy metal door with a placard showing they were about to enter the dock.

Jack let Camaro go first despite the only one being armed. They were in an empty, dead place, neither man worried about running into human trouble.

Entering a large area full of metal shelves, Jack's flashlight illuminated several boxes. In a rush of excitement, Camaro bolted toward the first container, his miner's lamp making a wide pool of light.

Ripping open the box, the mine boss reached inside and pulled out a can. Holding it up like a world championship trophy, he shouted, "Pork and Beans! I can't believe it!"

With adrenaline-fueled movements, Camaro went to a second container, this time producing canned corn. "Oh my God!" he exclaimed through the filtered mask. "They're all full of food!"

As his hostage explored the treasure trove of groceries, Jack's attention turned to the dark, open storage area of a semi-trailer at the loading dock. It was at least a quarter full of similar crates and boxes.

"According to the log book I found," the commander began, "the deputies were diverting trucks from the interstate to this school during the last few hours before the ash began to fall. There are several more trailers outside. Hell, they all might be full of food."

Camaro, for his part, was nothing short of giddy as he tore open more cases of grub. Every few seconds, Jack heard the excited miner declaring the contents with glee. "I've got bags of pasta here!" followed soon after by, "There's powdered milk... a lot of it!"

It took nearly twenty minutes before the mining honcho began to slow down. Finally bleeding off all his adrenaline, Cam's pallor indicated he was about to be overwhelmed by the flurry of activity. "Let's eat," Jack suggested. "You're going to need to renew your strength to make it back. Let's prepare a feast to celebrate."

"Now that's one hell of an idea," Camaro agreed, reaching for the nearest carton. "What would you like?"

Pointing at a pot resting on a nearby shelf, Jack replied, "You pick, Mr. Butler. I'll get started on the fire."

An hour later, both men were stuffed. It was the first time in weeks Jack had felt so satiated.

"I can feel the energy surging through my bones," Camaro commented, leaning back, and patting his midsection. "I thought I'd never experience a stuffed gut like this again."

"We need to get moving soon," Jack replied with a nod. "It will be nightfall before long, and even though I haven't seen any other people around, traveling after sunset isn't a good idea these days."

"Agreed," Camaro said. "Where are you heading now, Commander?"

"I'm going into Austin," Jack lied, still not trusting the man beside him. "I'm going to see if anyone has any information about where my family might have gone."

"Be careful going into the city. We've lost some people there," Cam warned.

"Really? How long ago?" Cisco asked.

"We lost two teams of three men each. They just simply vanished. I stopped sending more men in that direction. Some of my crew believe Austin is full of roving bands of zombies."

The commander had to laugh at the superstition, but inside, he was concerned. Camaro was the second person to warn him about traveling through Austin.

Rising and stretching, Jack quickly configured a hobo bundle and began filling that temporary pack with as much food as he could carry. Trying to select the highest weight to calorie ratio possible, he concentrated on peanut butter, beans, and bags of high-carb noodles.

After watching the commander, Camaro began doing the same. "I'll bring this sample back so that all of the guys can put on the feedbag," he stated. "We'll build some sort of wagon or sled to take all of these goodies back to the mine. There should be enough here to last us for a while, maybe more if we're careful."

"Good luck," Jack smiled, extending his hand. "I hope this buys you enough time to find a long-term source of nourishment. Maybe Sheng will be a little more willing to barter now."

"And good luck to you as well, Commander," Camaro replied, accepting Jack's handshake with vigor. "If you're ever in this area again, you're always welcome at the mine."

Leaving his former hostage to his packing, Jack headed for the main lobby. Once outside, he judged that he had just enough daylight left to make it back to Sheng's dugout if he hurried. Happy to be reunited with his bicycle, the commander attached his grocery sack to the rack and began pedaling. Tomorrow, he would take Hannah up on her offer and return with the beautiful woman to the airport.

As he began riding, Jack's mind digested the miner's accusations regarding Sheng and his attempt to poison them. "There are always two sides to every coin," he mumbled through the mask. "Maybe the old Chinaman did, and maybe he didn't. It will be interesting to hear his side of the story."

Periodically checking that his valuable hobo bundle was secure, the commander decided that he would turn down any offer of a meal from the old man. "Better safe than sorry," Jack grinned. "Besides, Hannah should be eager to get back to her people. She'll be chomping at the bit to get on the road."

Chapter 44

Jack arrived back at Sheng's just as the sun hung low in the west. Careful to avoid the old man's traps, the commander carefully worked his way through the junkyard, each step placed with as much caution as possible.

Finally reaching the cave-like opening, he yelled a greeting. "Hello! It's Jack Cisco! Don't shoot! I'm coming in!"

After waiting several seconds without a response, Jack repeated the warning.

Worry began to fill the commander's head has he cautiously peered into the manmade cavern that was Sheng's front door. Had the miners he'd left behind decided to get revenge? Had Sheng and Hannah been killed?

Continuing into the zigzagging tunnel, Jack gently pushed open the wooden door. The dugout was completely dark inside, the commander's senses informing him that the place was abandoned. "What the hell?"

With his flashlight, Jack began searching the interior, half expecting to find Hannah and Sheng lying dead on the floor. Instead, he found the place unoccupied, either by the living or the dead. Several bundles of the Asian's tubers were missing, as was all of Hannah's gear. Only the commander's remaining kit, alongside the miner's confiscated weapons, were left behind.

Pivoting quickly, Jack headed to check the barn. Hannah had parked her motorcycle there.

He found several sets of footprints, the signs indicating that someone had been busy inside the crumbling structure. Jack spied the same type of weird track left behind by Hannah's sleigh.

"They bugged out," Jack finally admitted. "They must have thought I was dead."

Sighing in disappointment, Jack trudged back to the dugout and stepped inside. After securing the door, the commander checked the woodburning stove and found it cold. "They left several hours ago," he reasoned.

Starting a new fire, Jack struggled to overcome his disappointment. He had been looking forward to seeing Hannah again, had been eager to experience the community she had described.

It then dawned on the commander that his new friend had taken Sheng back to Austin. "She doesn't know that old bastard may have tried to poison the miners! What if he does the same thing to the people at the airport?"

Glancing down at the gauges between the handlebars, Hannah frowned with concern. Sheng, his arms wrapped around her waist, seemed to sense her worry.

"What is wrong with your machine?" he asked.

"Your weight and all the stuff on the sled are draining my battery like crazy," she replied. "I'm worried that we don't have enough juice to make it back to the airport."

"You wanted me to come. You asked me to bring samples of all my tubers and roots. You shouldn't have asked if there wasn't enough power to make the trip," the old man quipped.

"I didn't realize how much your belongings weighed," Hannah defended.

"Why do you drive so far south?" Sheng asked. "I know the airport is east, not south. We have no time to tour the countryside. It will be dark soon!"

"We can't ride through Austin; it's too dangerous. There is an area called the Forbidden Zone where violent people attack any traveler. We must come in from the south to avoid most of the city. It's safer that way."

The electric bike's passenger didn't appreciate her excuse. "I thought you said I would be safer here than in my home! Did you lie to me, young woman? I feel so exposed out here. There are no walls or dirt to protect us."

"We'll be fine. Don't worry. Even if my motorcycle runs out of juice, it will get us close enough that it will be a short hike. I can drag your sled the rest of the way if necessary," the rider explained.

"Then why do you get so tense every time you look down at that instrument?" Sheng countered.

"Because I don't want to walk if I don't have to," she answered with a shrug. "And, like you said, it's getting dark."

The road they were following entered a valley, the ash becoming deeper as the electric bike plowed into several wind-blown drifts. At the next bend, Sheng heard a crashing noise behind them.

"Shit!" Hannah barked, her eyes locked onto the rearview mirror mounted to the handlebars. A few moments later and they had come to a complete stop.

Dismounting, Sheng turned and looked back at the sled they were towing. A high drift of pumice had flipped the makeshift device, the contents now a scattered field of debris alongside the road. "My tubers and roots!" the old man snapped. "What have you done?"

Both driver and passenger rushed back, Hannah righting the sled while Sheng bent and carefully began gathering his possessions, all of which were strewn along the side the road for several yards.

Sighing as she began helping clear the debris field, Hannah looked up to see a sign next to the pavement, "Littering. Five hundred dollar fine," she read. She couldn't help but chuckle.

"What are you laughing about?" Sheng asked, still hustling to salvage his belongings.

Hannah, not wanting to insult her guest by explaining that their precious cargo might be considered by some as litter, told a white lie. "I'm sorry," Hannah began, "but this motorcycle isn't designed

143

for two riders and a heavy, unbalanced sled. It makes me quite clumsy."

"Well, I don't think anything was damaged," Sheng admitted, his arms loaded with a bundle of wild onions and other herbs. "Still, we will have to wash everything carefully before we can eat."

As she pitched in to help her frustrated passenger, Hannah said, "This time we'll make sure to tie our cargo more securely. I think it would also help if we could balance the load a little more to the rear of the sled."

It was almost thirty minutes later before they were ready to ride again, the delay causing Hannah to check not only her battery indicator but the sun's position as well. "We're not going to make it before dark," she announced with a frown.

"Are you sure?" Sheng responded, his own face now wrinkled with concern.

"The extra weight, my battery charge, and now dusk are all fighting against us. We should look for someplace to set up a camp," Hannah declared.

"I don't like that idea," Sheng replied, his eyes now studying the suburban landscape with suspicion. "I wasn't prepared for a camping trip. Isn't there a shortcut?"

"That's a bad idea," Hannah replied as she threw her leg over the bike's seat. "Like I said, there are certain areas of the city that we don't travel through. Some sections are still very dangerous," she said, trying to downplay the threat.

"You never mentioned that before we left my home," Sheng growled. "You promised that we would go to this airport building you're so proud of... you said that we would be safe there."

Shaking her head, Hannah tried to soothe her jittery friend. "You will be far safer at the airport than you were before. We'll be fine holing up here for the night. I've done it dozens of times."

Crossing his arms in defiance, Sheng spat, "I have no desire to spend the night out among all these buildings. They could be hiding any number of hideous individuals. Take me home."

"What?" Hannah said. "What are you talking about? We're almost there."

"I didn't agree to this…. This isn't what you promised me. I refuse to spend the night in some abandoned building, unable to sleep and jumping at every little noise. Take me home. I demand that you do so."

With the panic of failure now building, Hannah tried to reason with her paranoid guest. She had worked so hard to convince the stubborn old man to leave his shack, she couldn't fail now. Hundreds of hungry souls were depending on her. "We can't make it back to your place before nightfall, Sheng. One way or the other, we're going to be spending the night alone in the darkness. At least here, we can have walls and a roof for protection. Neither of us wants to be caught out in the open if one of those storms comes rolling in. Hang in there… trust me."

"I do not like this place, or these structures, or being hemmed in," Sheng pushed back. "I would prefer to sleep under the trees and among the rocks than in this eerie, haunted place. It smells of bad spirits here. I want to go home."

With the airport's best hope of salvation quickly fading away, Hannah looked to the east and said, "I suppose we could take a direct route through Austin. We could easily make the airport before nightfall if we went that way."

"But you said it isn't safe," Sheng countered.

"Safe is a relative term, my friend. When we first started venturing away from the airport, we tried to avoid other people at all costs. If a scout saw footprints, or any sign of human activity, we declared the area unsafe. That was months ago. Those people could have been just passing through or are dead by now. And even if there were survivors in the area, the chances of us running into them are probably very slim."

It was Sheng's turn to be conflicted. "I want to go with you. I want to help your people if I can. But… I am an old man and can't

145

fight or run as I used to. I survive by listening to my instincts and trusting my karma. If we can make it safely to your airport before dark, then I will go. Otherwise, take me home."

For a moment, Hannah considered her options. She knew Sheng well enough to know that if she refused to take him back to the dugout, he would simply start walking back. He was that pigheaded. She could try to force him, perhaps even at gunpoint, but that would be the end of his cooperation.

Her mind then returned to Captain Bascom and the issues faced by her community. Sheng, and the specialized knowledge he possessed would help solve a critical problem that was growing worse every day. Again, glancing to the east, she weighed the possibilities.

Her decision came quickly. "Get on," she smiled, patting the motorcycle's seat. "We'll take the shortcut. We can be at the airport in just over an hour."

Nodding his acceptance, Sheng climbed aboard.

Hannah engaged the throttle, and soon enough, Sheng was warily scanning the city's outskirts as they rolled deeper into the heart of Austin.

Years had passed since Sheng had ventured this far from his home. Even before Yellowstone's explosion, it had been a rare event to visit civilization.

Once a year, he would drive into Clover Springs and pay his property taxes. When his sculpture had been presented at the Austin Museum of Fine Art, he had been chauffeured into the city by one of the curators. Then there was the trip to the Department of Motor Vehicles every four years to renew his license. Being a recluse was one thing, being stranded another.

Mrs. Ross, a kind woman who lived down by Pearl Creek, filled out his taxes every year. Sheng would take a shoebox full of receipts and notes to the retired accountant in February and return to scrawl his signature in April. She always made oatmeal cookies and hot tea. He hated the sugary snack and found her herbal brew barely consumable. Still, the lonely widow charged very little to prepare the necessary annual documents, and most importantly, she was close by.

Visiting the Social Security complex in San Antonio had been another of his grand adventures, that trip a result of a conversation Sheng had when removing an antiquated tractor from a retired fellow's barnyard. "Heard we're going to get a raise in our monthly checks," the old-timey rancher had announced as Sheng winched the rusting machine onto his trailer.

"What checks?" Sheng had asked, the answer leading the naturalized citizen to the big city and the free money offered by the US government.

Now and then, Sheng had driven his beat-up pickup through the rural Hill Country, looking for an inspirational piece of machinery or hoping to catch a glimpse of an animal new to his eyes. Most of his collection, however, came from local ranchers who visited his property. Many offered to deliver their discarded equipment just to be rid of an eyesore.

The Texas Hill Country hadn't been an accidental destination for Sheng, the topography reminding the newly arrived immigrant of his native Yunnan Province back home.

Born into a large family of peasant farmers, he had toiled in the sculpted hillsides since the age of three. It was the same work his father had performed, and his father before that. Only Sheng's great-great-great grandfather… his namesake… had escaped their tiny village and labor-intensive lifestyle.

The elder Sheng's story was the stuff that fueled larger than life legends throughout the rural community.

Word of the California Gold Rush in the late 1840s had finally reached rural Yunnan over two decades later. Like his descendent four generations later, the original Sheng had been a dreamer and malcontent. According to family lore, he had packed his bags and made off for Hong Kong and a ship to America, promising to return a wealthy man.

The rest of the elder Sheng's legend was pure speculation and most likely exaggeration. A few letters had arrived over the years, penned by a man who claimed that the United States was a "Golden Mountain" and extolling the virtues of the distant land. Each message home concluded with the promise of a triumphant return bringing many riches.

Yet, Sheng had never returned, and after only three letters, the correspondence stopped. Generations passed, each likely embellishing the local hero's story.

In the early 1930s, Japan invaded China, more than ten years before the Asian powerhouse would attack Pearl Harbor and bring the USA into an already-vicious global conflict.

China became an ally of the United States during World War II, desperately trying to defend her country against the Japanese Imperial Army. After the war, immigration to the United States was again in vogue.

A more critical influence on the younger Sheng was that China emerged from the war as a communist nation. Decades before the Cultural Revolution was official, local politicians and leaders made it clear that Chairman Mao didn't appreciate artists, professors, scholars, and revisionists. There was no room in a Marxist–Leninist society for those who believed creating music that could speak to your soul, or sculpture so moving that it lifted your spirits, or masterful paintings that spoke to your heart were just as important as growing rice or producing steel.

Sheng, like his ancestor, had always been different. As a small child in the paddies, he was constantly being scolded for making tiny statues and figurines out of mud and sticks rather than doing his share of the work.

As a teen, he would often sneak away and carve on a piece of wood instead of harvesting the crops. Many of the neighboring villagers complained, Sheng's mother forced to apologize for her son's nonconformist behavior.

It was a warning from one of the regional communist officials that finally sent Sheng packing. At eighteen years of age, the youth's mother had received a public dressing-down over her wayward son's lack of production. In the middle of the night, with only a small bundle of clothes and money borrowed from sympathetic family members, the teenager had slipped away and made the difficult overland journey to Hong Kong.

After a harrowing adventure that eventually landed him in San Francisco, Sheng was stunned to discover that Chinese people weren't welcome in the new world. Laws were still on the books that forbade him from marrying Caucasian women. There were special taxes in place meant to keep Asian immigrants corralled in slum-like "Chinatowns." His race wasn't allowed to own property.

Still, no one in authority tried to stop the young transplant from doing what he loved the most – creating works of art. Soon, Sheng's talent caught the eye of a local businessman. He was given a job creating ornate carvings on furniture. Two years later, he had saved enough money to get out of California and escape its heavy bias against the Chinese.

At that time, rumors ran rampant throughout Chinatown about a place called Texas. There were cowboys there, men, who according to the movies, respected freedom for all races. The economy was reportedly booming in the Lone Star State. It was reputed to be a place where people of all colors... whether they be white, brown, or yellow... could thrive.

Sheng bought a train ticket, packed his bags, and boarded a coach for Austin.

His original intent had been to arrive in Houston, a larger, more robust city. The rolling terrain of the Hill Country, passing by his coach's window, changed the young sculptor's mind. This place reminded him of his home in China. This was a land where he could create great art while at one with the land.

He found work in a small Austin shop that manufactured boots and tack. Within a few weeks, Sheng's masterpieces had gained an outstanding reputation. He was paid more money that he had ever thought existed in the world as he tooled rawhide and buckskin into works of art.

After five years, he had stashed away a significant amount of savings. A co-worker had suggested that the budding artist invest in land. He had purchased thirty-two acres the following summer.

Now, riding behind Hannah, he wondered if leaving his homestead had been a mistake. The terrain had flattened out, the number of homes and businesses increasing with each passing mile. He didn't like the city, didn't trust people. He had seen more than his fair share of discrimination, had plenty of experience with the darker attributes of mankind. "What are you getting yourself into?" he whispered in a voice that his driver couldn't hear.

Straighten up and be a man, he thought. He'd been brave enough to travel halfway across China without permission, as a youth. He'd managed passage on a ship bound for the Golden Mountain. He'd survived and even thrived in the New World. *You can do this*, he assured himself. *You've overcome far greater obstacles.*

It didn't take five minutes before Hannah was regretting her decision. The population density, along with its accompanying stores, businesses, intersections, and gas stations, was increasing with each passing block. Not since before the apocalypse had she navigated through such cluttered streets.

More and more relic vehicles clogged the pavement, blocking her view and limiting her avenues of escape. There had been a terrible accident at the last intersection, two cars and a pickup colliding at high speeds and leaving crumpled sheet metal and a debris field of plastic body parts and broken glass. She saw a skeleton behind the wheel of a sedan.

A minute later, Hannah squeezed the brake, a fallen utility pole completely blocking the street. A semi had clipped the aluminum base.

Turning onto a narrower side road, Hannah had to slow their pace ever further due to a gauntlet of ash-covered cars and trucks scattered over the pavement. "I feel like I'm being herded into a trap," she whispered.

At the next cross-street, Hannah saw the nooses. There were three ropes, all hanging from the stout metal arms of street lights. Two were anchored by human remains, enough flesh still clinging to the corpses to catch the slight breeze, the deceased swaying a lonely dance in the wind. Squeezing the bike's brake, she came to a stop in the middle of the avenue, her eyes unable to look away.

She'd seen plenty of decaying bodies since the collapse. Blackened, rotting flesh was nothing new to her eyes and nose. What focused Hannah's gaze with laser intensity was the empty hangman's noose.

The dark rope looked like someone had used a marker to draw the grizzly black symbol against the grey canvas of the sky. It was a stark illustration, a metaphor that predicted the future without any distortion or pretense. The empty loop seemed to call her, a siren song of death. "Your neck is going to end up in such a place," she whispered, physically shuddering as a cold chill flooded her core. "It's a sign… a premonition."

"Stop being such a spooked, little girl," she swore quietly. "Hanging around Sheng is making you extra jumpy. Pull it together!"

Shaking off the vision while continuing to curse her out of control imagination, Hannah applied a gentle turn of the motorcycle's throttle. She forced herself to keep her eyes on the pavement ahead as they passed under the gallows.

Less than a block later, they approached the warnings.

Using sheets of plywood and ample spray paint, someone had placed three large, unavoidable signs in the middle of the street. "Stay out or die!" the first read.

The next bulletin board had been tagged with skull and crossbones, the universal icon of death.

"Trespassers will be burned alive!" read the third. "Do not pass!"

"Are you sure this is a safe route?" Sheng asked, his skepticism at an all-time high.

"I told you it was dangerous taking the short cut. Still, those notices were probably erected shortly after the volcano blew. There was bedlam and anarchy for a few weeks before everybody started succumbing to the ash and starvation. The people who painted those warnings are probably long dead and gone."

Sheng didn't seem convinced. "If that is true, why did you say that you avoid some places?"

"We know there are survivors in Austin. They are very hostile. We have skirmished with them a few times. They occupy the north side of the city. We've never encountered them this far south."

"If you say so," Sheng grunted from behind. "I am at your mercy back here. Helpless as a child and not enjoying the scenery."

Hannah continued past the warning signs, her eyes alert and scanning both sides of the road. The motorcycle was her secret weapon, its speed giving her confidence. If hostiles came out looking for a fight, she could accelerate to safety. Even with Sheng's added weight and the pull of the sled, her electric machine was far, far faster than even the most gifted sprinter. Moving targets were difficult to shoot.

Her tactic soon came into question, however. The streets here were lined with cars and trucks on both sides. A hefty pile of partially burned tires, blown debris from a burned-out structure, and a host of objects littered the pavement.

Barely able to weave between some of the abandoned wrecks, Hannah's eyes continued to search the surrounding buildings. "This is an excellent place for an ambush," she hissed, her heart now pounding in her chest.

Again, she had to hit the brakes and slow their pace.

The end of the street was completely blocked, the barricade composed of a perfectly-placed pickup, a stack of old furniture, and a mound of shopping carts and firewood. "Somebody tried to build a fortress," she whispered, coming to a complete stop forty yards from the roadblock while clutching her rifle.

Yet, nothing moved, shot, or made a sound. Was the barricade a relic? A place forgotten after the battle had moved on?

With her eyes darting left and right, Hannah smiled when she realized that the roadblock had been designed to keep four-wheeled vehicles from passing. There was a home on the left, its front yard clear of any debris. There was more than enough room for her bike to pass.

"Hang on," she warned Sheng. "We're going around."

Twisting the throttle, Hannah pointed the bike toward the narrow opening.

The motorcycle bounced hard as it went up the curb and across the sidewalk, Hannah taking it slow so as not to upset the sled again. She was halfway across the ash-covered yard when the ground disappeared under her front wheel.

Before she could shout a warning, the bike dove into a pit and hit bottom, the bone-jarring impact and downward angle sending both driver and passenger flying over the handlebars.

Landing hard, Hannah's helmet hit first, her body doing a summersault before coming to rest. Sheng, flying over her head, slammed into the structure with a whoosh and thump. The old man ended up half in, half out of the pit.

Disoriented and dazed, it took Hannah a few seconds to regroup. Lying in the bottom of a casket-sized hole, it dawned on her that someone had purposely left the yard open to lure any passerby into the pit. What if they were on their way right now to finish off the prey?

As she tried to move, a sharp pain shot through Hannah's arm. Looking down at the burning limb, she saw the bloody tip of a spike that had sliced open her flesh. After a quick scan of her surroundings, Hannah realized that she had just missed being impaled on a dozen of the wicked barbs, most of the pit's floor being covered with sharp, protruding spearheads.

Only the motorcycle's speed had saved them. The pit had been designed to snare a pedestrian. Hannah had been going fast enough that she and her passenger had been thrown over the spikes… but just barely.

Gently checking each limb for injury, she carefully stood and did a quick scan of her surroundings. The area was still void of human life as far as she could see, but there was no telling how long that would last.

Sheng was her next priority.

She found the old man on the edge of the pit, laying half in and half out of the trap. He was trying to rise up and perch on one elbow. "Are you okay?" she whispered with an urgent tone.

"I think so. My ankle and arm hurt, but I don't think they're broken," he gasped.

"Can you stand?" she asked, moving to his side for support.

"Maybe," he said while gingerly testing his leg.

After a careful transfer of weight, Sheng nodded his head to indicate that he could stand. "Walking is going to be difficult," the elderly passenger added.

Hannah's next move was to check her motorcycle. She found the front wheel bent, the associated tire flat. One of the spikes had performed well, piercing the rubber. "Shit!" she barked.

Stepping carefully around the spearheads, Hannah tried to lift the motorcycle out of the pit. A minute later, the wounded machine was back in the yard, but clearly not in riding condition. Even if she had a spare tire or patch kit, the aluminum wheel was badly out of round and wouldn't hold air.

Again, she scanned their surroundings. Some instinct told her that being caught out in the open like this would be the end. Her body was beginning to feel the trauma of impacting the ground as the adrenaline burned away. Her arm was still bleeding.

"We have to find shelter," she explained, scouting the nearby structures for a potential hide. "I have a bad feeling that somebody is going to be checking this punji pit before long. We don't want to be caught here."

Sheng joined her, his eyes darting up and down the street. "I can't go far. I am in a lot of pain."

"I understand," Hannah replied, her gaze now focused on a steeple visible in the distance. "Let's head toward that church I can see down the street. I'm betting it is well constructed… might make a good Alamo."

Leaving the motorcycle and sled behind, Hannah offered Sheng a shoulder as they begin the three-block journey. Each punishing step reminded the two of them that they had just survived a motorcycle accident.

After a grueling trek, the duo arrived at St. Mary's Episcopal Church, a modest house of worship constructed of red brick and sporting stained glass windows.

Hannah handed Sheng her pistol and pointed at a nearby doorway. "Stay here. Cover my back. I'm going to check that church to make sure it isn't occupied."

The old man's only reply was a nod, his lack of a comeback causing Hannah even more concern. It was the first time since he had met him that she could ever remember Sheng not getting in the last word.

With her AR15 up and ready, Hannah crossed the street and climbed up the three steps leading to the double-wide front door. While there were no footprints in the ash, she was sure there was at least one other entrance. The building was unlocked. Cautiously, she stepped inside the small foyer and listened.

One of the most valuable lessons learned, since becoming a scout, was to use her ears and nose just as much as her eyes. People didn't bathe nearly as much since Yellowstone blew its top. Humans made noise.

For over a minute, Hannah did nothing but control her own breathing while listening for even the smallest hint that someone was inside St. Mary's. "Not a creature is stirring, not even a church mouse," she whispered, raising her weapon as she entered the sanctuary.

As expected, Hannah noticed rows of pews separated by the main aisle. At the far end of the building stood the pulpit and lectern. A choir box rounded out the primary features of the room.

Again, she checked the thick carpeting near the entrance, looking for any sign that someone had tracked the grey ash inside. She saw no footprints. In fact, St. Mary's was one of the cleanest buildings she had visited since the eruption.

Cutting left, Hannah headed up one of the outside aisles, her instincts craving the comfort of a wall for cover… just in case someone popped up and started blasting away.

She reached the pulpit and spotted a doorway leading off each side.

For five minutes, Hannah searched St. Mary's facilities. There was a basement full of classrooms and storage. She checked the church's offices, small kitchen, and restrooms carefully. The entire building was completely empty of any life forms.

Returning to the front, Hannah whistled for Sheng to join her. "It's clear," she reported, meeting him in the middle of the street. "It's not the Ritz Carlton, but for now, it's the best we can do."

Pain seemed to temper the old man's reply. Again, a curt nod was his only response.

Once her passenger was inside the sanctuary, Hannah returned to the spike pit, disconnected the sled, and began pulling their supplies toward the sanctuary. Sheng seemed happy to see his collection of roots, tubers, and other possessions, managing to mumble a soft, "Thank you."

Again, Hannah left the church and returned to the punji trap.

Pushing her wounded motorcycle, even along the street's smooth pavement, was back-breaking work. With the front rim severely bent and the tire flat, she was exhausted by the time she arrived at the church's front steps. She was accessing her body's reserves by the time she managed to stash the bike inside the front doors.

Still, there was work to do. After a two-minute breather and wrapping her arm in a makeshift bandage, she hefted her weapon and went back outside.

Scanning the surrounding neighborhood, Hannah spied a row of dead bushes separating two nearby bungalows. Hustling to take advantage of the fading light, she pulled her knife and quickly cut away a bundle of lifeless twigs and branches.

Returning to the pit, she began sweeping the ash with the makeshift broom. There wasn't time to backtrack very far, but at least she could slow down anyone following their trail.

Working quickly, she then began erasing their path to the church.

By the time Hannah had swept three more false trails, darkness had fallen. With a shrug, she mumbled, "That's the best I can do," and returned to the sanctuary.

She found Sheng in the church's basement kitchen, the savvy old Asian having built a small cooking fire in the stainless-steel sink. The smoke was already beginning to form a hazy layer against the ceiling.

"Should we let in some fresh air?" she questioned.

"People might smell the smoke… if there's anyone around," Sheng responded.

Stifling a cough, Hannah moved to a small window. "I've not seen any sign of survivors out there. I think it's worth the risk."

"Suit yourself," Sheng shrugged. "These tubers have to be cooked before they're safe to eat. Besides, I need a hot meal."

"Are you okay?" she asked again. "You're not acting normal."

"I am bruised and battered," he replied, his eyes never leaving the small frying pan of sizzling food. "These old bones aren't meant to take a beating like that."

"I'm sorry," she said. "I didn't see the pit. It was well disguised."

Turning to face her, Sheng's eyes flashed with unbridled anger. "I knew this was a bad idea. I should have listened to my instincts and stayed at home. Tomorrow, I am going to start walking back there... to a place where I know I can be safe."

Shaking her head, Hannah countered, "The miners will overwhelm you within an hour. You don't have enough ammunition or guns to keep them at bay."

"At least I will die defending my home," he snapped. "That sounds like a far better end to my time on this earth than being hunted down like a wild animal in some strange place that holds no meaning to my life."

"We can walk to the airport in the morning," she offered, trying to minimize the frustration in her voice. "I think it will take us about two hours to reach safety. That's a lot less than what it would take you to hike back home."

Sheng's eyes drifted to the open window and the dark landscape beyond. "If we're still alive in the morning, I'll make my decision then. In the meantime, we should enjoy our last meal."

Choosing to ignore the ill-tempered old fart, Hannah went about properly dressing her wound. She had read that during the Vietnam war, the Viet Cong had dipped their punji sticks in human feces so those who bumbled into the trap would have to fight deadly infections. "Let's hope my Austin neighbors weren't as diligent," she whispered, forcing away the urge to shudder.

Still, it was a nasty cut. "I pray the doc still has some antibiotics," she worried. "If we make it back...."

Chapter 45

Jack was up before dawn, eager to begin the day's ride. Glancing out from Sheng's front door tunnel, he scanned the junkyard, waiting for enough light to travel. "The sky looks like a well-used ashtray," he grumbled, turning back to the dugout with a frown.

One of his tires was low again, the discovery causing the commander to grimace. The front rubber had been giving him trouble since entering Texas and was yet another reminder of how precarious his situation had become. He'd struggled through applying a patch in New Mexico and didn't want to expend the time or energy required by the arduous task. About the only thing worse would be his chain suffering a broken link.

Pulling the small pump from the bike's rear pannier, Jack screwed on the nozzle and began the process of refilling the tortured tube with air. After several cycles, he checked the gauge and was relieved to see that the tire was holding pressure. "How many more miles of life do you have left?" he questioned the well-worn tread.

The sun, disguised as a slightly-lighter patch of grey in the overcast sky, was well above the horizon by the time Jack finished packing his two-wheel steed. After pushing his companion through Sheng's matrix of traps, the commander swung a leg over the seat and tested the bike's balance.

"Here we go again," he groaned as he put weight down on the pedal. "Over the hills and through the woods."

The map showed Austin International Airport was just under forty miles to the east. That measurement was as the crow flies, or via a direct route.

Hannah, however, had warned of traveling directly through urban Austin. "We always approach from the south," she had stated. "It's a few extra miles, but the population density is lighter

159

on that side of the city. Fewer people translates into a lower chance of a bad encounter."

That tactic, trading miles for safety, made sense to Jack. After all, he had significantly increased his frequent flyer mileage by avoiding even the smallest of villages on the way east. It only made sense according to his thinking. "What's an extra day of pedaling?" he grunted, rolling down Sheng's lane.

Arriving at the country road bordering the old man's property, Jack turned to the south. Hannah's tracks were still visible in the ash, and for a moment, Jack wondered how long he would be able to follow the motorcycle's trail. "At least you won't get lost," he smirked.

With the extra weight of his scavenged canned goods filling every nook and cranny of his pack and saddlebags, Jack soon found the hills were nothing short of torture. Working the gears on his bike, the commander repeatedly complained about the strain on his legs.

"If I never ride a bicycle again, it will be too soon," he bitched as he struggled up one especially steep grade.

Sheng's hand shook Hannah's shoulder with urgency. "Woman! Wake up," the old man hissed.

Blinking away the sleep from her eyes, Hannah half rose after a deep breath. "What's wrong?"

"There are men outside. I saw them through the window. They have guns," the frightened, old man responded.

With a surge of energy now racing through her veins, Hannah managed to stand and reach for her rifle in the same motion. "Where?"

Waving for her to follow, Sheng stepped to the nearest window and pointed with a shaking hand. "Back by the spike pit. They are looking around."

Sure enough, Hannah could see at least three men through the dirty glass. One of the shadowy figures was pointing at the snare, two others listening intently. A moment later, a fourth appeared from behind the house.

"Shit," Hannah barked. "Our secret is out. Damn it!"

Her mind began creating a variety of escape plans and evaluating each in turn. Sheng didn't move so quickly and would definitely slow down any retreat. Without her motorcycle, they would be easy to catch.

The next possibility was to stay inside the church and hide, hoping that the men outside weren't very skilled at tracking. Even as that plan was passing through her mind, Hannah saw one of the dark figures point along the ground, his gloved figure finally indicating the church. "So much for my attempt to brush away our prints," she grumbled.

She was down to two magazines for the AR15 and only one spare magazine for her pistol. Scouts didn't fight, according to Captain Bascom. They were only to carry enough ammo to break contact and escape. "Speed is life. No one can keep up with your electric rides," he former fighter-jock had preached.

Now, that logic seemed a bit short-sighted given her bike was inoperable. Why hadn't she thought about that possibility before?

Shaking her head to clear what was essentially a worthless use of brainpower, Hannah went back to the immediate problem – how to survive the next fifteen to twenty minutes.

"Maybe they're not hostile," Sheng offered, the shorter Asian trying to peer over her shoulder. "Maybe they're just curious."

Hannah doubted that was the case. "Perhaps. They sure are carrying a lot of firepower and ammo for peaceful explorers," she noted, nodding toward the military-looking load vests bristling with magazines.

On cue, the leader made a circular motion with his hand and then gestured toward the church. The other men were quick to form a skirmish line and then as a unit, they began moving toward the sanctuary.

161

Their spacing showed experience, Hannah observed. Each of the approaching strangers stayed at least twenty feet from his nearest comrade. Their weapons were high and sweeping. Every bit of cover was utilized as they drew closer.

"Damn. These guys are pros," Hannah hissed, her mind desperately trying to figure a way out.

It dawned on the scout that Sheng was the prize. The knowledge inside of the old man's head was the most important thing in her world right now. He was also an anchor around her neck. Alone, she might have a chance to outdistance and avoid the heavily-armed men.

"Sheng, I want you to go to the basement and hide. Those guys out there have no way of knowing how many of us are inside this church. That's why they are being extra cautious. I want you to get down there and find the best hiding place you can, and then wait. Take some water. Take my pistol," she instructed in a rush.

"Where are you going?" the puzzled, old man asked.

"I'm going to try and draw them away from the church. I can move quicker without you. Now, if I am not back by dusk, then wait here until the morning and start walking toward the airport. Here's my map," she replied, handing over the folded chart.

"But... but...." he started to protest.

Hannah didn't let him form the words, "We don't have time for a debate. I'm going to make them chase me. Hopefully, they'll give up after a while, and I can circle back around and pick you up. You'll be safe as long as you stay hidden. Understood?"

Clearly, Sheng didn't like her plan, but couldn't produce a better option. Nodding his agreement, he then turned and headed for the basement door, mumbling, "I knew I should have stayed at home. I just knew it!"

With her gaze returning to the window, Hannah estimated she had another two minutes before the hunting party reached the church's door. They were moving very carefully, a sign of command, control, and experience. "This is very disturbing," she whispered as she began gathering her gear.

After hastily pocketing everything she could, the scout moved to the front entrance and took a deep breath while mentally rehearsing the next few steps.

Pulling open the heavy, wooden door, she burst outside and darted for the church's sign near the sidewalk. She prayed that its heavy concrete base was thick enough to stop bullets.

The first shout of warning came as she bounded down the front steps. Other voices soon followed as she dove for the ground and then brought her weapon up from behind the sign's foundation.

"What do you want?" she shouted at the approaching party.

"A woman?" one of the hunters asked from a relic car just half a block away.

"Who are you? What are you doing in our territory?" shouted a male voice.

"I'm just passing through," Hannah replied, her barrel tracking the voice's position.

"Put down your weapon and let's talk," the same male replied.

Hannah managed a chuckle at the suggestion. "No chance of that happening. This isn't my first rodeo," she yelled back. "Leave me alone, and I will be out of your territory in less than an hour."

"We don't cotton to scavengers or looters," sounded a heavy southern accent. "Put down your rifle, and we'll escort you out."

"Sorry, but I'm not in the mood to play the defenseless female role today, fellas. Back off, and I'll be out of your hair before you know it. If you come any closer, somebody's going to get hurt, and to be blunt, I'm not worth it," Hannah replied.

Instead of a vocal response, Hannah spied one of the strangers stand and move for a closer position. That was a bad sign. They were going to try and flank her.

She also noticed that the rifleman was wearing one of the full masks she had heard about from one of the other scouts. That observation sent a cold bolt of fear down her spine. The only people that wore such equipment were the Horns – from the Forbidden Zone.

Shaking off the cold chill of terror, Hannah realized she had to move, and she had to do so at once. They were jockeying to cut her off. She had to run.

Rising from behind the sign, she bolted with all the strength her legs could muster, running hard for a corner convenience store at the next intersection. Ash-covered cars were parked along both sides of the street, and Hannah intended on keeping their bulk between her and the men behind her.

Weaving quickly between a small sedan and a delivery van, Hannah winced as the car's mirror exploded from a bullet's impact, that first shot followed by a series of rounds chasing her to the ground by the front bumper. "So much for a peaceful conversation," she mumbled as she tried to draw air into her pounding chest.

Rising to the fender, Hannah loosed two random shots back at her attackers. She knew it was unlikely that the bullets would find flesh or bone; she was sending a message. "I will fight," she whispered. "Don't follow too closely."

Hugging the delivery van's side, she made another mad dash away from the followers. More rounds hissed through the air, zipping past like angry insects looking for flesh to bite and sting.

She cut hard in front of the van, and then, without hesitation, continued running along the sidewalk toward an older SUV that was next in line.

The bold move worked, for about two seconds, as a string of high-velocity lead began to whack and thump into the ash at her feet. She felt a tug on her pant leg, one of the lead missiles slicing through the thick material but missing flesh.

She dove for the SUV's hood, landing so hard she felt the sheet metal bend and pop with her weight. Momentum pushed her over the hood ornament, the cheap metal snapping off as it gouged into her hip.

Rolling off the vehicle, Hannah landed badly on the street by the front bumper. Her legs were burning with exertion, the pain in her arm and hip screaming for relief.

After another breath, she scurried across the street toward the cover of the now-defunct convenience food store.

More lead messages sizzled past Hannah's head, their song making it clear that the men behind her weren't in the mood for hide and seek.

She reached the corner of the building just as three rounds slammed into the concrete block exterior.

Hannah's instinct was to continue running while she had the building between her and the attackers. A quick glance to identify her next cover, showed a thick oak three halfway up the block. *Those guys are right on my heels,* she swore under her breath. *Guess this is where I make my stand.*

Turning back, she poked the AR15's barrel around the building's edge and scanned for a target.

She spotted two human shapes rushing along the opposite side the street in pursuit. They were bent at the waist and running hard. Her finger tightened on the trigger, her mind screaming for her to squeeze.

A small puff of red flash, followed by a gentle nudge against her shoulder, signaled that Hannah was returning fire. The lead target pulled up short, dropped his rifle, and then crumpled in a heap to the ground.

With no time for celebration, she moved her front post to the second runner. Seeing his buddy go down in a heap, he was diving for the ground. Hannah waited until he'd landed and then snap-fired three shots at the prone figure.

She didn't wait to see the results, some instinct telling her to scoot. Pivoting smartly, she was off and running toward the oak. "They won't follow so closely now," she grunted as her footfalls didn't draw any more bullets.

Captain Bascom's words came back into her head as Hannah approached the oak, "Speed is life. Distance is life."

When a quick glance over her shoulder didn't reveal any pursuing hunters, she bypassed the oak and continued running.

At the next intersection, she cut right. Halfway up the block, she made a hard-left turn between two bungalow style homes. Pausing only to open a wooden gate leading to the backyard, Hannah continued to zig and zag away from the men chasing her. "How far will you go to catch me?" she mouthed after looking over her shoulder. "How much am I worth to you?"

She knew that there were a half-dozen reasons why she would be considered a valuable prize. First and foremost was the fact that she was a woman. Despite starvation, desperation, and a lack of hope, the male sex drive seemed to be alive and well in post-apocalyptic Texas. Stories of gang rapes, using females for currency while bartering, and other horrific practices had been repeated to the scouts. While Hannah thought a lot of it was mostly exaggeration and rumor, she had little doubt that some parts of the tall tales were rooted in the truth.

Secondly, she had a weapon and ammunition. More than once, she had met stragglers and desperados who wanted her AR15 more than her body, nourishment, or anything else.

Then there was what the hunting party's leader had stated so clearly back at the church. Every breathing soul on earth knew that food, ammunition, medical supplies, and other necessities of life were now limited. Between the ash and the lack of sunshine, nothing was being grown or manufactured. There was a fixed supply, and that made every other human on the planet a competitor. Scavengers and looters depleted finite resources. It was every man for himself. I might eat tomorrow what you would eat today. If I'm able, I should just take it.

Competition bred tribal behavior. Territory had taken on a whole new level of significance in day-to-day existence. Sheng was one example, the miners another. Many of the survivors Hannah had encountered had become like wild animals protecting their turfs.

In the end, it didn't matter whether the men chasing Hannah considered her a threat or a prize. So much had changed since the eruption. There was no longer a risk of punishment for bad deeds. Survival was everyone's top priority. Anyone not part of the clan was the enemy.

Struggling to climb a privacy fence, Hannah finally dropped over the wooden barrier and into another yard. Reaching the next street, she cut away from her pursuers, hoping to draw them even further from the church and Sheng's hiding place.

Just as she was beginning to believe she had out-distanced the Horns, she heard a male voice issuing orders a short distance away. "You're not going to give up, are you?" she mumbled.

Increasing her pace, Hannah hurried away from the sound. Cutting right and left at every opportunity, she crossed through yards, hustled up alleys, and dashed across intersections.

Stopping beside a Spanish-style stucco home, she leaned heavily against the wall to catch her breath. "I have to be at least twelve blocks away from the church by now," she considered in a hushed tone. "How long are you going to chase the rabbit?" she queried, glancing in the direction of her pursuers.

A few moments later, Hannah again heard the same male throat shouting commands. He sounded close.

"What is it going to take to shake you people?" Hannah hissed as she forced her exhausted legs to move. "I'm not worth it... really, I'm not."

Jogging with her rifle cradled in her arms, she darted directly away from the position of the hunter's voice. After two blocks of low-rise apartment buildings, she approached a freeway.

Cursing the open terrain, Hannah paused and scanned her surroundings. "They have been herding me," she realized. "There is no place to hide... no place to run without being seen. They will pick me off if I try to cross that much open space. It would be an easy shot."

She heard more voices behind her. "Is the entire city of Austin chasing me?" she quipped, again looking for an opportunity to cross the open lanes of pavement and reach the wooded area beyond.

Less than a football field away, Hannah spotted salvation. There was a huge culvert, a steel drainage tunnel that appeared to run under all four lanes of the freeway. While the thought of running through the dark, dingy, metal cave was frightening, that fear paled in comparison to what she knew would happen if the Horns captured their prey.

She made a mad dash, racing for the only possible escape route. Down the incline she sprinted, the ash thick and slippery under her feet.

At the bottom, she assessed the drain, taking a cautious peek at the dark, circular opening. She could see the light on the other side. "At least it's not blocked by debris," she whispered, moving for the mouth.

The bottom of the cave-like drain was covered in several inches of wet mud and spongy, saturated pumice. With careful footfalls, Hannah ducked low and entered the culvert. "There are no snakes left alive," she tried to reassure herself. "No critters in here to bite you. Now… run for your life!"

Each step produced a dull, metallic echo, Hannah sure the noise would attract the men trying to kill her. "What if they start shooting down this tunnel?" she questioned at the halfway point. "This was stupid."

There was, however, no turning back, the thought of hot lead ricocheting off the steel walls and ripping through her body motivating Hannah to increase her pace.

Claustrophobia began to squeeze her head as the circle of light to her front grew larger. Hannah was having trouble drawing enough breath, the narrow passage feeling like a band of steel tightening around her chest.

The last twenty yards were passing quickly now, the light streaming in from the far side allowing her to increase her stride without stumbling. "You're going to make it!" she proclaimed.

Bursting out of the far opening and into the light, Hannah stopped running and stood upright, desperately filling her lungs with air. She was just exhaling that first chest-full of relief when something large and heavy struck across her shoulder blades.

Knocked the ground, Hannah was stunned and bewildered. She sensed more than saw a man on top of her. A second later, strong hands had pinned her to the ground while another heavy body sat on her legs.

Fighting a hopeless battle to free her limbs, Hannah finally stopped struggling long enough to focus on the face hovering over her own. Instead of a human shape, she saw an insect-like image, huge, flat eyes that reflected light, a circular wire grid where the nose should be, a tiny slit for a mouth. It was robotic… alien in appearance, a cross between a praying mantis on steroids and one of Satan's astronauts. She had never seen anything like it before, and it sent another flash of revulsion through her body.

Motivated by fear, she began fighting with all her remaining strength.

Cocking his arm while making a huge, gloved fist, the insect-face barked, "Stop it, bitch, or I'll knock out every one of your teeth!"

Realizing it was hopeless, Hannah ceased her struggle.

After being frisked and groped, she was hauled roughly to her feet. Someone produced a set of shiny steel handcuffs as the sound of several pairs of boots caught up with her captors. "I knew she'd go for the drainage ditch!"

With her hands securely bound behind her back, Hannah looked up to see a huge man examining her. He didn't look happy.

"You killed one of my team," he growled. "Give me one good reason why I shouldn't put a pistol to your head and end this right now?"

With her heart beating like a jackhammer and a stomach curdling from fear, Hannah couldn't form any words. Her lack of response didn't seem to surprise him.

"Who are you?" the evil astronaut snapped, stepping close to her face to intimidate her.

"My name is Hannah," she managed through a parched throat.

"Where are you from, Hannah?"

She hesitated before responding, that slight pause angering the interrogator. As she started to say, "I was just passing through," a gloved hand slapped her hard enough that she tumbled to the ash.

"Don't bullshit me, lady!" the oversized bug roared, hovering over her like a beast about to devour its prey. "I don't have time for lies! Where are you from?"

"Central Texas," she managed through the blood in her mouth.

Her response drew a kick, the heavy boot slamming into her shoulder, landing with enough force to send Hannah rolling across the ground. "You are lying, bitch!" the questioner screamed. "You're from the airport, you piece of shit! We found that fucking electric motorcycle you all ride. You're the only ones that have those machines."

Cascading waves of pain crashed through Hannah's body, fighting with her terror for control of her thoughts. Still, despite the intense emotions and physical agony surging through her, her mind returned to Sheng. If they had found the bike inside the church, had they found the old man?

"Yes, I'm from the airport," Hannah gasped, trying to catch her wind.

"And what were you doing on our turf? Haven't we made it absolutely clear that we don't allow trespassers?"

"My battery was too low," she nodded. "I thought I could take a shortcut to get home, but the road was blocked, and I didn't have any choice but to come this way. When I hit the booby-trap, I was hurt and stuck."

Extraterrestrial-face paused, his mind seemingly contemplating Hannah's response. Finally, he continued, "We found a sled full of roots in the church. Where did you find them?"

"Out in the countryside. I dug them up," she lied, happy that Sheng had indeed managed to avoid capture.

"And how do you know where to dig for these roots? Are they edible?"

A small ray of hope came to Hannah, a glimmer of potential salvation if she played her cards just right. She had been willing to do practically anything to get Sheng safely to the airport so that his skills and knowledge could save the community there. Would the men standing over her have the same mindset? Where they as desperate? Would they let her live if they believed she could feed them? "Yes, they are edible. I was taking them back to help feed my people," Hannah said.

A snarl of frustration sounded from beneath the man's mask, his hands clenching into massive fists in preparation to strike. "How do you know where to dig?" he bellowed. "Answer my damn questions!"

Nodding, Hannah told another lie, "My grandmother taught me how to find herbs, roots, and tubers when I was a little girl. I still remember what a few of them look like. I was taking them back for my friends."

For several, long seconds, the behemoth in front of Hannah digested her words. He then pivoted to face the band of men surrounding the prisoner and said, "Take her back to the station. The chief will want to question her."

Pulled to her feet, Hannah was shoved back toward the freeway. "Walk. Now!" her captor instructed.

Relief flooded her mind as Hannah plodded along. She had expected to be killed immediately, perhaps after being gang-raped by the Horns. Now, with her quickly invented ruse, she had bought herself some time. The end might be near, but she had managed to delay her demise for some period. Who knew what might happen in the minutes and hours that followed?

Her thoughts then returned to the words of her interrogator as she dissected their meaning. The chief? The station? What did those terms mean?

No one had lived to relay information about the men who controlled the Forbidden Zone. There had been speculation that the north side of Austin was controlled by rogue policemen, other theories offering that National Guard units had banded together and created their own community. Hannah had even heard one version that had a group of fraternities had formed a government there.

Whoever was running the show was obviously well organized, ruthless, and not afraid to unleash violence. Any time a scout had crossed certain boundaries, a vicious attack had quickly followed. Numerous booby-traps, roadblocks, and barriers had been erected, most of them well after Yellowstone's impact had annihilated the general population.

Now, for the first time since the scouts had ventured forth from the airport, Hannah had hard intel. The giant Horn had used the words chief and station. The men had produced handcuffs to secure her wrists. They had hunted her down using advanced tactics. They had to be units of the Austin Police Department that had somehow managed to survive the ash and had formed a community.

Perhaps it was her desperate situation or the fact that she had avoided certain death that gave Hannah a small sliver of optimism. If they were police officers, there should be some level of morality… some need to bring justice remaining within their ranks. *Better to deal with the cops than some random assortment of ruffians who suddenly found themselves in charge*, she decided.

Chapter 46

Over an hour had passed since he'd heard the men in the church, and his legs were beginning to protest their cramped position. Still, Sheng hesitated to leave his hiding spot.

Finally, believing that the church was clear of her visitors, he resolved to leave the cupboard's safety. Grimacing from his complaining joints, he gently pushed open the door and peered out from under the church's kitchen cabinet. The building seemed quiet.

He held his position for a few minutes longer, his ears straining to detect the slightest squeaking on the stairs. Satisfied that he was, indeed alone, he gradually and cautiously uncoiled his body from its awkward position, freeing himself from his hide. He maintained absolute stealth, quite aware of the consequences of divulging his location. Eventually, able to unfold his limbs and stand, he remained ready to duck back inside given the slightest rustle, whisper, or peep.

When nothing but silence met his appearance, he began moving with small steps toward the staircase that led to the main sanctuary above. All the while his ears were on high alert, trying to reach out and detect any threat.

He had heard several voices and the creaking of floorboards as the armed party had searched the building. He thought his heart was going to come bounding out of his chest when two of the ruffians had ventured down to the basement and began opening doors in the kitchen. He couldn't remember ever being so relieved as when he heard their heavy boots climbing back to the main floor.

With Hannah's pistol clutched tightly in his hand, Sheng entered the main sanctuary. Scanning the evenly spaced rows of pews, the old man then stepped to the closest window and peered outside.

He exhaled with relief when he observed nothing but footprints through the glass. The men had left the area, or at least as much of it as he could see.

Moving to another vantage point, Sheng carefully scanned up and down the nearby streets. He studied every window and doorway. He detected nothing but an abandoned neighborhood.

Returning to the interior, Sheng noted that Hannah's motorcycle had been taken, as well as his sled full of tubers. All the girl's equipment, with the exception of her motorcycle helmet, was missing as well. "Raiders," he hissed. "No better than those miners. They'll steal anything that isn't nailed down."

His thoughts then turned to Hannah. *Had she escaped? Would she be returning to the church soon? Or had she been killed?* He wished he could recall what had she told him to do as she darted out the door. His heart had been pounding inside his ears at the time, and much of what she had said was a blur. He was supposed to wait for her for a while, but he couldn't remember how long. However, he was certain that she had wanted him to continue to the airport if she didn't return.

For over an hour, Sheng patiently sat and stared out the window, waiting for the high-spirited woman to return. "How far away can she be?" he wondered. "A person can walk a great distance in an hour."

It then occurred to the old man that it would be getting dark soon. He had no food or water and didn't like being in the city. There were too many buildings blocking his sight, too much concrete and glass for him to breathe freely. This was a haunted place. He didn't want to be here at night, alone, without nourishment or liquids.

Quickly making his decision, Sheng picked up the motorcycle helmet and tucked it under his arm. The woman from the airport would want it, he supposed. She would know where to find him.

He exited the church slowly, exposing only his head as he peered up and down the abandoned street. Making sure his cloth mask was tight against his nose and mouth, he took a deep breath and began walking back toward his home. "I've had enough of strange places and abandoned buildings," he mumbled. "I didn't want to leave my property, and now I'm going to go back. Hannah knows where to find her pistol and helmet, and if I hurry, I can be back before the sun rises in the morning."

Jack broke for lunch earlier than normal, offsetting his misery with the promise of a heartier than usual meal. "I'll make a feast," he mumbled. "You've earned a few hundred extra calories today," he whispered as he gathered wood for a fire.

As he prepared his lunch, Jack fought the urge to rush. "Why are you so eager to get on the road?" he wondered. "Take your time… there's no hurry."

That first fork of food reminded him of the miner's tale, his entire body tensing as Camaro Butler's words replayed in his mind. *Hannah is taking Sheng back to Austin with her*, he thought. *What if Cam was telling the truth? What if the old man is a mass murderer on the sly? What if he tries to kill everybody at the airport?*

Shaking his head to clear the conjured images, Jack mumbled, "I just can't fathom that old pain in the ass being a homicidal maniac. Still, I need to warn Hannah about the miners' claims. She needs to know."

Finishing his meal, Jack quickly cleaned his utensils and extinguished the fire. He still had several hours of usable daylight left. The hills and ravines had, unfortunately, slowed his pace significantly. Even if he could make Austin International before nightfall, he knew that a stranger approaching an armed camp at dusk would be risking his life.

"Sheng's not going to poison them all in less than a day," he said, staring to the east. "I'll be there in plenty of time to thwart any homicidal rampage."

175

Given its position of prominence, the empty pickle jar looked completely out of place.

Centered at the front edge of the chief's desk, the common, clear-glass container was an oddity when compared to the many plaques, awards, and framed photographs adorning the office walls. There were images of the Texas governor, past presidents, and other important politicians, all of them standing next to the same uniformed man, smiling, shaking hands, or with their arm draped over the fireman's shoulder.

Chief Paxton Woods was obviously a very important individual who had achieved success at the highest levels of his profession.

A custom shelf behind the desk housed a detailed, handcrafted model of the Austin Fire Department's first official mobile unit, a horse-drawn wagon with rain barrels for tanks and a handpump for pressure. The emergency signal was a brass bell. The hose was less than an inch in diameter and could project a small stream of water that reached almost thirty feet. High technology for the period.

Although the department had been officially formed in 1841, the date painted on the toy-sized wagon was 1858. Things had evidently progressed slowly in Austin before the civil war, at least as far as firefighting was concerned.

An elaborate trophy case sat next to the rustic, wooden model, its glass shelves packed with plaques, awards, and other memorabilia that served to highlight the department's image and prestige.

The ornate mahogany placard next to the pickle jar read, "Battalion Commander Paxton S. Woods, Austin Fire Department." Pax's long-time superior, Chief Morton, had been killed during the riots at city hall. The mayor had issued a field promotion during those final hours before the city government had completely collapsed.

Most of the rare visitors to this inner-sanctum ignored the pickle jar's quirky existence, wrongfully assuming that the chief had just enjoyed the last of his gherkins and had forgotten to toss the container in the trash.

Others couldn't help themselves and asked about the jar's presence.

"That jar of pickle juice was the last thing we had left in the refrigerator," Paxton would explain. "I remember drinking half of the brine and handing the rest over to my wife. It was all that remained in the house. We were starving… ravenous… weak and losing hope. For our previous meal, we had spread hotdog relish on stale tortilla chips. Nothing will change a man like a deep, gnawing, hollow hunger. I keep that reminder sitting right there so I'll never, ever forget that… especially in times like these."

As Hannah was forcefully shoved into the chief's office, she had more important things on her mind than the jar.

"Well now, what do we have here," Chief Woods questioned in an even tone. While it was rare that his men would bring a captive into his enclave, this wasn't the first time.

"We caught this one in the southwest district. She's one of the airport's motorcycle riders. We have her bike downstairs, as well as her weapons and supplies."

Ignoring the prisoner, the chief addressed his subordinate, "How did you catch her?"

"She fell into an old booby-trap and damaged the bike. She led us on a merry foot chase after that. Hopkins was killed, a bullet from her rifle," the captor reported.

Anger flashed behind the chief's eyes, but it passed quickly, and his gaze returned to neutral. All business, he asked, "And why is she here instead of lying dead out in the ash?"

A second subordinate stepped forward, a small batch of tubers and roots in his hand. "She was pulling a sled behind her bike. It was full of these. She claims to know which plants are edible and where they can be found."

177

Still handcuffed and forced to her knees by the Horns who had seized her, Hannah fought the urge to flinch as the chief's eyes bored into her soul. "Is this true?" he asked.

"Yes. My grandmother was an outdoor type. She taught me a lot when I was younger," Hannah lied, pleased that her voice had remained steady.

Rising from behind his desk, Woods approached the man holding Sheng's tubers. "What is this root?" the chief asked, pointing to a specific example.

"Greenbriar," Hannah replied, hoping the wee bit of knowledge she had learned from her Asian friend would be enough to save her life.

"And it is edible?"

"Yes," the captive nodded. "You have to roast or boil it for a while to remove the bitterness, but it is very similar to a potato after that."

"How common is this root?" Woods inquired, his voice still skeptical.

"It is probably one of the most common plants around. It has unique qualities which makes it identifiable, even when there are no leaves. The Native Americans harvested it to make flour in the winter," Hannah replied, repeating Sheng's words as best she could remember.

Handing the bundle of tubers back to his man, Woods then turned to another fellow and said, "Take one of the students to the library. See if there are any books available on local edibles. If we can verify what this young lady is telling us, perhaps we can open the door to a new food source."

Nodding briskly, the subordinate rushed out to execute the chief's orders. After he had left, Paxton returned to his desk chair, his eyes now studying Hannah.

"You have three death sentences hanging over your head. Count number one is the fact that you're from the airport. Number two is your trespass, and the third is that you killed one of my men. I would normally execute you immediately and bring this matter to a close. However, your knowledge about these roots and tubers might be valuable, so I'm going to wait and pass judgment after we have gathered additional information," Woods declared.

"Why do you fight us? Why do you shoot at our scouts every time we try to make contact? We have no quarrel with you. We want to work *with* other survivors, not against," Hannah countered.

For a moment, she thought Chief Woods was going to ignore her questions. After a long pause, his brows knotted as he growled, "Because you people killed my wife and the families of a lot of other men in this building."

"We didn't kill anybody's wife or family," Hannah pushed back. "What are you talking about? We're not murderers!"

With a grunt, Woods stood and squared his shoulders. A blistering rage flashed in the fireman's eyes, and for a second, Hannah braced for what she thought would be a horrible beating. The man standing before her was that angry.

Instead of pummeling the captive, Woods strolled past, heading to the window and peering outside. "What did you do before the apocalypse?" he asked calmly.

"I was a TSA agent at the airport," she replied honestly.

"A public servant, just like me," he mumbled. "Then, perhaps you are capable of understanding."

Without waiting for a reply, Woods stepped to the front of his desk and perched on the corner. "The day Yellowstone blew, I was the shift commander for the 2nd Battalion and on duty here at the station. We weren't overly concerned about the news. It was a disaster that was over a thousand miles away. But by lunch, that changed. Our call volume began to rise. The newscasts were painting an ugly picture, and anxiety grew by the minute across our fair city. In my business, that translated into

179

gridlock and a substantial increase in automobile accidents, mostly due to road rage and impatient drivers."

Nodding Hannah replied, "I remember that day well. We experienced a similar reaction amongst the trapped passengers. There for a while, we thought things were going to get out of hand."

Ignoring her comments, Woods continued, his empty stare now indicative of a man who was mentally traveling back in time. "Chaos ruled the day. By five o'clock, we were responding to a police request at a local grocery store. The cops needed one of our engines there to use a high-pressure hose on rioters. We answered over 500 calls from dispatch in the next few hours, most of the fires, accidents, and injuries due to the fear that was taking over the streets."

The chief slowly shook his head from side to side, his expression betraying the misery of his resurfacing memories. "My battalion worked for forty-eight hours straight during those first two days. We were exhausted, unable to answer any but the most desperate of dispatches. My men were worried about their own families. The police were feeling the stress as well, their commanders calling in reserves as they tried to quell the panic evident in the streets."

"When the first flakes of ash started falling, absolute bedlam erupted. I had entire shifts of firemen who didn't report for duty, either unable or unwilling to make it to their station. The motors in our pumpers and engines were failing, clogged by the grit. The governor called out the National Guard, but I heard that only about forty percent of their ranks reported for duty. When their vehicles started rolling into Austin, we still had hope that we could turn the tide of anarchy."

Hannah was listening intently now, her mind having joined Paxton's timeline, her thoughts correlating his experience with those she endured at the airport.

"I went on a call with a rescue truck… a horrible, multi-car accident less than a mile from the station. According to the 9-1-1 dispatcher, there were children trapped inside one of the vehicles," Woods continued. "The streets were in pandemonium; it was every man for himself. The college student population was trying to get home, some of them walking while dragging their suitcases along. Other folks were out shopping, trying to stock up on supplies. You could see a dozen columns of smoke on the horizon, fires that we couldn't even think about responding to. Still, we rolled when we could, in an effort to save as many lives as possible, praying that the mayor and the National Guard would regain control of the population soon."

"When we arrived, we found a multiple vehicle accident... and a pretty bad one at that. With the ash falling like a winter snowstorm, my men had already been briefed to wear their rebreathers at all times while outside. It's a small miracle we had just been issued the new, high-tech air scrubbers. We wouldn't have survived with the old compressed air SCBU units."

"SCBU units?" Hannah asked.

"Self-Contained Breathing Units," Woods explained, his tone suddenly absent of malice toward Hannah. He was now a teacher, a leader of men, and seemed to welcome the distraction from reliving those painful days of the past. "We had used them for years. They held about half an hour of clean air before having to be refilled. These new units, however, are based off the air-scrubbing technology like what is used on the space station. They make oxygen out of water using electrolysis and can last for days without having to be recharged. Those devices saved us and have kept us alive ever since."

Remembering the strange mask she'd seen on one of the men who captured her, Hannah now understood. Captain Bascom's efforts had been to seal the airport to keep out the deadly ash. The firemen had used their new space-age equipment to protect their ranks.

"Normally, we would wait for the police to arrive at any accident before taking action. What we found that day was a father and two children trapped in an SUV that had been t-boned. Gasoline was leaking from the tank, and it was only a matter of time before it caught fire. We couldn't wait. There was just no telling how long it would have taken to get a squad car to respond. The police officers were in worse shape than we were. So, I ordered my guys to use a hydraulic tool to free the victims."

Anger replaced the sadness on Paxton Woods's face, his eyes becoming slits of despair as he continued his story. "We pulled the two children out and then the father. Less than a half a minute later, the pooling gasoline met hot metal and ignited, and the entire SUV was engulfed in a blink of the eye. We had gotten them all out just in the nick of time. But you know what happened next? That man… the guy who had just watched us rescue his little kids… let our paramedic check them out and then pulled a gun on us. We were stunned."

"A gun? Pointed at your men? Why?" Hannah asked, now completely immersed in the chief's tale.

"He demanded that my lieutenant hand over his mask and tank. He started screaming at us to take off our breathing equipment and give all of it to him. He was sweeping us with that pistol, obviously on the edge of insanity. I'll never forget the crazed look in his eyes. Firemen regularly encounter violent PCP users, out of control opioid addicts, and a host of individuals who are transformed into chemically enhanced demons with superhuman strength and aggression. Still, I'd never seen any other human being that irrational. It wasn't a man or father threatening us, he was a wild animal… a vicious beast."

"What happened?" Hannah whispered, already suspecting where her captor's story was headed.

"My lieutenant began taking off his equipment. As he reached to unbuckle the harness, the gunman must have thought he was going for a weapon and fired. Lieutenant James had three kids, about the same age as the two children he'd just rescued. He was hit in the chest with three rounds and was dead before he hit the pavement."

Hannah shook her head in disgust. "I'm sorry, Chief. There were a lot of terrible acts during those horrible days. It's amazing how brutal people can become when stressed."

Nodding his agreement, Woods continued with his story. "I watched that murderer scoop up James's rebreather, grab his children, and rush off into the crowd that had gathered. No one did a damn thing to stop him, everybody just looking at us as if thinking, 'What in the hell did you expect?' It then dawned on me that there might be other armed animals in the mob who might get the same idea. As I ordered my men back to our truck, we found four guys trying to siphon the fuel out of our engine's tank. The entire episode was repulsive, grotesque, and infuriating. I wanted to puke, but I was too furious to vomit. Here we were, doing our best to serve the public, and those we were trying to protect were gunning us down in the street. That moment changed me… all of us. It altered every fireman's perspective from that point forward. As I drove back to the station, I decided right then and there that we weren't going to answer any more dispatches until the National Guard got things back under control."

As Hannah digested the chief's words, Paxton continued. "In fact, we parked the fire truck, and I had a quick meeting with the guys. We had been working over fifty hours straight by that time and were about worthless, so I told them to go home and take care of their families. I did the same, locking the door behind me before walking home. I found my terrified my wife huddling in the closet, clutching an old revolver we kept in the nightstand. Gangs of youth had been roaming the streets, knocking on doors and throwing rocks at windows. She had seen them break into a neighbor's house, pull the housewife into the front yard, and brutally rape the woman. My wife was scared to death."

183

"My better half hadn't been able to make it to the grocery store," Woods sighed. "She worked full time at city hall, and with just to the two of us living in the house, we didn't keep a lot of groceries in the pantry or fridge. We thought it was the high life to be able to eat out whenever we wanted. The electricity went out later that afternoon, and it never came back on."

Paxton Woods's recalling of those days made Hannah realize just how lucky she had been. Captain Bascom had taken over at the airport, his style of command, rugged features, and pilot's uniform combined to reinforce him a figure of leadership, a man of authority. Were it not for his foresight, management skills, creative problem-solving, and rock-solid personality….

"We rationed what little food we had," Woods stated. "We ate cold soup after the gas stove stopped working. We licked the mayonnaise jar clean and divided a few slices of bread. Man, I can remember thinking about all the things I would have traded for a toaster that worked! All the while, we kept waiting for the National Guard, or Mother Green, or somebody to take control of the city."

Hannah nodded, "We kept believing authority would be reestablished as well. The police officers at the airport were listening to their radios, our control tower in contact with other FAA sites. Those were dark days. No one knew what was happening, and the ash kept falling. I thought it would never quit."

Pointing toward the empty pickle jar, Paxton continued, "About an hour after I shared our last little bit of nourishment with my wife, one of my firemen walked up to our front door. After several nights of hearing random gunfire and blood-curdling screams… and seeing roving gangs walking the streets, I was a little jumpy. I almost shot my own man. Anyway, he told us that he had talked to another member of our department, a firefighter stationed at your airport. He said that the people at Austin International were organizing… that there was food and the rule of law, along with a plan to filter the air. He claimed that he and a bunch of the other guys from our station were sending their families there."

With the chief's mention of the airport, Hannah piqued. She knew about the firemen who manned the substation next to the runways. Was that what was Woods talking about?

"My wife's Suburban hadn't been driven since the ash began falling. From what I had heard, the engine should last long enough to get her there. We loaded up our clothes, and I told her I would meet her at Terminal A. I wanted to go by the firehouse... I wanted to tell any men who might be staying there to join us at the airport."

Confused, Hannah shook her head. "We didn't have any new people from the Austin Fire Department arrive at the airport after the ash began falling. I would have known about that. What happened?"

With a sudden outburst, Chief Woods slammed both of his fists on the desk, the pickle jar and Hannah both jumping in surprise. "You fucking killed her! You gunned her down in cold blood!"

"We did nothing of the sort," Hannah retorted after she had regrouped. "Yes, we stopped gate crashers, and a lot of them, but we didn't kill anyone in cold blood."

Now an evil grin spread across Paxton's face, his smirk cold and dark. "I was there, young lady. I found her shot-up SUV. I touched her dead, cold body, still sitting behind the wheel, less than a block from the airport's main entrance. There were lots of other dead bodies alongside her, all of them gunned down trying to do nothing more than save their own lives. I saw people with little children, an elderly couple, and even a car full of Austin cops, all lying in their own blood by the barricade your people had erected to keep them out. Don't lie to me. I witnessed all of this with my own eyes."

Hannah became defensive, "Yes, we had people trying to force their way in, and yes, we had to stop them with gunfire. But... we didn't kill in cold blood. We warned them, tried to wave them off and even fired warning shots to keep them away. For a while, we

185

were even using a water cannon to discourage gate crashing. Still, they kept coming, trying to shoot, or sneak, or force their way in. They tried to ram our people, run them over, or blast their way into the facility. What choice did we have?"

"Who elected you God?" Woods shouted back, the spittle of rage flying from his mouth. "Who was it that decided to close the airport? To make it an exclusive club? Who gave any of you the right to do that?"

Pausing, in the hope that the Paxton would regain his composure, Hannah chose her next words carefully. In truth, she had asked herself those very same questions a dozen times since the collapse and felt at peace with the answer. Finally, when Woods's breathing had settled, she said, "The passengers stranded at the airport had zero options, Chief. They had no home in Austin, no place to go. Most were thousands of miles away from their loved ones and their regular lives. The airlines, as well as the people who worked there, were responsible for those desperate, helpless souls. What were we supposed to do? Open the gates and let anyone come in? We had limited food, limited water, and no place to sleep, bathe, or care for those travelers. You, your wife, and all those who tried to crash our gates had a choice. You all had homes, or apartments, or family to turn to. Our guests had none of that, and we made the decision to protect them."

For a nanosecond, Woods seemed taken aback by the captive woman's spirited defense of her community's crimes. Then, with a stern tone, he said, "I'm not going to waste my time debating you. If your explanation of those roots and herbs is accurate, I will give you a choice. You can teach us what you know, and I will execute you painlessly and quickly. If you decide not to share your knowledge, or you're lying to us, then your death will be slow and agonizing.

Before Hannah could form a response, Woods nodded toward one of the men standing behind her. Roughly hauled to her feet, she was manhandled toward the door, her interview obviously over. "It doesn't have to be this way, Chief," she pleaded over her shoulder. "We can help each other. We can make everyone's lives better through cooperation. We can stop all of this fighting and killing."

"We don't need help from people like you," Woods spat. "We only need for all of you to stop using the limited resources around here and die."

After Hannah had been removed from the room, the chief looked at the remaining subordinate and said, "You know the airport people will be coming to look for her. They'll send several of their men to track her down."

"We'll be ready. I'm already forming our best shooters, and we'll be waiting for them."

"Good," Woods nodded. "Perhaps this will be an opportunity to eliminate a pestilence sooner rather than later. Make sure nothing happens to the woman. She may become even more valuable as time goes on."

Nodding his understanding, the younger man then relaxed to a casual stance. "You okay, Dad?"

The chief didn't answer for a few beats, the exchange with the airport scout obviously stirring his emotions. "Thank goodness I've still got you," he finally answered in a hush. "Your mother would be proud of you, Junior. That's all I'm going to say."

"We'll take care of those scum," the younger Woods replied with a steady voice. "And the sooner, the better. We can't bring mom back, but we can make them pay for what they did."

Jack had been following Hannah's tracks since lunch, thankful that the worst of the hills were behind him.

As the miles passed, he tried to force his thoughts into an optimistic lane. It was a method he had used multiple times while crossing the post-apocalyptic landscape of America's southwest. "At least you don't have to worry about some asshole texting while driving," he mumbled as he shifted gears. "There are no drunk drivers to hurt your family, no badly maintained 18-wheelers to crush Mylie's sedan."

As the terrain flattened out, the population density, or at least the remnants of civilization, increased dramatically. By midafternoon, he was passing by the subdivisions, gas stations, strip malls, and low-rise apartment buildings that formed the far southwestern reaches of Austin.

"Today would be a busy shopping day," he noted as he passed an outlet mall. "You and Miley would be fretting over a parking space, or how long the wait was for a table at lunch. Look at the bright side… those problems are no longer part of your life."

Hannah had been clear about avoiding the city, which made the commander wonder when her path would turn south. As he pedaled deeper and deeper into developed real estate, his concerns grew.

"No income tax, no IRS, no mortgage due date, no watching the stock market to see how the 401K is doing," he whispered, trying to compensate for the stress. "See, there are positive aspects to being one of the few survivors of doomsday."

He came upon a change in Hannah's tracks, stopping the bike and dismounting to investigate the odd patterns in the ash. "Something happened here," he grunted, scanning the strange impressions along the side of the road.

After playing detective for a minute, Jack brightened. "She dumped the sled. It was probably full of Sheng's tubers and the old man's gear. I wonder if he brought the good roots or the poison ones?"

As he remounted the two-wheeler, Jack glanced again at the scope and scale of the impressions in the ash. "That little tumble delayed her," he noted. "Now she's running late. Did that influence her route? Did she decide to change course and take a risk?"

Continuing, Jack began to notice the same corralling effect Hannah had detected the day before. Between the traffic accidents, downed utility pole, and the presence of low-rise buildings, he was beginning to understand why his new friend had taken this specific path. His nerves were getting frayed by the proximity and density of buildings, homes, vehicles, and piles of debris. "The streets are too confining here," he mumbled. "There's no room to maneuver, too few escape routes."

There was another stark contrast with the rural, wide-open spaces he had grown accustomed to.

It was one thing to look upon a dead desert and see nothing but emptiness. There was a strange familiarity to the desolation and lack of life. That scorched earth had never been home to lush gardens or exotic fish. Nor had the badlands ever vibrated with the energy, effervescence, or bustle of a city.

The desert seemed almost comfortable with her absence of life. Her landscape was accustomed to the void, at home with the emptiness.

Not so with the city, however. Jack's surroundings had once blossomed with life. Dogs had walked these sidewalks; lawns were green and growing; cats had ambushed birds in the bushes. Busy shoppers had hustled along with their bags; joggers had listened to the favorite tunes while taking in the air. The commander could almost hear the background hum of society still echoing off concrete facades.

The storefronts the commander passed now were like the faces of long-departed giants, their empty windows the hollow, lifeless eyes of the deceased. The desert had never been as alive, and somehow, that made its demise a bit more acceptable. Here, there had been a vivacious, throbbing pulse of growth and progress, and that made its death even more stark and melancholy.

Shaking his head to clear the funk building inside, Jack tried to concentrate on his surroundings with security in mind. This was a dangerous place – he could feel it.

His fears were reinforced when he spotted to the hangman's nooses and the corpses dangling from the sky. While he'd seen his share of death and destruction since leaving the safety of *Utah*'s steel hull, the commander couldn't help but feel disgust at the scene. "What the hell happened here?" he pondered. "Vendetta? Looters caught by vigilantes? Payback for the tool your brother-in-law borrowed and never returned?"

His forced humor had little effect. For several minutes, Jack could only sit and stare at the spectacle. Like a bloody automobile accident on the freeway, he couldn't tear his eyes away.

It was the crunch of ash under a foot that broke the spell.

In a flash, Jack was off his bike, carbine in hand. After a single second scan of the area, he quickly pushed his bike twenty feet to take cover behind a delivery van.

Nothing moved for several seconds, the commander beginning to wonder if the noise he'd heard was just the settling of ash or due to some other natural cause. It was pure luck that he spotted a sliver of lime-green brightness against the pewter background. He recognized it immediately as the same color as Hannah's motorcycle helmet. After another search of the surrounding buildings, he took a chance. "Hannah? Sheng? It's Jack... Jack Cisco!"

The patch of color disappeared for a moment, pulled back into the doorway that concealed whoever was holding the helmet. Then, with hesitation, Sheng's head appeared for second before ducking back out of sight.

"Sheng? It's Commander Cisco! Are you okay?"

The old man stepped out then, his weight forward, as ready to run as any pair elderly limbs could be. "Navy man?" he shouted back. "Is that you? I thought you were dead?"

Jack rose from behind the van, lowering his weapon as he waved a greeting. "Yes, it's me. Are you okay?"

They met in the middle of the street, Sheng's hands still shaking from the encounter. "Thank goodness it is you, Commander. I only saw a person with a rifle in the street and thought you were one of the raiders who attacked us."

"Attacked you? Where is Hannah?" Jack responded with urgency as his eyes darted up and down the avenue.

"I don't know where she is," Sheng explained, pointing back over his shoulder.

Chatting in a major intersection, surrounded by a million hiding places, while knowing hostiles were in the area didn't seem like a good idea to the commander. "Let's get someplace a little more secluded," Jack offered, pointing toward his bicycle and the van.

Nodding his agreement, Sheng followed Jack back to the place where his bike was propped. Both men ducked low as Jack started firing questions. "Where is Hannah? Is she hurt?"

It took Sheng several minutes to recount the previous day's events. "She never came back to the church," he finally concluded. "I don't know if she was killed, or became lost, or is wounded and lying in a ditch someplace. There was a lot of gunfire when she first bolted from the sanctuary, but after that, I heard nothing but the sound of the shouting voices."

As Jack digested the old man's tale, Sheng announced, "I'm going home. I am not safe here. I don't like this place. I should never have agreed to come along with her."

Knowing how important the Chinaman was to Hannah's plans, Jack doubted that she was in good health. She just wasn't the type to abandon a frightened, old man, and given his knowledge and potential to feed her community, the commander was sure she would have breached the gates of hell to make it back… if she were able.

That meant Hannah had either been killed, captured, or wounded. Any serious injury was probably a death sentence without medical care. The scenario left him with a difficult dilemma.

191

Clearly, Sheng didn't want to continue, and given the haunting surroundings and his recent experiences, Jack didn't blame the old guy.

He could let the herbalist try and return to his dugout alone while he searched for Hannah, but that plan seemed irresponsible on so many levels. The old gent was a treasure trove of critical information and skills – turning him loose in the wilderness was just wrong.

Yet, Jack didn't know the area and had zero local knowledge. Just like there were a million places where a hostile rifle could be waiting in ambush, the wounded woman could be lying in just as many nooks and crannies. How would he ever find her? Walking through the streets-turned-gallows while shouting Hannah's name was about the most foolish course of action he could imagine.

It occurred to Jack that he needed help.

"We're going to the airport," he explained to Sheng. "It is the closest, safest place I know."

Shaking his head with firm resolve, Sheng disagreed. "No. I want to go home."

"Your home isn't safe anymore," Jack explained. "The miners think you tried to kill them. While I found them enough food to last for a few weeks, that grub will eventually run out, and they have a score to settle with you."

"They are liars. I didn't try to kill anybody," the old man retorted in a decidedly defensive tone.

"Then why did they all get so sick after you showed them which roots to eat?"

With a dismissive wave of his hand, Sheng said, "They were either too stupid or too impatient to follow my instructions. Some of the tubers are disagreeable if not properly prepared. They ignored my warnings and consumed them too quickly like greedy animals."

Frowning, Jack had to wonder about the old man's explanation. He was wise enough to know that there were typically two sides to every story. Being a commander on a ship of the line had taught him that. Life after the eruption had driven that lesson home with even more stark consequences.

Yet, Camaro had been adamant that Sheng had attempted mass murder by poisoning them. According to the miner, the botanist had both motive *and* opportunity.

Shaking his head, Jack pushed aside Sheng's guilt or innocence. Now wasn't the time. "I believe you," the commander lied while looking the old man directly in the eye. "But... the miners will not. You are going to the airport with me. I don't care if I have to hog tie your arms and legs and drag you there behind the bike. I need you to come for Hannah. You can show the rescue party where the church is located. You can give them a first-hand account of what happened. We both owe her at least that much."

For a moment, Jack thought Sheng was going to either run or shoot him with Hannah's pistol. Finally, after several uncomfortable seconds, the Asian nodded. "I suppose you're right. The woman has been kind to me, and I did agree to go with her."

"Good. Let's get the hell out of here as soon as possible," Jack nodded.

Sheng couldn't argue with that.

Chapter 47

A child, no more than seven years old, darted in front of Captain Bascom. The pilot's reflexes were tested as he twisted mid-stride to avoid plowing into the excited youth. A second later, three more of the school-aged kids followed, their eager eyes focused upward as they ran past, oblivious to anything but the main terminal's ceiling.

"Children! No running!" Mrs. Ward demanded, the airport's teacher hustled to catch up with her young charges.

Throwing Alex an exasperated look that said, "I'm sorry," she continued after the gaggle, demanding that the brood slow down. "They're a little wound up."

Now curious about what was motivating the enthusiastic young ones, Alex turned and followed. Normally, Mrs. Ward kept her class's nose to the grindstone, the makeshift school's blackboards full of equations, sentence structure, history bullet-points, and other basic lessons.

Books, worthy of a learning environment, were rare. Mrs. Ward, a teacher for nearly three decades before being marooned at Austin International, had done yeoman's work, cobbling together a curriculum that would keep the forty-three stranded children on a positive development path.

To make up for the lack of learning materials, volunteers served as guest instructors at the school. Of the more than 400 survivors, Bascom had been pleasantly surprised at the variety of skills, occupations, and advanced knowledge available in the community. Apparently, engineers, writers, politicians, pilots, and scientists with a wealth of worldly experience to share all flew the friendly skies. At one point, Mrs. Ward had stated that no less than six languages were spoken among their ranks. The kids might not be receiving as many book lessons as before, but they were definitely benefiting from a valuable education.

The class, it turns out, was on their way to Gate 17. As Alex hustled to catch up, he heard eager young voices chattering about a nest and eggs. Had the birds finally mated? Even the stoic captain felt a tingling rush of excitement.

Like most large buildings, local sparrows and other species of birds occasionally managed to get inside the terminal. It wasn't unusual for passengers to see and hear the feathered flyers while traveling.

Just a few days after sealing the doors and windows, the captain had heard reports of at least one bird being trapped inside. At first, there was concern that the restricted animal might cause damage while trying to escape, might poke a hole in one of their makeshift barriers. There was, apparently, no good way to catch the winged fugitives.

After two weeks of watching the ash blow and drift outside, someone had commented that the terminal's non-human occupants might be the last of their kind to survive – anywhere.

In addition to the birds, spiders and other insects had suddenly achieved a new level of respect by the stranded population of humans. A wave of conservatory awareness had swept through the community. It had been one of the few heart-warming experiences since the eruption.

Rather than being immediately squashed by the sole of a shoe, creepy-crawlers were carefully captured and moved to one of Mrs. Ward's makeshift aquariums. The school now boasted several containers of small wildlife, protecting everything from silverfish to cockroaches as if they were precious gems.

Plates with crumbs and scraps of food were left out for any birds, rodents, or insects that remained uncaged. Missing the normalcy of household pets like cats and dogs, the schoolchildren had begun taking regular safaris around the facility, trying to spot, identify, and catalog any non-human survivors in their midst.

Just feet from the Gate 17 jetway, the group of students pulled up short and began pointing toward the exposed metal rafters above. Following their small fingers, Alex spotted a cluster of shredded paper, carpet strings, and other materials that had been skillfully woven into a circular nest.

A beak and dark pair of eyes peeked over the edge of the elevated homestead, unabashedly staring down at the class and teacher. A moment later, a flutter of movement signaled that a second bird had joined the first. A cheer rose out from the students, their enthusiasm bringing a wide grin to the adult's face.

As he watched, Alex realized that the occupied nest held a much deeper meaning than just a field trip for the children. The birds above, if reproducing, might be the Adam and Eve of their species. They truly could be only ones left of their kind. They might eventually be able to repopulate the skies outside, and that was a ray of hope they all so desperately needed. It gave Bascom a sense of optimism, a glimmer of hope that one day, things might return to normal.

Now late for his meeting, Alex forced himself to turn away. As he hustled to make up time, he found himself unable to quit smiling. "I wonder if there are eggs in that nest?" he pondered. "I guess we'll know in a few weeks."

Alex hadn't made it twenty steps when Deiter's anxious voice called. "Captain Bascom! Sir!"

Pausing to let the hustling man catch up, Alex realized that Deiter was out of breath from running. "There's a strange pair of men at the main entrance. One of them is holding up a lime-green motorcycle helmet. The other appears to be an old man, at least from what the sentries at the control tower could discern."

Bascom's pulse jumped at the mention of the headgear. Only Hannah wore a helmet that color, and she was two days overdue. Was the elder man this Sheng character she had talked about recruiting? The Asian artist who knew about the roots and tubers? How did he get here without the help of the scout? And who is this stranger?

"Something's happened to Hannah," Bascom mumbled under his breath. Then, turning to Deiter, he instructed, "Get a team ready and then meet me at the luggage area."

"Yes, sir," the subordinate nodded and then rushed off to execute the captain's orders.

Jogging back to his office, Alex unlocked a closet and pulled out an AR15 rifle and bandolier of magazines. He then opened a desk drawer and removed a long piece of heavy cotton cloth scavenged from the hundreds of suitcases left behind at the airport. After two attempts, he had the breathing mask secured around his nose and mouth.

He hustled to the staircase that led to the terminal's lower floor. Deiter was already in the air-lock, his own weapon primed for action.

"We'll take a cart outside to the control tower," the captain explained. "I want to get eyes on these people before we send out a team. Is everyone ready?"

"Yes, sir. They are armed and masked-up."

"Good. Now, let's have a look at our visitors," Bascom stated. "This might be a trap set by the Horns. They've been getting a little frisky lately."

It was an unusual event for the captain to leave the pressurized terminal, the need for his presence outside the air-lock having declined since the early days after the eruption. After passing through the outer door and into the world of dangerous air, the two men stepped toward one of the electric carts that had pulled small freight trains of bags and suitcases around the facility.

With Deiter driving, the duo hurried to the control tower, the concrete structure rising several stories above the otherwise flat grounds that contained tarmacs, runways, and access roads. Arriving at the base, Bascom dismounted and stepped to the heavy, steel door that guarded the facility.

During those troubling first few weeks after Yellowstone's outburst, security had monitored several spots along the perimeter and manned the tower as well. Over time, as the threats diminished, Bascom had ordered that only the control room be staffed with lookouts.

It was the perfect position to keep them safe. The octagon-shaped room crowned the tower and was fitted with oversized glass windows, affording an unobstructed view of the entire area. After all, it had been designed for just such a purpose and was elevated enough to provide a 360-degree vantage.

It also came equipped with several pairs of large, powerful binoculars, access doors that were nearly as thick as a tank's armor, and a high, barbed wire fence surrounding the base. It had been planned and built during a time when terrorists liked to highjack aircraft and use them as weapons. After the events of 9-11, every airport in North America had hardened their perimeters and control facilities.

Deiter banged four times on the substantial, metal door and then waited for a response. It was the agreed-upon code for entry.

"Seems odd to think of the times when a control tower was considered a target as the good ol' days," Bascom offered while they waited.

"Yes, sir," Deiter replied.

With the heavy rake of metal grinding against metal, the door opened. A masked head appeared, the pistol in his hand pointed skyward. After seeing the familiar faces of Deiter and Alex, the sentry relaxed and waved them inside.

The tower wasn't considered a clean space, so Bascom was forced to keep the cloth filter tight against his head as he climbed several flights of stairs.

Out of breath by the time they reached the top floor, he panted, "I need to get more exercise."

They entered a large, circular room that contained a dozen workstations. Now dark and dusty from months without being used, the computer consoles, radar screens, and flat panel displays were more clutter than valuable instruments.

There were always three men inside the tower, each shift lasting twelve hours, seven days a week. One of the individuals assigned to the duty once compared it to playing baseball in the outfield. "You spend hours and hours bored to death, and then all of a sudden, there are about three seconds of extreme excitement… sometimes too exciting!"

Walking to the window where one of the sentries was watching through a massive pair of binoculars, Bascom was handed an identical optic. "They are just sitting there waiting," the guard reported. "They haven't moved, other than to take a drink and wave a bedsheet taped to a broom handle as a white flag. They just walked up twenty minutes ago, the bigger guy pushing a bicycle. I haven't seen any other movement."

After focusing the optic, Bascom steadied his elbow on a desk and zeroed in on the subjects. The sentry's description had been accurate.

Body language gave away the older man's age, his slightly-bent gait clearly that of a man with more than a few years on him. Bascom decided the younger man's posture indicated impatience, perhaps even aggravation.

"Send the team. If the old man's name is Sheng, bring them both to the luggage bay. If not, send them packing, with a lead escort if necessary."

"I'm on it," Deiter responded, removing the radio from his belt.

Alex stayed in the tower long enough to see the bustling movements of six men next to the terminal, the response team loaded for bear and prepared to fight. The captain knew at least that number of shooters were still inside, ready to respond if the activity at the entrance was an ambush, or if the initial force needed backup.

As soon as the luggage tractor was rolling across the ash-covered tarmac, Bascom turned to Deiter and said, "We better get started back. If there's trouble, I want to go out with the second team."

"No one is here," Sheng complained, taking another draw of water from Jack's Camelbak. "We're wasting our time. The woman lied to both of us."

"Oh, they are here," Jack retorted, his patience with Mr. Grumpyass wearing thin. "No doubt that lime green helmet has grabbed their attention. They are watching us… assessing our every move. They are discussing their options – making sure we're not bait for a trap."

Shaking his head, Sheng added, "Well, I wish they would hurry and make a decision. I am tired, cold, and hungry. I want to get this over to go home."

Before the commander could respond, he detected movement from the main terminal building. A luggage tractor approached them, bristling with armed men.

"Get over behind that wreck," Jack spat, reaching to help Sheng to his feet. "Keep your head down."

The old man was eager to cooperate after spotting the rather impressive show of force that was racing their way. For his part, Jack moved to a wide-open space, clearly visible from the barrier that had been erected to close the entrance. He made a point of directing the barrel of his rifle toward the ground, holding it casually with one hand.

The electric tractor stopped fifty meters from the gate, all six of its passengers disembarking and forming a skirmish line. Their weapons remained high and ready, the barrels sweeping the fence line, roadblock, and surrounding terrain.

Not knowing what else to say or do, Jack held up his hands in the "don't shoot," position and shouted, "I mean no harm. I don't want any trouble."

"Put your weapon down on the ground!" shouted the closest man.

"That's not going to happen," Jack replied. "I was invited here by Hannah. She asked me to come here and speak to a Captain Bascom."

"Who is the other man with you?" the approaching gunman shouted.

"His name is Sheng. He was invited here by Hannah as well," Jack yelled back.

The mention of the master herbalist's name seemed to take the starch out of their posture, several of the riflemen relaxing enough that their movement was noticeable. They advanced as a single unit toward the two strangers. Not another word was exchanged until the six airport defenders reached the barricade.

"Where is Hannah?" the head rifleman demanded.

"She was ambushed by highwaymen or other black hats," Jack replied. "That's why we are here. We need help searching for her, and Sheng is a little long in the tooth to be involved in a rescue."

Without waiting for a response, Jack turned and motioned for Sheng to join him, the old-timer holding Hannah's helmet forward like it was a diplomatic passport.

Three of the airport gunmen quickly huddled, while the other half of them covered the party crashers. Finally, one of them pulled a walkie-talkie from his belt and relayed an update. Seconds later, the transmission terminated, and the jefe gestured toward the right. "There is a narrow passageway over there. Unload your weapons and then come through. You will not be harmed; you have Captain Bascom's word on it."

"What is it with these Central Texas bigwigs?" Jack cursed under his breath. "Everybody expects me to take their word for shit, yet nobody is willing to issue an ounce of trust in return."

Still, he didn't have much choice. Taking Hannah's pistol from Sheng, Jack made a show of unloading it and his rifle. The two men then stepped toward the indicated opening, the commander pushing his bicycle alongside them.

"You won't need that," the leader snarled. "Leave it here."

"The bike goes where I go," Jack countered. "It has kept me alive, and it doesn't bite." And then, to lighten the mood, he added, "And *you* have *my* word on *that*."

The attempt at comic relief was totally lost on the airport's defenders, and again, a quick conversation over the radio followed.

"Fine," the gatekeeper eventually retorted. "You want to push it to the terminal, then be my guest."

Just to show that he wasn't about to be bullied, Jack mounted the bicycle and countered, "Lead the way. I can keep up with your battery-powered buggy."

They loaded Sheng onto the luggage wagon, the old man glancing around nervously, unsure why he was being treated like a captive. "They're just being cautious," Jack said, trying to reassure the elderly gent.

Sheng didn't seem comforted by his words, throwing the commander a disconcerted, almost pleading look. Jack was sure that it said, "You know that I want to go home. Why did you bring me here?" For his part, the commander didn't blame the man who had risked travelling so far just to share his knowledge. While the resourceful survivalist didn't expect a ticker tape parade, he had thought he would be welcomed at the colony with open arms. "You expected to be treated like a hero, not a trespasser," Cisco mumbled.

Another officer checked Jack's backpack, rustling around in the interior before declaring that there was nothing dangerous inside. "He's got military-issued body armor, but he is carrying no explosives," he added.

After the security check, they headed toward the terminal, Jack pedaling behind the electric tractor. They rolled up the main entrance like a group of passengers trying to make their flight on time.

Just before reaching the departure area, the utility vehicle took a hard-left turn through a narrow opening in a chain-link fence. Jack had never been in the restricted section before and soon found himself riding underneath the wings of an enormous commercial aircraft. In the distance, he could hear the whine of running jet engines.

The security team came to a stop in front of what appeared to be a household garage door. One of the guards jumped off, maneuvering to open the door while the others kept an eye on Sheng and Jack. "I'll need to check your weapons. No one is allowed to be armed inside."

When Jack hesitated, the sentry said, "Captain Bascom has given his word. You will not be harmed."

"And you, sir, have my word as an officer of the United States Navy, I won't use my blaster unless somebody else shoots first," Jack countered.

"As far as I know, fella, the US Navy no longer exists. No one is allowed to be armed inside. That's not negotiable."

Finally capitulating, Jack handed over his carbine, pistol, and Hannah's sidearm as well. "That pistol belongs to your scout," he informed the sentry. "She gave it to Sheng before disappearing."

The guard accepted the weapons, his suspicious eyes slowly and deliberately scrutinizing the commander from head to toe when he recognized Hannah's gun.

Entering the terminal, Jack spotted a matrix of conveyor belts, metal racks, and other apparatus used to sort and transport thousands of suitcases. He could smell jet fuel, oil, and other mechanical scents. There were tools, more of the electric tractors, and one small office.

"We call this the air-lock," the security boss instructed. "You are to go inside, strip down to your underwear and wait. Someone will give you clothing and then you can redress. Once inside the inner door, you still need to keep your masks."

"I don't wear underwear," Sheng announced, almost as if he was proud of being different.

"No one cares," the guard replied. "We have to keep the ash out of the terminal."

Jack and Sheng did as instructed, the guards keeping a careful watch through the glass door. "I knew I should have trimmed my chest hair yesterday," the commander mumbled as he took off his shirt.

"I vaguely remember having body hair," Sheng replied with a grunt. "Stop bitching about every little thing. This was your idea, Sailor Man."

Near the end of the process, Cisco noticed that additional armed men were waiting on them inside the safe area.

Exiting the room, Jack was handed a jumpsuit complete with an airline logo and a clean roll of socks. After he and Sheng quickly dressed, they were escorted to a stairwell and told to climb.

At the top, another guard waited. With a curt nod, he opened a heavy door. Jack could feel the overpressure inside the terminal as a slight breeze rushed through his hair.

Once inside, the sentry said, "You can take off your masks in here. No need for them."

Once his face scarf was unwrapped, Jack drank in a deep chest full of air, savoring the freedom. Sheng did the same, the older man seemingly unimpressed. "It smells musty in here," he grumbled.

Continuing into the terminal, the high ceilings and open expanse seemed to impact both visitors, but in different ways. Jack first noticed the smells of cooking food. Sheng was amazed at the size of the interior. "I've never been in an airport before," the old man muttered, his eyes wide. "Are they all this big?"

"Most are even larger," Jack replied. "On the grand scale of things, this facility is actually quite small."

They were escorted a short distance down the main corridor, the commander able to see throngs of onlookers who seemed content to keep their distance. "Either they're scared of us, or they've been told to keep away," he whispered to Sheng.

"Given how much hair you have on your body, I don't blame them," Sheng whispered.

The guard opened an unmarked, side door and motioned them inside. "This is Captain Bascom's office. He will see you now," he stated.

"All hail the king," Jack grunted. "Make sure to bow deeply to his royal highness."

Stepping inside, Jack was surprised at how small was the space the community leader had reserved for himself. In fact, there was barely enough room for the commander, Sheng, and their guard.

Behind the desk, a tall, grey-haired man stood and extended his hand. He was obviously fit and carried himself with an air normally reserved for military officers or corporate executives. "My name is Alex Bascom. I am the mayor of our little town."

"Commander Jack Cisco, US Navy," Jack replied, accepting the handshake, and hoping that his own military rank would buy some good will.

"Sheng," the older man introduced, accepting the offered greeting.

"Do either of you need food, water, or medical care?" Alex asked with a smile that Jack thought was forced.

"No," they both responded.

Nodding, Bascom then got right to the point. "Where is Hannah?"

It took Sheng ten minutes to explain what had happened to the scout. While the Chinaman rambled on, Jack took the opportunity to study his surroundings.

The captain's modest desk was sparsely furnished, organized and neat, and completely clear of any clutter. A single ornament adorned the space… a small, metal replica of an F-22 Raptor, the Air Force's frontline interceptor aircraft. The base that it sat on was engraved with the words, "Colonel Alexander Bascom, Commander, 57th Squadron, Gunfighters."

It makes sense that Captain Bascom would be an ex-Air Force jock, Jack thought. *The flyboys always get the cushy assignments.*

While Sheng droned on, Jack's attention shifted to an oversized map of Austin mounted on the wall behind Bascom's desk. Someone had notated the chart with dozens of colored pushpins, rubber bands, and highlighted areas. The commander couldn't make heads or tails of the code.

After the older man had finished his tale, Bascom had a few questions for his botanist guest. "Can you point to the location of the church on the map?" he asked, nodding toward the same chart Jack had just been studying.

"No," Sheng replied. "I've never used those things. I stop and ask directions if I'm lost."

Clearly frustrated, Bascom's attention switched to Jack. "What about you?"

"I don't know the exact coordinates or address of the church, but I can get close to the place where I found Sheng. Maybe he can backtrack from there?" Jack replied.

With a nod from their host, Jack stood and studied the map. He knew the general direction he and Sheng had traveled since meeting. Finding the airport, the commander then began tracing his finger along a southwestern direction. Both Bascom and the sentry keenly watched his progress.

Remembering a few landmarks, and trying to recall the distance traveled, Jack finally drew a small circle on the map with his finger. "It was in this general vicinity," he declared.

After exchanging troubled glances with his subordinate, Bascom said, "Are you sure?"

"Reasonably sure. I don't know this area and had no method of calculating speed over ground," Jack responded. "I didn't have a GPS handy, but it is a realistic estimate."

Again, the airport leader threw his subordinate a troubling glance. Jack couldn't let it go a second time. "What's wrong, Captain?"

Ignoring the commander's query, Bascom turned to Sheng and said, "We can't mount a rescue without more specific information. Would you happen to remember the name of the church?" he asked the old-timer.

"Yes. I'll never forget it," Sheng nodded. "While the hooligans searched the building, I was hiding in a cabinet that was full of signs. They were the last words I thought I would ever see, 'Bake Sale Saturday. St. Mary's Episcopal Church.' Exactly, what *is* a bake sale?"

Jack wanted to laugh but suppressed the chuckle. Now wasn't the time, Hannah's life might depend on how quickly a rescue could be organized.

Bascom ignored Sheng's question about brownies and fundraisers. To Deiter he commanded, "Go get a phone book out of the library. We'll look up the address."

The security type clearly didn't want to leave his boss alone with the two strangers, but Bascom's stern expression prevailed over his concerns. In a flash, the loyal man rushed out of the office.

"And just how did you become involved in all this, Commander Cisco?" Bascom inquired while his man was away.

Jack's narrative was short and to the point. "I was aboard the *USS Utah* when Yellowstone erupted. My wife and daughters were supposed to be at my father-in-law's ranch about fifty miles west of Austin. After receiving leave from my commanding officer, I took off from San Diego and traveled here to Texas to find them. That's where I ran into Hannah, and she offered to bring me here for a variety of reasons. On the way, we stopped by Sheng's home, ran into a few problems, and since then I've been a part of this merry, little band."

"You traveled all the way from California on a bicycle? After the eruption?" Alex asked, his expression betraying his obvious skepticism.

"Yes, sir, I did. It wasn't easy, but there was no way I was going to rest until I found my family, either dead or alive."

It didn't take Bascom a second to ask the obvious question. "And? Did you find them, Commander?"

"No," Jack sighed. "My father-in-law's ranch was under a lake of mud and water. I have no idea what happened to them. That was part of the reason why I agreed to accompany Hannah back here to the airport... she said you might have information regarding where they might have gone."

"I see," he whispered, his chin coming to rest on a triangle made from his fingertips.

A few seconds passed before the captain returned his attention to Sheng. "Hannah had reported to me that you had amassed a tremendous amount of knowledge about local plants, Mr. Sheng. She informed me that you eat better than any other survivor she has encountered. Is this true?"

Sheng wasn't humble. "I was raised in rural China, Mr. Captain. We had to know how to harvest and preserve all of nature's bounty and to do so winter, spring, fall, and summer. Hannah wanted me to come here and teach your people how to identify and process what little food is still available in the wild. I agreed to do so because the woman was very kind to me."

"I'm so very happy you've decided to join our community, Mr. Sheng. You are more than welcome here. We have a physician if you have any concerns or needs, as well as a social environment that I'm sure will keep you entertained."

Shaking his head, Sheng didn't seem accepting of Bascom's offers. "I have no interest or need of Western medicine, Mr. Captain, and I do not wish to stay here for very long. Hannah said that you would help me deal with the only threat to my happy existence if I agreed to educate your foragers. That is why I'm here."

209

Jack, stunned at Sheng's statement, couldn't keep the surprise off his face. "You mean the miners? Are they the threat you're talking about?"

Nodding the old Chinaman responded, "Hannah said that Captain Bascom would help eliminate them."

"You want the miners killed?" the commander snapped, his anger growing by the second.

"I don't care if they are killed, or relocated, or chased away. Hannah promised," he argued.

Before the disagreement could blossom, Deiter pushed through the office door carrying a thick phonebook. His finger held open a page.

Quickly moving to the map, the security man's eyes darted between the hanging chart and the phonebook's page. "Here is the church," he announced, stabbing a specific point, then adding, "This is a serious development, sir."

Bascom rose from behind his desk and stared hard at the location indicated by Deiter's digit. "That's in the Forbidden Zone. What was she thinking... why would Hannah go there?"

"The sled carrying my tubers overturned, and it took us a long time to pick everything up," Sheng explained. "I wanted the woman to take me home. We didn't want to spend the night among all of the haunted buildings, so she agreed to take a shortcut."

"What is the Forbidden Zone, Captain?" Jack asked.

"We are not the only community of survivors in Austin, Commander," Bascom answered. "We're not sure who or what they are, but there is another organized group that has reacted with violence every time we send scouts to a certain area. After we lost several of our people there, we dubbed that part of the city as the Forbidden Zone."

"And you don't know anything about the people who occupy that area?" Jack frowned.

"No. We have tried to make contact with them on several occasions, but they refuse to respond with anything other than firearms and attacks. My people call them 'Horns.'"

Given the worried expressions on Bascom's and Deiter's faces, Jack didn't press for more details. Both of his hosts seemed lost in thought.

"Hannah might be lying hurt… or hiding and afraid to move, sir," Deiter offered.

"I know, I know," Bascom snapped back. "Yet we can't afford to lose any more people, Deiter. The chances are slim that she has survived, especially in the Zone. Do we risk more lives and loss of resources on what seems to be only a flicker of hope?"

Jack couldn't' believe his ears. Without thinking, he threw Bascom a scolding look and growled, "No man left behind, **Colonel**."

Whether it was the use of his military rank or Jack's challenge to his authority, Bascom reacted poorly to the comment. "I will not have my decisions questioned, **Commander**. You are a stranger here, with zero local knowledge or experience. You have no idea regarding our resources, tactical capabilities, or strategic outlook."

Jack sighed at Bascom's invoking their respective military ranks. A naval commander, on the Pentagon's pay scale, was an O-5. An Air Force Colonel was an O-6 and the superior officer.

"I could lead a team no larger than the squad you sent to greet us at the gate," Jack countered. "We could track her from the church and search the area in a few hours with that many men. Are these Forbidden Zone badasses so aggressive that they would attack a force of such size?"

"We don't know," Bascom exhaled. "And that's the problem. They are becoming more and more antagonistic. Just yesterday, they fired on one of our scouts who wasn't that close to their turf. We've seen evidence that they are expanding their scavenging efforts. Other small groups of survivors we have contacted were scared to death of them. And in the last month, some of them have vanished."

While Jack could respect the amount of stress involved with Bascom's role, something in his core beliefs just wouldn't accept abandoning Hannah.

"What if she's been captured?" Deiter asked in a hushed voice. Then, more forcefully, he added, "I've only been thinking that she is either dead or wounded, but what if they have taken her prisoner? She knows our defenses, radio codes, and procedures."

Bascom's eyes flew wide at the suggestion. "That would make us even more vulnerable. Information is more powerful than any rifle. If they know our situation, they could…."

Listening to Bascom's voice fade, Jack wondered if life here at the airport was as wonderful as Hannah had led him to believe.

"The commander is right," Bascom then announced. "No man… or woman, left behind. Prepare a team, Deiter. Take whatever resources you need. Be ready to leave at first light."

"Yes, sir!" the security man snapped, pivoting to leave the room.

"I want to go," Jack announced as Deiter's backside was about to clear the doorway. "I considered Hannah my friend. I can help."

"Deiter!" Bascom called, causing his man to do an about-face. "Take the commander with you. He is to report to you and might prove useful."

"But, sir, he doesn't know our methods, he's not trained with my team members or…" the security man protested.

"I've fought my way across half the continent.," Jack interrupted. With a softer voice, he added, "Besides, my streak of stubbornness is partly to blame for Hannah's predicament. I want to go."

"You can always use another shooter, Deiter," Bascom advised. "Take the commander with you."

Nodding his agreement, Deiter waved for Jack to join him. "Don't get in our way, Navy man," he whispered as they went out into the hallway. "If you give us away or screw things up, one of my bullets will accidentally end up in your head. Understood?"

"Don't worry," Jack grinned. "I have a bad feeling that we're both going to have more to worry about than your bad aim."

Chapter 48

Jack was escorted to the staircase and then led down into the unpressurized area of the first floor. "I can't sleep with the civilized people?" the commander asked.

"I'm just following Captain Bascom's orders," Deiter responded with a shrug. "You and the Chinese guy are the first strangers we've ever allowed into the building period. I wouldn't complain too loudly, or he might toss you out on the tarmac."

"I haven't slept without a mask on my face for weeks," Jack pushed back. "I was kind of looking forward to it."

"Sorry," the security chief responded simply.

"Does Bascom think I have cooties or something?" Jack continued, sniffing his armpit for emphasis. "I just bathed a couple days ago. That's pretty good hygiene for a post-apocalyptic world."

The humor seemed to lighten Deiter's mood. "I've smelled worse. But to answer your question, I don't think body odor has anything to do with the captain's decision."

"What gives then? You guys have my weapons. I'm sure I haven't shown any disconcerting indicators of mental issues. Why make the guest sleep in the doghouse?"

Bascom stopped walking and squared to face the commander. "I don't think he wants you talking to our people, if you really want to know."

"Huh? Did I swear like a sailor before?" Jack questioned.

"No, you were very professional, if not a bit aggressive. I think Captain Bascom is worried about what impact your presence might have on our young people. To be blunt, I'm a little concerned myself."

"Why? I have no idea what you mean," Jack frowned, his sense of humor evaporating quickly.

Deiter began walking again, his stride indicating that the conversation was over. After three steps he changed his mind, pulling up short to address Jack. "You don't realize the problems the captain faces on a daily basis. We have hundreds of people here, most of the stranded far, far away from their homes. The older people have adjusted, for the most part, willing to accept that they might never see their children, homes, or businesses again. They are not physically able to travel great distances on foot, so returning to their previous life is impossible."

"And the younger people?" Jack asked, already sensing how the story was going to end.

"We've already had issues with bolters, or people who leave the airport without permission. The younger men are the most likely to try and return to their families or their homes," Deiter paused, briefly indulging in a moment of reflection. "Do you remember what you were like when you hit sixteen or seventeen years of age, Commander? I'll bet you were ready to take the world by storm. Well, that has not changed. Guys that age think they are smarter, faster, and stronger than anyone else. They believe nothing can touch them… that they are immortal. They are brimming with confidence and are physically fit. They make grandiose plans of saving the world. Then, they abandon the safety of the airport, and we rarely ever hear from them again. I've lost count of how many we have lost."

Shaking his head, Jack finished Deiter's explanation. "The only thing that has kept them here is the perceived dangers of traveling outside these walls. The ash. The Forbidden Zone. The violence your scouts encounter and the vast emptiness out there. That keeps the young men and women here."

Nodding, Deiter added, "Now you show up, claiming to have traveled alone across half of the doomsday landscape. One guy, not specially trained like a Green Beret or Navy Seal, and not especially impressive physically. A submariner who bumbled ashore and took off on a bicycle. I know a dozen men here who would take one look at you and say, 'If he can do it, so can I.'"

Rubbing his chin, Jack said, "And what if they did decide to leave? What if they did take the chance and bug out? I don't see how that hurts you or the community. Fewer mouths to feed. Fewer people taking oxygen out of the room."

"We need them," Deiter countered. "We need guards in the tower, mechanics working on the planes, and sentries to stand watch. Just like a regular society, there is a lot of manual labor involved with sustaining life here. The filters must be maintained, food loaded and unloaded at the warehouse, and the planes refueled. We find at least two holes a week in the seals and vents. Most of our younger population works their asses off at least ten hours a day. The workload is necessary to keep everyone alive."

"And the older folks?" Jack inquired, his mind trying to digest everything Deiter was saying.

"Everybody works here," Deiter stated with pride. "If you want to eat, drink, and breathe, you have to pull your share. But… Yellowstone erupted during a weekend. The flights that were canceled had a significant number of older citizens aboard, not the normal mix of businessmen and women. More than eighty percent of our residents are over fifty-five years old. In fact, were it not for the TSA agents and the substation cops who were here, I wouldn't be able to put together the rescue team that's going out in the morning."

"I see," Jack nodded, still trying to process Deiter's words. "Why did you stay here?"

"I did eight years in the Army after high school. I didn't reenlist because I was just tired of Mother Green and all the chicken shit that went along with wearing the uniform. I got a job at the TSA and a one-bedroom apartment close by. I was an only child, and my folks had passed away years ago. My wife died of breast cancer shortly after I started working here. Long story short, I didn't have any place else to go."

217

"Why is Bascom so uptight about letting a stranger in?" the commander then asked.

Happy that the subject had changed from his personal life, Deiter replied, "He's got a long list of very good reasons. You weren't here. You didn't see what we went through."

"Tell me about it," Jack suggested. "You're right about my not understanding. I was under about a mile of the Pacific Ocean when the volcano blew. The worst of it was over by the time we docked."

Waving Jack up to walk beside him, Deiter didn't seem to know where to start describing those first few days. As they entered a small room with a cot, the security man said, "These are your quarters for the night. I should be going."

"Hang around for a bit," Jack offered, throwing his pack on the cot. "I don't get to talk to people all that often. I really want to know what it was like."

Shrugging, Deiter moved to a plastic chair in the corner and took a seat. "I'll never forget Captain Bascom coming into the TSA officers' break room that morning. We had all been glued to the television, watching Yellowstone spew death and destruction. Everybody was waiting for the eruption to stop, but it just kept getting worse and worse. By mid-afternoon, we all were becoming paranoid and jumpy."

"I don't get it?" Jack asked, taking a seat on the cot. "What made you realize that it was more than just the Midwest that was in trouble?"

"Oh, I suppose the main thing was the newscasts. They kept bringing on these experts, so-and-so from the National Geographical Society, Dr. Such-and-Such from the government offices of emergency management, and a whole parade of doom and gloom cheerleaders. By then, the ash was starting to fall as far east as Chicago. There were already roofs collapsing in Kansas City and St. Louis. All the while the volcano kept throwing millions of tons of junk into the air."

"Did they show videos of those cities?" Jack asked, now enthralled.

"They sure did," Deiter spat. "Kept repeating them, over and again. St. Louis looked like it was being hit with a winter blizzard. The station we were watching showed a before and after shot of the river. You could barely see the damn thing after the pumice started falling."

"And that's when you first met Bascom?"

"Yeah, I'd probably seen him around before, but I didn't interact much with the pilots. In the travel ecosystem, they tend to be elite and a little standoffish. Anyway, in walks this guy wearing his captain's uniform, all ramrod straight and formal. The anxiety and fear in the room were as thick as a San Francisco fog. Without any introduction or greeting, he strolls to the front of the room and stops when he's blocking the television. He says, "I am Captain Alex Bascom. If you want to live more than a few more days, please pay attention."

"That's when he made his pitch?"

Nodding, Deiter continued, "At first, we thought he was a nut job, driven stark, raving mad by the news of the eruption and the stress it was causing. But, as the day went on, we all were looking at each other and saying, 'Maybe that old fighter jock isn't so crazy after all.' It was about then that the first reports of glass being in the ash started broadcasting. From the TV pictures, the entire world was going over the edge. Grocery store riots over the last loaves of bread... itinerant preachers standing on street corners telling people the end was near... every National Guard unit in the country being called in... runs on banks and gas stations. I stepped outside to get some air at one point. I remember counting seventeen columns of smoke on the horizon. One of the skyscrapers downtown looked like the World Trade Center after 9-11, flames boiling into the air. You couldn't hear anything but sirens. It was absolute chaos out there."

219

"How did Bascom know about the volcano before the newscasts?" Jack asked, trying to fill in the timeline.

"He said he'd been grounded before, some volcano in Iceland closing all of Europe's airspace for days. He told us that the military had given them all a briefing, and he had spent the downtime researching what the effects of an eruption could have on Air Force operations. A group of us found him a little later and basically said, 'Okay, Captain, what do we have to do to live?'"

"Is that when he came up with the idea to seal the airport and create an overpressure using the planes?" Jack inquired.

"Yes and no. First, he had the idea of everyone sleeping in the planes. The plan to use their air systems came a bit later," Deiter replied. "We gathered all the passengers, crews, mechanics, workers from the food courts and ticket agents... anybody who was still in the building. We had a great big powwow at Gate 20. Bascom stood on a chair and took over. He was calm, forceful, had the credentials, and commanded a presence. We were lucky he was here."

"Still, there had to be a lot of people who thought he was off his rocker?" Jack supposed.

"Maybe at first," Deiter replied. "We still hadn't closed the entrance at that point. There were still a lot of people coming and going. We had airport employees who left to go home and then turned around and came back, bringing their families with them, other folks who just kind of drifted in. They all told stories of horrific events happening around the city, and that kind of reinforced the captain's words... convinced us all to keep our noses to the grindstone and silenced the naysayers."

"What made you close the entrances?"

The former TSA agent paused for a bit, images from that terrible time rolling through his mind. When he did start speaking again, the words became rushed and urgent. "Word must have spread about what we were doing here. People started coming in droves. At first, we welcomed anybody, but then we caught some desperados trying to make off with cases of food. One of my agents was shot by another man during an argument. About then, we finished counting all the food in the warehouses. After dividing it by the number of mouths to feed, the captain announced, 'We have to close this down. We can't save everybody. If we don't do something, the looters will pick us clean in a matter of hours.' So, we blocked the main entrance and started mounting patrols. Those were the worst few days of the entire affair. We had lines of traffic backed up at the entrance. Some people thought the planes were still able to fly, and they wanted to get out of town. Others had heard we had warehouses full of grub and wanted their share. The captain ordered the fire engines into position, and we used their water cannons to break up a couple of mobs. Twice, we had armed masses try to breach the gate, which resulted in a massive firefight. We barely held our ground and lost fourteen people during that first battle."

"Sounds awful," Jack offered. "I've heard similar stories as I crossed the country. Everybody panicked. Anarchy ruled. People became very tribal… almost overnight."

Deiter agreed. "I would have never thought my fellow Americans were capable of such behavior. Four days later, with the ash falling like a January blizzard in Maine, we had a guy who somehow made it through our security. To this day, I still don't know how, but he did it. A minivan, hauling a family, pulled up at the passenger drop-off, right outside the terminal. I was there, working to seal the automatic doors. The power had just gone out a few hours before. The occupants were desperate to gain entry. "We must fly to the equator," the father had begged, pounding on the glass, blood trickling out of his nose. 'The air will be breathable there! My wife and children… they are dying,' he pleaded."

With his eyes growing moist, Deiter's voice grew soft and sad. "The wind was so strong that ash was blowing horizontally past the windows. This guy stood outside, just pounding on the glass,

221

demanding that we let him in. For over ten minutes, we tried to reason with him. He pulled his kids out of the van, a toddler and an infant. Both were already coughing up blood. He held them up as if they were some sort of ticket to get inside. If we had opened the doors, we would have contaminated the entire terminal. We tried to convince him that no planes were flying... that he should put on some sort of mask... that he should go home and stay inside... that there was absolutely no evidence that the equator would be spared. He was inconsolable, switching from incomplete, blabbering sentences to harsh, screamed, threats."

Wiping his eyes, Deiter then added, "In the end, he returned to his minivan, opened the back latch, and retrieved a tire iron. We drew our weapons, screaming at him, begging him not to do it. Everyone was shouting orders, pleading with the irrational father to stop. He didn't. With a crazed look on his face, he raised the bar to strike our protective layer of glass. One of our police officers shot him in the chest, the bullet making a perfectly round, neat hole in the window and the dude's shirt. I'll never forget his blood mixing with the pewter flakes falling from the sky. It gave me nightmares for weeks."

"Lord have mercy," Jack mumbled, a scowl on his face.

Deiter wasn't done. "The face of the older child was pressed against the van's window, crying for his father to get up... to come back... to take them home. A woman darted from the vehicle. She stayed there, right beside the glass, weeping over her husbands' body for nearly five minutes while he bled out. I couldn't turn away. I couldn't help myself. Finally, she stood and wiped the tears from her cheeks. Her gaze turned to the small crowd that had gathered on the safe side of the airport glass. 'There is a special place in hell for all of you!' she screamed. 'I will see you there soon enough.'"

With a sniffle, Deiter said, "Eventually, she returned to the van and drove away. No one spoke a word as the red taillights disappeared into the storm cloud of grey. We repaired the window with tape, and to this day, I can't walk past it without thinking of that family. That wasn't the last time someone was killed trying to gain entry, but it was the most disturbing. Even now, I wonder sometimes what we have become… what kind of vicious beasts has Yellowstone has created?"

"No wonder Bascom doesn't welcome outsiders," Jack grunted. "I probably wouldn't send out the welcome wagon either."

"Those days changed us all, Commander Cisco. Every single man, woman, and child was altered by that damned volcano. I don't value human life like I once did. I don't give a shit about anybody but the people inside this building. Not you, not Sheng, not anybody else. The world has forced me to think that way. I don't like it, but I don't have any choice."

Without another word, Deiter rose and left Jack alone in his assigned quarters. After the security official had closed the door, the commander whispered, "But you're all going to have to change, my friend. Survival will require an open heart and mind. You just don't know it yet."

Two of the airport's electric motorcycles led a small convoy through urban Austin. Following the pair of riders trailed one of the facility's luggage tractors, a single car hooked to the hitch.

Jack, Deiter, and six of his best shooters were along for the ride.

The battery-powered tractor only had enough range to take them halfway. "Come back for us at dark," Deiter ordered the driver. "Bring an extra cart. We might have wounded or dead."

"Such optimism," Jack whispered in a voice only he could hear.

The rescue party continued toward the church on foot, Deiter sending the faster motorcycles ahead as an advance force. Again, the commander butted heads with the man. "I wouldn't do that," Jack advised. "I would keep those go-fasts back as a reserve. They could swoop in quickly and get us out of a jam."

223

"Your advice isn't appreciated or necessary, Cisco," Deiter pushed back. "We know how to do this."

Shrugging, Jack replied, "You're in charge. Lead on."

Deiter's influence over his team was obvious as they moved out. Jack was impressed by their spacing and coordinated movements. Each rifleman kept a reasonable distance between himself and the next in line. Everybody's head was on a swivel, moving left and right, their rifle barrels' movements coordinated with that of their eyes.

They arrived at the church around mid-day. After scrutinizing the house of worship for a few minutes, Deiter ordered his scouts to begin following Hannah's tracks.

Jack had to admit the two riders were good. They took turns being in the lead, leapfrogging each other as they traveled through the streets. When the gap between the foot soldiers and wheeled scouts became too great, they always seem to pick a good defensive spot to wait for their slower comrades.

For his part, the commander concentrated on analyzing Hannah's tracks. Her footprints were slightly shorter and narrowing than the men who had obviously been following the fleeing woman. "You were luring them away from Sheng," Jack whispered at one point. "Smart girl."

Twice they found empty brass casings lying on top of the ash. The first scene had a large pool of crimson darkening the ground. "That's not Hannah's blood," Jack observed. "See the shell casings? She was carrying an AR15. The bleeder was shooting a larger caliber weapon. She got one of them pretty good."

After a half an hour of carefully tracking Hannah's escape route, it became clear to Jack that she had been zigzagging toward the southeast, cutting at right angles. What was even more impressive was the fact that the men following her seemed to be aware of some intended destination or goal.

Jack saw multiple examples where the hunters had bypassed a leg of her travels, seemingly jumping ahead or taking a shortcut in an attempt to get in front of their prey. The commander's level of respect for the Zombies, or Horns, or whatever they were called, was growing by the minute.

"How in the hell did they know where she was going to pop out of that particular neighborhood in that exact spot?" Jack asked at one point, his finger indicating tracks that showed two men pre-positioned less than a block from Hannah's route.

"It's like they had an observation drone or some shit," Deiter agreed, his eyes travelling toward the heavens, a worried expression covering his face.

"Did they have people in the trees? A helicopter? A plane?" Jack speculated, his eyes taking in the skyline. "These guys are damn good."

A block later, one of the scouts zoomed up to Deiter. "There's a highway up ahead. Hannah's tracks lead right to it. There's no cover there… it's wide open for at least a mile in both directions. Be careful."

"Bring the other bike back, and let's scout the highway on foot," Jack suggested, his instincts now bristling with apprehension. "I'm liking this setup less and less."

As usual, Deiter ignored the commander's words. "Go back to the freeway, and ride in both directions. We'll move forward and wait until you report," he ordered the scout.

Shaking his head, there was little Jack could do. Even the greenest of officers knew better than to divide forces when in such close proximity to the enemy.

As the motorbike sped away, Deiter motioned his unit forward. Everyone could feel the tension in the air, all hands gripping their weapons tighter than before.

Entering an apartment complex, Jack detected a difference in Hannah's trail. She was being less careful now, the space between her footfalls growing wider than before. She didn't stop for cover, wasn't taking advantage of the buildings or grounds on both sides of the street. Now she was running in a straight line, her legs pumping to save her life. "She must have seen or felt the hunters closing in," he whispered to no one.

They approached the freeway and stopped, all eyes scanning up and down the open expanse of pavement. Now Hannah's trail was confused and difficult to follow, partially obscured by dozens of other footprints. Still, they could all see where their comrade had gone, a straight line of well-packed ash leading to a large drainage culvert running under the blacktop lanes.

Motion distracted Jack, the commander catching one of the speeding motorcycles as it came flying toward the team. Something was wrong. Jack could tell by the rider's body language and haste.

Less than two football fields away, the electric bike began crossing a small bridge. A rope magically appeared from beneath the carpet of ash, pulled taut over the abutments, directly in front of the oncoming scout.

The rider didn't even have time to hit the brakes before his body was flung off the rear of the speeding machine as it was snagged by the rope. "They clotheslined the scout!" someone screamed.

Before the rider's flopping arms and legs had stopped rolling, two men appeared from under the bridge and began firing into the prone form. Jack watched the scout's body dance a sickening series of jerks and twitches as their lead shredded flesh and pulverized bone.

Without even a glance at the remaining rescue team, the two shooters jumped back over the railing and disappeared. So quickly did they vanish, Jack would have wondered if he'd really seen anything at all. The unmoving body of the scout, however, was proof enough.

"Get those bastards!" Deiter screamed, the team leader furious with rage.

Before Jack could shout a warning, Deiter was up and running after the ambushers, waving his men forward with the bloodlust of revenge in his eyes.

"Don't do it!" the commander tried to warn the men still beside him. "It's a trap!"

None of the airport shooters listened, leaving Jack behind as they bounded down the embankment after their fearless leader. They were almost to the closest lane of pavement when a dozen rifles opened up from the across the freeway.

Jack knew instantly how the trap had been sprung. The Zombies had been hiding in the drainage tunnel, waiting for the bikes. The rope couldn't have been an accident, its perfect placement and timing a sure indicator that the black hats were aware of how the airport personnel operated.

Flicking the safety off his carbine, Jack tried to buy his comrades time to escape the kill zone. Switching to full-automatic, he sent a burst of rounds raking the far edge of the blacktop. Then another, and another.

The effort, however, was practically wasted.

All of Deiter's men were on the ground and either bleeding or trying dig themselves a hole for cover as round after round tore into their ranks. The commander's return fire might be buying them a few seconds, but that was about it.

Jack had never been so frustrated... had never felt so hopeless as the men below were shredded into raw meat. It was a slaughterhouse down there, volley after volley of merciless lead slicing Deiter's team to pieces.

Slamming home a new magazine, he considered popping up and charging the other side. His gut knew it was suicide, but he had to do something. Good men were dying down there.

Movement disturbed the commander's peripheral vision, the other scout now returning, drawn by the sound of the one-sided battle. Jack saw the rider's weapon propped on the handlebars, red flashes of gunfire spewing from the muzzle.

Another weapon soon joined his side, the commander stunned to see Deiter firing back from behind a barricade made of two dead bodies. Now the ambushers were facing gunfire from three different angles, and that development gave them pause.

Regrouping during the lull, Jack took his time with the second magazine. Using his optic and picking a target, he could see the top of one man's head… just a mop of hair visible from the ear up. Centered the crosshairs of his optic, the commander squeezed the trigger.

A billowing haze of flesh and blood signaled that Jack had hit his mark. A second later, two other bushwhackers became visible, changing positions to address the charging scout. Jack killed one of them but was unable to zero in on the second man before he disappeared from the circle of his optic.

Now it was the commander's turn to receive fire, his marksmanship rewarded by a hailstorm of incoming rounds slapping and popping into the earth around his head.

Jack retreated down the slight rise, pushing his body backward to avoid the volley, dragging his weapon by the sling.

A scream of agony sounded from the far side of the road, either Deiter or the scout getting in a lucky shot. Sensing that someone else was now the target, Jack crawled back to his original position and began scanning for any exposed body part.

The volume of fire from the other side suddenly dissipated. Jack could make out two, maybe three weapons now barking in their direction. "They're breaking contact," the commander realized. "They've accomplished their mission, and now they'll fade away into the woods. It's only the rearguard shooting at us now."

Sure enough, the tempo of incoming lead declined again, the commander sure there was only one weapon sniping at them now. Jack waited, forcing his trigger finger to relax until he could identify a clear target.

A shoulder appeared, just a few inches of a coat or shirt breaking cover. Jack squeezed the trigger, the M4 pushing back as it made its report.

A wail of distress across the freeway broke the silence, a rifle flying into view as it tumbled end over end, through the air. Then the man stood to escape, trying to run while holding his arm. Jack fired again, this time striking center mass with his shot. The runner fell face-first into the ash, his body landing with an awkward flop and roll.

Then, as suddenly as it had all started, the firefight was over. It took the commander several seconds to reacclimate to the quiet, noiseless afternoon. That silence, however, didn't last long.

A moan of pain from below his position brought Jack up and out of his hide. Rushing bent at the waist, just in case some of the Zombies were still around, the commander hurried to the pile of dead and dying men below.

His first objective was Deiter, but the security honcho motioned him away, grunting, "Check the others, I'm okay."

One by one, Jack felt for pulses while the surviving scout went to check on the other rider.

Sadly, Jack returned to Deiter. "They're all gone," the commander reported. "Where are you hit?"

Half of Deiter's upper thigh was missing, nothing left but bleeding, raw flesh. Quickly pulling off a dead man's belt, the commander did his best to apply a tourniquet to stop the flow.

By then, the surviving scout had returned, a quick shake of his head telling Jack that there were only three of the rescue party still alive. "We have to get him back to the doc at the airport," the commander said to the scout. "He's lost a lot of blood and probably that leg."

Pointing toward the woods on the far side of the freeway, the rider said, "I'll get some branches. We can make a gurney."

"Hurry," the commander snapped.

While the scout began breaking off saplings with his boot, Jack went to examine the fallen enemy. All four of the Zombies were dead, and as the commander reached to check one of the corpse's pockets, he noticed an odd emblem on the man's shirt. "Austin Fire Department," he read.

It was then that Jack noticed something else odd. Stepping briskly to another deceased ambusher, the commander bent and studied the man's breathing mask.

"I've seen this before," Jack whispered, reaching for the unit. "The United States Navy was thinking of buying these for our submarines and ships."

While the commander hadn't been directly involved in the evaluation, he did remember one remarkable feature of the masks. They came equipped with a built-in, heads-up display of forward-looking infrared technology. Being able to see heat was touted as an enormous benefit to those who fought fires. It would allow the wearer to see hot spots, human bodies, and all kinds of hazards that were invisible to the naked eye.

"It would also allow the wearer to track Hannah through a neighborhood. You would be able to see her footprints glowing like a neon sign in the desert. That's how they took her so easily. That's part of the reason why these guys are so good. They have a technological advantage."

Pulling on the mask, Jack instantly could see an entirely new world superimposed on the viewports covering his eyes. Turning toward the woods, he could see the scout still gathering branches, the man's body heat glowing like a searchlight on a dark night. "Smoke, fog, darkness… none of it would matter to the guy wearing this thing," the commander mumbled.

Jack's attention then returned to the body at his feet. Reaching down, he pulled open the victim's heavy coat. Again, the same emblem was embroidered on the dead man's chest. *Both guys wearing the same looted shirt? That's a stretch,* he thought. Knowing that was far too great a coincidence, Jack had to consider other possibilities. "Maybe the Zombies are firefighters?" Jack muttered. "That's hard to believe. Why would they be so hostile and unapproachable? Maybe some gang just looted a firehouse and found this gear?"

Like the average person, Jack had always considered firefighters as trustworthy men and women who served their communities and risked their lives to help others. "First responders?" he grunted. "I just can't believe it."

Removing the sophisticated mask, Jack's attention was drawn by the returning scout, bringing materials for the homemade stretcher. Quickly, the two men salvaged rifle slings and began to weave a web of saplings and nylon that would support Deiter's body. All the electric bikes were equipped with makeshift tow rings, and within twenty minutes, the field gurney was hooked to the motorcycle. The patient would have a bumpy ride, but given the alternative, the commander was sure he wouldn't mind.

"What are you going to do?" the scout asked as he prepared to rush Deiter back to the airport.

"I'm going to follow the Zombies into Zombieland… or what is it you guys call it? The Forbidden Zone," the commander replied. "I think Hannah is still alive, and even if I'm wrong about that, I still want to know more about these asshats."

"They'll kill you, too, Jack," the scout predicted. "The Horns kill everybody."

Shrugging, Jack said, "It's been tried before. Now get Deiter back to medical care. I'll see you at the airport's gate in a day or two."

"Wait!" Deiter grunted from the stretcher. "Commander, a word please?"

Jack stepped to the wounded man and took a knee.

"Your wife. Her name is Mylie, right?" Deiter began. "You have two beautiful girls, too?"

"How in the hell did you know that?" Jack spat, his face moving closer to the injured man as his head began to spin.

"I went to high school with Mylie. A few months before the collapse, I went home to visit a friend in Fredericksburg and ran into her on the sidewalk. She told me she was staying at her father's ranch for a while."

231

Stunned and confused by Deiter's words, Jack just hovered, his lips moving but no words coming out. Finally, he managed, "Why didn't you say something, Deiter? Why the big secret?"

A slight smile crossed Deiter's lips, "She was always the prettiest girl in school, Jack. I always had a huge crush on her. I went out the ranch the next weekend, and we sat on the porch swing and talked for two hours. She told me that we could see each other after her divorce was finalized, but not before."

"And?" Jack barked. "Was that the last time you saw her?"

"No," Deiter confessed. "After Yellowstone blew, I bribed one of the scouts to take me out to the ranch. Her father was real sick from breathing the ash. She said she expected him to pass away any minute. She was packing up to leave. She said something about a cousin in Galveston. That was the last time I saw her."

Reaching to grab Deiter by the shoulders, it was all Jack could do to restrain himself and not try to shake more information out of the seriously injured man. "She didn't say anything else? That's it? You just let her go off on her own?"

"Her cousin was supposedly coming to get her, had some sort of electric car. Plus, I couldn't be gone too long, or Bascom would know I'd left without permission. One way or the other, she had no intention of returning to the airport with me, so I left her to finish packing. That's all I know. I hope you find her, Jack. I hope you can make her happy again."

A bolt of pain shot through Deiter's frame just then, the wounded man groaning in discomfort. Realizing he wasn't going to get any more information, Jack motioned for the scout to take off.

Without another word, the rider twisted the throttle and was rolling. Jack watched the two men leave, his mind reeling from what he'd just been told. Galveston? Jack knew Mylie's parents both came from large families, many of her relatives spread across much of Texas and the Gulf Coast. For several seconds, the commander tried to remember any mention of the island city. Nothing came to mind.

Shaking his head to regroup, Jack forced himself back to the present. He was, after all, standing alone in Forbidden Horn-Zombie Land, exposed, and without his bicycle.

That realization caused the commander to turn until he was staring at the first scout's wrecked motorcycle. It was on lying on its side, not far away. "I wonder…" he mumbled, jogging toward the machine.

The paint was badly scratched, two spokes dangling from the front rim. Other than that minor damage, the electric two-wheeler looked to be in workable condition.

With his pack on his back and his carbine across the handlebars, Jack twisted the throttle and was nearly thrown off the back of the accelerating machine. "Damn! This thing is fast!" he gleefully proclaimed after recovering his balance and wits.

It had been years since Jack had ridden a motorcycle, but it quickly came back. "I got to get me one of these," he grinned as he rolled down the pavement to the point where the highwaymen had retreated off into the woods.

For a moment, Jack considered his options. Mylie might be in Galveston, probably 300 miles away. The electric horse between his legs wouldn't make it that far, but it sure could eat up a lot of the distance. He could walk the rest of the way.

Recalling Deiter's words, the commander then considered another possibility. Was the local security man lying? Did he have some hidden agenda? Was he pissed because Jack had made the right call concerning the ambush? Could he be spinning a tale just to get rid of the competition?

"How did he know about Mylie and the girls?" Jack considered. "How did he know their names? I never mentioned any details in the airport. I don't have anything in my saddlebags with their names on it."

Hannah had stated that Captain Bascom thrived on information. "He thinks knowledge will be what saves us. As a scout, I was always looking for reference guides, phone books, listings, and directories. He even sent me to retrieve the logs from the local bus station on one excursion," she had claimed. "Said it might be important to know who had taken a Greyhound out of Austin in the days following the eruption."

Forcing the paranoia out of his head, Jack returned to the task at hand. "Galveston will have to wait. If Mylie has endured this long, a few more days won't matter."

It was easy to pick up the ambushers' trail. Flush with victory and convinced of their superiority in both numbers and firepower, they were doing nothing to hide their tracks.

Given the electric bike's silent mode of operation, Jack wasn't worried about being detected, at least not from any noise he might be making.

It then dawned on the commander that the infrared mask he'd scavenged had nearly a full charge. That meant that somebody, probably at a fire station, had electricity. It would take special equipment to top off that unit's batteries. That fact, combined with the emblem on the fireman's shirts, gave Jack an idea.

Instead of following the firemen through the woods, Jack turned left, following along the freeway. Rolling up to the next exit, he spied a truck stop along the feeder road.

Phone booths had virtually disappeared across the American landscape, a huge percentage of the population now utilizing wireless communications. Many truckers, however, were still old school. "Maybe Bascom isn't so eccentric after all," the commander grunted. "Maybe phone books are our salvation."

The truck stop had been thoroughly looted, the interior looking like a hurricane had been turned loose inside. Jack wasn't here to look for snack food or valuables. He wanted information.

Stepping gingerly over the overturned shelving and broken glass, he spied a sign dangling from the ceiling. "Showers and Restrooms."

There, mounted on the wall, was a row of old-fashioned pay phones. Hanging from each by a thin, steel cable was a phone book.

Jack had seen the number "2" embroidered on both of the shirts as part of the Austin Fire Department's logo. Turning the pages quickly, he found the listing for city's fire stations.

Frowning, Jack realized that the number "2" might refer to either a station or battalion. Glancing around at the destroyed interior, he then headed for the front counter where the cash register had once rested.

Kicking aside a lottery ticket dispenser and empty beef jerky display, Jack found several folding maps under the debris. The first one was a geographical depiction of the state of Texas… the second another a map of the southwestern United States. The last provided a detailed, street by street diagram of the city of Austin.

Triumphally snatching up the map, Jack returned to the phone book. Along the way, he passed by a small display of ink pens and grabbed a sharpie.

It took the commander five minutes to mark the location of every firehouse in the book. After all, Austin was a big town.

Once that task had been completed, he was squinting with concentration as he tried to recall the map on Bascom's office wall. The captain had marked the Forbidden Zone with his pushpins and highlighters. While there was no way Jack could remember the exact boundaries, he did have a general idea of where the firemen were operating.

Finally, Jack identified his own location on the map. The ambush had occurred a short distance down the freeway. He knew the general direction the firemen were traveling.

Studying the map, the commander exhaled. There were only three fire stations that would qualify as a headquarters for the ambushers. One of them was listed in the books as "Station No. 9, Second Battalion Administration Offices."

"That's where they're going," Jack concluded.

He then took another few minutes to study the map. With the electric bike, he could easily get out in front of the triumphant ambushers. He would extract a little payback, and perhaps learn where Hannah was being held.

Rushing outside, Jack mounted the motorcycle and zipped away, whizzing down the freeway for another mile. He exited, took a right, and sped through a series of empty streets.

He approached a shopping mall and slowed, the wide, expansive parking lot and broad streets the perfect setup. Quickly circling the facility, Jack found a semi-trailer at one of the anchor store's loading docks. A moment later, he was scampering up its side. From the top of the semi, Jack could access the mall's flat roof. With rifle in hand, the commander rushed for the southern end of the building, praying he wasn't too late.

He walked along the edge and picked the best vantage point available. From his elevated perch, Jack could watch not only the parking lot, but also two intersecting streets. "The Zombies should be strolling this way. I only need to catch them out in the open for a few seconds."

Diligently dedicated to reducing the enemy, Jack sat and kept his vigil for what seemed an eternity. Right and left he scanned with his magnified optic, trying to detect any sign of movement or human forms. "Am I too late?" he grumbled after seeing nothing but a desolate, empty urban landscape. "Did they take another route? Are they moving faster than I thought?"

A minute later, relief flooded the commander's stiff body, and his mood lightened. At the perimeter of the parking lot, just beyond a fast food restaurant's drive-up menu board, Jack spotted movement.

A man appeared there, holding a rifle as he swaggered across the pavement. A few seconds later, a column of men followed.

Jack immediately recognized the Horny horde that had executed the ambush.

Jack estimated that they were 600 yards away. "Too far for me," he grimaced, wishing for the Nth time that he had been more interested in firearms and marksmanship as a youth.

Worse yet, it appeared as if the firemen were taking a path that wouldn't bring them any closer to his position.

Turning to scan the expansive roof, Jack decided that he might have a chance if he darted to the north side of the mall. "Depending on where they go," he hissed, "that might work."

Running bent at the waist to reduce his silhouette, Jack hustled for the opposite end of the shopping complex. Finally arriving at the spot closest to the column's expected route, he carefully raised his rifle to the end of the roof's metal drip edge and waited.

With a single point man out front, the firemen continued their stroll along the edge of the mall's parking lot at a casual clip. "You're in your own territory," Jack whispered, observing the targets through his optic. "Why should you be worried? You just pulled off a major victory."

When the Zombie convoy had advanced as close to his position as they would get, Jack flipped off his carbine's safety and then elevated his crosshairs to the very top of a target's head. He knew his bullet would drop, the distance about four football fields away. What he couldn't calculate was exactly how much his shot would fall.

Even if he were wrong, he should still hit flesh and bone. Jack didn't care about killing. In fact, he knew enough about small unit tactics to understand that wounding one of the enemy was actually a more effective strategy. "The others will have to help their injured comrade. It will slow them down, cause morale to plummet, and consume resources," he whispered.

He next flicked the M4's fire selector to full automatic. Wounding more than one of the Zombies would really ruin their day. With his crosshairs centered on a short man at the center of the convoy, Jack pulled the trigger.

The M4 pushed against his shoulder as it made a buzz-saw sound. At least six rounds left the barrel with the burst, a parade of brass arching through the air as the lead streamed toward the target.

Adjusting for the barrel rise, Jack then loosed a second volley while the men below scattered for cover.

He didn't wait to see how much damage his attack had caused. He wasn't here to win a battle or defeat a larger force. Ducking low and crawling away from the edge, Jack hoped he could gain some distance before the men down there could figure out where the shots had come from.

Keeping his head down, Jack darted across the roof at top speed, making a beeline for the loading dock. Jumping on the semi-trailer's roof, he was scrambling down the access rungs, hitting the earth a few seconds later.

Without looking back, Jack leaped onto the motorcycle and cranked the throttle.

Keeping the massive mall between himself and the ambushed Horns, he sped across the parking lot and then started zigzagging through an area of upscale homes and stores. After three minutes, Jack slowed the bike and then rolled to a stop.

Both adrenaline and the rush of success surged through Jack's veins. He had no idea if he had hit any of his targets, but he was sure that the men back there didn't appreciate being sniped on their own turf. "They'll be more cautious now," Jack whispered, pulling out the city map from his pocket. "The next chapter won't be so easy."

Chapter 49

Her cell was a repurposed storage closet. There was no bed, pillow, chair, or blanket. The guard had slid in a five-gallon bucket and ordered, "Don't piss on the floor, or I'll kick the shit out of you," and then slammed the door. It was cold, dark, and terrifying.

Hannah had no idea how long she sat in the corner. Only a small slit of light, seeping in from a crack under the door, illuminated the interior. Occasionally she could hear footsteps walking by. Once there had been the distant tones of a human voice. That was the extent of her sensory perception.

Alone and undistracted, her mind automatically shifted to torture and death. At first, she cried out of self-pity. Later, anger began to take over. She had never been so distraught, had never experienced anything like the emotions that seemed to be tearing her mind apart from the inside.

By the time she heard a key being inserted in the lock, Hannah had reached a place where she would welcome torture, a beating, rape, or anything else they might throw at her. As long as there was human interaction, something to distract her from her own thoughts.

Light flooded the room, Hannah having to squint from the sudden brightness. It was a different man standing in the doorway this time, but she didn't care. "Stand up," the guard growled. "You're going to be put to work."

She didn't understand, but that didn't matter. Hannah's self-defense mechanisms were far, far beyond worrying about her own personal safety. She only wanted the isolation of solitary confinement to end. Nothing could be worse for her.

She walked out of the closet blinking and confused. The plain, undecorated hallway beyond her closet-prison launched a rush of joy that immediately bolstered her spirit. Freedom! A space larger than a coffin! Light!

"Walk," the guard ordered, pointing down the corridor. "And don't even think about getting cute."

Doing as ordered, Hannah began taking the first of several tentative strides. She had just regained her full motor skills when the two approached a staircase. "Up," the less-than-verbose sentry commanded.

They climbed two flights of stairs and entered another hall via the emergency fire door and its push-bar latch. From there, Hannah was led to a large room that contained all kinds of exercise equipment.

There, along the far wall, sat a row of stationary bicycles. All but one of them was occupied, the gym rats pedaling hard. The sentry pointed toward the empty machine. "Ride," he scowled.

"You want me to get in a workout?" Hannah questioned, still not comprehending what was being asked of her.

"No, I want you to pedal your legs off. Those bikes aren't for shaving pounds off your ass. They generate our electricity," the guard replied.

Glancing at the row of sweaty riders, Hanna noticed that each stationary had an extra set of wires running to a large electronic control panel. With a shrug, she moved toward the open bike. A minute later, she was pedaling at a steady clip.

For fifteen minutes, the prisoner performed her hard labor. In reality, the exercise and human presence was more than welcome. "People pay good money for gym memberships, but I even have my own personal trainer here for free. No doubt I'll be able to outpace Jack after a few weeks of this."

A teenage boy appeared, carrying a bucket and several coffee cups on a string. One by one, he moved down the row of riders offering each a drink of water. Hannah, now parched, accepted.

Stepping off her machine like she'd seen the other human-generators do, she took a quick sip and then asked the waterer about the bikes. "How did you guys come up with this clever idea?" she inquired.

"There was a fitness center at the university that installed these generator bikes a few years ago. All the college students loved the idea of converting their exercise into kilowatts and helping the environment. When the electricity went out, the firefighters needed a way to recharge their lights and breathing systems. One of the guys did his workouts there, so we scavenged the equipment and hooked them up to every car battery we could salvage. That has helped keep us alive."

"Very ingenious," Hannah cooed to the youngster. "Can I have some more water?"

"No. I'm sorry, but everyone is only allowed one cup."

"Oh? Is there a shortage of water around here?"

"We have to filter the river water through carbon and other stuff," the lad began to answer. "That takes a lot of time and manpower, and sometimes we run short."

The sentry appeared at that moment, scowling at the water boy. "She doesn't need to have her questions answered. Move on."

"Sure enough," he replied, lifting the bucket, and taking the cup out of Hannah's hands.

Once he was out of earshot, the sentry turned to Hannah and said, "Get back on the bike. You put in another half hour of hard work, and you'll be fed and then returned to the holding cell."

Shaking her head in protest, Hannah offered, "I'd prefer to earn my keep and stay here. I can ride that bike for hours."

"We'll see," grunted the muscular watchman.

Returning to the generator's seat, Hannah began pushing the pedals and studying the other members of the turbine gym. After glancing up and down the line of stationary units, she thought, *They're just like us. I could be in the airport right now. Other than these crazy bikes, I wouldn't be able to tell any difference.*

There were people from all age groups, races, shapes, and sizes. All of them were thin, but not malnourished. A friendly-looking lady at the end smiled when she caught Hannah throwing a glance her way. The twenty-something young man one bike over couldn't seem to stop staring at her chest.

"What did you expect?" Hannah said under her breath. "Monsters? Boogeymen? Lions, tigers, and bears?"

It occurred to her that, less than a year ago, the dreaded occupants of the Forbidden Zone had been her next-door neighbors out mowing their lawns… or the customers who bought groceries in the same store that she frequented… or the thrill seekers watching the latest horror flick in the seat next to hers. They were her fellow citizens that she had run into every day… the same chatty woman standing in line at the checkout counter… the millennial who never could decide between regular and decaf at the coffee shop… the guy honking at the rude driver one lane over.

"Nothing has changed," she whispered. "So why are we killing each other?"

Her thoughts then returned to her visit to the principal's office and the subsequent discussion with Chief Woods. A shudder traveled down her spine as she recalled the hatred in his eyes. *I need to get him and his henchmen inside the airport,* she thought. *He needs to have the exact same experience I am having at this very moment. Maybe then, peace could gain momentum.*

With her legs pumping hard, Hannah's mind started conjuring up images of Woods meeting Bascom for the first time. The two men would smile, but it would be forced. They would shake hands, but it wouldn't be friendly. They would sit at a table and calmly discuss their differences and grievances.

Her mind-movie was so ridiculous, the images caused Hannah to let out a short burst of laughter before she quickly covered her mouth in embarrassment. There was no way that was going to happen. Bascom would never tolerate letting anyone from the Forbidden Zone into the terminal. He would die before allowing such a thing.

"What's so funny?" growled the nearby sentry. "What's going on?"

"Sorry," Hannah replied. "I was just thinking about something amusing. There's nothing going on."

The guard checked her out, his eyes moving from toe to forehead as Hannah continued to pedal away. He then glanced at the bike's control panel, which displayed several statistics about how fast and far she had ridden.

"You're slacking off. If you want to stay out of that cell, I'd suggest you give it a little more effort," he threatened.

Nodding her agreement, Hannah increased her pace slightly. She had no idea what was expected, but the thought of being thrown back in that dark broom closet gave her a burst of extra energy.

Her legs settling into the increased rhythm, her mind returned to the daydream that had led to the outburst. "It will never happen," she whispered. "Both Bascom and Woods are filled with too much hatred and distrust. What a shame."

She had to admit that she wouldn't want to be the one who suggested allowing the Forbidden Zone leader into the terminal building. She knew the captain well enough to predict his reaction, and it wouldn't be pretty.

She was perspiring heavily when the sentry glanced at his watch and said, "Stop. It's time to eat."

The Horn took her through a different door, pausing by the ladies' locker room. "Inside you'll find three tubs of water. One is to wash with; the second is to rinse your body; the third is to rinse your clothes. Do not drink any of that water. It is unfiltered and full of glass. Take something that fits from the shelf. Don't be picky. Wash your outfit and hang it on the line. You have three minutes, and then I'm coming in there and, dragging you out, clothed or not. Understand?"

Nodding, Hannah stepped into the locker room.

Just as the thug had described, three large tubs made of corrugated tin lined one wall. She recognized them as livestock watering troughs. One was full of cold, soapy water. The next topped off with clear, clean liquid. The third, just as the guard had stated, was full of murky fluid that smelled like laundry detergent.

Shucking off her clothes, she tossed them into the wash tub. Next, she found a pile of washcloths and rags on a shelf. The soft liquid felt good against her skin, despite being chilly. The sparse amount of water reserved for the rinse made it hit or miss, but better than nothing. It had been a while since she'd bathed. She thought about dipping her hair into the tank, but then reconsidered. There wasn't time. She didn't have a brush or comb. The provided towels were only rags.

Being tall for a lady, she had trouble finding anything that fit. While there were several boxes of folded articles present, she couldn't figure out any order or how the sizes had been sorted. "This looks like somebody raided a second-hand store," she whispered.

A pair of denim overalls caught her eye because they just might cover her ankles. Adding a cotton T-shirt to her attire, she couldn't help but feel she looked like a farmer. "Sheng would think I was ready to start digging in the fields," she said, catching a glance of her form in the mirror.

With a clean pair of socks and her boots back on her feet, Hannah rushed out the locker room to find the guard impatiently staring at his watch. "That took too long. The next time… if there is a next time… you'd better not be late, or I will cut your rations in half."

They continued toward the cafeteria, passing by several occupied rooms. A dozen questions popped into her mind as the tour continued. "How do you keep the ash out of this building?" she asked at one point.

"None of your business," he gruffly responded.

"How many people are here?" she tried again.

"Shut your mouth and walk," the guard ordered.

Finally, they approached the lunchroom. Just like the ash controls in place at the airport, a small box of rags sat next to the heavy, sliding glass doors. "We have to wear a mask in here," the Horn announced.

Wrapping a dishtowel around her face, Hannah was escorted inside the large room. It was immediately evident why a nose-filter was necessary here.

One window against a far wall had been punched out, a homemade chimney made of sheet metal now occupying that space. Under the makeshift exhaust hood, two BBQ grills were producing a steady stream of smoke. Even through her mask, Hannah detected the heavy odor of cooking fires. The walls about the grills were dark with soot.

She was led to a table in the corner, her fellow occupants casting suspicious glances at the new diner and her escort. Once she was seated next to her captor, a woman delivered two bowls of a greasy-looking soup.

"Not the hobo stew again?" the sentry complained.

"We're doing the best we can with what we have. Do you want me to give your rations to somebody else? There are plenty of hungry mouths around here to feed," the server countered.

Shaking his head, the watchman dug in. Hannah, realizing that she hadn't eaten in nearly two days, followed suit. The stew wasn't terrible but was far from a gourmet dish.

As she gingerly shoveled hot spoons of the gruel into her mouth, Hannah spent her chewing time studying her cafeteria patrons.

Just as she had seen in the fitness center, she noted what would have been a typical cross-section of any American city population. An older couple ate in silence at the next table, their masks leaving just enough of their eyes exposed to show deep wrinkles of age and stress. Both seemed healthy enough, however, the woman pointing at her mate and making an unheard joke that caused him to laugh.

245

Across the room, a young mother sat, trying to keep her two toddlers from pulling off their lung filters. It was difficult enough for Hannah to eat while moving aside the cloth for every bite. She couldn't imagine how badly a child would struggle with the safety routine.

Hannah wanted to strike up a conversation with her guard, felt a strong urge to let him know that if their roles were reversed, they would be sitting in the airport's food court, surrounded by a nearly identical crowd.

When the sentry grumbled about the smaller portions, she almost broke her silence again. "We're running out of food, too," she wanted to say, but held her tongue. That information could be used against her community. It was strategic. It was top secret.

You're still thinking of them as the enemy, she realized, swallowing one last spoonful of stew. *They're no different than us. We're all Americans. We're all Texans. Why are we having a civil war?*

While she wasn't much of a history buff, Hannah knew enough about the American Civil War to draw several parallels. That conflict had pitted brother against brother. Only total defeat, defined by the obliteration of large swaths of the lands below the Mason-Dixon line, had ended that war. Even decades later, there were still hard feelings between the northern United States and the Deep South.

Only a few months before Yellowstone's blowout, Hannah had been watching a newscast about statues of Civil War heroes being dismantled in several southern cities. Like so many things before the eruption, those squabbles seemed so petty and dividing now.

Shoving the empty bowl away, Hannah couldn't help but feel downcast. As far as she was concerned, the conflict between the firemen and the airport survivors made no sense to her at all; people should be working together toward a full recovery instead. Considering the stupidity and the waste of it all made her head ache. However, she only had to look at the War Between the

States as proof that her fellow Texans shared a tradition of violent and short-sided behavior.

We'll both do anything to win, because we're both convinced that fighting is the only way to survive, she surmised. *How sad. How very, very tragic for all of us.*

It then occurred to Hannah that she was as guilty as anybody. She had defended the airport's main gate, firing her AR15 multiple times to keep the mob at bay. She had scavenged supplies as a scout, unaware and uncaring about any others who might be in the area. She had pulled Sheng from his home, killed some of the miners, and worse.

"There is plenty of guilt to go around," she muttered under her breath.

Jack had heard naval aviators tout the adage, "Speed is life," with regard to aerial combat. After his ambush at the mall and subsequent escape on the electric bike, he now had a deeper understanding of that saying.

Being so much faster than your adversary provided several distinct advantages, not the least of which was to implement a hit-and-run strategy. Jack was far outnumbered and outgunned, so any direct, force-on-force engagement was out of the question.

What he could do is whittle them down – peel the skin off the Horn's onion one layer at a time.

The only countering tactics available to the men on the trail was to set a trap or avoid contact. In the ash, hiding from Jack was going to be difficult. He planned to make it extremely difficult for the pokey turtles to snare the much quicker hare.

Circling around, the commander couldn't help but feel a sense of accomplishment. So much had happened this day, and he still had over an hour of daylight left.

For the first time since docking in San Diego, he had evidence that Mylie had indeed gone to her family's ranch. While he had

247

assumed as much before embarking on a cross-country tour of hell, his wife's location had never been a certainty. "Congratulations, Commander. At least you didn't travel all this way to find out she'd stayed in Virginia," he grunted.

Forcing his mind to concentrate on the convoy of Zombies, Jack piloted the bike back toward the west. He had laid in wait for them before; this time, he was going to hit them from the rear.

Picking up the path of the Horns was easy. That many men didn't move without leaving undeniable signs.

He followed their passing to the location where his attack had occurred. Here, the trail got sloppy, no doubt a symptom of raining bullets that scattered their single-file column. Jack noted two bloody spots in the ash. He had hit at least one man. There was no telling how badly.

From this point forward, Jack knew he had to be cautious. He had wounded the beast, and that tended to bring out either the best, or worst, behavior in men. The commander assumed he was dealing with intelligent, experienced enemies. He was not going to underestimate them.

They had used a rearguard before. They had managed to track Hannah and most likely had captured her alive. They had executed a very effective ambush against an alert team of men. They were not fools.

Cutting two blocks left on his silent machine, Jack glanced at his watch. "The average person walks between 3.5 and 4.0 miles per hour," he whispered. "They have a wounded party and must advance with some level of caution. That means they are probably about a mile up the road, give or take."

Taking the bike up to 60 miles per hour, Jack traveled one and a half miles just to be sure. He knew their path, had a good idea of their destination. His next move wasn't going to be easy, but it was definitely logistically achievable.

His top priority was to find a location to hide with the bike. The firemen weren't the only ones leaving a trail, and the motorbike's tires were unmistakable. If his prey happened across his tracks, the gig would be over before it ever began.

His map showed a city park up ahead. If he was guessing correctly, the column of ambushers would pass along its northern edge.

He cut a wide swath around the park, approaching on the opposite side from where he estimated the firemen would cross. There was a baseball diamond ahead, complete with bleachers, dugouts, and a bullpen. The home run fence was about waist high on the commander.

Pulling the motorcycle to a stop behind the home team's dugout, Jack noticed the concession stand behind home plate. The door had been broken open, hanging by one hinge at an odd angle. A hot dog machine partially blocked the doorway, and a sleeve of crushed paper cups laid on the stoop.

Dismounting quickly, Jack jogged to the opening and marveled at the chaos inside. "Somebody wanted a footlong and a beer pretty badly," he quipped.

The interior was covered with a carpet of stampeded paper plates, popcorn bags, and plastic spoons. "The bike will fit," he estimated.

Hustling back to his electric chariot, Jack pushed the heavy machine inside the concession stand and then executed a three-point turn within the crowded space. His escape vehicle was ready – just in case the anticipated ballgame became a red-hot affair.

Jack's first instinct was to climb the bleachers. He quickly dismissed that option because he had hit the convoy from above at the mall. If he were walking in the other guys' shoes, his eyes would be working overtime, but especially focused on every elevated vantage.

Instead, the commander studied the dugout's slightly-pitched roof. It wasn't overly high but would provide enough angle to see the entire park.

The ash was thin here, a ridge of dead, blown leaves having been caught by the wire backstop that ran behind the plate and batter's boxes. That barrier, originally designed to protect the crowd from foul balls, served as an accidental snow fence for the pumice, catching the grey grit on the other side.

Using the crunchy pathway between the concession stand and the dugout, Jack swung his carbine's sling to his back and pulled himself onto the visitors' roof. He stayed low, crawling across the tin until he reached the far side.

It wasn't perfect, but as far as he was concerned, it was the best cover available. There, he waited, hoping the Horns would arrive before darkness complicated his plan.

On a whim, Jack found the infrared mask in his pack and pulled it on. Barely lifting his head, he scanned the park looking for heat signatures or other signs of human activity. The press of a button illuminated a different world.

His vision was filled with a palette of reds, blacks, and whites. Using the control panel just behind his right ear, the commander started pressing buttons until the display read, "White = Hot."

The technology wasn't as advanced as the FLIR system on *Utah*'s periscope mast but was still quite impressive. Given a world of low sunlight, cold temperatures, and a lack of vegetation, most of what Jack saw was the darker background of a lifeless void. There was still enough thermal difference to discern the outline of the dead trees, unheated homes, and other inanimate objects, but not the brightness of life. It reminded the commander of black and white television and made him sad.

As Jack scanned the park's perimeter, a small spot of white popped into his field of vision. It was underneath a car parked along the closest street. "Is that a rat? A cat? What the hell?" he grunted, now intrigued.

The object didn't move, just far enough away that Jack couldn't make out any details.

Still, it was the only hot signature in the area.

A minute later, Jack spotted another similarly-sized point of heat. The second example was also low to the ground, two blocks over and on another avenue that led to the park. "Let me guess. The cockroaches couldn't survive this apocalypse, but the chihuahuas did?" he wondered out loud.

When Jack's gaze returned to the first hot spot, he inhaled sharply. Whatever had generated the heat was gone. Nothing but cold ash and metal registered in the mask.

"Did this damn thing get broken during the ambush?" Jack wondered, tempted to pull the mask off his face and trust his own eyes. Just as he was reaching for the chin strap, the first area of brightness reappeared – this time about fifty feet closer than before. It was a man's boot, the owner hiding behind the wheel well of a minivan.

Jack could see all of them less than a minute later, three men walking point, spread out like the tips of a pitchfork. They were moving with extreme caution, hustling from tree to porch to automobile and then staying put while the area ahead was searched. Whoever was in charge of the Zombie fire brigade wasn't taking any chances.

The problem was, they were headed straight for Jack.

Either the commander had miscalculated the enemy's course, or they had changed their direction. It didn't matter. Jack had about two minutes before they would be on him.

Assuming the firemen were wearing the same thermal imager as the one he had scavenged, Jack looked around for a good place to hide. There wasn't any cover for a hundred yards in any direction.

The commander had hit them from the front before, and just as he had anticipated, they had reacted. This time, his plan had been to let them pass and then strike from behind. That strategy was obviously backfiring. If they pinned him down on this baseball field, even the top speed of the electric bike wouldn't bail him out.

Keeping low, Jack back-crawled to the edge of the tin, doing his best stay off the horizon. Dropping off the roof of the dugout, the commander immediately started looking for cover… anyplace to hide.

His first instinct was to push the motorcycle out of the snack shed and zoom away. Scanning that escape route, Jack realized that wasn't going to work. The entire baseball diamond was surrounded by a chain-link fence, the nearest opening far down the left field line. That route would take him directly at the approaching point man. Even if he managed to escape that guy's bullets, there was a parking lot just beyond, at least a football field in width. It would be like shooting fish in a barrel, and he would be the guppy. They would cut him to shreds before the bike even reached half-speed.

Besides, Jack wanted to keep the Zombies guessing. Even if he raced away and managed to dodge what was sure to be a maelstrom of bullets, he wanted to remain anonymous. He wanted the Horns to keep wondering who was picking them off. It would deplete their morale and multiply the effectiveness of his attacks.

He spied a banner hanging from the backstop, the plastic sign announcing, "Little League Tryouts This Saturday!" An idea popped into Jack's head as he pulled his knife. It was a huge risk, but he didn't see any other option.

Cutting down the banner, Jack placed the heavy hot dog machine on one end, then proceeded along the track back and forth, wearing the long sheet of plastic like a superhero's cape. A quick glance over his shoulder confirmed that his tracks in the ash were at least being disguised. "It won't pass a close examination, but at least it isn't obvious I've been stomping around back here," he mumbled.

He then burrowed into the heap of leaves, praying the dead foliage would obscure enough of his body heat to leave him undetected by the mask-wearing scouts. As a final precaution, Jack pulled the banner over his pile, threw two more handfuls of leaves over the plastic sheet, and waited.

It seemed like an hour to Jack, but he supposed less than a minute passed. Peeking out through a narrow slit, the commander spied the first Horn's head appear over the left field fence. The Zombie was cautious, peering right and left through the insect-like mask covering his head.

Jack's heart began racing faster when his antagonist appeared again, this time moving directly down the left field foul line. He was running across the exposed space, looking like an outfielder who was heading to the dugout after making the last out of the inning. "Instead of a glove, this guy's carrying an AR15," Jack whispered from beneath the leaves.

The point man then paused beside the bleachers, his head pivoting right, then left, then back again as he made sure no threat existed in the parking lot or the wooded area beyond.

He mounted the bleachers, the heavy footsteps sending a resounding thud across the diamond as he thumped his way to the top. There, with an elevated vantage, the scout stopped and swept the area with his thermal mask.

When his head started turning Jack's way, the commander closed the slit. He had detected this guy's boot from clear across the park using the thermal technology. Even the tiniest heat signature would make the Horn suspicious, and that would result in several bullets cavitating his organs.

Lying in the dark, completely unaware of what was going on around him, Jack waited. He wanted to hear the scout's boots thumping down the bleachers and then running past. The silence out there was maddening.

It was all Jack could do to keep from jumping up and sending a wild, desperate spray of hot lead in all directions. Despite only a few seconds having passed, his mind was already playing tricks on him. He had visions of a scout staring down at the clear thermal image of Jack's body lying in the leaves. Then the point man would wait patiently while the rest of the Zombies surrounded the trapped animal. The guy would snicker inside his praying mantis mask, wondering how anybody so stupid could have survived so long. A signal would be given when they were all in position, and then a dozen weapons would pour a relentless torrent of lead into the commander's prone body. "That will teach you to ambush us, asshole!" they would laugh.

Jack decided that he couldn't stand it any longer. He had to take a chance and peek outside. He had to know what his opponents were doing.

As he slowly moved his hand to make an opening in the leaves, the commander heard the first descending footfall on the bleachers. "Damn," Jack exhaled. "That was close."

After dismounting from the metal stands, the commander heard the scout running away. Now more secure, Jack spread the decaying foliage just in time to see the masked man running across the pitcher's mound, hustling to catch up with his group. He crossed to first base and then continued trotting toward the outfield. A few seconds later, he disappeared beyond the homerun fence.

Knowing that the main body of the Zombie column wouldn't be far behind, Jack crawled out from under his blanket of leaves and scurried to follow the scout. Even if someone saw him now, it would be difficult to tell the commander's masked face from one of their own.

Hustling like a batter who had just laid down a bunt, Jack raced toward first base. He kept on running, reaching the home run fence a short time later. Now breathing hard, he looked for even the smallest gap in the plywood barrier. There it was, a small slit between two of the wooden sheets. Taking a knee, Jack had to pull off the fireman's mask to see through the narrow opening. Just as he had anticipated, a dozen men were entering the far side of the park.

They were walking in a single file, probably no more than 300 yards from the commander's position. Jack had to smile when he noticed that two of his enemy were carrying a stretcher. His aim at the mall had been true.

Jack waited until the convoy was almost past his hide. Then he moved to the very end of the fence, went prone, double-checked that his magazine was fully seated, and then rolled out into foul territory.

It took less than a blink for the commander to zero in on the farthest man. The stretcher bearers were closer and grouped together, but he ignored the easy target. Their weapons were hanging by slings from their backs. They couldn't return fire.

Jack pulled the trigger, his weapon's report echoing loudly across the quiet park.

As fast as he could reacquire, Jack fired into the stunned, bewildered line of men. His third round was just leaving the barrel when the Horns finally recovered the shock of his attack and began diving for the ground, seeking cover, or scurrying away.

Sending five more shots into their screaming, panicked masses, Jack then rolled back behind the fence, scrambled for his feet, and ran like hell for the snack shack.

With the fence between him and the confused firemen, Jack managed home plate before he turned and wasted three more pain pills, firing blindly toward the last known position of his foe. "That will keep you from following too closely," he hissed, racing around the backstop and into the concession stand.

He didn't bother to push the bike out the door. With a burst of the throttle, the bike came flying out the opening, Jack barely managing to keep the soaring machine upright as it began to accelerate away.

For the first hundred yards, he was completely exposed. With his muscles involuntarily tensing as he anticipated sizzling lead impacting his body at any moment, Jack raced down the foul line and through the opening in the fence. A moment later, he was zooming across the parking lot. No return fire came his way.

Once safe on a residential street, Jack rolled to a stop to catch his breath and regather his wits. While he had intended on sniping the ambushers all the way to their station, the last encounter could have gone completely wrong. He began to reevaluate his plan.

The firemen, or whoever they were, weren't going to make it back before darkness fell if they were heading for Station No. 9. With the thermal masks being employed by both sides, Jack believed the odds were still in his favor.

His justification for attacking the Horns was simple enough – the best defense was a strong offense.

Bascom and the airport clan seemed to be scared shitless of the Forbidden Zone, and given the technological advantages of the opposing side, the commander didn't blame them. The Zombies, according to Deiter, were growing bolder with each passing day.

It was time, Jack was convinced, to reverse that trend.

Deiter and his crew had acted more like police officers than infantry during the freeway ambush. Cops always had superiority in numbers. If they got into a fight, they were typically assured that more and more backup was on the way. If they didn't have that numerical advantage, they normally didn't engage until overwhelming force was assured. The rescue team from the airport had been mistaken about the size of its opposition, and most of them had paid the ultimate price for that error.

Jack, being a submariner, had been taught to fight in situations where he was always outnumbered. In the Navy's war colleges, the officers of the Silent Service were schooled in tactics similar to those employed by guerrilla forces on land. Hit and run. Shoot and scoot. Live to fight another day. Kill the enemy via a thousand small cuts.

If Jack's boat encountered an enemy surface force in wartime, chances were that there were multiple ships above. The opponent was typically faster, possessed overwhelming firepower, and had superior maneuverability. Charging in with guns blazing was suicide. Submarines didn't last long in pitched battles. They used stealth, surprise, and maneuver to survive and ultimately achieve victory.

Germany's wolfpacks had wreaked havoc on Allied shipping during the early days of WWII. The US Navy's Pacific submarine force had done the same to the Japanese, sending millions of tons of critical cargo to the bottom of the sea. Submarines were still considered to be one of the most effective weapons ever created. Jack saw no reason why those same tactics wouldn't work in post-apocalyptic Texas.

Yet, he was going to have to be smarter. The baseball diamond had almost been a critical mistake. One he vowed not to repeat.

Sliding the map from his pocket, the commander studied the matrix of streets, parks, interstates, and lakes ahead. He estimated that the firemen still had a good three hours of walking before they arrived at their headquarters, unless Jack could slow them down even more.

Between his current position and downtown Austin, the commander noted the Colorado River as a natural chokepoint. "They'll have to use a bridge to cross. They'll send people on ahead to make sure the route is clear. They'll be on high alert and in defensive positions. I have to hit them before they reach the river." Such a plan represented an extremely risky proposition.

Frustration and doubt began to plague Jack's thoughts. Why was he doing this? He didn't have a dog in this fight. Mylie and his girls, if still alive, were far away from Austin. Every minute he invested here delayed any potential reunion with his family.

Yet, without Hannah, he would still be wandering around the Texas Hill Country, aimlessly trying to pick up any sign of Mylie's trail. How long would it be before he had been murdered, starved to death, or simply gave up? Jack couldn't help but feel a sense of debt to his new friend.

That thought was followed by images of Hannah being tortured, abused, or violated. He felt a special kinship with the woman, despite having only known her for a few days. "She doesn't deserve that," he whispered, his entire frame shuddering at the grim prospect. "She was just like me, trying to save as many lives as she could."

His primary issue with simply heading toward Galveston, however, had nothing to do with any perceived IOU or rescuing a damsel in distress. Just like the caves at Carlsbad, or the cattle at the Cliff House, Jack couldn't help but consider mankind's future and the world his daughters would inherit. The airport was the largest community the commander had encountered. Bascom's trick of using pressurized air had saved more lives than any other situation he'd found. Could it be replicated on a larger scale? If the ash persisted, was living in domed cities or underground structures the only option for humans to survive?

Jack didn't know the answers to those questions. One nagging, reoccurring thought recurring his thoughts – it was going to take a lot of people with a catalog of specialized skills to rebuild society. The survivors at the airport were a critical resource for the species.

He also knew that there was a strong possibility that Mylie had never made it to Galveston Island. Deiter had said his last visit had occurred after the eruption. From everything Jack had learned, anarchy and chaos were already taking hold by that time. Traveling, even the relatively short distance of 300 miles, would have been fraught with peril during those early days. A million things could have detoured Mylie, or worse yet, lead to her demise.

Any journey to Galveston posed its own set of risks and challenges. How would he find his wife and children? He'd never been to the island city but could guess it was a sizable place. "Far too large for one guy to search on a bicycle," Jack whispered to the empty street.

And then there was Hannah… The captain had hesitated far too long about mounting a rescue for his scout. If Jack managed to figure out a way to save Hannah, would Bascom offer to help? In the captain's mind, was the enemy of my enemy a friend?

While Jack had his doubts, he had to admit that the airport crowd was running up quite a debt on the balance sheet of good deeds. The commander had brought Sheng in. He had badly hurt the Forbidden Zone Horns. He would have been responsible for saving Deiter's life, if the ex-cop lived. Would Bascom pay the debt? Would the airport honcho choose to even up the score a little?

In the end, it was Cisco's sense of right and wrong that pointed his motorbike toward the Colorado River. Taking Hannah was wrong. Killing the airport's scouts was felonious. Jack had seen his share of tin pan dictators since the collapse. It was easy to put whoever was running the show at the fire station into the same category. If he and his family were going to have any chance of making a new life in this world of ash and clouds, megalomaniacs were going to have to be put down.

Chapter 50

It was movie night, one of Captain Bascom's favorite events.

Once a week, the unmodified 757 at Gate 21 was turned into a movie theater for the airport's residents. One of the few aircraft that hadn't had its seats removed, the cabin was filled by excited children and adults, all eager to watch a DVD film on the headrests' small screens.

Up until a few weeks ago, small cups of popcorn had been served during the show. That scavenged case of buttered goodness had run out during the spy thriller last month, but no one really seemed to mind.

This week's flick was a space opera that had been released just a short time before Yellowstone erupted. Captain Bascom had rejected the original choice, a tearjerker about a dog who died in a war. "Our people have enough sorrow on their minds. We don't need to make them cry any more than necessary," he explained to the event organizers.

Alex didn't care one iota about the flick. He'd never been a big fan of the cinema. No, what pleased Bascom about the event was the fact that most of the community would be occupied and entertained. He would get a night off from settling minor disputes and listening to petty bickering.

He attended the "opening" of the new release solely for reasons of morale. The people wanted to see their leader confident and relaxed. He needed to show the flag.

After the cabin lights had dimmed and the video began playing, Bascom exited the plane. He'd just stepped into the main terminal when one of Deiter's men made a mad dash toward the improvised movie theatre.

"Sir, one of the scouts has returned. He is carrying a wounded man on his sled," the young man reported.

"Damn it!" Bascom cursed, moving to jog beside the messenger. "Any idea who is hurt?"

"No, sir."

"Has anyone informed the doctor that he's about to get a new patient?"

"Yes, sir."

Rushing to the lower level, the two men stepped into a hectic scene. As Bascom darted to the wounded man's side, his face blanched white. "Oh, no, not Deiter," he mumbled.

A proper stretcher was produced, the unconscious, wounded man lifted gently and then hefted toward the stairs.

Turning to the scout, Bascom's famous temper was on the rise. "What in the hell happened? Where are the other men?" he demanded.

Pulling off his helmet, T.J. Pierce began his report. "The Horns were waiting for us along the freeway. It was nearly a perfect ambush. We followed Hannah's trail to the spot, and they came at us out of nowhere."

"Did that bastard Cisco lead you into the trap?" Bascom snapped, the veins on his forehead beginning to bulge.

Shaking his head, T.J. replied, "No, sir, he actually saved Deiter and me. None of us would have made it out alive if it had not been for the commander's actions."

For a fleeting moment, Bascom seemed disappointed. "How many are left?"

"Commander Cisco is the only other survivor," the scout stated.

"And where is the commander?"

"He was going after the bushwhackers. He said he was going to get a little payback and hopefully find Hannah in the process," T.J. announced.

His face red with fury, Bascom began pacing the luggage area, his mind reeling from the scout's report. Finally regaining his composure, the captain said, "Get cleaned up. Take care of your equipment and then come and find me. You're officially promoted to head of security. We have a lot to talk about."

"Yes, sir," Pierce replied. "Thank you, sir."

"Oh, don't thank me just yet," the ex-fighter jock grumbled. "This is an escalation… an act of war. We are not going to let this go unanswered. I'll be in the infirmary, checking on Deiter."

It was easy to narrow the firemen's route down to three bridges crossing the Colorado River.

He was careful to avoid a direct line of sight with the skyscrapers looming on the horizon. Bascom had reported that his scouts had, in every case, been shot at if they ever ventured close to the Forbidden Zone. Glancing up at Austin's skyline of high-rise buildings, the commander assumed that there were men in those towers with binoculars, radios, and sniper rifles.

Using dead patches of trees, narrow alleys, and the cover of mid-rise buildings along the way slowed Jack's progress. He wasn't worried. After the ballfield encounter, it was going to take the column of Zombies a while to regroup and change their underwear.

After blasting through Austin's city streets, Jack arrived at the banks of the wide, slow-moving river. Here he could see what remained of the bridges now that civilization had fallen. Pulling up to the first crossing, Jack could eliminate it as the Zombies' escape route. An edge-to-edge wall of city busses blocked its entrance, the lanes leading to the barricade jammed with burned out relics of what had once been shiny sports cars resting next to farming pickups and high-occupancy SUVs.

One of the vehicles consumed by the fires had been a gasoline tanker truck, Jack braking to a stop less than fifty feet away from the skeletal remains of the big rig. The inferno from the tanker's fuel had burned completely through the pavement, destroying portions of the bridge's deck, and leaving a gaping hole to the river below. Even if Jack could have navigated passage through the carnage, he wouldn't have trusted the bridge's surface to support his weight.

His assessment narrowed the Horn's escape route down to two possibilities.

The second crossing was almost clear of vehicles but showed no signs of any foot traffic at all. Jack couldn't detect a single print or track, only an undisturbed blanket of ash. *That's odd. I wonder why people aren't using this bridge?* he mused. *Maybe it isn't structurally sound either.* Jack knew that given enough time, he would like to solve the mystery, but time was a luxury that he did not have right now. He had to stay focused on his next objective, so he twisted the throttle and sped away.

The third bridge, just a short distance beyond, displayed a clearly marked trail that had been heavily traveled. Here, the pumice was worn away, a five-foot wide, dark lane of blacktop visible all the way to the opposite side.

He scanned the area, trying to anticipate their approach. He had hit the Horns from the front and the rear so far, both attacks reducing their number. If by chance he had managed to wound one or more at the ballpark, their defensive posture would be degraded even further.

Jack tried to visualize his adversary's predicament. They wanted to get to the safety of their home port. They had wounded men and probably a limited amount of food and water. Their mission had likely been planned as a quick in and out, no need for overnight provisions or gear. During the last two encounters, the commander couldn't recall seeing heavy backpacks or a lot of equipment within their ranks.

It was easy to assume that they were also pissed to the extreme. Jack knew there was nothing more frustrating than not being able to strike back when attacked. They couldn't even be sure who was hunting them or why. If he had been one of the firemen heading back to headquarters, the commander knew he would be spoiling for payback.

They had left the highway ambush in triumph. Sure, the loss of four of their own had been unfortunate, but they had killed nearly twice that number and accomplished their goal. Now those body counts, and the associated victory, were being reversed. "I wouldn't want to be the Horn team leader who had to report today's final results," Jack grinned.

Faced with a coin flip whose outcome he had no way to predict, a deep scowl furrowed the commander's brow. Either the Zombies would be hyper-aggressive and sloppy, or overly cautious and reserved. He had to design a plan that would accommodate both possibilities, and that was going to require some thought.

As he pulled the motorcycle behind a mid-rise apartment building, Jack began a mental roll call of the various tactics he'd been taught. Covering everything from holding attacks to envelopment, the commander quickly dismissed several options. "I can't do a pincer movement or deploy encirclement by myself," he complained.

He then remembered diversion, and a grin threatened to turn up the corners of Cisco's lips. "Just like the old cowboy movies," he grunted. "Works every time."

Throwing a rock to draw a sentry's attention wasn't going to be effective against a large force of paranoid riflemen. Jack needed something a little more creative than a trick born of old horse operas.

He sorted through every example of a diversion he could remember. There was the age-old feint attack, but that required more than one guy doing the dirty work. How would he draw the enemy's attention?

"I need help," Jack concluded. "I need a few more cowboys to shoot at the convoy. Hell, they don't even have to be good marksmen. Just keep their attention long enough so that I can…."

Glancing down at his load vest, Jack eyed one of his spare magazines. A spark shone in the commander's eyes as an idea popped into his head.

Glancing up and down the street, Jack realized that he was in a residential area. A wall of apartment buildings bordered one side of the avenue approaching the river, the other occupied by low-rise office space. What had once been beautiful, mature oak trees separated the paved lanes. There weren't any nearby stores to loot. What about the goodies stored in his pack? The commander began a mental inventory or his kit, and soon, his smile broadened.

Engaging the bike's kickstand, Jack removed his pack and began rummaging through its contents.

Pulling out a roll of duct tape, the commander began to smile in earnest as his plan developed. Before he'd left San Diego, one of *Utah*'s crew had recommended he pack the handy product. "It will burn like a torch. It will patch or fix just about anything. Hell, half the ships in the US Navy wouldn't be at sea without duct tape. Take it along. It doesn't weigh all that much and takes up very little space."

Jack had thrown the roll in his pack and forgotten about it.

The sailor had claimed that it would burn. Stretching out a length about one foot long, Jack glanced at his watch and then flicked his disposable butane lighter, normally used to start campfires, to set the tape ablaze.

Concealed in a pickup's bed, Jack conducted a little science experiment, timing how quickly the tape burned. He was amazed.

It took nearly five minutes for the flames to reach the far end. "I wouldn't want to breathe the fumes," Jack stated, "but it does burn well."

Doing a quick calculation in his head, the commander tore off several inches of the tape while commenting, "I need this to make the fuse. Now for the firecrackers."

Pulling a spare mag from his vest, Jack began thumbing out the cartridges. After each bullet was ejected, he wrapped the base with the tape and then pulled off another few inches of length from the roll.

It took him nearly ten minutes to finish constructing his diversion, a snake-like trail of tape and bullets spread across the truck's tailgate and bed.

Next, he began searching for just the right place to stage his new invention.

His first thought was one of the apartment balconies cascading above his head. Thinking it over, Jack decided against that possibility. It would be difficult to climb up, set the device and then, after lighting the fuse, scramble quickly back down to his bike. That would make the timing more complicated.

At the corner, he noticed a city trash can, the logo of a local bank painted on the side. Moving quickly, Jack removed and upended the bin to dump what little refuse was inside, leaving himself with an empty metal container.

Turning to judge the distance to the river, Jack liked the trashcan's position. It was three blocks to the bridge. Too far for the Zombies to make a break for safety, too close for them to automatically retreat. Even if they did manage to run away from the water, he would be waiting.

He began adhering the tape to the inside of the oversized garbage pail, careful to leave part of the surface unattached so that it would burn evenly. Finally satisfied that his creation had a good chance of success, Jack replaced the bin inside the outer shell. "The trash collectors are going to get a bang out of that," he mumbled.

Jack then positioned his motorcycle for a quick getaway. Now, all that remained was to wait for the Horns to come parading down the avenue leading to the bridge. He would add some fireworks to the festivities. The thermal mask would announce their approach despite the fading light.

He didn't have to wait long.

The sun, or what was left of it, had just set when Jack spotted the first hot spot appear in his mask's thermal projection. Just like before, it was an exposed body part that announced the point man's approach.

Once again, the Horns were deploying one of their number a few blocks in front of the main body. Given the events of the day, Jack assumed that there was now a rearguard, and perhaps even wingmen running parallel to their course.

It was also clear that their leadership had decided that speed was their best defense.

With his prey moving much quicker than before, Jack contemplated the length of his fuse. He had trimmed the tape for a three-minute burn. Was that now too long?

Watching their progress, Cisco did his best to judge the timing of his diversion. If the bullets in the trash can went off too soon, the Zombies would retreat, regroup, and cross at another time, maybe use a different bridge.

If his fake ambush was sprung too late, they would merely charge across the bridge to avoid the kill zone.

With his lighter in hand, Jack waited, pining for one of the ballistic battle computers aboard *Utah* that would plot his firing solution in a nanosecond. Painfully aware of his own limitations, the commander's hand trembled so badly that he had trouble lighting the fuse. After verifying that the tape was burning, he dashed for the e-bike and zoomed away.

He steered south, making sure he gave the approaching column, and any of their scouts, a wide berth. Jack almost crashed into a delivery van while glancing at his watch. At the two-minute mark, he was six blocks behind the Zombies.

Slamming on the brakes, he slid the bike to a stop between a minivan and a tow truck parked at the curb. Dismounting with his weapon and backpack, the commander began jogging toward the targets. While Bascom's scouts might be able to shoot while riding their e-bikes, Jack wanted his boots planted on terra firma when the lead started flying.

Not wanting to run into any rearguard, the commander took cover in the doorway of a dry-cleaning store and waited. At the three-minute mark, he coiled for the first round to cook off, but nothing happened. At three minutes and fifteen seconds, he was beginning to worry that something had gone wrong in the trash can.

Fifteen seconds later, panic was welling up inside his chest. "Did the tape go out? Did it get wet or something? Did one of their guys detect the smoke with a thermal imager?"

He was just about to retreat when a distant boom echoed through the city.

Before Jack could move out of the doorway, another small explosion sounded. By the time he'd taken five steps, a third and fourth detonation rumbled down the street, one on the heels of the other.

Someone up ahead began shouting orders. He could see men running, the nearest Zombie taking cover behind a tree and raising a rifle. Jack rushed forward, using as much cover as possible, bound and determined to hit the Horns from the rear while they were distracted.

The trash can was now giving the Zombies hell, multiple cartridges cooking off in quick succession. Somebody was returning fire, a long burst of muzzle flashes pinpointing the shooter's position. The commander took comfort in the fact that his plan seemed to be working after all.

"Is anybody hit?" an excited voice demanded.

"Where is the bastard?" somebody else shouted.

"I can't see him!" another adversary screamed, followed by several shots ripping holes in the offending garbage can.

Now with three clear targets visible in his infrared display, Jack took cover behind a low retaining wall bordering the street. A fourth man appeared, the guy actually retreating toward Jack's position. The garbage pail was winning!

269

The commander tore into their ranks with gusto, his M4 sending three quick rounds at the farthest tango. Before his last brass was tinkling across the stone wall, he reacquired another Zombie, fired three times, and then repeated.

Realizing that there was a second assaulter behind them sent the Horns into a panic. Jack saw men leave good cover and run, exposing themselves unnecessarily. He made them pay.

It seemed like only a few seconds had passed when his rifle's bolt locked back, the weapon empty. "Thirty rounds already," Jack hissed, slamming home a new box of misery missiles.

After the reload, Jack continued pouring lead into the enemy's ranks, raining havoc on the confused swirling mass of men ahead. Many of the Zombies seemed unable to discern friendly fire from hostile muzzle flashes. Orders were being shouted, mixed with the shrieks of the wounded. Bedlam ruled their ranks.

Rising from his cover, Jack charged forward in search of more tangos.

The street ahead was lined with old oak trees, their trunks blocking his field of fire. He wanted to take out as many of the bastards as he could.

Mercy wasn't even a consideration in Jack's mind. As he ran deeper into their midst, images of the freeway slaughter bounced through his mind's eye. He was giving them exactly what they had delivered to Deiter's men. No quarter. No reserve.

As he neared the first oak, Jack noticed a man step out from his hiding place. Seeing a familiar mask on the commander's face, he said, "Where are they? Can you see them with the thermal?"

With all his strength, Jack launched his rifle's stock at the man's face, delivering a bone-crushing butt-stroke to the victim's forehead and sending him reeling to the ground.

The commander paused for a second, waiting to see if the guy tried to get up. He didn't, so Jack resumed the hunt.

Halfway up the next block, Jack heard a strong voice rising above all the others. "Get across the bridge! Get across the bridge!" he was shouting. "Do it, now!"

Running toward the voice, Jack approached an intersection just a block from the river crossing. Pausing before entering into the open space, the commander spied a tall man wearing a mask identical to his own. The Zombie leader was waving his remaining troops forward, his arm making wide circles in the air as he repeatedly screeched his orders.

Using a utility pole as cover, Jack brought his weapon up and centered the crosshairs on the Horn boss. Just as his finger began pulling on the trigger, the metal post next to the commander's head exploded with the impact of several shots.

Diving to the sidewalk, Jack felt a hot, stinging bolt of pain rushing up his arm. Twisting toward the gutter, he reached for the burning limb, trying to ascertain the extent of his wound.

Pulling back a bloody hand, Jack was relieved to find that his hand and wrist were still attached to his body. He couldn't feel them, had no control over his muscles, but his body was intact. It was time to break contact. He'd done far more damage than he could have ever imagined.

Crawling backward, Jack retreated until he entered an alley. Taking a deep breath, the commander got to his feet and began running down the backstreet, hoping the surrounding buildings would provide enough cover.

He cut back at the next street and headed toward his bike. He couldn't run at full speed, his unresponsive, dangling, arm disrupting his balance.

Three blocks away from the center of the firefight, the commander finally slowed his pace. It was completely dark now, the entire area covered by a silence that Jack found unnatural, almost spooky.

His first inclination was to get back to his wheels, address his wounded hand, and then make for the airport.

He found the motorcycle right where he'd left it. After a quick scan of the area to make sure the Zombies hadn't regrouped, he pulled off his pack and one-handed, began digging for his blow-out bag.

The medical kit he'd brought from San Diego was standard issue for the Marines. Jack found bandages, antibiotic cream, and a couple of ibuprofen tablets for the pain that was sure to come.

He found that his wrist has suffered a long gash, but believed the underlying bones were all okay. He couldn't detect any shrapnel. Pre-apocalypse, the wound was a worthy candidate for at least a dozen staples. Now, sitting on an ash-covered street in Zombieville, a couple of butterfly bandages and a length of gauze wrap would have to do.

After finishing with the first aid, Jack tried to flex and move his injured wing. Some feeling was coming back into the hand, but it still was mostly unresponsive. Repacking his kit, Jack eyed the motorbike and then frowned. His wounded limb was the one that controls the bike's throttle. Could he drive cross-handed? He doubted it.

It then occurred to Jack that he could inflict an even deeper wound on the hostile firemen, and do so without increasing the risk to himself. The airport crew had lost several valuable weapons after the freeway ambush. While the Zombies hadn't been able to gather the dead's rifles and ammo at the time, the commander had little doubt those assets wouldn't be there by the time a salvage operation was mounted. With Deiter on the stretcher, there simply wasn't room to take them back where they belonged.

Since he couldn't operate the bike just yet, Jack decided to mount his own treasure hunt. The infrared mask had proven invaluable during the hostilities. Perhaps there were more of the rare units on the men he'd killed. Ammo would eventually become as important as food. Having a stash couldn't hurt.

In addition to weapons and masks, Jack wanted to know more about the men he was facing. If all of them were firemen, that intelligence might go a long way to ending the conflict.

Rising, he again flexed his right arm. It was recovering, and with any luck, it would be usable soon. He could shoot with his left hand if necessary, but Jack didn't think the routed Horns would be back for more.

Retracing his original steps, Jack soon came to the first men he'd hit from behind. None of them had the high-tech breathing units, all their faces covered by simple outlaw masks. He quickly snatched their weapons and ammo… then he searched the bodies for any identification or personal effects.

Unable to carry all the hardware he was gathering, Jack found a good hiding spot for the cache. Later, he could sneak back in and recover the hoard if necessary.

The fourth victim was the man Jack had butt-stroked. The commander was surprised to find the guy up on one elbow, trying to get to his feet. He was young, probably early twenties. His breathing cloth had been knocked from his face. Blood ran down one side of his cheek, a vicious gash oozing crimson from just above his eyelid. Pulling his pistol with his off hand, Jack barked, "Just stay down, pal. You're not going anywhere."

Already fighting the headache from hell, the Zombie fighter's eyes grew wide at the commander's surprise appearance. "What do you want?" he mumbled through the blood streaming down his face.

"You lost. We won. I'll be asking the questions," Jack barked. "Who are you? What is your name?"

"Garrett. Patrolman Noah Garrett. I'm a cop… or I was before the shit hit the fan," the wounded man replied.

"And now you're a murdering son of a bitch?" Jack growled. "Why did you ambush the men from the airport?"

"They were in our territory. The chief ordered us to make sure they never came back. We've warned you airport heathens several times to stop raiding our resources, but you keep coming back. Who the hell are you?"

Ignoring Noah's question, Jack asked his own. "You said 'chief'? Did you mean the chief of police?"

"The chief of the fire department, Chief Paxton Woods."

"Is the woman you captured two days ago still alive?"

"I'm done talking," Noah spat, finally regaining a little composure. "Go ahead and kill me. I'll be damned if I'm going to help you airport scumbags with anything."

"Get up," Jack ordered, extending his weapon for emphasis. "If you cooperate, you'll see tomorrow's sunrise. If not, well, you'll join your comrades in hell. Your call."

"Fuck you," Noah barked. "Like I said, I'm not going to do shit for you, asshole."

Restraining the strike to avoid doing more damage, Jack tapped Officer Garrett on the head with his pistol, the impact to his tender flesh making the wounded man howl in pain. "Get up and start walking before I turn the other side of your skull into mush."

"Okay… okay…" Garrett conceded, holding up a hand to ward off any more blows.

Jack stood back as the officer struggled to his feet. While the man's eyes blazed with fiery hatred, his movements were feeble at best. "You're about to be demoted, young man. I'm busting you down from patrolman to jackass. I hope you're strong enough to carry a few things for me."

Indeed, Jack's intent was to enlist the stout-looking fellow as a manual laborer. Despite having a belly full of hatred for what Noah and his cohorts had done to Deiter's team, the commander couldn't just summarily execute any man who still had a layer of peach fuzz on his face.

With his pistol covering the prisoner, Jack began patting the ex-cop down for weapons. The only thing he found was a miniature, folding knife, two spare magazines and a small, plastic bottle of water. Less than an inch of clear liquid covered the bottom. He noticed Noah's eyes open wide as he held up the container.

Handing the container back to the bleeding man, Jack said, "Drink that if you want. Blood loss can make a man thirsty. Believe me, I know."

"I'll save it for later, if you don't mind. It's the last of my rations," the kid replied, relieved that Jack wasn't going to confiscate his water.

"You ration water?" Jack asked, realizing he'd misinterpreted Garrett's reaction. He had been scared to lose a couple of ounces of liquid.

"Yes. Doesn't everybody?" the former cop spat.

"Interesting," the commander whispered, finishing his pat-down and then stepping back.

Just as Jack was about to explain his need for a gun bearer, a moan of anguish drifted on the wind, originating somewhere down the street.

"One of your buddies is still alive," the commander observed. "Let's go take a look," he added, motioning Noah forward with his sidearm.

The duo stepped to the intersection where Jack had been hit, another low groan close to their position. It took them less than a minute to find the wounded man.

Jack recognized the tall leader by his thermal breathing unit. Evidently, the commander's one shot had hit the order-shouting honcho.

Noah knew exactly who it was. "Lieutenant Woods!" the younger man shouted, rushing to the downed Zombie. "Lieutenant, are you okay? Talk to me!"

The commander joined him at the wounded man's side, Noah reaching to tear open the victim's coat while Jack offered his flashlight to get a better look.

The small pool of light shed by the commander's torch illuminated a nasty wound just below the Lieutenant's rib cage. Jack also noticed something else.

275

There, just above the left breast pocket, was another embroidered emblem of the Austin Fire Department. Below the ornate symbol were the words, "Lieutenant Paxton Woods, Jr."

Setting aside his observation for the moment, Jack switched his gaze to the downed fireman's wound. The news wasn't good.

"He has been shot in the gut," Jack stated, announcing the obvious. "That's way, way beyond my capability to treat. Do you guys have doctors back at the fire station?"

"No. We only have EMTs," Noah replied in a dejected tone. "They don't do surgery."

"There is a doctor at the airport," Jack stated.

Glancing up to stare into Jack's face, Noah's eyes betrayed the hatred he felt. "He'd rather die than be a prisoner there. Just put him out of his misery… please."

Frowning, Jack responded, "But we might be able to save him. Hasn't there already been enough killing on both sides, Noah? Don't you think Chief Woods wants his son back?"

Jack's deduction that it was the chief's son lying on the ground seemed to shock Noah. "How did you…" he sputtered, just before realizing that he'd run his mouth a little too much.

"We didn't start this," the young cop began, his tone thick with embarrassment over the inadvertent disclosure. "Every time we sent out a team to scavenge for medical supplies or food or anything else, you bitches from the airport had already been there and cleaned everything out. We saw your fucking motorcycles hauling off load after load of valuables, like you were the last people left on earth. All the while, our wives and children were starving, a lot of our men drowning in their own blood."

"I'm not from the airport, son. I just got here and found myself in the middle of your shitstorm. What I can tell you is that the people there don't want to fight and kill anymore. They're trying to survive, just like you."

A whimper from Lt. Woods interrupted their exchange, the vile fading from Noah's eyes. "L.T., talk to me, man. Hang in there. We're going to get you some help."

"He's your friend," Jack stated, the softness in the cop's voice telling the commander everything he needed to know. "Let's put aside all this bickering and bullshit and save his life."

"How?" Noah snapped, his voice returning to a state of anger and distrust.

"I will take him back to the airport. I give you my word that he'll receive the best care we can give him. I'll cut you loose so that you can go back to Chief Woods. Bring the woman you captured to the airport's main entrance tomorrow at noon, and we'll do an exchange. Hopefully, that will get a dialogue started... maybe establish a little trust on both sides."

"You would do that?" Noah questioned. "You would give him medical care?"

Nodding, Jack said, "I can't guarantee he'll make it. He's in pretty bad shape. What I can promise, as an officer of the United States Navy is that he will be treated as one of our own."

"And if he doesn't make it? What does that do to the exchange?"

Flashing a knowing smile, Jack's voice was kind. "Do you have children, Noah?"

"No. Hadn't gotten around to it just yet," the cop admitted.

"Believe me, young man. A father will do almost anything to see his child one last time. I know this from first-hand experience. Chief Woods will want his boy back, even if it's just his body."

"I will try," the young policeman promised. "That's all I can do. Chief Woods can be a little unpredictable at times."

"Trust me," Jack said with confidence. "He'll do anything to save his son. Now, help me build a stretcher so we can at least salvage one life out of this mess."

Jack didn't stick around to watch the fireman cross the bridge and enter downtown Austin. If he was going to have any success

277

turning this situation around, it would help to have Chief Woods reunite with his son, preferably alive and well.

Speeding through the deserted streets of America's eleventh largest city, the commander was thankful for the green and white information signs posted along the roadways that guided him toward the airport.

He arrived at the main entrance a little more than fifteen minutes later. Dismounting and engaging the kickstand, his first act was to check on Junior's pulse. "He's still breathing," Jack whispered. "Hang in there, Lieutenant."

Returning to the motorcycle, Jack flashed the headlights three times, praying that the watchmen in the control tower were awake and alert. He then mounted the bike and guided it through the narrow pathway that led to the terminal.

Racing across along the primary service road, Jack cut through the gate just like before. There were three armed men waiting for him when he arrived at the luggage area's garage doors.

"I've got a wounded man here," Jack announced, hoping the sentries wouldn't shoot him on sight. "We need to get him to the doc right away."

Just like with Deiter a few hours before, the airport crew took one look at Jack's makeshift gurney and launched into action. Again, a stretcher was produced, two of them moving to lift the wounded man from behind Jack's bike.

"Who is this?" the commander heard someone say.

"What is this device on his face?"

"It's one of the Forbidden Zone shooters!" another declared. "What the hell...."

Moving closer, Jack said, "I shot him during a firefight. He's somebody important to them."

One of the helpers lifted his rifle, pointing the weapon at Junior's face. "I will show you how fucking important he is," the man growled, flicking off the weapon's safety.

Jack shoved the barrel away, his voice going into command mode. "I plan on trading him for Hannah, idiot. Stow that weapon and lend a hand. You do want Hannah back, right?"

"They won't make a trade," one of the others hissed. "She's already dead, and this fucker should join her in hell!"

Bascom rushed up, T.J. Pierce at his side. "What's going on here, Commander Cisco? Who is this injured man?"

"I captured him during an ambush I set up for the Horns," Jack explained in a rush. "I have reason to believe he is the son of the man who controls the Forbidden Zone. I want to trade him for Hannah."

Bascom's brow wrinkled as he digested Jack's words, the captain's eyes darting between the wounded firefighter and Cisco's mask-covered face.

"Why should I waste our valuable resources on this murdering piece of shit?" Bascom snarled.

"Do you want Hannah back? Do you still have any humanity left inside? Because it's the right thing to do, **Colonel**," Jack countered. "Our kind has always treated the wounded enemy with kindness and respect. Remember?"

Several seconds passed, Jack unsure of what Bascom's decision would be. Finally, with exasperation, he turned and ordered, "Take the prisoner to the doctor. I want two armed men guarding him at all times. Understood?"

Begrudgingly, the others bent to lift the stretcher. Jack was more than relieved as he watched them climb the stairs toward the main terminal. "That was smart, Captain. Good decision."

Without a word to Jack, Bascom turned to the remaining security men. "Take the commander's weapons. Bring him to my office, under guard."

"What?" Jack snapped, unable to keep the shock and surprise off his face. "What the hell is wrong with you?"

279

Bascom didn't respond. Pivoting smartly, the captain headed for the stairs in a huff as the airport team began patting Jack down for weapons.

There were only three security officers, and the commander wasn't all that impressed with their skills. It took all of his mental discipline not to make a play for one of their rifles, secure his freedom, and ride off into the darkness. Bascom was an ass, an idiot who was out of control and not exhibiting a shred of logic.

Disarmed, Jack was then escorted to the staircase. At the top, his pulled off his mask and turned to see T.J. standing nearby. "How many of them did you get?" the newly promoted scout asked first.

"A lot," Jack replied. "At least seven or eight, I would guess. I didn't hang around long enough to do a formal body count."

"Good," T.J. replied. "Let's go see Bascom. Just keep in mind, he's had a pretty rough day."

"He's not the only one," Jack quipped, wishing instantly he hadn't uttered the snide remark.

The found the captain's office empty, but neither was surprised. "The man has a lot on his plate," Pierce defended. "I'm sure he'll be back soon."

Sure enough, Bascom charged in a few minutes later. Jack decided to take the initiative, "How's Deiter?"

"He lost the leg," the captain announced, his tone bitter. "How does a man survive in this world with only one leg?"

"Sorry to hear that," Jack replied in a softer tone.

"Now, Commander, I want to hear of your escapades. Don't leave anything out," Bascom warned.

Jack started from when they'd discovered Hannah's trail. Just as the captain had requested, he didn't leave anything out. "I tried to warn Deiter. I tried to tell him not to charge into that open ground, but he was hell-bent for leather and wanted payback. You realize that revenge can be a dangerous thing, don't you, *Colonel*?"

Again, Jack's use of Bascom's military rank was like a punch to the man's gut. "Go on, Cisco. Without the editorials, if you please," the captain coldly stated.

Continuing with the debriefing, Jack described the ambush at the mall, the shootout at the ball diamond, and his trick at the bridge. "That's when I came across the young Horn I had butt-stroked," the commander stated casually. "He and I had a little conversation; then I persuaded him to help me gather the spoils of war."

After the commander had described finding Paxton Woods, Jr., Jack added, "That's when the idea of a prisoner exchange occurred to me. We have the chance to get Hannah back and open a dialog. Who knows, we might be able to cooperate with each other rather than continuing this running sequence of gun battles and killing. My message was to meet at the main entrance tomorrow at noon. I'm sure they will be there with bells on."

Given what he'd accomplished, Jack expected at least an acknowledgment of his effort. In any military organization, turning the lemon of the freeway ambush into the lemonade of inflicting significant enemy causalities would be considered a positive. The fact that he'd pulled it off alone should have at least earned a sincere "thank you."

Bascom didn't see it that way. "Who on God's earth authorized you to do any negotiating for our community, Commander?" the captain fumed. "Furthermore, I don't appreciate you poking the hornet's nest that is the Forbidden Zone. Yes, they've been sniping at our people, but until today, there were no organized attacks or significant causalities. Now, thanks to you, I've got an extremely motivated, openly hostile force just off our northern perimeter. They're probably rallying every man they can find to annihilate us, even as we speak."

Jack was stunned, unable to believe what his ears were hearing. Still, years of service to his country had instilled a discipline that he couldn't shun. In a steady voice that he would use to disagree with a senior officer, Jack replied, "I do not concur, sir. You yourself told me that the people in the Forbidden Zone were becoming more and more aggressive. That much was clear when they killed seven of your people without mercy this morning. I've opened a door for you, Bascom. Bringing that wounded man here gives you the chance to stop all of this insanity. Those guys in the Forbidden Zone aren't MS-13 gangbangers, rogue outlaw bikers, or three-headed monsters from Mars. They're cops, firemen, and other people you would have trusted with your life before Yellowstone blew."

The captain wasn't used to anyone talking back, and it showed on his face. "I want you out of my airport, Commander. Now!"

"Suit yourself," Jack shrugged.

"T.J., take the commander to his bicycle. Issue him a ration of water and then escort him to the side gate."

Standing to leave, Jack couldn't help but make one last effort to persuade the man. "Tomorrow at noon, some of Chief Woods's men are going to show up at the front gate with Hannah. I would suggest you hand over that boy, dead or alive. I would also strongly advise you to start negotiations with those people. Invite them in here to see what your community has accomplished. I have been told about the man who organized and saved all these people. When you see them tomorrow, Captain, be that man again. Show them who you were before everything went to hell in a handbasket."

When Bascom didn't reply, Jack continued out the door, T.J. right on his tail.

"T.J., before you go, I want you to call a meeting," Bascom announced from behind his desk. "I want all hands on deck. Anybody who can carry a weapon should be present. We're going to set up a little surprise for our friends from the Forbidden Zone," Bascom ordered.

"Yes, sir," Pierce responded, his eyes clouding with trouble.

"Did he just say what I thought he said?" Jack asked after the two men had walked a few steps down the terminal's main corridor.

"Yes," the scout answered, not sure what else to say.

"You guys can't do that, T.J. You can still stop this madness before it turns into an all-out fight to the death," Jack pleaded. "Nobody is going to win if this thing continues to spiral out of control."

"Captain Bascom has saved all of our lives with his guidance and leadership," T.J. responded with a frown. "I'm going to follow his orders, and so will every man, woman, and child in this community."

Still, Jack could tell T.J. didn't like it. He was, predictably, being a loyal soldier, trusting in the man who had led him through hell. The commander had seen the exact same thing a hundred times in the Navy. The military would cease to function without such discipline. It wasn't going to do any good to debate the subordinate.

Escorted to the location where his bicycle had been stored, T.J. ordered one of his comrades to retrieve a ration of water and then handed Jack back his weapons. The food Jack has stored in his saddlebags was missing. "Where is my chow?" he asked.

"I have no idea, sir," T.J. responded with a hint of embarrassment.

"So now you're not only pigheaded, you're thieves as well? Hell, I had two weeks of grub stored in there. Is this what your stand for, Mr. Pierce?" Jack complained.

Not knowing what else to do, T.J. said, "If you want, I will go and see if anybody knows where your supplies are stored and return them to you."

"I want," Jack grunted. "Casting a man into the wilderness without any provisions would keep me up and night. I'd hate to cause you any nightmares, T.J."

Pivoting quickly, T.J. rushed away on a mission to recover Cisco's food. The commander waited until he heard the man's footfalls on the metal stairs, and then moved with purpose.

On the far wall, the scouts' e-bikes were secured, all the battery-powered units plugged in and recharging. Hoisting his pack onto his shoulder, Jack then pulled his saddlebags free of his bike and headed to the closest electro-cycle.

After securing his belongings, Jack pulled his pistol, chambered a round, and then threw his leg over the bike's seat.

With a twist of the throttle, Jack launched out of the luggage area, the darkness giving the commander excellent cover. It took him less than a minute to reach the main entrance, and then he was soaring through the streets.

Chapter 51

After her meal of greasy stew, Hannah's guard returned her to the broom closet.

Again, panic began to swell up in her core, the confined space and lack of light ripping at her sanity. "Keep it together," she demanded of the walls. "At least you know they'll let you out now and then to pedal."

She hadn't been confined more than thirty minutes where she heard the key entering the lock. Rising in anticipation of being escorted back to the gym, she was stunned when two large men burst into the narrow space and grabbed her by the hair. "Come on, biker bitch," one of them growled, dragging her across the floor as she cried out in pain.

Once in the hall, she was yanked to her feet, a burly man grasping each arm. "Who is Commander Jack Cisco?" Chief Woods demanded, his gruff tone and expression making it clear that he was mad as hell.

"It doesn't matter. He's dead," Hannah announced.

Her answer elicited a round of grunts and chuckles from the surrounding men. Only Woods spoke, "Dead? For a ghost, Commander Cisco is certainly most lethal. Now answer my question. Who is Jack Cisco?"

"A man I met on the trail," Hannah replied honestly, a glimmer of hope raising her spirits. *What had Jack done? What did he mean by 'lethal'?* she wondered. *How did Woods know about him?*

Tilting his head in consideration of her answer, the chief quickly came to a conclusion. Without hesitation, he took one step forward and slapped his prisoner hard across the face.

White-hot streaks of pain rocked Hannah's skull, her face burning as if someone had poured molten lava down her cheek. "Don't mess with me, young woman. I don't have the time or patience. Who is Commander Jack Cisco?"

"I'm telling you the truth," Hannah whimpered, her lips barely able to move after the assault. "He's a naval officer than I met only a few days ago on the trail west of the city."

From behind her, Hannah heard another voice say, "Maybe she fucked this Cisco guy. Maybe he's in love. She looks like she's built for pleasure. He's probably butt-hurt that we have taken away the best piece of ass he's ever had."

A round of raucous laughter bellowed from the men in the corridor, but Chief Woods wasn't amused. "Why would a man you just met on the trail attack us? Why would he kill for you?"

"He's a submariner. His boat docked in San Diego after Yellowstone. His wife was supposed to be staying at a ranch just west of the city. He rode a bicycle all the way here, trying to find his family. That's really all I know," Hannah pleaded.

Woods swung again, the second strike even more powerful than the first. Waves of nausea now accompanied her pounding grey matter, her body fighting to maintain consciousness. Her legs buckled from the intense pain, her fall broken by the two ruffians clutching her arms.

"I'm telling you the truth!" she pleaded, once she'd regained control of her facial muscles. "I swear it!"

"How many able-bodied men are at the airport?" Bascom barked, holding up his hand as if ready to deliver another blow.

Hannah hadn't been prepared for questions about Jack. She had believed he had died at the hands of the miners. Woods's mention of the forgotten man's name had surprised her. Questions about the airport, however, were expected, and the rehearsed resistance in her mind kicked in. "I don't know," she lied.

Bracing for another strike to her face, Hannah was surprised when no impact occurred. Chancing to open her eyes, she saw Woods nod at the two brutes holding her arms.

One of the Neanderthals loosened his grip to just one hand, the other paw grabbing the front of Hannah's overalls and pulling down with enough force to rip the straps from her shoulder. Her

T-shirt was next, torn from her body as if were a piece of paper being tossed into the trash.

Left topless, her chest rising and falling as she struggled to fill her lungs with air, Hannah was forced violently to the floor. A moment later, her overalls were pulled away, leaving her completely exposed.

She had wondered a dozen times about being raped since she'd been captured. How would she react? What would such a violation be like? How bad would the physical pain be? Would it be worse than the mental anguish that was sure to follow?

Trying to cover herself with her arms, Hannah looked up to see four men leering down at her nakedness, apparently readying for a sexual assault.

Instead of reaching for their zippers or buttons, only Woods moved, his hand producing a black device with two metal prongs. She knew instantly that it was a stun gun.

"One of our police comrades gave me this device," Woods began. "He confiscated it from a Mexican drug dealer a few years ago. This is a stun gun, but a design that is illegal here in the United States. That is because it is deadly if not used in limited doses. You see, this particular unit has been modified to issue over 100,000 volts and was used by the cartel enforcers. Now, how many shooters are at the airport?"

Hannah hesitated, considering the best avenue of approach, but Woods did not. The chief pulled the gun's trigger, a loud zapping sound buzzing through the hall when a blue bolt of electrical current jumped between the prongs.

"How many?" he demanded, lowering the device toward Hannah's heaving stomach.

Surprised that her resolve was still in place, the scout heard her own, voice say, "I don't know."

A thousand stinging wasps attacked Hannah's body at the same instant, her arms and legs jumping and twitching involuntarily.

287

The pain was off the scale, her vision narrowing to a small circle of blackness. On the edge of losing consciousness, Hannah was on the verge of slipping into a deep, black hole, when the debilitating suffering suddenly stopped.

"How many shooters?" Woods's voice insisted from somewhere far away.

Hannah's brain began making adjustments, her mind shifting into a defensive state while trying to reason her way out of receiving more abuse. Why would it hurt to tell them how many men are at the airport? What harm could possibly come from her telling this madman what he wanted to know? Or maybe she could feed him false information? How would he know if she told him a lie?

Before she could formulate a dishonest response, the searing agony returned to her torso, her legs seizing in a series of short jerks and spasms as the unbearable current jolted her core.

Again, the torture stopped as quickly as it had begun, Hannah's skin tingling with the aftershock. She heard a woman's scream echoing down the hall, a full two seconds passing before she realized the sound had come from her own throat.

"She pissed herself," one of the henchmen laughed. "Who's going to clean that up?"

For her part, Hannah no longer cared about her nakedness or personal hygiene. The entire focus of her being was on those two cold, metal prongs in the chief's hand.

"I can do this all night," Woods announced with terrifying calm. "You can't. I've been told that permanent neurological damage is possible if the body is exposed to this level of voltage for an extended period. How many shooters?" Again, the chief switched on the device, this time pushing the prongs into her exposed skin as he loomed over her.

With every beat of her heart, Hannah's brain thumped against her skull, and she was convinced her intestines were being ripped from her torso. "There are fifty-four," she blurted out, surprised at her honesty, and no longer feeling like she could control her own words.

Woods pressed the device deeper even into her flesh, "How many?" he snapped.

"Oh, gawd, please, no! I'm telling the truth! There are fifty-four including the scouts!" she pleaded.

"We know there are hundreds of people at the airport. Do you really expect me to believe that there are only fifty-four armed men?" Woods spat.

"We killed seven at the ambush this morning," one of the guards added. "That means there are less than fifty defenders if she's telling the truth – which I doubt."

Seeming to ignore his henchman's comment, Woods again addressed the helpless woman at his feet. "How much ammunition do you have?"

The exchange had given Hannah time to regroup, if only a little. A wave of embarrassment over her weakness began to grow in her head. "I don't know how much ammunition we have," she lied. "That wasn't my job."

Woods intentionally dragged the stun gun's prongs down Hannah's stomach, the hideous device stopping just above her bikini cut. "I don't believe you," he said.

"Seriously. Please. I have no idea how much…."

Woods squeezed the trigger, Hannah's mid-section arching high into the air as another scream escaped from deep inside her chest. Hot, burning waves of misery consumed her body, her bones feeling like they had burst into flames. Her wildly pumping heart would surely explode.

"We're running low on ammunition!" Hannah confessed after her breathing allowed. Her brain had surrendered. She would tell Woods anything he wanted to know, do anything he asked.

For another ten minutes, the chief asked a series of questions regarding food, radio frequencies, and the defensive capabilities of the airport. Most surprising was his desire to hear a complete bio on Captain Bascom.

Then, a second surprise. "The roots you were captured with – are they poisonous?"

"No," she replied, her mind unable to resist.

"And how do you know they are harmless?"

"There is an old Chinese man named Sheng. I was taking him to the airport from his home when your men found me. He is the expert. He knows what practically every plant and herb is used for. I believed that his knowledge would allow us to harvest enough food for years."

"Interesting," Woods replied, rubbing his chin.

Finally satisfied with the results of his interrogation, Paxton pocketed the stun gun and turned to his henchmen. "Clean her up. Give her something to drink and then put her back in the cell. I want all the unit commanders in my office. We're going to pull an all-nighter and then end this conflict by sunset tomorrow."

Riding the electric-bike through the streets at night was a challenge. Heavy, grey clouds dominated the earth's skies, there wasn't any moonlight or illumination from the stars. The phrase "pitch black" came to Jack's mind.

With the inky darkness, risk grew exponentially. Worried about an ambush or triggering a booby-trap, his movements were cautious and deliberate. His progress through suburban Austin was slow, really not much faster than pedaling his bike. Still, his legs appreciated the battery-powered luxury that afforded them rest.

It didn't help that his mind was distracted by replaying yesterday's events. His head was filled with conflicting emotions, and that made it difficult to concentrate on the road ahead.

He was emotionally and physically exhausted, and focus was almost impossible. He had survived a deadly physical assault by the Zombies, performed three taxing counter-attacks, and had eaten very little between. He needed sleep, food, and a chance to let his mind digest everything that had happened in the last twenty-four hours.

His first inclination was to ride the battery-cycle as far as he could toward Galveston. "Screw Austin, Texas and all of the pig-headed assholes who had survived there. I'll head east, run this thing until it's dry, and then find a bicycle shop and a new set of wheels."

That course of action, carefully dissected as the blocks passed by, didn't stand up to scrutiny and logic. Where would he find another bicycle shop? He would have to rely on pure luck. After all, he couldn't do an internet search or stop in the local gas station and ask directions. Phone books were sparse. He wasn't likely to simply stumble on a well-equipped store in rural America. So, he wouldn't be able to avoid the city, and that increased a traveler's risk.

Another worry was finding food during the trip. His complaint at the airport had been only partially to provide a distraction. His stomach was already eating his backbone. He had only a day's worth of water provided by T.J., and that wasn't going to get him far in post-apocalyptic Texas.

Walking, even half the distance to Galveston, was going to be an insurmountable task. Even if his batteries held out for 150 miles, he was still going to have days and days of footwork ahead. Hoofing it was slow going, making Jack a target for who knew what kind of trouble that might exist between here and the coast.

Even if the commander had possessed the resources to make the journey, he wasn't convinced he should bug out just yet. He was deeply troubled by the building confrontation between the Zombies and the fly boys. They were going to butt heads, and a lot of people were going to die in the aftermath. The ill-conceived confrontation seemed as inevitable as the ash.

Most of the people living in Austin, on both sides of the dispute, were good souls. Jack could even excuse Bascom and Chief Woods for a lot of their behavior. Hell, in their shoes, he might have acted in much the same way. It wasn't those two leaders or their lieutenants that were the primary issue – it was the twisted world that Yellowstone had fashioned.

Unlike Norval Pickett back in Carlsbad, neither of the local leaders were driven by visions of conquest or empire-building as far as the commander could tell. Megalomania wasn't the issue here, at least not yet.

Bascom had booted him from the airport because there was only room for one hero in that community. Jack had underestimated the man's ego, but then again, hadn't his establishment of command and control allowed hundreds to survive? Chief Woods was probably just as self-centered, most likely cut from nearly identical cloth.

No, the problem in Austin was competition. Both Bascom and Woods were smart enough to realize that their only hope of survival was to consume what already existed. Nothing new was being manufactured, grown, or harvested. The finite amount of food, medicine, clothing, ammunition, and shelter limited the number of people it could support. Once that was consumed, there would be nothing left. No replenishment. No reserves. Only certain, slow, agonizing death.

Even Sheng's solution was inadequate. How long would the roots and tubers remain alive and dormant underground? How long before they decomposed and became part of the soil? Plus, Jack realized that mankind had a history of over-harvesting food without adequate replacement strategies. The disappearance of the American buffalo immediately came to mind. If new growth wasn't part of the cycle, eventually even the most plentiful resources would be depleted.

While loyal to their communities to a fault, both leaders were looking at a fixed amount of critical necessities that were within reach. From that realization, it was an easy journey to make any competitor the bad guy… an evil that must be eradicated from the face of the earth… a nemesis that was as threatening as a plague of Biblical locusts.

In fact, were it not for the indelible spirit of hope embedded in most human souls, both communities would have already thrown in the towel. We all sense that the end is near, so why wait? Why suffer? What reason is there for living? Life is never going to get any better, only worse.

Jack knew the answer. He'd seen it in Archie's greenhouses. He'd eaten fresh eggs and watched live cattle. He was also certain that eventually, Mother Earth would heal herself and allow life to reestablish its broad and bountiful presence. The commander also knew that both Bascom and Woods shared the same core belief.

That translated into a waiting game. The community that lasted the longest, that held out until seeds began to grow again and the air was safe to breathe would win the marathon of survival. Bascom wasn't stupid, and the commander assumed the same of Chief Woods. They could do the math. Eliminate the other side, and their communities would last twice as long. It was really that simple.

Or was it?

Neither of those two men had seen what Jack had witnessed on his journey across the Southwest. They didn't know about herds of livestock, blossoming plants, or edible moss and mushrooms growing in caves. If he had any regrets about the past few days, they centered on his inability to speak to the heart of either leader… to let these men know that there were alternatives that could alter their future courses for the better. He'd miscalculated. He hadn't played his hand well, and that bothered the commander more than anything.

The fact that a complete ecosystem had been established at the airport was nothing short of fantastic. Somehow, the firemen had not only survived the glass-filled air, but they had organized and supported a sizable community. The brilliance demonstrated by both groups was exactly what mankind would need to continue into the next century. Yet, both were so shortsighted they couldn't see the forest for the trees… the forest of hope for the trees of need.

It dawned on Cisco that both the warring leaders operated as if they existed in bubbles. Austin, Texas was the extent of their worlds, limiting their thinking, decision-making, and planning. As sure as Jack was riding on an electric bike, Bascom believed eliminating the firemen would double the area his scouts could forage. Woods was no doubt wringing his hands as well, eager to send his salvage teams into new territory. Both sides were probably starving, convinced that the grass was greener on the other side of the fence, especially if they eliminated the cows that were grazing over there.

Engaging the e-bike's brake, Jack rolled to a stop.

"I can't let them do it," he mumbled, his eyes wandering around the desolate landscape of the abandoned city. "There are hundreds of precious lives about to be lost due to nothing more than short-sighted ignorance. I have to try and stop it."

He mulled over several potential solutions. He could assassinate Bascom and Woods, but they would just be replaced by subordinates who knew no other course or process.

He could throw his skills behind Bascom and then try to reason with the man before it was too late. Sighing loudly, Jack knew there was a slim chance of that strategy's success. The captain was as tough as a pig's nose. He'd already had firsthand experience with that. No doubt, Chief Woods was probably a mirror image of his archenemy. The style and methods of both men had been what was required to survive in those early days after the eruption. Now, that mindset was ingrained in both communities and wouldn't be dislodged by anything short of total defeat.

It occurred to Jack that education was the solution. If he could just get both those stubborn men to realize what was a stake, a war might be avoided. "They aren't going to listen to words. Austin is now the new Missouri. I'm must show them."

Then a eureka moment lit every neuron in his brain, his lips forming into a broad smile as the commander marinated a possible solution.

Engaging the bike's throttle, Jack turned back toward the west. He had a favor to call in. He would give Bascom and Woods something to think about. He would demonstrate to both sides that not even victory on the battlefield would ensure their futures.

As the miles rolled by, Jack worked on refining his plan. Once on country roads, the commander increased his speed and began enjoying the cold night air blowing past his head. "I can make this work," he whispered to the night. "We can salvage this."

Leaping from the luggage tractor, Bascom entered a terminal bustling with activity.

Men hustled in every direction, most carrying weapons and packs. Glancing at his watch, the captain whispered, "The sun will rise in two more hours. Much still needs to be done."

He hurried to the long, folding table, its surface covered in a hodgepodge mixture of glass jars. T.J. Pierce was there, pouring a clear liquid into the containers as another tore strips off a blanket. "How did it go at the main entrance?" the new security head asked.

"We couldn't test it for obvious reasons, but the mechanics think our little surprise will work well. They did the best they could, given such short notice," Bascom reported. "How goes this effort?"

"We'll have twenty-plus Molotov cocktails pre-positioned before dawn," Pierce replied. "Filling them with a mixture of JP5 jet fuel mixed with a couple of special ingredients should give them a little extra punch."

"Excellent," the captain replied. "I'm going inside to check on our other preparations."

Stepping toward the staircase, Bascom was approached by a young man holding out his radio. "The spotters on the hotel roof have a report, sir."

Taking the communication device, the captain pushed the talk button, "Bascom here. What's happening?"

"We've seen movement beyond the perimeter, just on the other side of runway number two," a faint voice declared. "My best guess is that it's the snipers that you anticipated would be deployed. Definitely not a large force."

"Keep your head down," Bascom replied. "Send an update the moment anything changes. Don't expose yourselves no matter what. They could become ambitious at any time."

Handing back the radio, the captain proceeded to climb the stairs, a knowing smile spreading across his face as he glanced to the north where Cisco believed the enemy camp was headquartered. "I knew you'd put long-range shooters on us before dawn. Do you really think I'm stupid enough to expose my people like that? This isn't going to go down on your terms, Mr. Woods, or whatever your name is. We're going to play by my rules."

Reaching the top of the stairs, Bascom was surprised to see Sheng walking down the main terminal, the old man obviously upset and intent on bending the captain's ear. The old bastard had done nothing but bitch and complain since arriving at the facility.

"Hello, Sheng," Bascom greeted with as much calm as he could manage. "Now isn't a good time."

"Who can sleep with all this racket going on?" Sheng barked, launching his first verbal salvo of the day. "Why are all these young men making so much racket at this wee hour of the morning?"

"We're preparing for an attack," the captain explained, wanting nothing more than for the ancient relic to drink some warm milk and nod off to sleep.

"I want to go back to my land. Your city is a mad house. The woman told me I would be safe here. The sailor said the same thing. Take me home," Sheng demanded.

"Everything will be fine," Bascom replied with a reassuring hand on the Chinaman's shoulder. "You will be safe here."

"Not with all these men running around with guns," Sheng countered. "And how are you going to breathe once this building is full of bullet holes? Where is the Navy man? He will take me back to my property."

The mention of Jack brought a scowl to Bascom's face. "I'm afraid the commander was not an officer or a gentleman. He was nothing more than a petty thief who slinked away in the middle of the night with some of our most valuable equipment."

For the first time since he'd met the disagreeable codger, Bascom saw surprise and indecision behind Sheng's eyes. "The commander left? He must have known you are about to be defeated."

Shaking his head, Bascom said, "No, that wasn't the reason, but now is not the time. I'm incredibly busy and have a lot of work to do before sunrise. Now, if you please…."

Ignoring the captain's brush-off, Sheng pointed to a group of armed men hustling past. "Your people are preparing to die. I've seen a lot of war and strife in my time. Their eyes brim with defeat."

Something in the old man's tone gave Bascom pause. He had been raised to respect his elders, his own grandfather one of the wisest men the captain had ever met. "You should avoid this fight," Sheng continued. "The karma isn't right."

Glancing around at the bustling activity in the terminal, doubt began to flood Bascom's mind. Yes, his people *were* afraid. That

297

was to be expected given the threat that loomed on the horizon. Yet, the captain detected something more, a deeper apprehension that was announced by their body language.

There was a message being communicated to anyone astute enough to read it. "Hasn't there already been enough death and killing? Haven't we already suffered through hell? When will this violence all end?" lamented the silent voices of those passing by.

Shaking his head to clear away his doubts, Bascom became stern with his guest. "Tomorrow or the day after, I'm going to assign several men to accompany you into the countryside. They will be yours to teach for as long as it takes to learn your skills. Once we know how to harvest the available food from nature, I'll provide an armed escort to take you back to your home. Is that acceptable, sir?"

"And what do I get in return?" Sheng frowned.

"Anything that I have to give," Bascom replied, a forced smile forming on his lips. When Sheng didn't respond, the captain said, "Now, if you'll excuse me," and pushed past the older gent.

Hustling to the infirmary, Bascom found the exhausted doctor standing over his patient. "How is our guest?" he asked the sawbones.

"He's stable, but that's about it. This facility isn't equipped to deal with battlefield wounds, Alex. I have neither the equipment, nor the necessary medications, nor the skills to deal with the type of damage this man has suffered. He could live a long life, or he could die in five minutes. That's all I can say."

"Isn't that the case with all of us?" Bascom asked, patting the doc on the shoulder with a reassuring gesture.

"One thing you should know, Alex. He can't be moved. Even the slightest jolt or bump could restart his internal bleeding. I've patched him up the best I can, but he's in a precarious state now, and probably will be for at least another forty-eight hours."

With his eyebrows jacked, Bascom's expression changed instantly. "He can't be moved? Are you sure?"

"Positive," the doctor announced, his voice firmed by his own resolve. "Move him, and you virtually guarantee his death."

Turning away, Bascom's mind began reeling over this new development. Within a minute, a dozen different scenarios began playing out in his head. Their leadership would assume it was a trick or a delay for nefarious purposes. They might make alternative demands that would ruin his plans.

"Get him ready to be moved, Doctor. Do your best," Bascom ordered.

"He will die, Alex. I can't do that... my oath forbids it," the physician sternly replied.

Pointing his finger at the doctor's face, the captain was livid. "Do it, sir, or you may have dozens of patients in worse condition if you don't. Your oath is to save lives. In my world, sacrifices sometimes must be made to do just that. I expect this young man to be on a portable stretcher by 11:45."

After staring hard at his friend for several seconds, Bascom stormed out of the infirmary.

The sentry, stationed at the mine's entrance, seemed surprised to see Jack rolling up to the gate.

Throwing a friendly wave, Jack dismounted and stretched his legs. "Thought I should use the front door this time," the commander teased. "Everything okay?"

Jack didn't recognize Mike for a few moments, the man's color and body language completely changed. *Amazing what a few days' worth of chow will do for a guy*, he thought.

"Hello, Commander. What brings you back to town?" Mike greeted, moving to unlock the gate.

"Just dropping in to see how you folks are doing. How's your son?"

"Timmy is much better, sir. The wife and I were just joking last night that we almost miss those quiet times before he had so much energy."

Jack laughed at the proud father's humor, and then he got down to business. "Would Camaro be up and about at this early hour?"

"Yes, he's an early riser. I saw him just before my shift started, organizing another team to go back to the high school. We found a semi-trailer in the parking lot, stuffed to the gills with canned soup. It even has clam chowder!"

Watching as Jack pushed his e-bike to the entrance, Mike became solemn. "Commander, I'm... well... I'm sorry about that day in the mine.... You know, when I came at you with that knife. I really can't explain what was going through my mind. I was desperate. I didn't know... I didn't realize...."

Interrupting the apology with a wave of his hand, Jack said, "No need to say another word, Mike. It's all good. I hold zero ill will about that incident."

Smiling again, Mike walked with the commander to the mule. "Do you know how it works?" he asked.

"Yes. After three trips, I think I can make it go," Jack replied, throwing his weapon and pack onto the narrow bench.

A few minutes later, Jack was slowing down the electric train. Dismounting, he followed the same path he had used before, passing through the narrow rock corridors and carved stone rooms. He found Camaro Butler sitting at his desk.

The mine boss immediately brightened when he glanced up and spotted the visitor. "Jack! Damn it's good to see you. Couldn't stay away?"

"I need a favor, Cam. A big favor. I hate to ask so soon, but I've got no other choice, and it's a very, very critical situation."

"Sit down. Take a load off. Anything we can do to help, you know you can count on us," the beaming miner stated.

"Don't be so sure about that. What I'm about to ask is dangerous, will take all your manpower, and might even result in some causalities."

Butler's face became serious but not unfriendly. "What's going on?"

For the next twenty minutes, Jack described the situation in Austin. When he got to the point of explaining the Forbidden Zone, Butler interrupted, saying, "I knew something was going on around the downtown area. I sent two teams there, and neither one ever returned. We decided not to risk any more of our people."

Through Hannah, Camaro had also been aware of the airport community, but he had no idea about the size and scope of the operation there. "There are really that many people inside? That's amazing," the miner commented.

A young man appeared just then, delivering a bowl of noodles to Butler. "Are you hungry, Jack?"

"Damn, that does smell good. Do you have any to spare?" the commander responded.

Cam's hearty belly laugh shook the table. "We have plenty, my friend. Thanks to you."

After ordering his guest a bowl of carbohydrates with a side of meat, Camaro again became serious. "What can we do to help?"

"I believe that the presence of a third party, a large, well-armed third party, would give both sides of this conflict pause. I believe both Bascom and Woods are acting as if they'll be the only game in town after annihilating the other guy. If we show up with all your crew and make a big show of brandishing our weapons, I'm hopeful it will cause them both to rethink this craziness."

Rubbing his chin, Camaro said, "What if they decide to attack my guys instead of each other? Or they could probe us with force, and we'd have to fight back."

"There are a hundred different scenarios, Cam. This isn't just a walk in the park. Again, you'd be putting some of your guys at risk. On the other hand, if we can manipulate a peaceful co-existence with all parties, I believe trade, shared knowledge, and

301

the resources of all three camps will lead to a better quality of life for everybody, as well as a faster recovery."

"We don't have much here to trade or offer," Camaro stated, his mind contemplating the commander's words. "I'm not prepared to give up our food. Other than that, I'm not sure that we'd be welcome, even if we did help them avoid a war."

Laughing, Jack pointed to the cup of water resting near Butler's plate. "I disagree, Cam. In fact, I would say you have the most valuable resource of all. You have an abundance of clean, easily accessible water. That's something neither of the communities in Austin brings to the table."

"I hadn't thought of that," the mine boss smiled. "I guess one man's trash is another man's treasure."

"Your people also know how to dig. You know how to filter air and survive underground. If Yellowstone blows again, or the ash refuses to dissipate, those skills could save a lot of lives. Don't sell yourself short," Cisco added.

Jack sat quietly, giving Cam a minute to evaluate all that he had heard. On the one hand, three communities helping each other would be stronger than any one. However, the mine boss had to consider the possibility of putting his people in harm's way. How many more casualties could they sustain as a community? Suddenly, the growling rumble of Jack's stomach broke the silence, bringing both men out of the mental fog of analysis. The waiter appeared just then, carrying a steaming hot bowl of noodles and what appeared to be slices of canned ham.

"Dig in," Camaro grinned, apparently pleased with his own attempt at humor. "I need to talk to my men. This decision is too big for me to make alone. The guys are already organizing a large team in the crew room to recover a truckload of soup we found yesterday. We can talk to them right now. How many guys do you think we should take to Austin?"

"How many can you muster?"

Butler had to think about the question for a moment, his eyes shifting to the rock ceiling as he calculated his manpower. "I guess at least sixty, perhaps seventy. Hell, just two days ago, we had eighty volunteers hauling grub back from the school."

Smiling broadly, Jack responded, "That should be enough. Go talk to your guys. Please let them know how important this is, not only to them, but perhaps to mankind as a whole."

Jack had just finished his meal when Camaro returned. "We're in. My teams are forming up right now. I told them to pack enough supplies for two nights and a long hike. Most of them are eager to get out of this mine and see something different for a change. We'll have sixty-three rifles to discourage our neighbors in the city from their bad behavior."

Glancing at his watch, Jack said, "Great! We've got to hurry; the exchange is supposed to happen at noon. That gives us just over six hours, and it will take at least four of that to walk to the airport."

Chapter 52

Chief Woods watched as twenty-six of his best men prepared to leave the fire station. Every fifth individual wore one of the new infrared scrubber masks fitted to his head, the rest looked like outlaws, cloth-breathing filters disguising their faces from the nose down.

They were all dressed in black duty pants and chestnut brown shirts… and were bristling with extra magazines, medical kits, and battle rifles. Most of their garb was courtesy of an army surplus store just a few blocks away, the ammunition the result of finding the warehouse of a national sporting goods chain that had yet to be looted. His men had hauled tons of supplies out of that building, including camping food, sleeping bags, clothing, and of course, every single, case of bullets and buckshot they could find.

Strolling to the man in charge of Team 3, Woods watched as the leader helped one of his shooters with a stubborn buckle. Finally satisfied that the clasp wouldn't rattle or come undone, the officer patted his subordinate on the back and said, "That should do it. You nervous, Tom?"

"A little," the younger man replied.

"We all are. After today, things are going to be a lot better. Just keep your powder dry and listen to what I say. We'll all be back here celebrating in a few hours."

The team leader then turned to Chief Woods and said, "We're ready, sir."

"Good," Woods nodded. "You know your assigned area, jump off point, and radio frequencies, correct?"

Patting the map and notepad sticking out of his breast pocket, the lead responded, "Affirmative, sir."

"Any questions, son?" Woods asked.

"None, Chief. We're good to go."

With a smile, Woods extended his hand and gave the team leader a firm shake. He then turned to the assembled squad and cleared his throat.

"Gentlemen, if I may have a word?"

Catching on, the team leader barked, "Attention! The chief has something to say!"

The room became very quiet, all eyes on the man credited with having saved the community. Woods didn't waste any time.

"The other two teams have already departed. First to arrive at their assigned positions, well before dawn, were the sniper teams and forward observers. Next, our special weapons units deployed, again, before sunrise so they couldn't be detected by the enemy sentries. With their two belt-fed machine guns, they will provide overwhelming fire superiority. You men will be the only members of our force visible to the enemy. I expect you to remain alert, be professional, and show those animals at the airport how a proper security force is supposed to look and act. You, gentlemen, are our ambassadors for the first phase of this operation. During phase two, after we have Lieutenant Woods safely back in our ranks, we will eliminate that sub-human plague that occupies that facility. We will take control of that airport and dispose of those godless looters and thieves. Good luck men, and good hunting."

A cheer rose up from the line of troopers, several of the men letting out a hearty, "Hell, yeah!"

Then, without further ado, Woods turned to the team leader and nodded. "I'll see you at the main entrance," he added.

Continuing back to his office, the chief glanced at the pickle jar and vowed, "If we win this fight today, I'll throw you away. Victory will mean the dawning of a new age for our community. We will eliminate that scavenging horde and provide meaningful safety for our people. We will have the entire city at our disposal and will once again become builders instead of scavengers."

Rather than moving to his desk, the chief returned to a small coat closet along the far wall. Opening the solid-maple door, he ignored the dress uniforms, dinner jackets, and heavy turnout coat hanging inside.

Finally withdrawing with his own body armor, load vest, and rifle, the chief began pulling on the unfamiliar equipment.

His son had found the military gear on one of their first explorations. In a parking garage, one block away from where the National Guard had made a valiant last stand trying to defend city hall, Paxton Junior had come across a delivery truck, the logo of a well-known rental company on the side. It had been covered by a tarp for some unknown reason.

The younger Woods had noticed something peculiar about the van. On the barely-exposed, front bumper, a reflective sticker indicated that the occupant was a colonel in the Texas Guard. Evidently, their rapid deployment had led to a shortage of cargo haulers. The chief had to admire the unknown colonel's grit. Renting a van to move your troops was inspired, clearly a man who wasn't about to let anything stand in his way with regard to fulfilling a mission.

Chief Woods had used that example a dozen times during those first few months. "We need to be like that brave colonel who would stop at nothing to succeed," he had preached.

Inside the rental truck, they found what had to have been the guardsmen's secret stash. There were cases of ammunition, several sets of body armor, a box of hand grenades, and three pallets of MREs. That treasure trove had been an important find.

Several of the Humvees in the area had survived the riots intact, despite their crews being killed in the violence. Since their engines wouldn't run, and there was no fuel, most of the military vehicles had been ignored by initial roving bands of pillagers. Given the stash of belted ammunition discovered in the van, Chief Woods wasted little time in ordering his people to retrieve two of the .50 caliber machine guns mounted on the National Guard's vehicles. Now, those deadly devices were on their way to the airport, along with several belts of ammunition. Woods considered them his secret weapon.

Even without those heavy armaments, the chief wasn't worried about who would hold the airport after the sun had set. In fact, his only concern was Junior. Were those animals at Austin International torturing his son for information? Was he receiving medical care? Food? Water?

Noah Garrett had reported that the man who had captured Junior seemed reasonable. The ex-cop had taken a serious blow to the head, and many in the chief's commander structure doubted some of the man's observations. "He said that the airport people don't want a fight. He let me go so I could deliver the message. I really don't think they are all that much different than we are."

Those blasphemous words wouldn't have normally been tolerated, but again, Noah had survived a pitched battle and was obviously suffering from severe head trauma.

Hannah, under duress, had given the chief a pretty clear picture of the airport's defenses and modes of operation. He knew about the men in the control tower, how they used electric luggage carts to move their personnel and was especially pleased to discover how fragile the airport's system of overpressure had become. To eliminate the threat they represented, all his people had to do was put a few holes in the main terminal and eventually, the occupants would die.

Her information about the Asian man, Sheng, had required that he change that simple strategy. Now, with that special individual living among the airport scum, Woods could no longer just stand back and blast the terminal into smithereens. Now they would have to take the building intact.

Another advantage to keeping the airport in one piece was the equipment being utilized there. Currently Fire Station No. 9 was overcrowded. Having a secondary location that was ash-proof would allow his people to spread out.

While Woods considered the station house a superior shelter, it did have its faults. One of the last major buildings constructed before Yellowstone blew, the structure had been a model of energy efficiency and had incorporated the latest designs in heating, circulation, and air conditioning. It had been outfitted with a sophisticated heat pump, solar power, ultramodern filtration systems, and a host of other features. It had been a showplace for the city's administration, a posterchild for those who wanted to minimalize mankind's carbon footprint.

It had also proven to be ash-resistant and had saved hundreds of lives.

Now, with a second location within reach, and the chance that a new source of food was in the offering, the chief wanted to then this stalemate. He strongly desired an end to the conflict sooner rather than later, and if that meant causalities among his men, so be it. They all knew the risks when they signed up, and he was confident that any of them would willingly give their lives for the community.

A light knock on the door interrupted the chief's thoughts, one of his lieutenants announcing his presence. "The woman is ready, sir, as is your security team. It will be noon in another forty-five minutes. We should be going."

"I'm ready," Woods stated with confidence, taking one last glance at the pickle jar.

Bascom jumped from the luggage cart as it rolled to a stop fifty yards from the main entrance; T.J. and two other riflemen following suit.

Quickly, he scanned the hastily-constructed barricade that had blocked the four-lane entrance to Austin International since the early days of the eruption. Images of those terrible times flashed through the captain's memory like a slide show he couldn't turn off. This area had been a battleground, dozens of American citizens killed on both sides of the fence. The fighting had been desperate, vicious, and mostly at close range.

He could still remember giving the order to block the roadway with the two largest vehicles available. Only two of the airport's fire trucks, designed to disperse huge quantities of foam and water on burning aircraft, were still running. "We can use their water cannons to scatter the crowds," someone had ventured. At the time, it had seemed a more humane way of holding their ground.

The water inside the fire engine's tanks hadn't lasted very long, however. Soon after, the huge fluorescent-green machines had become nothing more than bullet stops and bastions.

Both trucks displayed evidence of the violence that occurred during those desperate times. Each sported a least a hundred or more holes, the high-velocity lead puncturing sheet metal and paint with ease. Red rings of rust now surrounded every violation, crimson streaks of corrosion leaking like blood draining from an open wound.

Surrounding the two hook and ladders was a host of other objects that had been used to reinforce the roadblock and fence. Airport employees had moved dozens of stacks of empty pallets to buttress the wall and had parked several civilian automobiles there before draining the tanks. Two police cars signaled the front of the wreckage, the officers assigned to the airport substation thinking that their flashing emergency lights and uniforms would keep the invading hordes at bay.

It had worked, but only for a few hours.

Bascom had been standing at the barrier when the desperation had eventually overwhelmed respect for authority. That tipping point, either triggered by time or some unknown event, had resulted in both policemen being slaughtered in a matter of seconds. The captain hadn't even known their names, nor had any recognizable part of their bodies ever been recovered. That wasn't surprising in the least, especially given the carnage that had occurred over the next few days.

Now the once-proud fire trucks were corroding hulks covered in a lethal pewter powder. Their tires were flat, the shiny chrome accents dulled by time, exposure to acid rain, and the ash.

The captain moved briskly, the presence of the enemy's snipers always in the back of his mind. His men had been tracking the adversary's activities most of the night, constant updates broadcasted over the new radio frequencies he had implemented since Hannah's capture. Everyone had been sure she would eventually tell her captors everything she knew, and that had caused the airport's defenders no small amount of effort to prepare to defend their home.

While the airport's personnel didn't include any formally-trained police officers or military snipers, T.J. had found three men who were experienced hunters. They were now stationed on the top third floor of the main parking garage, concealed in the host of passenger automobiles now residing there.

For his part, Bascom was reasonably sure that the Horns wouldn't attack before they had retrieved the chief's son. That was only an assumption, however, one of a dozen questions that wouldn't be answered until the sun was setting in the west. "We will know soon enough," he whispered to no one as he walked toward the rear bumper of the massive fire engine.

"I see men approaching," the radio in T.J.'s hand squawked. "At least two dozen armed men moving toward the entrance. Two blocks away. Hannah is with them."

Turning to his lieutenant, Bascom quipped, "At least our friends from the Forbidden Zone are punctual."

"Got to give them that," the ex-hunting guide replied nervously.

Bascom exhaled when he reached the cover of the fire truck. Given its shadowing bulk and the known positions of the enemy's long-distance shooters, he was safe for the time being. That, however, would soon change.

With only T.J. and one other man, Bascom headed for the narrow path his people had cleared through the barricade. It was what Deiter had once called a fatal funnel, an opening only wide enough for a single person to pass. The scouts had requested the entryway, and since it had been months since anyone had tried to breach the airport's considerable defenses, the captain had approved the hidden opening.

Once clear of the barricade, Bascom rushed to a small, open area just on the other side of the gate. He could now see the advancing line of gunmen making their way through the gridlock of shot-up cars and trucks that filled the street for several blocks.

The man leading the enemy parade was holding onto Hannah's arm, the scout evidently having trouble walking with her hands bound behind her back.

Focusing on the captive, a torrent of rage began to build inside Bascom. His scout, far and above the healthiest and most beautiful woman in the airport, looked like a walking pile of overcooked shit.

Bascom could see the dark circles under Hannah's eyes, which were nothing more swollen slits just above her mask. Her hair was flat and matted against her scalp, the angle of her head showing that she was weak and distraught. The man holding her arm wasn't helping her balance, he was making sure she didn't pass out and fall flat on her face.

The captain had been there when American prisoners had been released after the Iraq war. Those soldiers had looked better than the woman now approaching. The unsettling image was infuriating, disgusting, and served to reassure Bascom that he was taking the right course when it came to dealing with these crazed animals.

The man he suspected was Chief Woods turned and made a hand signal when they were fifty yards away. The lines of shooters immediately dispersed, half running left, the remaining to the right. With his heartbeat racing, Bascom noted that the enemy fanned out and began taking cover behind the collection of relics left by the gatecrashers. There was no shortage of hides.

Once his forces had spread out, Woods continued forward with Hannah.

When he reached the opening, there was no polite greeting, false pretense, or exchange of social amenities. "Where is my son, Lieutenant Woods?"

This isn't going to start well, Bascom thought, choosing his next words very carefully. "Your son has been in surgery for several hours. He is still alive, but barely. Our physician is extremely reluctant to move his patient. He has advised me that such an effort would increase his chances of contracting an infection or even dying."

"And you expect me to believe this story?" the chief responded.

"It is the truth. If you want to see for yourself, I will see to it that you are escorted into our infirmary. You have my word that you won't be harmed."

"Your word doesn't hold much value in my book, Bascom," the chief growled.

With an innocent shrug, the captain said, "I am telling you the truth."

"What now?" Woods proposed, his tone indicating that he probably wasn't going to believe anything that Bascom said.

"If you wish, I can order your son brought here immediately. His wellbeing, one way or the other, will be on your conscience. We can wait a few days until your son is well enough to be moved. We can fight it out right here and now and see who's left standing. Really, it's up to you. One thing is for certain, Hannah stays. She's obviously been tortured while in your care, and I'm not about to let that continue."

Tilting his head in thought, Woods didn't respond for several seconds. Finally, he said, "That's not going to happen, Bascom. I will, however, agree to send an EMT inside to assess my son's condition. If he can be moved, my man will supervise his transfer. If not, you and I will discuss the options. Agreed?"

It was the captain's turn to evaluate this new twist, his mind working through the chess game's future moves.

He had come to the gate willing to sacrifice Hannah. The loss of her life, when weighed against the potential damage that the occupants of the Forbidden Zone could inflict, was a bitter but clear choice. Now, after seeing her face to face, Bascom's resolve was wavering.

He hadn't thought of Woods sending in a subordinate. His original plan had been to get the enemy leader inside his compound and then spring his trap. Yet, the captain knew that most battle plans fell apart as soon as the first shot was fired. "Agreed," he called back. "You can send in one man."

Turning his back to Bascom, Chief Woods produced a handheld radio and said something that the airport defenders couldn't hear. A minute later, a single man rushed forward.

Bascom watched as the new arrival handed his boss a rifle, sidearm, and knife. After that exchange, Woods turned and shouted, "He is unarmed. Do I have your word no harm will come to him?"

"We don't murder people," Bascom replied. "That's in your playbook, not mine. He will not be harmed."

The EMT jogged forward, the young fellow obviously scared shitless. "Welcome to the lion's den," Bascom mumbled, turning to escort his new guest through the walkway and onto airport grounds.

Turning to the shooter standing next to T.J., Bascom ordered, "Pat him down, then take him to the doctor. Bring him back here, unharmed, once he has inspected the patient."

Nodding, the man hurried to the EMT and began a quick search. "He's clean."

The captain watched as the luggage tractor sped toward the main terminal, his mind occupied by what next step he would take. One thing was for certain, seeing Hannah's condition had hardened his resolve to make sure, one way or the other, that this reprehensible situation was concluded before the day's end.

Bascom wasn't the only one second-guessing his strategy.

An hour ago, realizing that the miners weren't going to make the airport showdown on time, Commander Cisco had sped ahead on his e-bike. While three days' worth of nutrition had helped the near-starving members of the underground community, they were far from robust.

To begin with, it had taken them almost a full hour before they were packed up and ready to roll. The commander had lost count of how many hugs had been issued by crying, concerned spouses and children. There was very little he could do – beggars just couldn't be choosey.

The situation deteriorated further once they were on the road. Within the first hour, the long column of joking, smiling men had turned ugly, the miners more resembling members of the Bataan Death March than an invading army of truth, justice, and the American way.

Five men had already dropped out by the end of the second hour, severe cramps, two pulled muscles, and a nasty bout of diarrhea all taking their toll.

Still, Camaro's men plodded along, the mine boss forced to call a break every half an hour due to the weakened condition of his ranks.

At ten minutes to noon, they had progressed to within a few miles of the airport's southern perimeter. "We're going to be too late," Jack had informed Cam. "I'm going on ahead to see what is going down. Who knows, maybe I've underestimated both of these guys, and they're already sitting down and smoking the peace pipe."

"Unlikely," Cam had responded. "I'm sorry, Jack. We'll be there as soon as we can."

After leaving his bike a safe distance away, Jack had carefully trod to the high fence surrounding the airport grounds just as the luggage tractor was speeding down the entrance road.

"At least a full-blown firefight hasn't broken out just yet. I wonder what's happening?" the commander mumbled, pulling a pair of borrowed wire-cutters from his pack.

Jack's original idea had been to sneak in his forces through a hole in the fence while Bascom's and Woods's troops were distracted by each other. He then had planned on somehow drawing both men's attention to his newly arrived army and inserting himself into the negotiations.

After that, he was just going to wing it, hoping to convince both leaders that their petty bickering was folly, and that even if they did manage victory, there was another sheriff in town.

Given hostilities hadn't broken out, perhaps there was still hope for his devious feint. As he snipped through several sections of wire, Jack prayed that Cam and his paper-tiger army would soon arrive. It was a long shot, but it was all he had left.

The EMT's eyes were wide as he entered the main terminal. Given the circumstances, T.J. had bypassed the need for the visitor to change his clothes in the clean room, instead indulging his guest by making the man suffer through only a quick brushing with a whisk broom.

As Pierce and the EMT passed through the main corridor, members of the community watched the stranger pass with silent voices and fearful expressions.

Several mothers clutched their children close, most of their spouses now outside and carrying a gun for the captain. The visitor noticed both the curiosity and the disdain. "How many kids are inside?" he asked Pierce.

"About thirty-five, give or take. Why?"

"I just didn't expect to see this many children. We have a similar number back at the station."

They arrived at the doctor's office, T.J. rapping lightly on the door. Opening barely an inch, the doc's grey beard showed through the crack.

Seeing who was outside, the physician pulled the entrance open holding a single finger up to his lips and making a hissing noise. "He's resting. Please be quiet."

Stepping through the door, the EMT did a double-take upon seeing Doc Leland. "Uncle?" he whispered. "Is that you, Uncle Bob?"

Blinking several times, Leland eagerly stepped toward the EMT a huge smile spreading from ear to ear. "Cory! My God, young man. I've not seen you for what? Two years?"

Embracing in an emotional hug, the EMT was nearly gushing with joy. "We thought you were dead, Uncle. Mom said you had flown out to Phoenix to play golf just before the volcano blew. When we hadn't heard anything…."

Nodding vigorously, the physician couldn't keep the obvious smile off his face. "I had to delay my trip by a day. Then I was trapped here and couldn't get home. That change of schedule probably saved my life."

Turning to T.J., the brewing conflict outside seemed forgotten. "Uncle Bob is the reason why I wanted to be an EMT," Cory gushed. "I've been saving to go back to school. I want to be a doctor, just like him."

For that snapshot in time, hope filled the infirmary. Watching the heartfelt reunion, T.J. allowed himself to wonder if there wasn't a chance the battle lines forming outside couldn't be avoided. Could the two sides get along? Weren't both communities made up of the same people, with identical dreams for the future?

That thought brought the former scout back to reality. Outside, waiting, were two heavily armed armies. Both staring down their gun barrels, both ramped up to wage war. There wasn't any time to catch up on family affairs. "The patient, doctor, please?" Pierce reminded. "The EMT is here to check on the wounded man."

"Oh, of course," Leland responded. "Come this way."

They were led into a larger room, several beds set up in preparation for the upcoming firefight. In the corner, between two armed men, laid Paxton Woods, Jr. An IV was hooked to his arm, blood from a clear plastic bag flowing into his veins.

"What is his status, Uncle?" Cory asked, his eyes scanning Woods's body up and down.

For three minutes, Dr. Leland explained what medical care, including the surgery, had been offered to the wounded lieutenant. "I did the best I could, given our limited resources. Perhaps you have better care available in your camp?" the physician asked.

"No," the EMT admitted. "A couple of other techs and I are all we've got. We couldn't have even attempted to perform the kind of surgery you've described."

The two medical minds then exchanged a quick round of short questions and answers. "Blood Pressure?" "Temperature?" "How much blood has he been given?"

Finally, Cory asked his uncle the critical question. "Can he be moved?"

Rubbing his chin, Leland replied, "Under normal circumstances, I'd say no. After my last conversation with Captain Bascom, however, I understand that there is a lot more at stake than this one man's life. I would put the odds at fifty-fifty that moving him will worsen his condition. There's a chance that being jostled around will cause his internal bleeding to resume, and that would be a death sentence."

For a long pause, Cory considered his uncle's words and then announced, "Get him ready. We should take him back."

"What?" T.J. barked, not believing what the EMT had just said. "You heard your uncle. Why take the risk?"

"Because Chief Woods ordered me to bring his son out of the airport unless I was convinced that moving him would be an automatic death sentence. While I'm positive his chances of recovery would be better if he stayed here with Uncle Bob, I have to follow orders."

All of T.J.'s optimism vanished in that second, his visions of peaceful coexistence with the men of the Forbidden Zone evaporating into thin, pressurized air.

Dr. Leland had already moved Paxton Jr. to a stretcher given Bascom's instructions. With a nod from T.J., the armed guards moved to grab each set of handles and lifted the patient.

After unhooking the IV bag from its pole and laying it gently beside the wounded man, Leland turned to his nephew and said, "I wish you luck, Cory. It was good to see that you survived. Tell my sister… err… your mother that I love her."

"She didn't make it, Uncle Bob," the EMT replied. "I am sorry that I have to tell you she was killed by looters at a shopping mall three days after the eruption. I wish you all the best as well."

The two men hugged, and then Cory nodded to the stretcher bearers that he was ready.

T.J., for his part, was still having trouble with the entire episode. Here were two long, lost family members reunited. Both men had assumed the other was dead. There were hundreds of people at the airport who would have given their right arm to have such a reunion.

Then, just a few minutes later, both Leland and his nephew were saying goodbye, both convinced that they would never see the other again. "What have we become?" T.J. whispered to no one.

For the first time in his short life, T.J. believed he was about to die. Both sides were so entrenched, the hatred so deep, he knew that war was unavoidable.

For a brief moment, he considered turning the tractor around and trying to make an escape. Fighting the firemen didn't make any sense to him. There was no good reason for all this. It was all a huge misunderstanding. Why should he die just because some volcano had erupted and made everybody crazy?

His thoughts turned to Captain Bascom. A parade of memories marched through the hunting guide's head, events recalled where the tall, straight, grey-haired man had saved countless lives. How many times had he been convinced the future was hopeless? That they were all going to drown in their own blood? It had always been the captain who had stepped up. His calming voice and sage eyes had never failed to take control and keep the calm.

"No," T.J. whispered as the air rushed past his head. "If Captain Bascom says we must do this, then I will fight like a rabid dog until either he orders me to stop or I'm dead. I owe the man that."

The first miners started streaming in behind Jack just as the luggage tractor reappeared. Through his rifle's magnified optic, Jack could see Lieutenant Woods being hauled back to the entrance.

As he drove toward the barricade, T.J. scanned the area along the way. Over a dozen of his men were stationed out there. They had been in position since before daybreak, hiding under ash-covered blankets, hunkered down in drainage culverts, scrunched in the nooks and crannies of the relic vehicles that made up the main roadblock at the entrance. He prayed they would be enough.

If Captain Bascom was surprised to see them return with Junior's stretcher, he didn't show it. Once the tractor had rolled to a stop behind the barricade, T.J. motioned for the two security men to carry the wounded man through the opening. "Stop on the other side," he warned. "This is going to be tricky."

Once the bearers made it through the tangle of twisted metal and rusting iron, they moved to the edge of the clearing and waited. Turning to the EMT, Bascom said, "Go on. Go tell your people what you have found."

As Cory strode across the opening, Chief Woods appeared from out of the wreckage and approached his man. All eyes were on the duo as they exchanged a quick, quiet set of words.

Cory continued on, disappearing into the gridlock of junk that filled the street. Woods waved to another man nearby, and Hannah was again produced. "Have them meet in the middle," the chief yelled toward Bascom. "Your men can set my son down. We'll take him from there."

"As you wish," Bascom shouted back, motioning the two stretcher bearers to carry their human cargo into the opening. Hannah's hands were quickly freed by a stroke of Woods's knife, and then, she too was hobbling toward freedom and the passageway.

After Hannah had limped by them, the two men carrying Paxton Jr. stopped and gently lowered the stretcher to the ground. Before they had taken three steps in retreat, a pair of firemen rushed out of the wreckage and took possession of the stretcher and its cargo.

For a minute, everyone thought the encounter might be over. Men on both sides, keyed up for bloodshed, battle, and death, had been watching the proceedings for nearly an hour. Were the two leaders going to back down? Had they had a change of heart?

Following Hannah through the opening, Bascom turned to one of the stretcher bearers and ordered, "Get her back to the doctor, right away." He then turned to T.J. and instructed, "Get into position. Hell is about to open a new branch at Austin International."

Bascom hustled for the nearest hook and ladder, climbing aboard the massive vehicle as if he'd scaled its hull a hundred times. From that elevated position, he could clearly see Chief Woods on the other side of the barricade.

321

"Remember the snipers," T.J. called from below, reminding his boss to take cover if things got hot.

For nearly two minutes, Woods stayed put, watching as the stretcher carrying his son meandered through the wreckage.

From atop the fire truck, Bascom noted that none of the firemen were withdrawing. He'd expected as much. There was only one reason why the shooters on the other side would maintain their positions. Turning to T.J., who was still hovering below, the captain announced, "Get everyone ready. This is about to begin."

Reaching for his radio, Pierce ordered, "Everybody up. Everybody up." He then repeated the same command, shouting to the men hidden in the barricade to get into fighting positions.

They came out of nowhere, carefully concealed in the ash, rust, and disfigured junkyard that marked the entrance to the airport. Next to Captain Bascom, two men appeared from the deck of the old fire engine and moved to the unit's water cannon.

Evidently, Chief Woods's spotters noticed the activity, the distant leader turning abruptly to cast a wary glance back at the barricade while listening to the radio in his hand.

In that critical moment, three things occurred at once.

From the top of a city bus two blocks away, one of the firemen's machine guns opened, firing a stream of massive .50 caliber bullets that slammed into the barricade, shredding metal, and punching through the barrier as if were made of paper.

That devastating salvo sent the airport defenders ducking for cover and diving into the ash, the machine gun's overwhelming rate of fire filling those men's hearts with a terror unlike anything they had ever experienced.

What had once been the protective cover of the blockade became a deathtrap of flesh-eating shrapnel as the big 50's weighty bullets tore through fenders, bumpers, and engine blocks, sending a blizzard of sharp metal flying at the defenders.

Men went down, screaming in agony, limbs ripped from their bodies, organs and bones shredded by the belt-fed meatgrinders peppering the barrier.

Bascom and the cannon crew, diving for the ash-covered deck beneath their feet, barely avoided the second event. From the hotel rooftop four blocks away, three snipers fired the same instant the machine guns unleashed their maelstrom of death.

Two bullets hit the steel deck next to Bascom's head, stinging shards of metal tearing the skin off his arm.

The third simultaneous action involved Woods's fire teams. As one, they rose from their positions just outside the barricade, adding a bombardment of rifle fire to the hailstorm of machine gun lead while charging toward the opening.

"Attack!" Bascom yelled at the top of his lungs. "Hit them now, with everything we've got!"

Below him, hugging the ground, T.J. repeated the captain's order into his radio. The men nearby were already on the move.

As the fire teams approached the open ground, three of the airport's gunmen rose from the wreckage, their arms sending glass bottles arching through the grey skies. "Whoosh, whoosh, whoosh," announced their impact, balls of boiling flame expanding in all directions as the Molotov cocktails ignited.

Now exposed, the snipers were themselves diving for cover, Bascom's hunters opening fire from the parking garage.

The roaring balls of burning jet fuel gave Woods's men pause, their progress slowed by the unexpected counterattack. As the chief continued to shout orders into his radio, three more firebombs exploded, sending blistering waves of heat against exposed Horn skin.

Seeing his men stalled less than sixty feet from the opening, the chief ordered his second machine gun into the fray. He'd been holding it in reserve, wanting to keep it back for after they had breached the barrier. Now, he'd have to improvise.

As the second big 50 began spewing lead, Woods jumped up and began motioning his men forward. "Take that opening!" he commanded. "Get in there and push them back!"

With two heavy machine guns pounding Bascom's men, the assault troops regained their momentum and continued their advance, closing the gap step by precarious step.

Bascom, still prone on the fire truck's deck, spotted the advancement. Turning to the two men at his side, he shouted, "Now! Do it now!"

Despite the flurry of lead launched their direction, the two defenders rose as one. The first man reached for a set of wires next to the cannon's base. The second grasped the water gun's handles and spun the barrel around to face the stream of charging Horns.

The wires were connected to a series of car batteries, installed by the mechanics in last night's mad rush to finalize preparations. The cannon's water tank had been topped off with several barrels of jet fuel.

The electrical connection made, a tube of high-pressure liquid blasted out of the cannon's muzzle, arching through the air toward the approaching invaders. Just as the stream began raining down from the sky, a butane torch's flame touched the flow. Bascom's men were now wielding the most powerful flamethrower ever deployed.

Searing heat bowled over several of the charging assaulters, the ground instantly covered by pools of liquid hell. One man, completely consumed in flames, ran screaming into the opening, two others trying to roll across the earth and extinguish the inferno that was melting the skin off their bones.

Stunned at the deployment of the homemade firestorm, Chief Woods's men fell back, running with all they could muster to escape the cannon's range.

Seeing their comrades being burned alive, the two machine gun crews quickly redirected their aim to the cannon, a nearly solid wall of 660-grain bullets tearing into the man aiming the deadly device.

Glancing up, Bascom saw his subordinate simply disappear, his body disintegrating into a fog of crimson and white vapor. A shower of gristle and bone rained down on the captain, covering him with minute scraps of bloody tissue and grit.

"Retreat!" Bascom shouted to anyone who could hear. "Fall back! Fall Back!"

The handful of remaining men defending the barricade rose, retreating toward the next line of defense. Still, the damage had been done. In less than two minutes, eleven dead men were scattered amongst the wreckage, joining the multitude of souls that had already died there during previous battles. Another half-dozen of Chief Woods's riflemen were wounded and out of the fight.

Both leaders were outwardly furious with their losses and the performance of their men. Bascom had expected to hold the barricade for at least an hour.

Chief Woods had planned on being through the barrier and onto the airport grounds with minimal losses. Both men hardened their resolve for round two. Neither hesitated to continue the fight.

Chapter 53

"Shit!" Jack barked, watching the battle through his optic, stunned by how quickly the fight had escalated.

When the hook and ladder's flamethrower had launched its deadly burst of burning liquid, Jack had been amazed at Bascom's creativity. "Damn! That is one serious area of denial weapon."

The miners, now arrayed in a single line and watching the battle unfold, were growing nervous. Camaro summed it up best, "I thought this was going to be a skirmish? You expect us to get between machine guns and flame cannons? I'm having second thoughts about this."

"No, I'm not going to risk any of your guys. Woods and Bascom are nuts… totally loco. I had no idea they would take things this far."

Form his vantage, Jack could see both sides regrouping. The airport teams were taking up positions in a drainage ditch, conceding roughly half of the open space leading to the terminal. There wasn't another defendable feature between them and the main gate. If Bascom couldn't hold his ground there, the battle would be over.

Despite taking heavy losses, Jack didn't think Woods was about to call it a day. The commander observed a host of men on the far side of the barrier, several leaders hustling here and there trying to rally the troops.

A few minutes later, Jack noticed the machine gun crews bring forward their tripod-mounted weapons. Shaking his head, he said, "The airport guys don't have a chance against those M2s. The firefighters can keep Bascom's boys pinned in that ditch while Woods's rifle teams advance. This is going to be over pretty quickly."

As Jack watched, the machine guns were hastily hauled into position, their crews setting up both weapons deployed inside the barricade.

As the remaining airport sharpshooter began harassing the crews, the snipers still atop the hotel tried to interdict, long-range lead flying back and forth across the open spaces of the airport's grounds.

Through his optic, Jack could see Chief Woods darting here and there, shouting orders and trying to get his men into position. Five minutes after the battle had begun, the two machine guns started pounding the ditch, sending Bascom's men scrambling for the safety of the bottom.

Five more of the airport's defenders were lying dead on the ground before a minute had passed.

After a few seconds of suppressive fire, Woods was again in front of his troops, waving them forward, encouraging them to charge into the remaining defenders.

Inhaling sharply, Jack spotted at least thirty gunmen rise from the wreckage and begin trotting toward the still scrambling airport crew. "This will be over in minutes," he proclaimed to Camaro. "We should be heading back to the mine about now. Woods's people might spot us, and given his recent victory, he might decide to chase us out of town."

Before Camaro could respond, a loud mechanical whine sounded from behind the terminal. "What the hell?" the mine boss snapped, all eyes darting in the direction of the peculiar and ever-increasing noise.

Just as the racket turned from a high-pitched scream to a roaring vibration, Jack noticed a hefty airliner roll out from behind the terminal. The damn thing was moving fast and increasing speed.

In seconds, it stormed around the main building and crashed through a chain-link fence like a bull charging through a bedsheet.

A rooster tail of ash rose up behind the powerful turbines driving the aircraft, creating a grey curtain that rose a hundred feet into the air. The plane was a rampaging dragon, its screaming wrath focused on the tiny humans in its path.

Woods's men saw it then, Jack noticing several of the advancing assaulters pointing and shouting. Whoever was driving the massive plane kept coming, the aircraft now rolling at over one hundred miles per hour.

The firemen turned around and began running back toward the barricade as the airliner barreled directly at their ranks. As the same instant, Bascom's men in the ditch stood up, pouring small arms fire into the retreating enemy.

With its enormous mass plowing across the open grounds, the plane's engines began contributing to the chaos and confusion. Their deafening roar made cohesive thought nearly impossible, any orders or broadcasts difficult to hear.

Woods was screaming at his machine gun crews, pointing like a madman at the approaching giant. After recovering from their initial shock at the monster's appearance, they moved their barrels and began laying long bursts into the rolling behemoth.

Sparks began flicking off the aircraft's nose as the machine gun crews found their range. Jack saw one of the cockpit's glass windows explode inward. Still, the airliner kept gaining momentum, closing the distance in only a few seconds.

Jack had no idea what the original plan had been. While sure that not even Bascom would ask one of his peers to commit suicide, the commander couldn't contemplate how the winged cavalry charge was supposed to end. Perhaps the pilot was planning to execute a last-second turn. Maybe the older plane's brakes had failed, or one of the initial .50 caliber rounds had killed the flight crew outright. Whatever the exit strategy had been for the men commandeering the airliner, it didn't work out.

The 737 slammed into the barricade at over 120 miles per hour, throwing the old fire trucks and any nearby relics high into the air. Woods's machine gun crews, scattering to avoid the jet-powered battering ram, were crushed by shrapnel that consisted of flying pickup trucks and airborne automobiles.

Still traveling at a high rate of speed, the aircraft was launched skyward, the wreckage of the barricade acting as a ramp. As it lifted into the air, the fuselage began to tilt.

A wingtip hit the pavement, a counterweight to the main body's forward momentum. The nose pointed down, the aircraft pinwheeling through the air as it struck the base of the hotel with irresistible force.

The entire fuselage virtually disappeared into the doomed structure, glass from the first three floors exploding outward, unable to contain the spike of pressure created by its winged guest entering the lobby. A second later, the fuel in the airliner's tanks detonated, the entire hotel disappearing in an expanding fireball, unlike anything Jack had ever seen.

A deafening thunderclap roared across the airport's grounds, the closest men dropping their rifles to clutch their ears. Wincing from the excruciating noise, Jack mumbled, "Mother of God. I can't believe this."

Staring numbly at the scene, Camaro's mouth was moving, but no words came. His brain, still not comprehending the scale of the destruction his eyes had just witnessed, struggled to cope.

The fireball subsided a few seconds later, replaced by boiling red and yellow flames clawing out of every window and door. No one spoke or moved, every man's thoughts still replaying an event that was simply beyond their ability to grasp.

Less than a minute passed before another odd sound reached Jack's ears. Just as he was starting to regain control of his faculties, a low, rumbling groan rose from the engulfed hotel. A bit later, the painful scream of tortured metal rose in pitch and volume. A vast puff of dust rose from the roof, and then the structure began collapsing, each floor cascading into the one below as a cloud of ash and debris shot into the air.

"This is truly hell on earth!" Jack heard Camaro proclaim. "In all my days… I could never have even imagined anything like this."

For several minutes, Jack and the miners milled about, the battlefield obscured by rolling clouds of ash, smoke, and soot. The hotel continued to burn and smolder, adding its share of pollution as well as the acidic odor of burning rubbish. The scene was like a major accident on the interstate, the gawkers unable to tear their eyes away from the wreckage.

"Bascom has pulled off an unbelievable victory," Jack offered at one point. "No sense in trying to reason with the man now. His head will be the size of a hot air balloon. We should be heading back to the mine."

"I want to see how this ends," Camaro replied. "We came all this way, and it's been one hell of a show. I have to see the last chapter."

Before long, the ash began to settle, the hotel's smoke diverted by a change in the wind's direction. Following Cam's pointing finger, Jack heard his friend say, "What's going on over there? What are they doing?"

Lifting his weapon, Jack zeroed in on the area that had been the barricade. He couldn't believe what showed in the circle of his optic.

Chief Woods was there, pointing and motioning for his men to gather around. The commander was surprised to see at least twenty survivors still holding their weapons and scurrying about in response to the order. "This isn't over," Jack proclaimed. "The firemen are still in the game."

Moving to view Bascom's ditch, Jack saw the two dozen or so defenders still in place. While it was impossible to tell, it looked as if the captain were trying to organize his own men to retake the entrance. "They're going to dance until the last man is down," Jack predicted.

It then occurred to Jack that his original plan might still be in play. Both sides were depleted. Both had used and lost their big guns. Could he stop the bloodshed? Was there still time?

Turning to Cam, Jack declared, "I'll be right back. I'm going to go get my bike. Have your men stay low. When you see me wave, stand and brandish your weapons. Try to look as menacing as possible."

After seeing Camaro nod his understanding, Jack took off at a quick clip, rushing through the hole in the fence and then disappearing in a sprint.

Once the commander was out of sight, Cam began passing along Jack's instructions, each man repeating his orders down the line.

Jack reappeared a few minutes later, his e-bike slowing only enough to squeeze through the hole in the wire. Once on the airport grounds, the commander rolled up to Camaro and asked, "All set?"

Nodding, Cam said, "Good luck!"

Just as he reached for the throttle, Jack paused and then quickly dismounted. Opening his pack, the commander pulled out a bleached piece of cloth, an old bath towel that he used as a breathing filter. It wasn't much of a white flag, but it would have to do.

With the towel flapping the air, Jack accelerated across the open grounds, racing for a spot directly between the two opposing forces. Stopping in the middle of no-man's land, the commander dismounted and again waved his tattered signal flag.

"What the hell is he doing?" Bascom asked, his men pointing to the commander.

Chief Woods was just as confused, his face forming a deep scowl. "Who the hell is that? One of their scouts?"

Jack remained unmoving for nearly a minute before becoming annoyed. At two minutes, without any reaction by either side, he turned and pointed toward the direction where the miners were stationed. He was close enough to see both Bascom and Woods glance in the direction indicated by his finger.

The commander gestured to Cam's men.

The miners rose, over sixty men standing in unison, shaking their weapons in the air while letting out a boisterous cheer. Crossing his arms in a cocky stance, Jack then turned and shouted at Bascom. "I'm going to make a deal with one side or the other. Do you really want to fight a second army?"

Without waiting for the captain's response, Jack then turned toward Chief Woods and repeated his request. "Work with me or against me, your call!"

Both leaders knew their men were still in shock, barely able to function. The appearance of the new armed presence on their private battlefield, however, elicited completely different reactions from the two honchos.

Bascom was furious at Jack's reappearance.

Woods, on the other hand, was more curious than annoyed.

Regardless of their personal feelings, the visual of the large, fresh foe sent waves of panic and disbelief through both of their crippled ranks.

Pulling his rifle's sling over his head, Bascom growled, "This won't take long," as he stormed out of the ditch.

Seeing his nemesis on his way to converse with this new contender, Woods decided to join the conversation, stomping his way toward the white flag. His initial thought was to convince Jack to join his side of the conflict. If he could get this newcomer to reinforce his depleted force, together they could still take the airport and win the day.

Waiting patiently as both leaders approached, Jack didn't have to fake the scowl on his face. When Bascom and Woods were standing ten feet away on their respective sides, his voice was steady and stern. "I'm going to make this short and simple," the commander began. "I'm not going to join either side. Either you stop this madness right fucking now, or I will wait until you tear each other to bits and then I'll have my men roll up here and finish off the survivors."

Neither Bascom nor Woods had expected Jack's aggressive stance, both men standing with their mouths open, trying to collect their thoughts. It was the chief who got his act together first. "What gives you the right to do anything in this city?" was the best comeback Paxton could manage.

"Those one hundred men standing over there give me all the rights I need," Jack answered calmly. "There are at least that many a few hours behind them. You're about to take a serious ass whooping and lose everything."

"Who are those men?" Bascom wanted to know.

"Just a bunch of guys I ran into while traveling," Jack grinned. "I told them about your nice, cozy airport terminal and bragged on the fact that you don't have to sleep with a mask over your face. They thought that sounded pretty good. They want a piece of the action."

"This is bullshit!" Woods barked, "You've got no business getting involved. This isn't your war!"

"Oh, it is now," Jack countered. "But enough of this friendly, small talk. Are you going to end this stupidity, or shall I take my place as the King of Austin, Texas?"

For a moment, Jack thought his appeal was working. Bascom looked exhausted, Woods still reeling from the shock and awe of the airliner's attack.

"It's that man and his vicious pack of murderers you should be attacking, not us!" Bascom shouted, pointing a shaking finger at the chief. "You know he and his men are nothing more than cold-blooded butchers. He even tried to kill you, Commander. Have you forgotten that?"

"Bullshit!" Woods snarled. "You airport scum are nothing more than a swarm of locusts, stealing everything, consuming every crumb in your path. Talk about murder? Go look at the junk heap on the other side of your barricade. How many people died there, Bascom? How many innocent lives were ended by your men over there?"

His fury mounting, Bascom reached into the small of his back and produced a pistol. After seeing the weapon in his mortal enemy's hand, Woods bent and drew a revolver from an ankle holster with a flash of motion. Both men went into a combat crouch, Jack sure they were going to start shooting.

The men under Woods's and Bascom's commands saw their leaders and began running toward the powwow. Now thinking he had made a terrible mistake, Jack coiled his legs to dive for the ground next to the electric cycle.

Just as Woods was cocking his hammer, a brilliant light rained down from the heavens. For a nanosecond, Jack thought the illumination was coming from the hotel, perhaps a secondary explosion. Blinking and squinting from the brightness, he looked skyward.

The sun was visible through a small patch of clear, blue sky. It has been months since anyone had seen the pulsating yellow orb.

Across both lines of charging fighters, men stopped mid-stride, the stunned expressions and wide eyes staring at the beam of sunlight that had challenged the charcoal grey clouds. Woods lowered his pistol, his thoughts no longer focused on killing Bascom. The captain's arms suddenly were unable to point his weapon, his reaction to the sun's visit so emotional.

For a few minutes, no one moved, their faces bathing in the warming rays. Jack could feel the heat on his cheeks, the blue heavens one of the most beautiful skies he could remember. Glancing down, he noticed his shadow on the ground and couldn't help but admire the image. Suddenly, the ash didn't look so grey, and neither did the future.

Over his shoulder, the commander heard someone laugh, an odd sound for a battlefield covered in blood and destruction. "Anybody got any sunscreen," another man joked. "I have sensitive skin."

Bascom was the first leader who found words, his voice barely a whisper. "Things will grow again," he muttered. "There can be life. Green things. Warmth."

"We can have solar power. The sun will help the earth heal. I thought I would never see it again," Woods added a short time later.

For several minutes, every eye on the battlefield turned skyward, the sun's glory dissolving the rage and bloodlust like winter ice melting away on a bright spring morning. Some men closed their eyes, absorbing the rejuvenating energy that seemed to purify their souls. Others couldn't help but smile, basking in the rays as if they were worshipping at the altar of life.

The chief eventually looked back to earth, his gaze focusing on the captain. "This is over. I don't feel like fighting anymore."

Nodding, the captain pointed toward the heavens and said, "I agree. This changes everything."

"There are a lot of hard feelings on both sides," Jack added. "If you want, I'll be glad to hang around and arbitrate. Given what we've all been through since the eruption, that actually sounds like I job I'd enjoy for a change."

Camaro eventually strolled out to the peace talks, his smile so large Jack thought the man's ears would be swallowed. When he heard the conversation, Butler's head began nodding in agreement. "We can all work together," the miner stated with confidence.

Jack introduced Cam to the men from the city, and after a few minutes, the miners were mixing with the shooters from both sides.

Medics from both camps rushed forward to tend to the wounded. Jack sighed with relief when he noted a fireman with a bleeding leg being loaded onto the airport's luggage tractor, the electric horse now being used as an ambulance.

The chief's voice boomed over the former battlefield, "Cory! Get our medical personnel inside the airport to assist their doctor. Take your bags with you. Give them anything they need."

A few minutes later, the bustling activity suddenly stopped when the sun disappeared behind the same old grey clouds that had owned the skies since the eruption. For a heartbeat, Jack worried that the event might reignite emotional flames.

Men from both sides looked up, and then returned to the task at hand. Exhaling, Jack surveyed the area and smiled. "Finally," he grinned. "Finally, a good day."

Epilogue

Strolling through the terminal, Jack spotted Mrs. Ward's class at one of the large windows, a child with a paintbrush drawing on the glass.

Curious, the commander stopped to see what the students were being taught.

He noted that there were several other markings on the window, each scrawled in a child's uneven hand. Jack could make out the days of the week, and beside each was a series of checkmarks.

Tilting his head, the commander studied the project intently, finally understanding the lesson. The children were keeping count of how many times the sun appeared each day. Mrs. Ward wanted her students to understand the progress that was being made, both inside and outside their still-confining world.

The day of the battle, the sun had remained hidden for the rest of the day. In the week since, it had reappeared twice the following day and had reached a peak of four visits yesterday. The bell curve was going the right direction.

Continuing, Jack noticed Hannah walking to intercept him. The commander paused for a moment, his gaze taking in the stunning woman coming his way. He had only seen her without a mask on a handful of occasions, those instances occurring while she was still recovering from her time at Station No. 9.

Now, well on her way down the road to recovery, Jack noticed a glow to her face, her freshly washed hair like strands of golden light. "I had no idea there was a goddess under that mask," he whispered, trying to keep his male instincts in check. Her height was accented by long, willowy legs that would draw any man's eye. Thin and flat in the middle while robust across the chest, the commander was amazed at the hourglass figure the scout's jumpsuit had been hiding. "She's drop-dead gorgeous," he observed, working hard not to openly gawk. "To top it off, she drives a motorcycle like Evel Knievel and shoots like Annie Oakley. Be careful, Commander. You're the new sailor in town."

She smiled as she approached. "Commander Cisco," she said as the two explorers shared an easy hug, "I have been looking for you."

"You doing okay?" Jack asked, slightly embarrassed that he hadn't had much time to visit with his friend. The past week had been hectic, playing the role of emissary taking most of his days and nights.

"Yeah. I'm getting there," she answered, managing a slight grin. "I've found that keeping busy helps with the healing process. I feel a little better every day."

"Good," the commander replied. "You went through a lot, but you're strong. You'll be fine, I'm sure of it."

Hannah changed the subject, embarrassed at Jack's praise. "So, I had lunch with Sheng today, and he is getting ready to conduct his first class on foraging. I thought you might want to drop in. There are teams from the fire station and the airport attending."

The mention of the old man brought a frown to Jack's face. He had almost forgotten. "Speaking of Sheng," he began, "There's something I wanted to discuss with you. Camaro and the miners are convinced that they were poisoned by that eccentric fellow. They swear on their mothers' graves that the roots and tubers they harvested made them very ill. Should we be trusting that old fart?"

Instead of protesting, or denying, or any of the other reactions Jack anticipated, Hannah surprised him by flashing the saddest pair of eyes he'd ever seen. "Yes, we can trust him. He wasn't the one who poisoned their food."

Jack's first thought was to debate Hannah, but then he replayed her words. "*He* wasn't the one? *You* poisoned their harvest?"

Nodding in guilt, she confessed, "Yes and no. Poisoned is a strong word. I *seasoned* their food. I knew that if the miners and Sheng became best buds, there was no way I would budge that old coot out of his house. Well, while we were in the hills digging, Sheng pointed toward a dead patch of stems and said, 'Avoid those. They will make you very sick.' So, when no one was looking, I cut off a few pieces and sprinkled them on the miner's food. Please forgive me. I was desperate. We were… still are… running out of food. And I only meant to discourage the miners from bonding so completely with Sheng. After all, I practically had to light a stick of dynamite under his artistic butt to get him here," she confessed.

Quickly recovering from the surprise of her guilty plea, Jack began laughing.

"What?" Hannah said. "Why are you laughing? I thought you would be mad, or disappointed, or something. What's so funny?"

Shaking his head and wiping a tear from the corner of his eye, Jack replied, "I like you, Hannah. That was devious, conniving, and unscrupulous. What a bold step to take in order to achieve your goals. It's people like you who are going to help us recover… folks who won't be denied, no matter what the circumstances."

With a wink, Hannah countered, "You mean like convincing Bascom and Woods that those poor, starving miners were your invincible, conquering army? Or was my little trick more akin to your telling both of our fearless leaders that there were a hundred more men on the way? Is that the kind of devious, conniving, unscrupulous behavior of which you speak?"

Feigned indignation covered Jack's face, the commander countering, "What, me? I'm innocent of all charges… as pure as the driven snow."

Grunting, "Bullshit!" Hannah began to laugh at Jack's playacting.

"Now, young lady," the commander said with a stern look on his face, "if you're willing to cooperate, I might be convinced to keep your misdeeds our little secret."

Thinking Jack was flirting with her and about to make an advance. Hannah batted her eyelids seductively and said, "Oh, and what kind of blackmail do you have in mind, Jack?"

The commander's cheeks blushed crimson, embarrassed that his message had been misread. Looking down, he muttered, "I'm sorry, Hannah. I didn't mean it that way. I was actually planning a trip to Galveston soon, and I wanted your help."

It was her turn to feel the flush cross her face as Hannah stuttered, "Oh, Jack, I'm sorry. We're both so tired given the events of the last week. I would be happy to help you search for your family. Let's get together tomorrow and begin working on the logistics."

Happy that he hadn't just insulted his new friend, Jack relaxed, and a smile spread across his face. "Thank you, Hannah. I think we're going to make a great team."

THE END

Made in the USA
Columbia, SC
24 August 2019